KEELEY & ASSOCIATES
COLLECTION #1

BOOKS #1-3

LAYLA LAWLOR

CONTENTS

DRAGON AND DETECTIVE

KEELEY & ASSOCIATES #1

Dragon & Detective

Keeley & Associates

FOREWORD

I can directly credit my mailing list readers with this book existing in its present form. This started out as a snippet from a flash fiction prompt about a detective being hired by a dragon from many years ago (probably written around 2014 or so) that I sent out in May 2020 as one of my mailing list freebies. That snippet is now the opening scene of this book.

I never meant to write more of it . . . until getting a cascade of emails asking me where the *rest* of the story was! I didn't expect it to be this long, let alone to produce an entire world in my head, but I guess that's what's happened.

This collection includes the first three books in the series: *Dragon & Detective, Ghost & Gumshoe, and Fae & Flatfoot.* The next book, Dick & Demon, is available for sale separately.

CHAPTER ONE

"SO YOU ARE THE PRIVATE INVESTIGATOR."

James looked up at his prospective client. Up . . . and up. He'd met dragons before, but only the playful little river dragons down by the harbor, about twice as big as otters with many of the same personality quirks. They liked fish, swimming, and mud, not necessarily in that order, and they hoarded shells and pieces of shiny junk in their nests underneath the docks. They were cute and friendly, and liked to beg shamelessly when the fishing boats came in.

Ozymandias, on the other hand, was the kind of dragon that legends spoke of: wealthy, powerful, and above all, *huge*.

"Yes, I am," James said, and added, "Uh . . . sir."

"Will you have tea?"

James blinked at the tea tray supported on the tip of two of the dragon's claws. A human-sized clutter of tea things huddled in the middle of a silver expanse of tray the size of a refrigerator door. He wasn't normally a tea drinker, but he found himself saying, "Yes, please—uh, Mr. Ozymandias."

When a dragon offers tea, you drink the tea. Especially

when the dragon is rich and wants to hire you and could probably eat you in a single bite.

"Please," the dragon said. "Call me Oz. The river dragons speak highly of you."

This was the first James had heard that they could speak at all. He stretched across the tray to pick up a steaming teacup. "Have you reported the theft to the police?"

Ozymandias snorted, releasing a perfect smoke ring. "The police indeed. I filed a report, certainly, but I don't expect anything to be done. Damned civil servants, hardly remember who pays the taxes that employ them—"

The last thing James wanted was a conversation with a giant *angry* dragon about taxes. He said quickly, "Well, why don't we start by looking at your collection, then."

He'd said the right words—Ozymandias's ruffled neck fringes smoothed down. The dragon set the tea tray on a shelf that was located at his height—fifteen feet above James's head—and dropped down to all fours. "This way, then."

Ozymandias led him across the gleaming marble tile of the mansion's main—foyer? Living room? Ballroom? In any case it was a huge open space with a dragon-scale staircase leading upstairs and potted plants the size of trees in the corners.

James was too fascinated by the dragon to spend much time staring around the mansion, however. Oz was armored in great overlapping scales the color of gunmetal, an irides-cent blue-gray. Even on all fours, despite a low-slung croco-dilian body, his back was as high as James's shoulder, with great masses of folded wings making it taller yet. His long neck folded in a sinuous S-curve, supporting a head the size of a passenger sedan. Behind his jaw and where his ears would be, if he'd had ears, multiple rows of spiny fringes fluttered in time with his steps. James hadn't figured out yet if those were some kind of functional sensory organ or simply there to display mood. The river dragons had little fins there.

"It's here," Oz said, pushing open a massive door.

The room on the other side was the size of an aircraft hangar, brilliantly lit with showroom-style spotlights illuminating rows of sleek sports cars. James didn't know much about cars, but he could see that these were quite expensive as well as immaculately cared for. Dragons loved shiny things, and loved showing them off to visitors, whether it was the river dragons holding up shells in their little paws, or . . . this.

In the old days, it had been jewels and gold. Now apparently it was Maseratis and Lamborghinis.

James made the requisite oohing and ahhing noises, then got down to business. "What's missing?"

"A first-generation 2002 Lamborghini Murcielago," Ozymandias said promptly. "It hasn't been gone for more than a few hours; I noticed it missing this morning immediately, of course. It was the one at the far end of the second row." He pointed with one claw. There was, indeed, an empty space in the neat rows of cars. "It was a gift from my daughter, with custom modifications. There's not another like it in the world."

James followed him between the rows of cars, looking to both sides—not at the cars but at the room's entrances and exits. Besides the door from the house that they'd come in through, which stood open, he saw two enormous garage doors that he guessed led to the outside. Each was capable of accommodating the dragon's bulk—and probably two or three car-carrying semi trucks side by side.

"Any signs of a break-in?"

The dragon shook his ponderous head.

"How do you open the doors? They're electronic, I'm guessing?"

Oz's tailtip twitched. "Yes. There are only two door openers —I have one, and my mechanic has the other. Of course it could not have been my mechanic, who I trust implicitly."

James merely nodded without saying anything. Draconic loyalty was also the stuff of legend; they trusted few, but when they did, they did so completely. Which unfortunately left them wide open for manipulation from rather less trust-worthy humans, but he wasn't going to say so. He would pursue the mechanic angle on his own.

"Who else has access to this room?"

"No one," Oz said, his tone very final. "I clean my collection myself, of course. Also, the security system would have shown if any of the doors were opened, either the doors to the outside or to the house. None were."

"So the Lamborghini vanished from a locked room."

"So it would seem," Oz said grimly.

James could feel his brain starting to click into problem-solving mode: making lists of things to check, people to talk to, questions to ask. This wasn't how he'd expected he'd spend his day when he arrived at the office this morning, but it certainly beat the hell out of doing background checks and tracking down deadbeat ex-husbands.

"What do you think, Detective?" the dragon asked, tilting his head to look down at James. "Will you take the case?"

Well, that was a no-brainer. It wasn't like people were beating down James's door trying to give him business. Everything he had at the moment was corporate busywork, plus a surveillance detail on a maybe-cheating spouse that he wouldn't mind taking a break from.

Besides, how many times in a private detective's career could you expect to have something like this drop into your lap? It was a genuine locked-room mystery.

James shifted his teacup to his left hand, and held out his

right to grasp the tip of one giant claw and give it a brisk shake. "Oz, you have yourself a detective."

∼

OZ SHOWED him to the security hub, a room built to dragon scale, with state-of-the-art banks of screens on the walls. There was a single human-sized terminal, but it was up on a desk ten feet off the ground. Oz lifted him up with a large clawed paw, a very disconcerting experience.

"My house is not designed for people your size," Oz said, sounding almost embarrassed.

"I wouldn't expect it to be. It's not like my office is sized for people like you," James pointed out. He couldn't resist asking, "Why did you hire a human detective? Aren't there dragon ones?"

"My kind are not really suited to it." Oz settled back on his haunches, looking enough like an enormous dog that James had to force himself not to slip into an inappropriate grin. "Humans, on the other hand, are busy and inquisitive and curious, like some sort of small industrious rodent. It is an ideal pursuit for your kind."

"Uh . . . thanks, I think." He looked up at the camera feeds, and after some trial and error, figured out how to manipulate them from his screen. There were various angles on the grounds around Oz's mansion, the entrances and exits, and the doors to the garage with the car collection, inside and outside. But no views of the inside.

"Do you have any camera angles that show the missing car?"

Oz's tail twitched. "If I did, I wouldn't need the help of a detective, would I?"

"Good point. Sorry." He switched to the outside view. "Do

you have any other security on the building? Human guards, that sort of thing?"

"There are wards on the walls, of course," Oz said with an offhand movement of his claw. "I do not employ other staff except for my mechanic, who doesn't live on site. Oh, and the gargoyle on the roof, but she didn't see anything."

James blinked. "I'll need to talk to her anyway. What's her actual job?"

"She keeps the birds off, mostly."

" . . . Okay," James murmured. He paged through the camera views. "Was anyone else here last night?"

"No one," Oz said firmly. "I was quite alone."

"Except for the gargoyle, I assume?"

"She is very undemanding company."

"Right. How about yesterday, or the previous few days? Any visitors?"

"No one who might have been involved in this thing," Oz said with another offhand movement of his claws.

"Yes, but specifically?"

"My daughter, Neith, was here about a week ago. And the classic auto enthusiasts' monthly meeting yesterday, of course."

James swiveled around from the terminal. "You don't say. Do you happen to have a list?"

～

IT TURNED out that Grand Bluffs ClassicWorks met on the first Tuesday of every month, rotating between members' homes. This month was Oz's turn to host.

"I can't think why you would suspect any of them," Oz complained as he tapped keys on a dragon-sized keyboard with his claw tips. He had donned a pair of reading glasses, slightly undersized for his face (but still large enough that a human would have had trouble carrying them), perched on the end of his long nose. "But I suppose this is what I hired you for. The inquisitiveness of humans may yet open doors that I had not thought to open."

It probably said a lot about Oz's likelihood of solving this on his own, James thought, that he'd had a house full of car enthusiasts yesterday and it hadn't occurred to him that one of them might have been involved in swiping the Lamborghini. As a newer car, it might be slightly outside the general scope of the club members' interests, but that didn't mean there wasn't a klepto in the club who couldn't pass up an automobile with a $280K price tag. (James had looked up some of Oz's collection on his phone while he was waiting, then boggled and quietly put the phone away.)

Oz looked up abruptly from the computer. "Pardon my poor manners, would you care for some refreshments?"

"Coffee?" James asked, hoping to forestall another cup of tea.

"Certainly. Just let me . . . this damned machine, back in my day we didn't have such things . . ."

"I can take a look if you want. You're just pulling up a spreadsheet, right?"

"More of a list really," the dragon said, but he watched as James pulled the human-scale terminal keyboard toward himself.

Oz clearly subscribed to the "all the files on the desktop" school of computer organization, most with filenames like *untitled 75*; no wonder he couldn't find anything. As James hunted through endless untitled documents for something that looked like it was associated with the classic car club, he asked, "Do you regularly have human guests?"

"I like to entertain," Oz said, pushing up his glasses.

"This classic car club . . . are they mostly human?"

"All of them," Oz said without any doubt.

That you know of, anyway, James thought, but didn't say. You weren't going to catch onto the true nature of a werewolf or a dryad unless you caught one at exactly the wrong moment. The more visibly nonhuman types like trolls and gargoyles and . . . well . . . dragons usually kept to themselves.

"Aha. Is this it?" James turned the screen so Oz could see it. The dragon leaned down until his nose almost bumped the flatscreen monitor—enormous by human standards, bigscreen-TV-sized, but still small for a dragon.

"Yes, that's it. That's our electronic mail list for staying in touch." Oz looked pleased with himself, as if he'd been the one to find it.

The spreadsheet didn't include physical addresses, but there were names and emails. A lot of names, more than James had expected. He scrolled down—seventy-two in total.

"Were all of these people here yesterday?"

"What? Oh, heavens no. Just the regulars."

"Can you show me which ones the regulars are?"

"Oh, well, Andrew of course, and Chad, and—"

"On the list," James said. "So I can mark them. I'll never remember."

"You can't? Ah. Quite. Human brains, very small, not much room. Just a moment." After a certain amount of hunting about, Oz tapped a key on the big keyboard, and a printer began to hum. "This will be simpler, I agree. Allow me to fetch your coffee."

James was left sitting on the desk with no clear way down, though he could probably have climbed down if he really had to. And he had access to all the security cameras, as well as Oz's files. It was amazing that dragons weren't robbed constantly, he thought.

On the other hand, a predator with a body the size of a semi-truck trailer and impervious to anything short of a rocket launcher was probably a significant deterrent to casual thieves. Dragons didn't need security guards because they themselves were better security than any they could hire. Oz seemed very polite, but James still wouldn't want to be on his bad side.

It was starting to occur to him that he'd better be able to solve this case.

~

JAMES LEFT the mansion with a printout the size of a large map rolled under his arm, annotated with scribbled notes in his own handwriting and Oz's enormous scrawl. He glanced back at the roof of the house as he got into his car. Gargoyles, Oz said, were not active by day, or at least didn't like to be, so Oz had promised to introduce him if he came back that evening.

Oz had identified fourteen club members at the previous day's meeting, a much more manageable suspect list. Which still didn't answer the question of how they'd gotten the car out. The floor in the garage was concrete, seemingly solid. The security footage showed nothing. It was as if the thief had walked right through the walls.

Hmm.

It seemed to him that there was someone else he needed to talk to.

CHAPTER TWO

THE OFFICE OF KEELEY & Associates (there were no associates, but James thought it sounded more professional) was located in a dockside warehouse converted to office space. The building had been a speakeasy in the 1920s, and a variety of other things before and after—a cigar shipping company's warehouse, a fish processing facility, a bank of ministorage units, a car decal painting place. It had, however, never been any of those things for very long, with long empty periods in between. Currently it was broken up into cheap and bare-bones office spaces with a block of apartments on the top floor. James's neighbors, along with a lot of FOR RENT signs, were a tattoo parlor, the home office of a beauty product pyramid scheme, and a takeout pizza place that never seemed to have any customers, which he strongly suspected was a front for a betting racket.

James stopped by his office just long enough to toss the name list into the clutter on his desk and pick up a couple of necessary items. Then he went around back of the building, behind the loading dock, to the back stairs that led down into the old speakeasy underneath the main warehouse.

There was an iron gate across the top of the stairs; James had picked the lock the first time (infernal curiosity was going to kill him one of these days) but since then, he'd obtained a set of keys from the property management company that owned the building, under the aegis of keeping up the place as a sort of informal maintenance man. He also got reduced rent for one of the top-floor apartments that way—one of the few apartments that was currently rented out.

There was a reason why the building had trouble keeping tenants. It was haunted.

Dead leaves were littered down the stairs, along with beer cans and fast-food takeout wrappers. James had opted to leave the trash because it made the stairs look unused and helped keep people out of the basement. The metal door at the bottom was wedged in its slightly warped frame and, as always, took some effort to break loose.

Unlike the above-ground part of the warehouse, with its thorough remodeling, the basement was relatively unchanged from the old days. There was even still some ancient, broken furniture along the bare brick walls, though the gorgeous bar with its oiled wooden top had long since gone. There were no functional lights down here; the long, low space, broken up with brick pillars supporting the weight of the floor above, was lit by shafts of wan daylight filtering in through a handful of small, dirty ground-level windows.

It was cold down here, and dank. Even on the hottest days, the warmth of the surface world didn't penetrate the chill earth.

Or perhaps the perpetual cold was because of the basement's ghostly tenant.

James shut the door and knelt to place his dented, junk-shop brazier on the old wooden floorboards. The first few times he'd used a tin coffee can, until Dolly asked him if he could possibly get something nicer. He twisted a piece of newspaper in the brazier and stuck a couple of cigarettes into it, then lit the whole thing. The tobacco smoke twisted up in the air, making him cough. It spread much faster than it should have, filling the air, curling between the pillars.

"Dolly?" James called. He stepped back from the brazier and walked down the length of the basement, away from the choking cigarette smell, toward the end where the bar used to be. "You're gonna give me lung cancer, you know. Couldn't you have a vice that at least smells a little better?"

"You modern people," Dolly's light voice said. "So worried about a little cigarette smoke."

As he got closer, the bar emerged slowly from the shadows, as if he was seeing something that had been there all along, but a little off to the side of his reality. The rest of the speakeasy was dimly visible now, coming up slowly around him like a lightbulb brightening: polished wooden floorboards, tables and chairs, flickers of moving people and snatches of faint, distant jazz music.

Where direct daylight came in through the windows, nothing of the speakeasy could be seen. It was only visible in the gray halflight in between, emerging dimly from the smoky air.

Dolly was fully present by the time he got there, a blonde flapper with a beaded wrap around her short hair and a sleeveless, sheer dress. She had an elbow on the counter and a cigarette in one hand. Behind her, the bare bricks of the wall could be seen faintly through the glasses and bottles of her bartender's trade.

"Ahhhhh," she moaned, inhaling. The cigarette was the same one he'd placed in the brazier, a rather anachronistic modern Chesterfield filter. "That's good. You don't know what you're missing out on."

"Easy for you to say. *You* don't have to worry about lung cancer. Thanks for showing up, by the way."

"I always like showing up for you. It's more interesting than haunting an empty building." Dolly hopped up on the bar and sat with her foot swinging. By now it looked so solid that James could almost have placed an elbow on it, or sat on one of the stools in front. He didn't try; breaking the illusion often made Dolly disappear, so he leaned against the cobwebby brick wall instead.

Up close, there were traces of blood on her dress. Her name was Dolly Mott, and according to the newspaper accounts he'd looked up after meeting her for the first time, she had died at a heartbreakingly young twenty-three in a shootout between rival gangs on the docks. With all the gang business that had gone down here, she wasn't the only ghost who hung around the waterfront, but she was by far the most tangible, coherent, and easy to talk to.

"If you've got a few minutes, I have some questions about ghosts."

"Ooh, fun," Dolly said, leaning forward. The cigarette shortened as she smoked it. She was holding the other one, unlit, in her other hand, tucked into the crook of her elbow. James knew from experience that she would last as long as the cigarettes did, unless something else made her vanish first. "Fire away, Valentino. Don't know if I can answer, but I'll try."

"Are all ghosts tied to a specific place, or can some of them move around?"

"Oh," she said thoughtfully. Smoke wreathed her head and the ornate wrap around her hair, glittering at the edges with elaborate beadwork. There was an equally ornate necklace clasped around her neck, a rosette of several large stones that might have been rubies or emeralds if they were real; it was impossible to tell, because there was always an odd monochrome quality to Dolly. It wasn't that she was black and white, not exactly, but he always had trouble remembering afterward what color any part of her outfit was.

"I don't know, actually," she went on. "I think for most, it's a place or an object. So you could move a ghost by moving the object they were associated with. With me . . ." She tapped the cigarette on the edge of an ashtray by her hip. "It's the place. But I don't know why, and I don't know how many different options are out there."

"So it's possible."

"Sure," Dolly said with a shrug. "Why not."

"If a ghost could move around on their own—walk into a building, say—could they take something out with them? I've seen you move things around, including through walls. I *know* there are a statistically unlikely number of ashtrays in my office, given that I don't smoke."

Dolly refused to acknowledge this. "How big a thing are we talking?"

"Car-sized," James said.

She was already shaking her head. "No way. Moving pennies is hard enough. You can do more with something that was meaningful for you in life—"

"Ashtrays, say."

"—but you could be the world's biggest motorhead and still not be able to fade a whole *car*. Although . . ." She lit the second cigarette off the butt of the first. "You could drive one, probably. Haunted cars are a thing. Sure. Just moving the gas pedal wouldn't be too hard."

"That gives me the same set of problems as a human being driving it. This car had to go through walls."

"Car thieves? Spectacular. What'd they take?"

"A Lamborghini," James said. She looked baffled. "A very expensive Italian car, belonging to a dragon."

"Italian? Could be the outfits."

James laughed. "Not likely. It's just the make of the car. Anyway, the Mafia isn't going to mess with a dragon; they're not that dumb."

"So who is that dumb?" Dolly asked, the corner of her mouth quirking up.

Strangely enough, he hadn't thought about it that way before. Anyone who would steal from a dragon's hoard was either the world's biggest idiot, or an adrenaline junkie who thought they were immune to dragon fire. And an idiot couldn't have pulled this off.

"Thanks, Dolly. That was helpful."

"Anytime. I like helping you with your cases." She took a regretful look at the second cigarette, nearly smoked down to the stub. "Awww, time to go."

"Can you stick around longer?"

"Why?" she asked, giving him a quick smile. "Miss me when I'm gone?"

He did, sometimes, which was ridiculous; she was the ghost of a woman who had died long before he was born. "Your smile brightens up this place," he said.

"Charmer. Next time," she added, "bring more cigs."

"Will do," James said, smiling slightly.

"You're a nice guy, James Keeley, when you let yourself be."

"Thanks, I think?"

She faded out. Cheshire-cat-like, her lipsticked smile was the last to go, though he still couldn't have said what color her lipstick was. The bar went pale and translucent, and wisped away as the smoke began to clear.

The only thing that didn't vanish was her ashtray, a cheap tin one, probably a dime a dozen back in the 1920s. It dropped through the vanishing bar and clattered to the floor.

"Did you smoke like a chimney when you were alive, too?" James asked the empty air. There was no answer, of course.

He knelt and picked up the ashtray. Although unused except for old soot stains and dust collected through the years, it was slightly warm to the touch, as if warm ashes really had rested in it a moment ago.

He had no idea how anything about Dolly worked, and the more he asked her about ghosts, the less he felt like he knew.

"Thank you," he said to the room.

Standing on a chair with a broken back, he cracked open one of the windows to clear the lingering traces of smoke from the room. Then he collected the brazier and went back upstairs to add the ashtray to his Dolly collection on the office windowsill.

～

SO HE WAS LOOKING for an idiot, or an adrenaline junkie, or someone who had nothing to lose. Which gave him a rough profile for the thief, something to help narrow down Oz's suspect list, such as it was.

He ordered in from the pizza place—bookie front or not, they made a good deep dish—and went down Oz's list of fourteen names. Most of the names were male; stereotype though it might be, this was a male hobby more often than not, he supposed. Oz's annotations were focused mainly on reminiscing about what kind of cars each of them owned and coveted, none of which was a Lamborghini specifically, but some of them had a more pronounced taste for American cars and some preferred foreign, so he focused on the latter first.

At times like this, he wished he could afford to hire an assistant. Maybe he could tack some temporary office help onto Oz's bill as a case expense.

He did a quick-and-dirty check on each name on the list

by the simple method of looking them up on the Internet. Most were on Facebook. All but one were over the age of forty, and most over fifty; apparently this wasn't a young man's hobby either.

Not everyone had much public information on their Facebook profile, but of those who did, he moved the ones whose pictures tilted heavily toward their kids, spouses, and grandkids down to the bottom of the suspect list.

Someone with nothing to lose.

Most of these men had a *lot* to lose.

Which didn't mean they might not be nursing a secret desire for a life of crime, a Lamborghini-fueled midlife crisis. But most people didn't undergo a sudden personality change in their fifties. It was true that people could surprise you. Most people, however, were fairly predictable.

He also moved people who were invested in their careers off the top of the suspect list. One man came up on the roster of doctors at Grand Bluffs General, also appearing occasionally on lists of volunteers at local free clinics. Another ran a successful fast-food franchise. Men successful in their careers were not, he thought, the kind of men who would risk it all to steal from a dragon.

He ended with two at the top of the list. One was the only under-forty, Adrian Kowalczyk, who also had next to no Internet presence—no Facebook, very few hits online. James had managed to find him on the university's list of graduates from six years ago (magna cum laude). The only other hits were some pictures on a snowboarding website and a triathlon winners' list. He potentially could fit the adrenaline junkie part of the profile. At the very least he seemed more capable of stealing a Lamborghini than the previous guy on the list, a seventy-year-old retired electrician.

Suspect number two was the group's sole regular female member, Gloria Tep, also lacking an Internet history; she did have a Facebook, but it was entirely locked and empty of personal details.

James sent her a Facebook friend request, and after some thought, composed emails to both her and Kowalczyk.

To Gloria Tep:

Hello, Ms. Tep. My name is James Keeley and I'm a freelance reporter hoping to write a feature on women in the classic automotive hobby scene. If you're interested, at your convenience, could we arrange a time and place to chat a bit about how you got into the hobby and your experiences with it? Thank you!

And to Adrian Kowalczyk, from a different email address, one of several he kept handy:

Hi, Adrian! I'm a reporter for the Grand Bluffs Register and we're looking ahead to running a series of features on home-grown athletes this summer/fall. I was just checking out your triathlon win from last year, and we don't have many triathletes yet. If you're interested, could we meet and chat a bit, at a time and place that works for you? Thank you!

He tacked his phone number onto both emails and sat back in his chair, back and shoulders aching; another thing he ought to do with Oz's retainer check was buy a chair that wasn't a broken-down garage-sale special. Red sunset light striped the wall through the blinds, and cast long black shadows from the row of antique ashtrays lined up on the windowsill—metal and glass, and one old snuff tin.

Time to go talk to a gargoyle.

James left an unlit cigarette in the newly acquired tin ashtray on the windowsill. Sometimes he would come back to his office in the morning to find his offering smoked down to ash. It was nice to think that Dolly hung around the place occasionally, even if he never saw her up here.

CHAPTER THREE

JAMES PHONED AHEAD to let Oz know he was coming, so the dragon was waiting on the lawn of the mansion, with his long tail lashing around his flanks like an impatient cat's. In the waning sunset light, Oz's scales gleamed like metal, reflecting back the sky's fiery colors and the floodlights illuminating the front of the house. Sometimes Oz looked a little like a car himself, James thought, as he stepped out of his considerably less impressive Subaru hatchback. Or maybe a tank.

In spite of Oz's air of barely concealed impatience, he lowered his table-sized head until his chin was almost resting on the grass so James could talk to him without getting neck strain.

"I've been looking into your list of car club members," James said. "I've got a couple of potential suspects for you— Adrian Kowalczyk and Gloria Tep. Have you noticed either of them behaving unusually, maybe looking around your house a lot, or finding excuses to use the bathroom or otherwise—okay, now what's wrong?"

"It's not either of them," Oz said, and James sighed.

"Why'd you bother hiring me if you're just going to ignore my suggestions?"

"Don't blame me if you insist on sticking to your pet theories in the absence of logical motives," Oz replied, half-lidding his gleaming dinner-plate eyes.

"It's a two-hundred-thousand-dollar car. How much more of a motive do you need?"

"There is no reason for anyone in the club to steal from me. They can see my collection any time they like."

"Yes, but—" James took a breath. The customer was always right. He could check out the suspects tomorrow on his own. "Anyway," he said, "I want to talk to your gargoyle."

"Of course." Oz reared up and held out a clawed paw, palm up. "Climb aboard; I'll take you up to her rooftop."

"Uh," James said, staring at the creased, scaly palm. Being picked up and set on Oz's desk was one thing, but at least it was over quickly. "Can't she come down here?"

Oz snorted, huffing out a smoke ring. "Why would she? She's a gargoyle. They prefer high places."

"*I* don't," James muttered, but he stepped into Oz's hand. It was a very strange feeling, the yielding scaly skin with muscles and bones slipping about underneath his feet, like walking on a framed-in but unfinished floor covered with futons.

Then Oz's other hand closed around the first, and both hands caged him gently, like a kid holding a frog. With a feeling of claustrophobia, James gripped Oz's scaly fingers, each as thick as his thigh. Claws the size and shape of swords rested lightly against his neck and shoulders.

"Are you sure there's not an elevator or a staircase or something?"

"Why would there be, when Gneiss and I both have wings?"

"Her name is Nice?"

"Gneiss," Oz said, somehow managing to emphasize the silent G. "A kind of rock." And he took off with a powerful downbeat of his wings and a boom like a thunderclap.

James would have lost his footing, but Oz's careful yet implacable grasp made it impossible; he was imprisoned in a cage of fingers. He tried not to look down as the lawn receded dizzyingly.

Oz landed on the rooftop with a thump that shook the house and unfolded his hands. "There you go. You can get off now."

The roof was less steep than it looked from below, but it was still a slanting, slate-tiled nightmare descending toward a terrifying drop to the lawn. The darkness was almost complete now, a blessing (because he couldn't see the drop) and also a curse (because he couldn't see his feet very well, either). He made himself release his steadying grip on Oz's fingers only with a vast effort of will.

"I'm not going to be much use to you if I fall off this roof and break my neck. *You* might have wings, but I don't."

"I'll catch you," Oz said with an easy confidence that was probably meant to be comforting. He straddled the roof contentedly, his glossy metallic coils sprawling and the tip of his tail tapping lightly against the roof tiles. "Oh, there she is."

The gargoyle was a fast-moving bit of darkness. She came out of the night, clattering across the roof toward them with a sound like hailstones. She was smaller than James would have expected. On all fours, she didn't even come up to his waist, and in the dim light she looked and moved not unlike a large dog, a Rottweiler or German Shepherd, as long as you didn't look too closely at the half-folded wings on her back.

She looked more gargoyle-like when she sat back on her haunches a few feet from him, allowing him to see her more clearly. Her eyes reflected what light there was, gleaming like a pair of lamps.

"You're the human detective," she said. Her voice was quick and light, making James realize he had expected something garbled and gravelly. Instead it could be the voice of an ordinary human woman. There was only a slight amount of slurring from the fangs jutting from her bottom jaw.

"That's right. I'm James Keeley." He hesitated, then held out a hand. Gneiss recoiled as if he'd pointed a gun at her.

"It's a human custom," Oz rumbled from above them. "They squeeze paws. I know, it's odd."

Gneiss took his hand hesitantly in hers. Her fingers were smaller than his, but they were tipped with sharp stony claws, and she squeezed his hand with terrifying strength. He got the feeling that she was trying to be delicate, but it still hurt. She could probably have pulped the bones in his hand if she'd wanted to. After squeezing just long enough that James was pretty sure he'd have bruises for days, she let go. He retrieved his hand and tried to surreptitiously make sure the fingers still worked.

"Nice—uh, good to meet you. So, Gneiss—that's your name, right?"

In the near-darkness, lit mainly by the city glow, he saw her head move in a slight nod. Her ears were set on either side of her head like a human's, but they were long and tapered, mobile as a cat's; they rotated to prick forward, her interest centered on him.

James tried not to think about the fact that if he angered either of these creatures, they could toss him off the roof to his death without breaking a sweat. Spying on cheating spouses and repossessing used cars was relatively safe and unproblematic by comparison. Sweat prickled his spine.

"Gneiss, I wanted to ask you about last night. Were you here all night?"

"I usually am," Gneiss said. "Unless I fly somewhere to

hunt, but I don't do that often. The hunting is good around here, on the rooftop and in the woods."

James hadn't realized until now that the mansion bordered a strip of forest. From up here it was a dark tide of trees unbroken by lights, lapping at the back of the house.

"What is that, anyway? A park? Or your private grounds?" He directed the question to Oz.

"Both," Oz said. He curled his supple neck around to look down. "It is a nature preserve. Oh, look! Fireflies. Excuse me, I must go see them."

With that, he slithered over the peak of the roof, his tail dragging behind him with a dry rattle. And James realized that he had been relying on Oz as his personal safety net considerably more than he'd realized.

"Wait—!"

For something so big, Oz had vanished with surprising speed. There wasn't even a tick of claws on roof tiles. James took a few steps farther up the roof, high enough to see over the peak. Oz was crouched on the other side, clinging to the eaves and absolutely motionless, staring down into the woods with rapt attention.

Gneiss clattered up beside him. "Did you have more questions?" she asked. "Because the night has come on, and I would like to hunt."

"Sorry. Yes, please, I do, if you don't mind."

He sat on the peak of the roof; it made him feel a little less like he was going to slide down the tiles and fall off the edge. Gneiss sat beside him, and James noticed that her legs bent backwards, like a dog's rather than a human's.

"The main thing I wanted to ask is whether you saw anything odd last night," he said. "Someone coming or going when you wouldn't normally expect it, that sort of thing."

"I pay little attention to what normally goes on at ground level, I'm afraid." Gneiss was perfectly still as she spoke; her only movement was the twitching of her ears and the slight swiveling of her head as she kept her attention on the roof around them, not on James. Otherwise she was utterly immobile, like Oz, who was still intently looking down.

James found himself hyper-aware of his own little twitches and shifts in position, the rustle of his jacket as he moved. No human could have held that still unless they were specially trained for it. *This is what it truly means to be a predator, these creatures whose entire being is focused on the hunt. Humans think we are, but we're not.*

"What kinds of things do you notice?" he asked.

"Birds," Gneiss said, her ears pricking. "Tasty, tasty birds."

"Tell me about the birds, then. What were the birds like last night?"

It was the right question. Gneiss lit up and positively gushed about night-sleeping sparrows and night-hunting owls; about the swallows nesting under the eves that she was allowing to remain undisturbed for now because swallows were so very tasty at a certain age; about pigeons sleeping under bridges with their plump feathery bodies, soft and cooing and full of flavor, and a very unusual night-flying auklet that had gotten into the attic somehow, which she regrettably had not been able to catch because she would have loved to eat one—

"A what?" James asked, jerking himself out of a haze of bird-induced lethargy.

"An auklet. Amazingly far out of its range. They're waterfowl of the Arctic coast, though they migrate south for the winter, thousands of miles, very impressive—they winter on the California coast, all the way over there; it must have gotten very badly lost in its last migration, perhaps somehow came up the St. Lawrence seaway or the Mississippi. Pity I couldn't catch it; who knows when I'll next have a chance to taste one." Gneiss smiled, showing a serrated row of fangs; it was hard to be sure in the dark, but there might be feathers caught in some of them.

"It was in the attic?" James said, wrenching his gaze away.

"I saw it just as it wiggled out. It was too fast for me. My kind are ambush predators, not chasers."

Now he had a mental image of a gargoyle crouching on a roof, waiting for a pigeon to land, and pouncing. Well, it made sense from an ecological-niche point of view . . .

"Do birds get into the attic often?" he asked.

"Every once in a while. It's a big house, you know, with lots of places to hide; one can't patrol every crevice no matter how one tries. Last year we had a chimney swift nesting up here. Oz said he didn't mind, so I observed them closely and then when they were grown to plump perfection—"

"Can you show me where it got in?" James cut in before she could elaborate.

"Certainly. This way."

She clattered cheerfully to the edge of the roof. James followed nervously, shoes slipping on the tiles.

"Right under here," Gneiss said. She hung over the edge while she held on with her rear claws, head dangling in empty space, completely unconcerned about the four-story drop. "Oh . . . you can't see, can you?"

"I'll give you a hand," a deep voice rumbled behind James. At some point Oz had returned; he could move astonishingly quietly when he wanted to, making no more sound than Gneiss. "Here."

Before James could explain that he didn't actually *want* a hand, he was gripped in Oz's enormous paw and lowered over the edge of the roof. He caught a swift breath, and tried to concentrate on looking across rather than down.

There was enough light coming up from the bright yard lights that he could see the stonework under the roof edge without having to strain his eyes. There were vents under here for attic ventilation, and he could see how a not-too-large bird might be able to squeeze in.

James reached through Oz's fingers to touch the vents, and tried not to think about what might happen if Oz's grip on the roof slipped. Oz had wings; he'd be fine. But that didn't mean he'd be able to keep hold of a small, fragile human body. Or avoid crushing James to pulp with a convulsive clutch of his fist.

"A bird didn't steal my car," Oz said from above, a questioning note in his deep, rumbling voice.

"It seems a little suspicious, though, doesn't it? An out-of-season water bird that Gneiss has never seen before? And she knows everything there is to know about birds." It never hurt to flatter informants a little bit.

"It's not that rare for unusual birds to show up outside their normal range," Gneiss said, sounding pleased. "But we're *way* outside its range. They nest on barren islands, so perhaps it thought this house was a cliff."

"Maybe," James said.

With a stomach-wrenching jolt, Oz lifted him back onto the roof. "What are you thinking?" the dragon asked.

"It just seems like a huge coincidence for such a rare bird to turn up the night the car went missing, and inside the house, too. You said your walls were warded, but that wouldn't apply to someone who entered the house through a physical opening in the wall, right?"

"A bird couldn't have driven my car out of the garage," Oz pointed out.

"No, but it might have had—I can't believe I'm saying this —an accomplice. Look, if you don't mind, could you let go of me?"

"Oh. Right." Oz opened his hand, and James stepped off his palm and sat down hard on the slate tiles, which felt much more stable and secure than they had a few minutes ago.

"Are you unwell?" Oz asked, tilting his head to study James sideways out of one glossy, reflective amber eye.

"I'm fine. Listen, what are some possibilities you can think of for people who might be able to turn into birds, or take up residence in a bird's head?"

"It could be a shapeshifter," Gneiss said. She frowned. "I wonder if shapeshifters taste like normal birds. Not that I'd eat one, of course. That would be rude."

There were shifters who could turn into almost anything. Werewolves of course were the best known, but James knew of others. An auklet shifter certainly wasn't out of the question.

"Some fae can also shapeshift," Oz said. "But I haven't done anything to upset any fae."

"How sure are you that your entire car club are human?"

"Well," Oz said, "they *look* human."

That was what he'd thought. So did shifters, until they transformed.

"Could I see the inside of the attic?" James asked.

∾

THIS HAD the advantage of getting him back to the ground, and the disadvantage of having to get there the same way he'd gone up.

Gneiss flapped off into the dusk to resume her nocturnal search for tasty nesting birds, and Oz insisted on a fortifying cup of tea for James's nerves before taking him upstairs. From the outside, the house looked tall enough to contain at least four human-sized floors inside, but with its draconic dimensions, there were only two. A sweeping ballroom-style staircase, scaled to dragon dimensions, led to the second floor. Oz picked up James again and carried him, mounting stairs that were five or six feet to the step.

"No flying?" James asked, trying to ignore the jolting and the long drop to the marble floor.

"Difficult to fly indoors. Wings keep breaking things."

Oz set him down upstairs. The "attic" that James had pictured was nothing like the reality, a long gabled space with lounging-around furniture—dragon-scale couches, he guessed, looking a bit like something from ancient Rome. The place looked one part living room, one part study. There were bookshelves everywhere, some with stacks of human-sized books, others containing dragon-scale books that James probably couldn't even pick up.

He couldn't resist peeking at the titles. Most of the nearest books were murder mysteries, especially cozy mystery series with punny titles.

"I'm learning more of human behavior by reading your literature," Oz said. "It's quite enlightening."

James picked up a book off the nearest shelf that was low enough for him to reach: *Bread to Murder*. "You know these are made up, right?"

"I understand the concept of fiction, yes," Oz scoffed. He reared up on his hind legs to investigate the vents.

James put the book back on its shelf, and looked up at the high ceiling. The enormous scale of Oz's dragon-sized furniture made him feel like Jack in the beanstalk tale, wandering around a giant's house.

"So if a bird got in here," he said, "it could easily fly downstairs."

"I suppose. I hadn't thought it was an issue, one bird in the house more or less. Gneiss always catches them eventually."

"Does it happen often?" James asked.

"Oh, now and then." Oz prodded at the vents and then

dropped back to all fours. "I quite like the fresh air, but perhaps I should cover these."

"It might be a good idea, in case the thieves come back."

Oz looked down at him. "You know, I think I'm starting to understand what you do a little better now."

That sounded ominous. "How so?" James asked.

"You let people talk about themselves. With Gneiss, for example. You didn't ask her too many questions; you just let her talk. It's how you are with the river dragons as well, why they recommended you to me. You let them show you their finds and don't get bored."

James found himself embarrassed, all the more so because he hadn't known he was doing that with the river dragons; they were just interesting to watch. "It's curiosity, that's all. I'm a terminally curious person. Speaking of which . . . can I look at your garage again? I'd like to see if we can figure out how they got the car out."

But there was no enlightenment to be had. Knowing that someone could have been in the house without Oz's knowledge didn't really help when the floor was still solid concrete, the security footage showing nothing unusual. The cameras could have been looped, in theory, though James didn't think most thieves were that organized or competent. But they still would have had to get the car out somehow.

"Oz, if someone started the engine of the car, would you have been able to hear it?"

"Immediately," Oz said with no hesitation. "Sound carries very well in this house. And I have sharp ears. I would have known."

"When did you last see it? I mean, exactly. You said last night?"

"Yes, the auto club meets in the evening, for the benefit of those who work human jobs during the day." Oz's tone suggested an amused indulgence of such human foibles as jobs. "We examined my collection, of course. They made many appreciative comments." He preened modestly.

"So you had them all in here?" James looked across the rows of gleaming cars, arranged as if in a showroom. "Did they stay together, or spread out?"

"Spread out, I suppose. We were walking about, looking at the cars. I was on hand to answer any questions. There were some *most* perspicacious comments from Hal—that's Hal Burton on your list," Oz added helpfully, "if you wanted to look him up. He has a 1969 Impala 327 that I was going to come over on Saturday to see. You could come if you want."

"I'll let you know." It might not be a bad way to meet some of the club, with Oz to introduce him—but that was still three days out. "Do they always do that when they're here, walk around unattended? I mean, could they have been wandering around the place all evening?"

"Of course not," Oz scoffed. "We were having a *meeting*. I'm not such a poor host as that."

"But did you keep track of all of them for the entire evening?"

"I assure you," Oz said, an edge creeping into his tone, "*every* car was here when I displayed my collection to the club."

"And it's not like they could just drive it right out in front of you." At least, they shouldn't have been able to. But if there was shapeshifter magic involved, perhaps there was other magic as well. "Did you check back afterward, or was the time you were in here with the club the last time you looked at the cars?"

"I didn't come back after. I was busy cleaning up and then went upstairs to read."

"So you were upstairs for the rest of the evening?" James asked, resolutely *not* allowing himself to veer into wondering how Oz read those tiny-for-him books (with a magnifying glass, perhaps?). "You didn't happen to notice a bird flying around, did you?"

"I did not," Oz said thoughtfully.

"When did the club leave?"

"They drifted off throughout the evening, as they often do. The last ones were here until . . . after ten, I believe. I wasn't paying close attention to the time. We had drinks and discussed Hal's Impala. Instead of the factory-standard small-block engine, it has an after-model 350 V8 with an Edelbrock four-barrel carburetor—"

"And who was here at the end of the evening?" James inserted hastily.

"Hal and Gloria."

Gloria Tep, who had been one of James's initial picks for top suspects. "Were you with them the entire time? Did you walk them to the door?"

"As if I would do anything else," Oz said, offended.

"Could any of them at any point have had a chance to wander around unattended?"

"I did not have my eyes on every single human at every point throughout the evening. Does that settle the matter for you?" His face settled into a scowl, an ominous look indeed on a creature that weighed several tons and could breathe fire.

James raised his hands. "Listen, I know they're your friends. I know you don't want to suspect them. Look at it this way—I'm a professional suspicious bastard. You hired me for that. I suspect them so you don't have to. I won't accuse anyone without evidence, I swear."

Oz's scowl relaxed slowly into a sort of smile, alarming on that long-nosed, scaly face. "Of course. That is an excellent way to put it. A professional suspicious bastard. I like that." He perked up. "Would you care to stay for dinner? I rarely have dinner guests, except for the auto club."

James wasn't sure why he had a sudden gut-kick of *nope*. That was the last thing he wanted to do, sticking around beyond the bounds of their professional relationship, indulging the dragon's apparent desire to make friends with every human he met.

"No, I need to get back to the office. You've given me a lot to work with. Oh, could you have your mechanic call me? I'd like to talk to him."

"Her," Oz said. "Gloria Tep handles that for me."

"You could have mentioned that earlier."

"I told you it wasn't her," Oz said.

James rubbed his eyes. "Okay, fine, then do me a favor and please don't mention any of this to her, or any of the rest of them. I'd like to question people in the club without letting them know I'm working for you."

"It's *not* Gloria." Oz brightened. "We could discuss it over dinner."

"Can't," James said firmly, "other commitments, sorry."

But he found himself oddly regretful, looking back at the house with his hand on his car door, standing in the penumbra of the brilliant light cast out by the floodlights scattered around the grounds. Lit up like that, with most of the interior lights on, the mansion looked big enough to be an event space, as if there should have been dozens of people inside.

But there was only Oz. It seemed like a lonely life for someone so gregarious.

Out of the dark sky, something landed on the roof with a thump, and a few feathers sifted down.

Okay . . . Oz and Gneiss.

James was smiling when he got into the car.

CHAPTER FOUR

GLORIA TEP WAS a perky dynamo of a woman who cheerfully showed him the two classic cars she owned, an Austin Healey Sprite Mk1 roadster and a refurbished Dodge Power Wagon. She was Cambodian, she said, and had come to the US as a child and had a successful career as a real estate agent before the housing market bubble crashed. The implosion of the real estate market shattered both her business and her marriage, so now she was divorced and worked as a gig mechanic while running a small lawn-care business.

James found himself liking her a lot, and also felt extremely guilty that he wasn't actually writing a story on her. He took down her contact information, tried to lower her expectations a bit by pointing out that the story might never make it to publication, and quietly wondered if he might be able to talk an actual reporter into coming by to chat with her.

He had to admit that he agreed with Oz that she hadn't been involved. There was no room for a Lamborghini in her pocket-sized backyard, and even though she could have had a buyer arranged, as the person who worked on Oz's cars she would have known it was a highly recognizable vehicle. Why that one, an extremely rare and noticeable car, out of all the ones in Oz's collection? And why stick around afterward, knowing she'd be the prime suspect? It was possible, but it just didn't fit.

Back at his office, he looked up auklets. Like Gneiss had said, the auklet was a small waterbird, mostly found around the coast of Alaska and Siberia. They wintered over farther south, but this was a deeply strange latitude to find them in the summer, especially this far inland.

James scribbled on a notepad: *The auklet is in on it.* And then he felt ridiculous. His phone rang as he scratched it out.

"Mr. Kelsey?" The voice on the other end was unfamiliar, and it wasn't until the caller added, "This is Adrian Kowalczyk" that he remembered Jim Kelsey was the sender on the email address he'd used to contact Kowalczyk last night. It was a believable typo for his real name if he needed plausible deniability.

He took a breath and swung into Salesman Mode. In his long and checkered employment history, he'd had several stints at trying to sell things, from telemarketing to off-brand bottled water to shoes. He wasn't exactly good at it, but he could do the patter for a short time.

"Adrian! Hi! Good of you to call me back, really appreciate it. What do you think of getting together for a chat? We'd love to put more of a spotlight on local athletics."

"I don't really like being in the spotlight, to tell you the truth," Adrian said with a laugh. His voice was light and friendly.

"No pressure. We won't run anything you aren't comfortable with. Hey, you get a free lunch out of it, on me."

"Takeout?" Adrian suggested. "I work from home, but if you wouldn't mind picking up something, I could give you a half-hour or so of my time."

~

ADRIAN KOWALCZYK LIVED in one of the newer housing developments that spilled down the bluffs toward the river. It was rugged here, with steep driveways plunging to nice houses half-hidden in brush and trees. Adrian's place was one of those, visible from the road only as glimpses of beige showing through dense willows and sumac. A turn of the driveway gave James a view of a split-level McMansion on a notch of flat land carved out of the hillside. The part of the bluff too steep to build on overhung the house.

James parked beside a low-slung, gleaming classic Corvette and a Mini Cooper. Adrian trotted down the stairs to meet him. He was compact and energetic, with a strong, firm handshake, his pale hair buzzed off in a tight cut.

"Gorgeous car," James said. Although Adrian was only wearing jeans and a T-shirt, James felt a little downscale here, in his worn jeans and beat-up brown leather jacket with its creases worn deep.

"She's a beaut, isn't she? I'm going to assume you don't mean the Mini."

James grinned and reached back into the car for the bag of takeout from the Indian restaurant Adrian had suggested. "No, I meant the 'Vette. Gorgeous view too."

From here, the neighbors were concealed behind trees, giving the illusion of total privacy. The river glistened gray and white below. The opposite bluff was dotted with houses and pale outcroppings of rock poking through the green blanket of trees. James could just glimpse downtown and the warehouse district where he had his office. Somehow the river always seemed muddier down there.

"Investments," Adrian said. "My siblings and I have a consulting business."

"I didn't find you online."

Adrian's pale eyebrows went up.

"I'm a reporter," James said. "I did a little background research so I wouldn't come out here and sound hopelessly ignorant."

Adrian grinned, a flash of white teeth. "It's not under my name. Cliffside Securities. Here."

He handed James a business card, cream-colored with gold letters. The name of the business was above *A. Kowalczyk, Consultant*, along with a phone number and email.

"Come on up to the deck," Adrian said. He led the way with that same coiled energy, bounding up the steps ahead of James.

The gym where James worked out was a seedy hole-in-the-wall where a guy like Adrian probably wouldn't be caught dead, but if James had run into him there, he was pretty sure his initial impression would have been *gymbro douche*. The kind of guy who ran everywhere, and worked out until he was a little too musclebound to move like a normal human being.

'Course, I guess that could just be jealousy, coming from a guy who's thirty-four and starting to feel every one of those years. His right leg still twinged where he'd been kicked in the hamstrings on a repo job last fall; it was all too noticeable climbing the steep stairs to the deck.

"Drink?" Adrian asked. He grabbed a couple of chairs and pulled them over to a wooden patio table with a shade umbrella. "Shake? Smoothie? Beer? I'm gonna crack open a cold one, me."

"Yeah, sure." James left the bag of takeout on the table and followed Adrian into the house, since he hadn't been specifically told not to.

Just inside the double doors from the deck, there was an enormous open-plan combination living room and kitchen. James wasn't expecting anyone else, so the sight of a blonde woman in the kitchen brought him up short. She had a pony-tail and wore a tank top showing off the female version of Adrian's thickly muscled shoulders—not as overbuilt, but definitely modeled on the same compact, powerful physique. She was pouring something out of a blender as Adrian got two beers out of the fridge. All she did was give James an unfriendly look before taking her tall glass of frothy brown-ish-green whatever elsewhere.

"Girlfriend?" James asked.

Adrian laughed, flashing those white teeth. "Sister. That's Ada."

"Your parents had a theme."

Adrian laughed again, cracked open the beers, and handed one to James. "Convenient for the business cards, though."

"She works with you? I'd've brought a curry for her too if I'd known."

"Don't worry about it. We all do our own thing. She just doesn't like strangers in the house."

With that not-at-all-suspicious comment hanging in the air, Adrian grabbed a handful of silverware from a drawer and went back out to the sun-drenched deck. James opened the takeout bag and began parceling out containers.

"There's probably enough here for your sister to clean up some of the leftovers if she wants to. Is it just the two of you?"

"One more of each," Adrian said, peeling back the foil from the still slightly oven-warm naan. "Adric, Ada's twin, lives with us. Aliette is just up the hill with her husband."

"Must be nice, having the whole family here," James said. It actually sounded like a nightmare to him, but then, he didn't have the best track record at getting along with family.

"Oh, you know, birds of a feather and all that," Adrian said cheerfully. James looked up quickly from spooning out rice.

"Auklets?" he said.

A quick sharp flash crossed Adrian's face, a spark in his eyes, hidden almost at once by the affable smile. "Say what?"

"Auklets. Waterfowl. They flock together."

"Oh. Good one." Adrian laughed. "And weirdly specific. But okay."

There was no point in keeping up the pretense, James decided. He'd played through with Gloria, but Adrian clearly knew something, so why the hell not push him a little? James dipped a piece of naan in the curry sauce and said, through a bite, "I ought to tell you that I'm not actually a reporter. I'm a private investigator looking into a car that was stolen the other night."

Adrian froze in the act of chewing, then finished and swallowed. He pushed his chair back, the movement quiet and dangerous. "What are you doing here, then?"

"I think you either stole it or you know who did."

Adrian gave him a long stare. His eyes had gone flat and reflective as marbles. "That's a hell of an accusation to make to a man on his own property. I think it's time for you to leave."

"Really? Do you have an alibi for your whereabouts two nights ago?"

"Not that I need to justify myself to you, but I have a dozen witnesses who can tell you exactly where I was," Adrian snapped. He rose from the table. James stood too; Adrian had the sort of leashed tension to him that could snap suddenly into violence. "I was at a meeting of a local hobby-ists' auto club, and then I came straight home. My siblings can corroborate."

"You know, I've hardly ever heard anybody say 'siblings' in real life."

"Get. Out."

James lifted his shoulders in a shrug and began returning

containers to the bag, though he did it with part of his attention on the table and most of it on Adrian. "Hope you don't mind if I take the leftovers. I hardly got to eat anything."

"I said *get out*. Don't make me say it again."

The glass door to the deck opened, and Adrian's sister came out. She moved the same way her brother did, a tense practiced grace combined with the slowness that came with a little too much bulking up. "What's going on out here?"

"Turns out this guy's a private dick." Adrian emphasized the word *dick*. "Who was just leaving."

Ada leaned against the wall beside the door and folded her arms. "Does he need help?"

"Kind of you to offer," James said, "but I've got it, thanks."

He went down the stairs with frequent glances above, where brother and sister flanked each other to block the top of the stairs. Ada was just a couple of inches shorter than her brother. James wouldn't want to tangle with either of them. He popped down the door locks after getting in the car.

It was tempting to stay in their yard for a little while and see what they did next, but he wouldn't put it past them to take a baseball bat to the car, or call the police.

Instead, he pulled out onto their road, then stopped at the next of the steep, partly hidden side driveways. Carefully he backed up the driveway until he was far enough off the road that the bushes obscured the car. He was blocking the driveway completely, but, well, if anyone came along and asked him to move, he'd deal with it then. He rolled his window down and occupied himself by pulling the bag of takeout into his lap and opening a carton.

When he saw the birds dart past the mouth of the driveway, he didn't realize at first that he'd just seen what he was waiting for. He was expecting a car. The image caught up with his brain a second after, a flash of two medium-sized, gray-and-white birds, a glimmer of orange beaks and fast-beating wings. They could have been pigeons or ducks. But they could just as easily have been two of the dark-gray sea birds he had looked up back at the office.

James shoved half a naan in his mouth, and followed those birds.

CHAPTER FIVE

It was easier said than done, but not impossible. The birds flew low, darting along the road rather than taking to the sky, as if they were trying not to be seen. Which was probably exactly what they were doing. Gneiss's reaction suggested that any bird watcher would notice a stray sea bird a thousand miles inland.

Still, James's Subaru, fifteen years old and held together mostly with dirt and hope, struggled with the tight turns of the steep and winding hillside roads. By the time he pulled out onto the clifftop road, he thought he'd lost the birds until he glimpsed them darting through the trees alongside the road.

The clifftop road was a long straight drag that ran directly into the center of Grand Bluffs' commercial district, so at least he could keep them in sight without difficulty for a while. The fact that there were a pair of them made it easier to be sure, or at least reasonably sure, that he had the right birds.

This is complete madness. You know that, right?

Birds didn't have to contend with traffic lights, so he lost them briefly when he hit the edge of town. He glimpsed the pair of birds again while stuck behind a slow-moving garbage truck—or *a* pair of birds, anyway. They darted over the roof of the railroad depot, soared high in the air, and abruptly folded their wings and dropped into the tangle of little residential streets around the railyards.

James pulled around the red-brick depot, skirting its parking lot. They were only a few blocks as the crow (or the auklet) flew from James's office in the warehouse district, but here it was all square frame ranch houses from the postwar building boom and apartment buildings with flaking paint and gravel parking lots. It was a neighborhood of old people who'd lived here all their lives, and college kids and minimum-wage working families who relied on the cheap rent. The railroad ran through the middle of it, behind a tall chain-link fence topped with wire.

There was no sign of a pair of fat-bodied gray birds in trees, on phone lines, on top of the railyard fence. James slowed to a crawl and cruised the narrow sidewalk-less streets, glancing at mailboxes. It was a long shot, but it was all he had at this point. Unless he caught sight of the birds again, he'd have to hope they had gone to one of the other members of the auto club, and that he would recognize the name from the mailbox.

And there it was. EAGAN MURPHY, on a tilting box shaped like a small red barn. An uncommon enough name that he couldn't help but recognize it, especially after looking everyone up on Facebook yesterday.

The house was a one-story white box, the lawn slightly overgrown with grass climbing up around a rusty swing set and an old bike. James parked behind a dismantled project car mostly covered with a frayed tarp, and reached into the backseat to retrieve Oz's list of names with James's annotations. Murphy was one of the club members that he'd put in the low-possibility category, an old dude whose Facebook was mostly family photos of potlucks and barbecues.

Well, you know what they say about people who ass-*ume* . . .

All seemed quiet; it was impossible to tell if anyone was home. He looked around carefully for suspiciously loitering gray birds, but saw none. There was a Jeep parked on the side of the street that might or might not belong to the owner of the house.

James drummed his fingers on the steering wheel. After weighing the pros and cons, he leaned under the seat and extracted a bundle wrapped in a reusable canvas shopping bag. When he unwrapped it, a snub-nosed revolver in a beat-up leather holster fell into his lap.

It looked like a Colt .38, and it very nearly was. He had a license to carry it. What he didn't have a license for was the ring of highly illegal spellgun sigils wrapping around the cylinder and grip. James regularly buffed them out with shoe polish and paint so the gun could pass for a normal gun at a cursory glance, but they inevitably started to glow through again.

For the most part, the spellgun was no more dangerous than an ordinary gun; in fact, in James's experience it was considerably less so. But, as well as working on creatures that were impervious to normal ammo, it made its bearer immune to most magic. While carrying this, he would shed spells and glamours like rain off a charmed raincoat.

He got out of the car, adjusting his jacket to cover the holster. The tarped-over car didn't look like a Lamborghini, even a stripped-down Lamborghini, but he lifted the edge of the tarp anyway, just to make sure. It was some kind of road-ster from the 1920s or 1930s, which was about as close as he could get on any car.

I'm not a car guy, but it's starting to look like I might be by the time this case is over.

A cracked concrete walkway led from the street to the porch. Children's toys were scattered about, half-lost in the grass: a toy car, a doll, a miniature dog.

James stepped up onto the porch, hesitated with his finger over the doorbell, then cupped his hands around his face and peered through the small diamond-shaped window instead. He couldn't see anything except the lacy pattern of a curtain.

He left the porch and went quietly around the side of the house. The weeds were long here, cluttered with garden tools. He had to step carefully to avoid making noise.

Voices up ahead. James slowed to a creep, one hand lightly trailing along the house's old aluminum siding. He couldn't make out what they were saying, only that there were two male voices. One sounded agitated, the other placating. James slid forward one careful step at a time.

"You have a moral problem with it?" one of the speakers was saying.

"No, I have a logistical problem with it!" That was definitely Adrian's voice. "Our business model relies on people not getting too curious about us. We have to stay under the radar. I fucking *knew* anything this high-profile was a mistake."

"It's not high-profile in the slightest," the other voice said —Eagan Murphy, maybe. He had some kind of light accent, hard to define: a certain lift to the vowels. "There's nothing in the paper about it, or the police blotter. There's exactly one—"

James never heard what there was only one of, because it was drowned out by a high-pitched screech. He looked up to see the orange beak and gray head of an auklet looking down over the gutter at him. Its beak opened and it screamed again.

Damn it. He'd momentarily forgotten there were two of them to watch out for.

Well, it wasn't like there was any point in stealth now. He rounded the corner of the house just in time to have a feathered explosion erupt in his face. This wasn't the same bird as the one on the roof, which was still shrieking up a storm, and this one was only trying to get away, not attack. James ducked aside and it streaked over his shoulder, wings beating madly. The other bird launched itself from the roof. They were both built along the lines of pigeons, with comparatively heavy bodies for their fast-beating wings, and it dropped a couple of feet before managing to catch the air and join its fleeing companion.

"You know, it's customary for guests to knock," Murphy said.

He was sitting at a patio table with a cup of coffee in one hand. He was easy enough to recognize from his Facebook photos, a little old guy with a shock of white hair underneath a flat tweed cap that James wasn't sure he'd ever seen anyone actually wear outside of British murder mystery shows. A potbelly strained against the buttons of Murphy's red plaid shirt.

Everything about him looked completely harmless, which made James glad he'd brought the spellgun.

"I knocked on the door," James lied. "No one answered."

There was no sign of anyone else on the back patio now, but it was impossible to miss signs of recent occupation: a second coffee cup on the table, a jacket slung over the arm of the other chair.

"So you decided to creep around the side of the house?" Murphy said. "I could call the police, you know."

"But you won't. Will you?" As he spoke, James took a quick look around the backyard. It was a typical yard for these WWII-era railroad houses, pocket-sized and surrounded by a low chain-link dog fence that butted up against the neighbors' yards on both sides. Like the front, it was not precisely run down, but it was somewhat over-grown. There was a sagging-roofed garden shed, and bushes covered with yellow flowers spilling out of the stakes that had been set up to contain them.

There was no sign of a Lamborghini or anywhere that one might be hidden. If Murphy had stolen it, or hired Adrian to do it, the car wasn't here.

"That's a lot of confidence for a man trespassing on private property." Murphy rose from the chair, and James realized that he hadn't been able to tell from the Facebook photos how short the guy was. He couldn't be much over five feet tall. "Who are you, anyway?"

"I'm—" James ran through a couple of possible lies, but settled on the truth. " . . .a private detective hired to look into a theft. I followed Adrian Kowalczyk here. That was him just now, wasn't it—the bird?"

Murphy gazed at him for a moment and then picked up the other coffee cup. "I just put on a fresh pot. Want some? I think there's some coffeecake too."

The prudent answer was probably "no," but James had no particular fear of being physically overwhelmed by a five-foot-tall retiree, and for everything else, he had the spellgun. "Yeah, sure."

Murphy held the door for him.

There was a small mudroom that opened directly onto the living room. The house was clean but slightly cluttered in a bachelor type of way. The majority of the clutter consisted of model cars. They were everywhere, on end tables and the coffee table and even the couch. The bookshelves on the walls held mostly models rather than books. Freestanding glassed-in cases held the ones that must be rare or expensive or simply the ones Murphy was the most proud of.

"Do you like my collection?" Murphy asked. He was smiling—beaming, rather.

"It's really impressive." James made a wordless, questioning gesture at the toys on the nearest shelf. Murphy nodded, and James picked one of them up.

It was heavy in his hand, a silver car about six inches long. Once again his general lack of knowledge about cars made it hard to guess the make or model, although the unusual doors —opening up, rather than out—triggered a movie-related memory.

"DeLorean?"

"1955 Mercedes-Benz 300 SL gullwing, actually," Murphy said. He reached over and touched some of the little details on the car with a proprietary sort of pride, brushing a thumb across the hood ornament and the tiny, delicately crafted door handles. "It's a real shame that auto designs have become so standardized now, don't you think? There used to be such a variety. Feel free to look at anything you like. Are you a collector?"

"I had a model phase like most kids, but it was more airplanes with me," James said. "I never finished any of them." *And Mom used to break them to punish me.* But he didn't think that particular detail needed to be shared. "What I'm looking for isn't a model, it's a full-sized car. A Lamborghini. Haven't seen one of those around, have you?"

"I've plenty of Lamborghinis." Murphy gestured at the walls and smiled. "Look around. You'll find one in no time."

"Yeah, but not the one I'm looking for." He gave the toy wheels a little spin with his fingertip and put the Mercedes back on its shelf. "There's no need for you to cover for Adrian Kowalczyk and his sister, you know. Being a shifter isn't illegal. Unpopular, maybe, but that's not the same thing."

"Asking questions must be part of your job. I won't hold it against you." Murphy went into the adjoining kitchen. There were model cars here too; shelves on the walls were full of them, as well as a promotional calendar featuring, naturally, classic cars. James was half-expecting cars all over the dishes too, but the mug Murphy took down from a shelf was just a chipped promotional mug with a radio station logo.

"Sugar? Milk?"

"Uh . . . little bit of milk. Look, I appreciate the hospitality, but I really need to ask you some questions about the other night."

"Which night?" Murphy turned to open the door of the fridge, which was elderly and decked out in classy 1970s olive green.

"Night before last. The night of the auto club meeting at Ozymandias's house."

"Ozymandias. You know, I'd never met a dragon before he joined the club. He's quite something, isn't he? Very curious about humans. Do you think they're all like that?"

"Since they're better known for living in caves on mountaintops, I doubt it." James accepted the mug, wrapping his fingers around its warmth. It didn't feel like Murphy was trying to work some kind of magic on him; while wearing the spellgun, he could often feel glamours and the like as they slid off him. "Ozymandias doesn't understand humans very well, he just likes them. He thinks we're all trustworthy and honorable. He refuses to entertain the idea that anyone from the car club would steal from him. It's really going to be a knife in his back when he finds out, isn't it?"

Murphy only shrugged, looking unconcerned as he topped off his own cup. "Why do you care? You're a hireling. You're only in it for the money."

That blow landed harder than it should have. "Yeah, I was hired to do a job," James said. He set his untouched coffee cup down between a model Volkswagen Beetle and a miniature truck. "Part of that means looking out for my employer's interests. Look, Murphy, I know you and Adrian did it. Where's the Lamborghini?"

"Pick one," Murphy said, waving a hand at the walls. He smiled, and two fingers lifted off his coffee mug and jerked in an imperious and curiously pointed gesture.

That was magic. James was already stepping backward quickly as he felt the tingling rush of some kind of spell hitting the spellgun's defensive shield and sliding off him. There was a soft, implosive *whoomph!* sound somewhere off to his left, and a clatter.

Murphy flinched back, staring at him. For the first time his composure cracked. "Why didn't that work?"

James's heart drummed in his chest. He glanced sideways to see what Murphy had tried to do to him. There was nothing visible, no scorch marks on the kitchen wallpaper or dripping, glowing anything. Just in case, he kept moving, backing into the living room, toward the door. His hip hit the couch and he edged to the side.

"Magic doesn't work on me." He left the spellgun in its holster, tucked under his jacket, because the last thing he wanted Murphy to realize was that the way to attack James was by separating him from the gun. "Look, I just want to know what you did with the damn car. I don't care about the rest of it. I'm here for the car, not you."

Frustration twisted Murphy's face. He jerked his fingers in the same imperious gesture, and again James had the sense of the spell sliding off him and hitting something in the vicinity. There was a soft thump from a corner of the living room. James risked a fast look but still couldn't see what it had done.

"Right," he muttered, and kept backing up, taking out his phone. He angled the phone so he could see it and Murphy at the same time, and brought up Oz's number before putting it to his ear.

"James," Oz rumbled, sounding pleased.

"Hey." James kept his eyes on Murphy. "I found your thief. Eagan Murphy. I haven't found the car yet, but—"

Oz was making some kind of protesting noise, probably along the lines of "Not one of *my* car club members!" but James only caught the beginning of it. Murphy gestured with his entire arm and body, slopping coffee over his hand, and the phone slipped out of James's hand and—

—vanished.

Except it hadn't. A tiny, toy-sized phone bounced off James's knee and clattered to the floor.

With his gaze fixed on Murphy, James knelt to scoop it up. The phone was too heavy to be plastic, but it appeared to be nonfunctional, a perfect miniature toy phone, about an inch long.

A cold chill slithered through him. Those toys on the lawn, and all the goddamn *cars* . . .

"Why doesn't it *work* on you?" Murphy sounded almost childlike, frustrated nearly to tears.

"Goodbye," James said. His back hit the front door, and he fumbled behind him to open it.

This was Oz's problem, not his. He had no interest in arresting Murphy or looking through his toy collection for the Lamborghini, let alone being added to it as a miniature driver. He'd never found out if the spellgun had a limited number of spell defenses in it, and he wasn't about to find out now.

He got the door open, stepped back, and slammed into someone tense and muscular who threw an arm around his neck and put him in a headlock.

CHAPTER SIX

IT WAS ADRIAN; James guessed that much without even being able to get a clear look at him. They thrashed across the porch. James slammed Adrian's back into the siding, but Adrian, with his gym-toned body, was as strong as an ox. James's vision began to telescope inward as Adrian's arm clamped down on his throat. He kicked backwards, nearly lost his balance as his bad knee buckled, then tried stomping on Adrian's feet. They both fell hard and rolled down the steps to the front walk. Adrian yelped when James's weight landed on him.

"Ow—*fuck*—Ada—!"

James had a brief glimpse of Ada Kowalczyk running at him across the lawn. Her foot connected with his stomach and drove the breath and most of the fight out of him. There were more blows to his neck and back, and the next thing he knew, he was facedown in the grass, choking for breath with a splitting headache and Adrian's knee in his back.

Firm hands patted him down and stripped him of the spellgun. James felt it go with a surge of acute panic. There was nothing to stop Murphy now from toy-ifying him.

"Damn it, I hate fighting right after shifting," Ada said from somewhere above him. "It's hard to get used to having depth perception again, and I keep expecting wings."

James managed to twist his head to the side, trying to get enough air. A few inches from his face, one of the toys in the grass stared back at him with a blank, unblinking gaze. It was a doll dressed like a miniature postman a few inches high.

"—doesn't *work* on him," Murphy said from a little farther away. "I tried three times. I don't know why."

So they hadn't figured out it was the spellgun yet. It was only a matter of time, though.

Then the ground shook with a terrific thump, and Oz's voice rumbled overhead, "What is happening here?"

The weight that was slowly pressing the air out of James's lungs abruptly stopped moving, and then eased up and withdrew. James sucked in a desperate breath, coughed, rolled over and sat up.

Oz had landed on the lawn. His coils spilled out into the street, and he'd flattened part of the fence. His wings were spread high above his back, casting shade across the lawns of the houses on either side. He looked even bigger than usual here, on this residential street, than at the mansion where everything was scaled to match him.

And he also looked furious. Smoke wreathed his head, curling from between his teeth.

"What are you people *doing*? James, are you well?"

"Fine." James coughed again and wiped dirt off his face.

"James says that you stole my Lamborghini. And I trust James." The dragon's face screwed up; he was clearly angry, but just as clearly struggling with the entire concept of betrayal. "But I also trusted you. Why would you do such a thing?"

"Oh, shut up," Murphy said, and jerked his hand.

James started to yell a warning. It had never really

occurred to him that Murphy's magic would work on Oz. Oz was—he was a *dragon*, powerful and huge, impervious to any normal form of injury.

But not, apparently, to magic.

It was instantaneous. Oz evaporated; there was the muffled crack of air rushing in to fill a dragon-sized space. An instant later, something small that flashed in the sun, Oz's metallic iridescent color, bounced off the top of James's car and fell into the driveway.

James was distantly aware that his hands were shaking. "You killed him," he said thickly.

"If it makes you feel any better," Murphy said, "he didn't feel a thing."

He strolled over to pick up the toy dragon, turned it over in his hand, and put it in his pocket. "There's something I still don't understand. Why doesn't my magic work on *you?*"

"I'm . . . immune," James lied. "It's natural resistance. No magic works on me." Rallying somewhat, he added, "I bet you could use a guy like me."

"If magic doesn't work, I bet bullets do," Adrian said, and James looked up quickly to find himself staring down the barrel of his own gun.

"For heaven's sake, don't shoot him on my lawn." Murphy sounded impatient rather than shocked. "The neighbors will notice."

"I don't really care," Adrian said between his teeth. "If any cops show up, just do your miniaturizing thing."

"That is not a solution," Murphy snapped. "I'd have to move. Put the damn gun down."

"Adrian, do as he says." Ada's voice was anxious. "We don't need a murder rap on top of everything else."

James held very still. The black hole in the barrel looked the size of a cave. Supposedly the spellgun had one other useful magical ability, but James had never found himself under circumstances that would test it—until now.

"I said *stop!*" Murphy's voice rang with authority.

At that point, everything happened at once.

Adrian squeezed the trigger, and Murphy moved his hand in one of those little gestures. There was the crack of a gunshot, a flash of green light, Adrian screamed—and then the world exploded in noise, the deafening sound of thousands of cars compacting themselves into an enormous ball of metal origami as they all rebounded to their normal size at once. The walls of the house burst outward, firing entire full-sized cars like metal missiles in all directions.

James flattened himself to the lawn, covering his head with his arms. He was distantly aware that a) he hadn't been shot, probably, and b) there was a decent chance he was going to get flattened by a car flying at bullet speed instead.

But he wasn't, and the noise died down after a few incredibly chaotic moments. The air was full of dust. James very cautiously and slowly sat up.

A few feet away from him, Ada was huddled with a small, limp gray bird in her arms, sobbing. Its feathers were a mass of blood. The spellgun had fallen to the ground.

James eased forward and retrieved it. Ada didn't even seem to notice; all she did was rock back and forth, holding her brother and weeping.

So it was true: the gun couldn't be used against its owner. Any harm would rebound on the person who fired it. Adrian, in this case.

"What happened?" Oz's voice asked, sounding uncharacteristically shaken.

The dragon, full-sized again, was crouched with his wings halfway wrapped around his head on the lawn . . . or what was left of it. All around the house, full-size objects littered the lawn and street and the lawns of neighboring houses: wrecked cars and furniture and tools, a full-sized tractor, a whimpering dog, and a very confused-looking letter carrier.

What used to be Murphy's house was now an incredibly complicated sculpture made up largely of crushed cars, with broken pieces of wall or roof visible here and there, bits of frame poking out like the spars of a wrecked ship.

Of Murphy, there was no sign.

James holstered the gun carefully. He had to run mentally through the last few seconds before the house exploded to understand what had happened. Adrian had tried to shoot him, and at the same time, Murphy tried to miniaturize Adrian. But Murphy's spell rebounded because Adrian had the spellgun, and hit Murphy himself, at the same time as the spellgun's shot rebounded on Adrian.

"What's happening?" the mail carrier asked plaintively, sitting up on the lawn.

James decided someone else could explain to the poor guy. "Oz," he said, and had to clear his throat to get his voice steady "Do you see a doll, around there anywhere? Would probably be a few inches high. Oh, never mind. I see him."

Murphy was lying on the walk near one of Oz's enormous claws. James struggled to his feet stiffly. As the adrenaline rush began to fade, he was starting to feel scrapes and bruises all over. He'd definitely twisted his knee, and the side of his head throbbed. Reaching up to touch it, he felt damp stickiness soaking his hair above his left ear.

"You killed my brother!" Ada screamed.

"I think I could make a case for self-defense." James limped over and picked up the Murphy doll. It was a perfectly formed miniature version of Murphy, with every detail exact. The doll's clothes were made of fabric, and the skin was cool and yielding, like soft plastic. Murphy's open eyes stared at nothing.

"What is that?" Oz asked. He turned his huge head and narrowed his dinner-plate-sized eye, squinting at the doll. "I don't have my reading glasses with me."

"It's Murphy," James said. He held up the doll so Oz could see it better. "He makes things small, and collects them. Er . . . maybe I should use the past tense now, since it's not like he can deminiaturize himself in his current state."

Oz closed first one eye, then the other, tilting his head back and forth. "Isn't he human?"

"I don't know what he is. It's possible he's a human magician, but I think more likely some kind of fae. Or maybe something no one's ever heard of, I'm not sure. He had these two steal your Lamborghini for his collection; I'm still not sure exactly how."

Ada spoke up, her voice thick with tears. Hatred curled around every word. "He shrank it before he left the mansion that night, and Adrian flew in later, and out again carrying it in his beak. That's all." She swiped at her face, unknowingly leaving a streak of her brother's blood. "I'm going to make you pay for this. You'll *pay*."

"Get in line," James said wearily. "Look, Oz, no offense, but I think I'd like to get out of here. I don't really want to have to explain any part of what just happened to the police." Especially the part where he was in possession of an illegal weapon that had just killed a guy. "If you'd move so I can get to my—" He stopped; Oz had shuffled a big hind leg out of the way, and now he could see that his Subaru had a large, extremely heavy-looking 1950s-era Cadillac on top of it. The flimsier, more modern car had buckled entirely. "Er, never mind."

Oz sat back on his haunches, and using both front paws, lifted the Cadillac. It came off with a screech of tortured metal. "Oh, my. Is that your car?"

"Was," James said. "Was my car. I, uh . . . don't suppose you could move it somewhere else. A few blocks away will do. I'm just going to leave. I suggest everyone else do the same."

"You'll pay," Ada said again, more softly. She drew in a shuddering breath, then laid Adrian's small, limp body on the lawn. Her body twisted and collapsed, and a small gray seabird, its feathers stained with blood, crouched beside the corpse.

There was something much sadder about the little bird than the furious woman. It beat its wings fiercely and took off in a long gradual climb, circled overhead and let fly a precisely targeted dropping. James dodged aside, too slow; he caught it on the shoulder of his jacket.

"Seriously, Oz, I need to get out of here." He waved the doll in Oz's direction. "Can you think of a place to put him? Just leaving him lying around seems like a bad idea."

Oz pinched the doll carefully between two enormous claws. "I can think of a few places." His voice was an ominous rumble. "And I believe I can carry both you and your car, for a short time."

CHAPTER SEVEN

THERE WERE PROBABLY MORE than a few witnesses who couldn't help noticing a dragon soaring overhead with a crushed car in its claws, but James didn't see how they could connect it to him, even if they also noticed the rider hunched down between the dragon's enormous wings, doing his best to keep from being blown off.

Oz dropped the car neatly at the loading dock behind the warehouse. Unfortunately he dropped it from about ten feet up. All four tires exploded and its remaining window glass burst out in a spray pattern around the vehicle.

"Sorry," Oz said.

"Forget it. It's not like it's ever going to drive again." Oz's scales were sharp, and James cut himself several times scrambling down, also ripping open one knee of his jeans. "Uh, thanks for the ride, I guess. I'm not sure if you could consider this a job well done or not. I found your thief, but your car is part of the filling in a thousand-ingredient car sandwich."

"It is not the outcome I hoped for, and I am not even sure that I am glad to know the truth. But I *am* glad that I am no longer ignorant, and that the thief is not still at large to plague me." Oz looked down his long muzzle at James. "Is this your residence? It is quite large, for a human dwelling. Or perhaps the other ones I've seen were more modest?"

"Er . . . no, this building is a converted warehouse, and my residence is in it."

"Are you sure you wouldn't prefer to go to the hospital? You seem unwell."

There were few things more annoying than being lectured by a client after he'd gotten himself beat up in the pursuit of said client's case. "I think our business is done," James said, clipping off the words. Mainly he just wanted to get through this conversation and hide out in his office before he crashed. "I'll draw up some paperwork and come by your place tomorrow to collect my fees." He glanced at the crumpled Subaru and made a snap decision. "I might claim my car as an expense."

"Oh, yes, you should," Oz said. "In fact, you may select one of my collection as your new transportation, as part of your payment, if you like."

James stared at him. The memory of that room full of hundred-thousand-dollar cars spun through his head. He had an instant of drooling covetousness and then shook himself back to reality, the reality being that Oz had no comprehension of what he was offering.

"Oz, the Subaru is worth probably a couple thousand, tops."

"And working for me cost you your transportation. So it is my responsibility to replace it." Oz raised his enormous clawed paw, and James couldn't stifle a flinch as it descended toward him, but all the dragon did was tap his shoulder with the pads of two fingers in a sort of pat. "I will look forward to seeing you on the morrow."

"Uh . . . yeah. Okay. Have a good evening."

There was a rear service door into the building that

opened with his key. The stairs to Dolly's basement were also back here, and he thought briefly of going down to let her know how the case had turned out. Not that it mattered much; he wasn't even sure how much she understood or remembered of what he said to her. She was the shade of a murdered woman, not a real live person. But he liked talking cases over with her.

Not now, though. Not yet.

Just inside the door, he sagged against the wall. The combination of adrenaline and willpower that had been carrying him forward was running out, his energy winding down like a watch spring. The memory surged forward of Adrian Kowalczyk covered in blood, and the shuddering hatred in Ada's blue eyes.

James rubbed his eyes and pushed off from the wall. Everything hurt. He didn't even feel up to climbing the stairs to his apartment. Maybe he should've had Oz take him to the hospital after all.

Still, he had aspirin and a bottle of bourbon in his desk; right now what sounded best was a handful of the former, a couple slugs of the latter, and a nap.

He opened the door to his office, and it was only belatedly, as the door swung open, that he registered the way the key had stuck, like something had gone a little bit wrong with the lock—and then blinding pain exploded in the side of his head.

He went down hard on the cheap, cigarette-burned industrial carpet. His head was a throbbing mass of pain; still, he managed to roll away from someone's attempt to kick him, only to roll into someone else's legs. A booted foot planted itself in his still-sore abdomen.

Breathing in short, painful gasps, he looked up at a vaguely familiar blond man gripping one of the bigger and heavier of Dolly's ashtrays in one hand. There was blood along the edge. James's head pulsed in time with his heartbeat.

For a dazed instant, he thought it was another ghost. A terribly familiar ghost.

"Adrian?" he gasped out.

"Adric, actually," the blond said, and James managed to pull together his blurred double vision. The family resemblance was clear, but Adric was more heavyset, with a nose that had a distinct crook in the middle from being broken, and a hard, cruel mouth. Adrian had fit seamlessly into the business world, but his brother had *cheap muscle* written all over him.

"This is him, right?" the owner of the boot asked. James looked up a jeans-clad leg to a leather jacket and a blonde ponytail slung over the shoulder of a woman who shared the general Kowalczyk family look. He fished around in his rattled brains for the name of the other sister. Aliette. Right.

"Your mom must've had a hell of a time calling you all in to dinner," he gasped out.

Aliette ground down with her boot, further abusing his sore stomach muscles. The spellgun dug into the small of his back.

"It's him," Ada's voice confirmed, and he thought, *Oh, hell.* "This is the scum that killed our brother."

Ada stepped into view. She must have flown directly to his office from Murphy's place in order to beat him here.

Which meant the other two had been here, waiting. And *that* meant while he had pursued Ada and Adrian to Murphy's place, the rest of the family had been heading over to his office to lay a trap. Apparently he hadn't been nearly as good at covering his tracks as he thought he was.

"Computers," he wheezed out, mostly to himself. "Adrian knows computers." And James's clumsy attempts to cover his trail had probably done nothing except make Adrian suspicious and lead to him checking up on the source of the mystery emails.

"Don't you *dare* speak his name." Ada crouched down, balling up a fist. James rolled his head to the side and took the blow on his jaw, with a sharp explosion of pain.

Systematically, with her teeth set and her face never changing, Ada punched him again. His teeth snapped together, and he tasted blood.

"He has a weapon. Where is it?" She pulled roughly at his clothing, and Aliette eased up on the boot so that Ada could roll him over. James tried to tense for an escape attempt, but his bruised stomach muscles cramped and he gasped aloud. Ada had her hand on the spellgun now, yanking it out of the holster. Too bad it wasn't spelled to resist *that*.

Go ahead and try to shoot me, he thought. *I dare you.*

But she didn't. Instead she examined the gun, turning it over, squinting at the barrel. Aliette's boot was now grinding into his ribs, pinning him down. He was probably a match for any single Kowalczyk one-on-one, but all three of them together, not so much. He'd be lucky if all they did was beat the shit out of him, and he had a feeling this wasn't his lucky day.

"This is charmed, isn't it? You somehow turned it on my brother. How does it work?"

"Try it and find out," James said, grinning through bloody lips.

Ada punched him again, snapping his head back against the floor. Stars whited out his vision for an instant.

"Let's try this again," Ada said. "What's up with the gun?"

James lay gazing with slowly returning vision at Ada, and above her, Aliette, with her boot planted firmly in his side. When he saw movement behind her, he thought at first that he was hallucinating. A heavy glass ashtray, a twin to the one

Adric had hit him with, hovered in the air behind Aliette's head.

No one had noticed it yet. James tried not to stare at it and give it away. Instead he turned to fix his gaze on Ada.

"It's a magic gun," he said. He ran his tongue over the inside of his mouth, where his teeth had cut his cheek. Getting punched in the face was the worst.

"I *know* that, asshole. What does it—"

The ashtray connected with Aliette's head with an audible crunch.

Aliette made a high-pitched, strangled noise of pain and went down. James lunged, from the feel of it leaving half his brains behind, and knocked the gun out of Ada's hands.

It skidded across the carpet under the desk. James flung himself after it. Someone stomped on the back of his knee, and he screamed, but his fingers closed over the spellgun's grip. He twisted around and fired blindly at whoever had stepped on him.

It was Adric, who hit the floor with a thump, not as a human but as a fat auklet.

With a vast sense of relief, James turned and fired again, taking down Ada. The gun was back to its usual mostly-nonlethal self.

Adric squawked indignantly and got a cross-eyed look of concentration as he tried to shift back.

Nothing happened. Adric shrieked in avian fury.

Aliette began to pick herself up, blood running into her eyes, and James shot her too. She went down in a tangle of confused legs and wings, squawking.

James still hadn't figured out a way to make the spellgun do exactly what he wanted with its charmed ammo. He was pretty sure there *was* a way; it stood to reason that the gun's results couldn't be totally random. He just hadn't figured it out yet. The gun did what it wanted.

Also, spelled bullets were damned expensive. He could only get them from the black market, and he'd used up four of them today.

"I didn't kill your brother on purpose, all right?" He levered himself painfully to his feet, wincing as his stomach muscles protested. The room swam around him whenever he moved, and he could barely put weight on his leg. Of course they'd trampled the bad leg. He limped over to open the window.

Two of the auklets were now attacking his shins, pecking furiously. James reached down and grabbed them one by one, getting thoroughly pecked for his trouble, and tossed them out the window.

The third—he wasn't sure which it was; he'd completely lost track—scuttled behind the wastebasket. James jerked the basket out of the way, and it retreated behind a filing cabinet.

"Oh, come *on.*"

Bright, furious bird eyes peeked out at him. James gritted his teeth and knelt down. The room swayed again. He stretched behind the cabinet as far as he could, got a fistful of feathers, and dragged out a biting, shrieking auklet, which he chucked out the window after its siblings.

He closed the window and collapsed into his chair. After a long moment of lying back and staring at the ceiling, feeling every last bruise, he said to the empty air, "Thanks, Dolly."

There was no answer, but he thought he smelled cigarette smoke.

He pushed himself to move before he stiffened up completely, and dug out the aspirin and bourbon from the top and bottom drawers respectively. He washed a couple of aspirin down with a slug of booze. Hell on the stomach, but that was the least of his problems right now.

After a moment to gather himself, he lurched down the hall to the shared public bathroom and locked the door.

His face looked like hell, but it was all superficial damage. Blood soaked his hair. He washed most of it out under the sink, and probed at the tender lump behind his ear. He was still occasionally seeing double and the aspirin hadn't yet taken the edge off his headache, but he didn't think he needed a hospital. For that, anyway. He rolled up his pants leg and tried to flex his swelling knee. With some effort, he could move his leg, but that was going to need ice and possibly an X-ray. His gut was still tender too.

He was abso-fucking-lutely taking Oz up on that offer of a new car after all of this.

CHAPTER EIGHT

"You sure you have the right address, friend?" the ride-share driver asked dubiously when he let James out in the mansion's sweeping driveway.

"Yeah, it's the place, all right." James was well aware of what he looked like. Ada's work on his face hadn't seemed too bad yesterday, but that was before everything had a chance to swell and turn purple. Meanwhile, his knee was a swollen mass of pain despite the ice and handfuls of aspirin taken at regular intervals, and his torso was fine as long as he didn't move, twist, or breathe.

Adding insult to injury, he'd had to put up with furious auklets pecking on his window all night.

They seemed to be permanently locked in their shift forms. He couldn't tell how much of their human minds had survived the transformation, but they'd spent the night trying to get in through the window, and dive-bombed him furiously when he left the warehouse in the morning.

Maybe he could hire Gneiss to keep them away.

The ride-share driver pulled away with a skeptical look, and James limped stiffly up to the mansion's enormous double doors. The doors opened just as he got there; James had a mental image of Oz hiding behind the door, waiting until his guests reached the exact distance from the door that he'd judged most polite and then opening it.

"You know," Oz said, looking down his long snout at James. "I wouldn't say I'm an expert on what color humans are supposed to be, but I don't recall some of those as part of your usual coloration."

"The rest of the Kowalczyks turned up at my office yesterday. They didn't have talking in mind."

"Are you all right?" Oz sounded genuinely concerned.

"I'll heal." James limped in. "And you know what'd make me feel better is a signed check in my hand."

He had been tempted to pad the bill in every possible direction. Oz would have paid it without knowing any better. And that was what stopped him. Oz had no defenses against human con artists. James didn't want to be one of them.

"Did you decide about a car?"

He was, however, only human.

"First of all, I'm not taking one of the really expensive ones," he said, and Oz *beamed* at him. There was really something wrong with this dragon. "Considering the neighborhoods I spend most of my time in, something like the Lamborghini is going to attract entirely the wrong kind of attention. Do you have something a little more . . . modest, maybe? But fast," he added, because moral fiber was one thing, but he didn't want to end up with a Honda Fit if he could have a Mustang. "Just maybe not quite that showy."

"That will not be a problem," Oz said. "I believe I know just the one; I've already picked it out. But first, refreshments? Coffee, tea?"

Dealing with Oz's effusive friendliness in his current

condition wore on his nerves. "No, thanks. Let's get the check signed. And—pick out my car, I guess."

They went to Oz's office first. James hadn't considered how signing a human-sized check might work for a dragon, but now he found out: Oz printed out the check itself from the computer, and then he had a mechanical device to sign it, a sort of pantograph that translated the sweeping motions of his large hand to a small grasping arm with a pen clamped in it.

"Clever," James said. He slid the check out from under the device. Oz's signature was an illegible scrawl, but that was true of most humans too. "Don't you even want to check my itemized bill? I can go over it with you."

"No need," Oz said airily. "I shall look over it at my leisure." He rattled his claws together in a considering motion. "There was something I was considering. A request, if I might. Or perhaps more of a suggestion. You may feel this is presumptuous, and if so, feel free to ignore it and we will never speak of it again."

James's knee was on fire after standing this long. "Go ahead," he said as politely as possible under the circumstances.

Oz was looking everywhere but at him. "I wonder if you had ever considered . . . taking on a partner?"

"*What.*"

Oz forged ahead eagerly. "I would love to learn from you. I wasn't thinking an equal partner, of course. Nor would I expect to be paid. Just an . . . an intern, of sorts? Perhaps on a part-time basis?"

"Oz . . ." He didn't know what to say. Literally. "It's not exciting and it's not glamorous, you know that, right? It's not like your books. This might be the first time I've actually investigated something that could be dignified with the term 'case.' Usually I serve legal papers, search court records, and stalk people's exes."

If anything, Oz looked even more interested. "That is exactly the sort of thing I don't know, but would love to learn. I think a court record search would be very exciting."

He would. But James couldn't help thinking of his own wish for someone to do the dull busywork so he didn't have to. Oz seemed detail-oriented and . . . he couldn't believe he was even considering it. Oz wouldn't even fit in the office.

But when else was he going to find someone halfway competent who would work for free?

"I'll . . . think about it," he said, and Oz lit up with that beaming expression again. "Listen, sorry to cut this short, but . . . leg . . ."

"Oh, of course." Oz was instantly all apologies. A giant paw swept down toward James. "I can carry you—"

"No!" James yelped. "I mean, I can walk, it's fine, look— humans don't like to be picked up and carried all the time. We're not used to it."

"Oh. Of course. Please accept my apologies." Oz gestured him onward. "This way."

As soon as they stepped into the hangar-sized garage, something struck James as slightly off from before, but it wasn't until they'd walked through several rows of show-room cars that he realized the cars had been rearranged to seamlessly fill the gap where the Lamborghini had been. He couldn't even remember its exact row.

"This one," Oz said. "I think it's very you. A 1976 Pontiac Firebird Trans Am."

It was long and sleek, black and gleaming, with the classic gold wings on the hood. James stared; that thing was straight out of his childhood movie daydreams.

"This is Burt Reynolds' car. This thing is from *Smokey and the Bandit.*"

"Well, not the *exact* car," Oz said, dipping his snout modestly. "Or even the exact model. Most people think the car in the movie is a 1977 model, but actually it's this model with a 1977 front end. Not many people know that."

James didn't really want to know what it was about him that made Oz think a fictional bootlegger's car would be the perfect fit for him, but he couldn't deny that it was love at first sight. He limped around it, watching his reflection ripple across the perfect, gleaming finish. The interior was black and gold to match the outside—black leather seats, gold accents on the dash and steering wheel. It even had the new-car smell. It couldn't possibly *be* new, but it had been restored so perfectly that it looked like it was.

"I can't take this, Oz."

Oz's long face fell . . . literally; he bowed his head. "But you must. I picked it out especially for you."

"Oz, I didn't even get your car back. And I damn near got you killed."

"You solved the case. You found my car and the thief. I am not unhappy with the outcome, James, except for you being hurt. Please." He held a claw near James's face, with a set of keys dangling from it. "Take the car. It would make me very happy."

"Oh, hell. Fine." James snatched the keys off the claw-tip. "I mean, thanks. Really. It's—a lot, that's all."

"No need to thank me, the look on your face when you saw it was enough," Oz said, and James wondered if Murphy had been even more of a shortsighted sack of dicks than he'd previously realized. There was a good chance that if Murphy had asked for the Lamborghini, Oz would have just *given* it to him. "I have the title paperwork ready for you. All you need to do is sign. And about my suggestion—please don't hesitate to contact me. We could do it on a trial basis, perhaps?"

"I said I'll think about it," James said, and what he remembered afterwards, even more than the roar of the Trans Am's powerful engine when he started it for the first time, was the look of cautious hope on Oz's face.

The auklets crapping thoroughly all over the car as soon as he got it back to the office wasn't even enough to ruin his cautiously cheerful mood.

EPILOGUE

IT TOOK three days and several summoning attempts before Dolly showed back up again. James thought she might be gone, whatever energy sustained her having dissipated in that final burst of poltergeist activity. The thought bothered him more than he felt it should.

But three nights later, when he lit a few cigarettes in the brazier, the 1920s ambiance of the speakeasy came up around him. The transformation was always more dramatic at night, as the gloomy, echoing darkness of the empty basement filled with the lights and music of a vanished world. It was more *there* at night, too, without the shafts of daylight cutting through the high windows to pierce the illusion.

And Dolly was at the bar, sitting on it with her feet swinging. She wore a different dress, this one flowered but still impossible to pin down to a particular color.

James grinned at her. "Hey, lady. I was wondering if I'd see you again."

"Was it long?" She leaned forward, peering at him. "You don't look too much older. Swell bruises, though."

"Three days," James said.

"Oh, is that all?" Dolly said. Smoke curled around her head as she took a long drag on the first of her handful of cigarettes. "Goodness, it's months sometimes, between times you come down to see me. I don't see why three days would put your nose out of joint." She stopped to light another cigarette off the butt of the first, and frowned at him. "You're staring at me."

"I just . . . never realized that you . . ."

He hadn't known she kept track. Hadn't known she *could* keep track. She didn't always remember their previous conversations; time and reality seemed to skip and stutter for her. There were signs of her presence around the warehouse sometimes—a hint of tobacco smoke in the air, the faint strains of jazz music, the ashtrays—but he had never actually seen her up there in person, not completely.

She was a fragment of reality, tied to this basement and lost in time.

Or at least he'd thought so.

"How'd you know I was in trouble?" he asked. It was a thought that he hadn't pushed at, until now. He was half expecting her to ask him what he was talking about.

"I'm not sure. I just did. I don't think I could really tell you exactly how. I know a few things about what happens in the building, when I'm paying attention."

"You saved my life, Dolly."

"Did I? That's the bee's knees." She beamed. "It wiped me out real bad. Like I said, ghosts can more easily touch and move things with some meaning to us. But I've never done anything like that before. I just had to."

"Well . . . thanks." He wished he could reach out—touch her, hug her, shake her hand, anything. But she usually evaporated when he tried, and he wasn't ready for the conversation to end yet. "Oh, hey, you want to hear some interesting news?"

"I love news," Dolly said eagerly, leaning forward.

His knee was starting to bother him. Being able to sit at the bar would have been nice, but since he couldn't, he brushed dust and cobwebs off one of the decrepit chairs against the wall, testing it carefully before sitting down to make sure it wasn't going to collapse.

"That dragon who hired me, Ozymandias?" He leaned back against the wall, propping himself with his good leg. "He wants to work with me."

"Really?" She looked dubious about it, not like her usual perky self. "Doing what?"

"Well . . . this. Being a private investigator. He has some kind of idea that it's glamorous and exciting." James massaged his knee. "I tried to convince him otherwise."

"You said no, then?"

"I haven't really decided yet." He frowned at her. "Are you *jealous?*"

"No!" she protested. "I just don't want you to leave."

"Who said I'm leaving?"

Her smile was like the sun coming out. "You're not?"

"Of course not. I didn't mean he's hiring me; at most he'd be working for me as a sort of unpaid intern." The idea that she might want him to stick around was a nice thought. "Don't want to break in a new upstairs tenant, huh?"

"It might be another thirty years before another tenant moves in who wants to talk to me." She lit the last of the four cigarettes he'd brought her. "You need to make more friends, gumshoe. Living friends. A dragon would be a good friend to have."

"*You're* a good friend to have, Dolly." It came out unexpectedly, and he wasn't sure it was true until he'd said it, but what else was she, if not a friend? Friends listened to you. Friends clonked your assailants over the head with ashtrays, when necessary.

Dolly caught a breath. She hopped off the bar onto the floor; it was the first time James had seen her on his side of it, without the bar as a sort of unbreachable buffer between them. He expected her to vanish now, taking her little slice of the 1920s with her, but in fact the ghostly nightclub was as solid and vivid around them as he'd ever seen it. He could almost make out the faces on some of the dancers.

Dolly leaned close to him. He'd caught whiffs of her perfume before, sometimes upstairs and sometimes down here, but it was strong tonight.

"You're a good guy, James," she said quietly, and kissed him on the cheek.

He actually felt it, not as the press of lips, but as a chill that brushed across his skin, raising the hairs on his arms.

As always, touch disrupted her presence in this world. The lights and music vanished as if a switch had been flipped. Only the smell of cigarette smoke lingered in the air, and perhaps the faintest vestige of perfume. The basement seemed very cold and very dark.

James sat in the dark for a moment, and then levered himself painfully out of the chair.

As he collected the ghost-summoning supplies, he thought maybe he'd bring down a spare chair from the office next time. Maybe even get a couch from upstairs, though he might need some help moving it down the stairs.

It'd be nice to be able to sit comfortably and talk to her, if he was going to come down here more often from now on.

GHOST AND GUMSHOE

KEELEY & ASSOCIATES #2

Ghost and Gumshoe

CHAPTER ONE

THE SUN HAD JUST RISEN across the warehouses and docks, peeking through cranes and gantries, lighting up the clay bluffs across the river. James Keeley was sitting on the end of a concrete pier, feeding the river dragons from a bucket of fish scraps, when a full-sized dragon landed behind him with a tremendous thump that jolted the entire structure and sent the bucket sailing into the water. James nearly followed, but managed to catch himself before he slid off the end of the dock.

The small river dragons, mud-colored and about twice the length of an otter, vanished beneath the surface with a series of small splashes.

"Oops," said the dragon.

James looked up at him and pried his hands off the edge of the pier. "Morning, Oz," he said after a moment, once his voice steadied. He reached for his cup of takeout coffee, only to discover that it had gone into the water too.

Ozymandias made a striking figure in the morning sun. He was enormous—his head alone was as big as a medium-sized sofa—and the sun caught his metallic gunmetal-blue scales in a glittering cascade of iridescent colors. Still, there was something slightly shy in the way that he ducked his head, looking at James sideways. He folded his wings with a nervous, pigeonlike rustling.

"I know I'm early," he said.

"Two hours early."

"I thought that I might get the lay of the land for my first day, so to speak? I really appreciate you employing me in this capacity," Oz said, "and I didn't want to do anything wrong."

"Oz . . . you're an intern. It's going to be things like sifting through twenty pages of phone records on the off chance that there's some kind of pattern to the calls from someone's cheating spouse. It's not fun, it's not exciting, and it's not really something that needs a lot of training."

Oz mantled his wings. "I understand that. I've been doing quite a bit of reading about it."

"In mystery novels? Because I told you, they exaggerate. The real life of a private investigator is not nearly that exciting."

"It's been extremely exciting so far."

"It's not usually like that," James said flatly. The bruises had faded, mostly, but his leg still gave him trouble after being stomped on from behind by one of the goons who'd roughed him up in his office. Speaking of which . . . a quick flicker of small shadows across the water gave him warning. "Oz, could you step over here for a minute? Spread out a wing a bit?"

"Uh, okay," Oz said, shuffling forward with surprising delicacy for a creature so huge. He unfurled one massive wing. "Like this?"

"Yes, exactly like that," James said, just as a diving auklet bounced off Oz's wing with a feathered thump.

The bird rolled off the end of the wing and recovered itself just before hitting the water; a resurfacing river dragon snapped at it, but missed. It flew off with a dirty look in James's direction.

"You can put the wing away now. It was just the one, and they're usually out fishing in the morning. Probably won't regroup 'til afternoon."

"They . . .?" Oz asked leadingly.

"The Kowalczyks. Remember them?"

"Thieves." Oz's wings rustled; his voice dropped to a growl. "They stole from me."

"Yeah, well, they're locked in their bird-shifter forms permanently. I'll explain later; long story. The point is, they blame me and they're now living underneath the air conditioning unit on top of my building. So if you stick around me, you can expect to be dive-bombed by furious auklets several times daily."

"I could have Gneiss come and handle the situation," Oz suggested.

Gneiss was the gargoyle who lived on the roof of Oz's mansion. She was an obligate birdovore.

"No! I mean, they're people. Not birds. They're just people who happen to *be* birds right now."

"I'm not sure I see the distinction—"

"We're not feeding them to a gargoyle, Oz. I'm your boss and I say so."

"You *are* my boss," Oz said. He seemed delighted at the prospect. "I've never had a boss before."

"Yeah, well, don't let the novelty of the experience go to your head." James got up and looked over the side of the pier into the ruffled brown river, where the little mud dragons had come back up to dart in and out of the water.

They were playing with the fish bucket, flipping it back and forth. One of them surfaced with its slender neck through the bucket handle, and James tensed; the last thing he needed was an early morning swim to play Doctor

Doolittle. But the dragon was merely puzzled, not trapped, and after flicking the little fins it had in place of ears, and nosing at the bucket a few times, it delicately backed its head out while its buddies bumped jealously at the bucket and then stole it away.

Oz's enormous head settled on the pier beside James, his gaze turned toward the little dragons too. This close, James could feel the heat radiating off him. He was warm as a radiator on a cold morning.

"Do you feed them every morning?" Oz asked.

"It's something to do while I wake up."

One of the river dragons popped up out of the water with a paper coffee cup clutched in its paws—maybe James's, maybe someone else's. It held it up proudly.

"Yeah, yeah, I see it. Show-off." The small dragon clutched the cup happily to its chest and dove beneath the surface of the water. "Look at that. Give them a piece of trash and they think they've found the Mona Lisa."

"They are fond of you," Oz said.

"I hate to break it to you, but they're fond of anyone who feeds them. You should see them follow the fishing boats around." James reached automatically for the fish bucket, before remembering he didn't have it anymore, and probably wasn't getting it back. "Also, we need to talk about your landings."

"How so?" Oz asked brightly.

"I—you—okay, never mind. We'll deal with that later."

∿

THE OFFICE OF KEELEY & Associates was in a turn-of-the-century warehouse, remodeled into office space and apartments, a short walk from the pier. James had added the *Associates* part to suggest that it wasn't a one-man show, even though it totally was, but it occurred to him that now he actually did have an associate.

Although his associate couldn't fit in the building. That was going to be a problem.

"Not to criticize," Oz said, a phrase that in James's experience was invariably followed by criticism. The dragon was curled in the alley outside the office, his chin (well, the tip of it anyway) resting on the sill of the open window. "But you may not have considered the accommodation of large clients."

"You're the largest client I've ever had." He knew it was a terrible argument; the problem was he'd never thought about it before.

"Perhaps because they couldn't get in the door."

"I know. Look, when I rented this place I was mainly thinking about whether I could afford it."

Oz brightened. "*I* can afford something much better. I could rent something better for you. Us. For us."

Good God. James had just glimpsed the long downward staircase of temptation that working with Oz was going to inflict on him. He had already let Oz give him a car, a mint-condition vintage Trans Am, which he had managed to justify as part of his fee for finding out who had stolen one of Oz's classic car collection. But that was business. Or at least he could convince himself that he'd earned it. Letting Oz rent him an office, though . . . no.

"Let's just work with what we've got for now, all right? No one ever uses the alley and the loading dock back there. You could work there for now. I might be able to work out cheap rent on one of the bigger spaces inside."

"I could buy the building—"

"Oz. Listen." James turned around from digging through files. "If you're going to work with me, you're going to need to shut up about being able to pay for things, all right?"

Mainly because it was too much damned temptation. He *wanted* it; he craved an office where the door didn't stick, an apartment with a full complement of working appliances. And that feeling, the craving for the easy out, was exactly what he didn't trust.

"Oh!" Oz said, brightening. "It's a matter of honor! Yes, of course. I fully understand."

"It's not—" James huffed out a breath. Somehow Oz thinking of him as a man of honor was worse, when *he* knew he was just a contrary bastard who didn't like owing people things. "Look, if you hate working in the alley—"

"Oh, no, not at all." Oz clattered his claws on the pavement. "I'm quite looking forward to it, actually. It's part of the entire working experience, is it not? One must work one's way up through difficulties; it's how it's done in books, anyway. I appreciate you allowing me to overcome some challenges so that I can better appreciate my circumstances later."

"I . . . uh, yeah. Okay. Look, Oz, it's not precisely—"

"What should I do first? Oh! Coffee. Or tea? But you prefer coffee." The alarmingly mobile spikes on Oz's head and neck pricked up, pointing forward. "The new employee in the office gets the coffee, isn't that right?"

"Sure," James said. It gave him something to do with Oz until he could figure out what actual work he could possibly give a dragon intern who had never held a job before and didn't fit in the office. "Yeah, you knocked my coffee in the harbor earlier, so sure. Go get us some coffee."

Oz took off with a downbeat of wings that drove a cloud of dust through the window, sent a swirl of papers flying everywhere, and knocked off several of the vintage ashtrays on the sill.

"And a muffin!" James yelled after him.

~

IT TOOK Oz almost an hour to come back. During that time, James shoveled the scattered papers into a heap on top of a filing cabinet and pinned them down with an ashtray for a paperweight. He didn't have much to do right now. The main thing was a background check that he finished with a few clicks of the mouse and sent off to the firm that had hired him, along with a faxed invoice. It took him longer to find the invoice form than the actual job had taken; it turned up in a stack of old receipts with a stale bagel on top.

A ground-shaking thump and a swirl of dust marked Oz's return, scattering everything else that wasn't nailed down. A moment later, an enormous set of claws extended through the open window and placed on the sill a tray with coffee things neatly arranged, along with a folded cloth napkin and a daisy in a vase. There was a gold-rimmed china plate with an array of muffins.

"I didn't know what kind you liked, so I got you several." Oz's clawtip ticked them off. "Bran, chocolate chip, blueberry, poppyseed—Oh, wait, I forgot something."

He picked up the cup between the tips of two claws and blew a tiny curl of flame into it. James felt the wash of heat. When Oz set the cup back down, it was steaming.

James picked it up cautiously. The handle was a bit hot, but the coffee was the perfect temperature. He added a dash of milk and took a sip. Hot and *very* good. Not that James was much of a coffee connoisseur, but even he could tell that this was fresh-ground and full-bodied. He hadn't had coffee like this since—hmmm. Since the last time Oz had served him coffee, actually.

Also, the china, bone-white and rimmed in gold, was familiar.

"Did you fly all the way back to your mansion to get this?"

"Shouldn't I have?" Oz asked, baffled.

"It's just unnecessary when there's a Starbucks in the strip mall on the corner."

"Starbucks next time. Got it." Oz clattered his claws. "I have never obtained coffee from a Starbucks before. It will be a new experience."

"For the baristas too, I imagine," James murmured. He got up, coffee cup in hand, and grabbed a poppyseed muffin off the tray. "You know, Oz, I think maybe it's time for you to meet someone. An informant of sorts, I guess you could call her."

"Ooh," Oz said happily. "Are we doing detective work already? I can't *wait* for this part."

"It's more that I need to show you why I don't want to move out of this building. One reason why, anyway. Meet me around back. There's a stairwell to the basement there."

He stuffed the muffin in his mouth and paused to grab a few things: a pack of cigarettes from the carton in his bottom desk drawer, a lighter that had been tucked into one of the ashtrays, and finally, last but not least, a dented and soot-stained brass brazier from the mess on the edge of his desk.

CHAPTER TWO

THE OLD BASEMENT speakeasy under the building, haunted by the ghost of a murdered flapper named Dolly Mott, was accessed through a recessed outside stairwell that went down the side of the building's foundation. There was a tall wrought-iron gate at the top that James had a key to, obtained from the property management company in exchange for some light maintenance around the place.

The concrete steps, as always, were littered with trash and dead leaves, which as always he left in place to enhance the abandoned look. He saw no sign that anyone had been there recently. Dolly was more than capable of keeping people out of her basement if she didn't want them there. The fact that the metal door at the bottom of the stairs opened with relative ease, after sticking briefly in its frame, indicated that she welcomed their company.

James looked back up the stairs at Oz, crouched at the top and blocking most of the light.

"Will you fit down here?"

"I'm not sure," Oz rumbled.

With great delicacy, he eeled his glossy, metallic body

through the open metal gate. It was an extremely tight fit. For a moment, the side of the gate snagged on his scales, and James winced as he anticipated the entire gate being folded into a pretzel as Oz pulled it down the stairs.

But Oz freed himself with a twitch of his shoulder and scraped down the stairwell after James. He made it to the door, but no further: his shoulders hung up. With a deep sigh, he lay down and rested his big head on the floor.

"That looks uncomfortable," James remarked. Standing by Oz's head, he could glimpse the dragon's body extending up the steps outside.

"I admit that I wouldn't mind if this was accomplished with all due haste. Who did you want me to meet?"

James crouched on the floor and set down the brazier. He'd brought a whole pack of Chesterfields, Dolly's favorite cigarette brand, because he wanted her to stick around for a while this time.

"She doesn't always show up," he explained as he shook the cigarettes out of their pack and arranged them in a little carcinogenic bouquet with some crumpled-up newspaper in the brazier. "I don't know why, and I don't think she does either. But she's usually around."

He flicked a lighter, then coughed as tobacco smoke curled up. As always, the smoke seemed to fill the room much faster and more completely than it should have, expanding out to a haze that all but blocked his view of the shadowy far end. He'd never tried doing this with the door open, letting in sunlight and fresh air. Even with Oz's head blocking most of the daylight, the air near the door was noticeably less hazy.

"Stay here," James said.

He crossed the room toward the end where Dolly had once tended bar. In the present day, there was nothing there, and nothing in the big, empty bricked-in space of the basement except a few broken pieces of furniture, some old piles of boards and bricks from long-abandoned renovation projects, and a lot of cobwebs.

But as he approached, the past emerged from the fug of cigarette smoke.

The dark basement faded slowly into a dim shadow of a 1920s speakeasy. At night it was more vivid and clear, with warm golden lamps lighting up the dance floor in a world that had vanished a century ago. With daylight slanting through the doorway and the basement's high windows, there were only flickering echoes of people and tables.

"Can you believe it's been a hundred years, James?" Dolly's light contralto asked.

He heard her before he saw her, but she was clear enough by the time he got there, standing behind the bar with her bobbed blonde hair under a beaded wrap and a cigarette pinched between two painted fingernails. A bright necklace glistened at her throat, a heavy rosette with inset stones that James guessed from their size were probably fake.

"That's right, isn't it?" Dolly said. "I think it's right. A hundred years, give or take a bit. Are people different now, James?"

"Not very," James said. A gangland shootout on the docks had killed her in the early 1920s, freezing her forever at age 23. No, people hadn't changed much.

As always, he had to resist the urge to lean on the bar or try to sit on one of the stools. Breaking the illusion usually made her vanish. You couldn't step back into the past.

"That's nice to know. What do you think it'll be like a hundred years from now?"

"I don't know, but if I get shot dead in my office by a cheating husband, I hope I'll haunt the building so we can find out."

Dolly smiled. "That's sweet." She'd already smoked her

first cigarette down to the filter. She lit the next from the glowing end, and dropped the butt in a glass ashtray on the glossy bar top. "Did you bring someone with you? I can't see over there very well."

James turned to gesture toward the doorway with Oz's big head wedged in it. Oz blinked slowly; it was about all he could do without being able to move.

"Hello, miss," he said.

"This is Ozymandias, the dragon I told you about. Oz, can you see her?"

"Sort of," Oz said in his deep rumble. "It's dim back there. Can she see me?"

"There's too much sun," Dolly said. "It's too bright. Can't he come in?"

"He doesn't fit."

She sucked thoughtfully on the cigarette. "He might be able to come in the loading doors."

"Wait, there's another door?"

Dolly swiveled with a clatter of beads and pointed to the wall behind her. "I don't know if it's still there. It's hard for me to see what's there in your time, you know, instead of left over from mine."

James went to investigate. The wall looked like ordinary brick, flaking with age. It seemed solid. But when he tugged at a loose brick, it came out, and there was dark wood beneath.

"Could it have been bricked over later?" he asked Dolly. She was still at the bar, but had turned to watch.

"It was always bricked to look like part of the wall. So the g-men didn't find it. On the other end it comes out underneath one of the wharves, where we used to unload the goods. There's a tunnel in between."

"Big enough to fit a dragon?" James asked. He stretched,

feeling along the wall. He found a crack, all of a sudden, running through the bricks.

"Should be. It's quite large. Nero didn't dig it, he just took advantage of an existing loading dock and bricked over the top."

Nero was the former owner of the speakeasy, or at least the person Dolly had dealt with in her role as barmaid. Nobody named Nero, or any name that could conceivably shorten to it, had ever appeared on the warehouse's paperwork; James had checked.

"Oz, do you want to go around to the other side and see if you can find the outside entrance?"

The dragon's massive head withdrew from the doorway, followed by the awkward shuffling sounds of a creature the size of a semi-truck trailer attempting to back up a flight of stairs. James, meanwhile, continued to explore the door, trying to get his fingers in the crack.

Suddenly he found it. The wall gave a faint cracking sound, and a shower of dust and cobwebs rattled down. James took a quick step back, wondering if Oz would be able to dig him out if the ceiling collapsed. A sharp dark line showed against the bricks, clear as a knife cut. Chill, musty air breathed out of the narrow gap.

"Just like that," Dolly said behind him. "Gosh, I had almost forgotten myself."

James looked around to see that she'd left the bar and wandered over to join him. She was smoking idly, the rest of the pack of Chesterfields dangling from her fingers. It seemed that he could smell smoke more strongly this close to her, though he knew it was most likely his imagination. The entire basement reeked of smoke from the brazier.

"Any other ghosts inside here?"

"I don't know," Dolly said, and she smiled, brief and sweet. "Let's find out, why don't we?"

The door's rusted hinges protested, but eventually gave in with a tortured shriek. It was one half of a set of double doors that opened barn-style into the speakeasy. The doors weren't overly tall—Oz was going to have to duck to get into the basement—but it was certainly more than wide enough for a dragon.

James shone his phone's light around inside. The basement had been stripped down for anything salable, though never remodeled and repurposed like the rest of the building, because of its ghostly occupant. But he might be the first person to open this tunnel since the 1920s. At the very least, it had been untouched for many years.

The walls were dirt and gravel riverbank fill, shored up with heavy wooden beams like mining timbers. Rather than the dirt floor James expected, there were wide crosswise floorboards, probably to make it easier to roll in their cargo.

And some of that cargo was still there. Wooden barrels and an occasional crate stood along the walls, with old cargo stamps barely visible beneath dust and cobwebs. There was a rumpled blanket or pile of clothing, eaten away to rags, and scattered glass bottles gone dingy with time.

James poked a bottle with his toe, then leaned down to pick it up. That was a surer sign than anything else that curious teens and other urban explorers hadn't made it this far. The bottle was the heavy glass kind that had long since been replaced by lighter, cheaper brands. These were collector's items now, if they weren't claimed by recyclers and turned in for cash.

It was incredibly quiet in here. The basement had always felt like its own world, slightly apart from the commercial district that had spread to envelop the old row of warehouses, but the tunnel was even more so. The air was stale and dusty. Up ahead, he glimpsed another set of wooden double doors ahead, dimly visible at the edge of the phone's light. They weren't actually that far from the river here.

"Dolly—" he began, looking back, and found that she hadn't followed. She was framed in a wreath of cigarette smoke in the relatively well-lighted mouth of the tunnel. Her shoulders were hunched; she looked small and unhappy.

He hadn't realized he'd come as far into the tunnel as he had, and he couldn't help being very aware of that freaky timeless hush, as he retreated back toward the light and —*safety*, was the thought that came to mind.

And his unsettled feeling cranked up a notch when he saw Dolly's tear-stained face. He'd never seen her cry before. Never seen her upset like this. She was visibly shivering, staring into the tunnel.

James looked behind him, back into the darkness, but there was nothing to be afraid of. At least nothing he could see.

"Dolly? What's wrong?" If she had been a living person, he would have put an arm around her. What would scare a ghost like that?

Dolly turned her wide eyes to his face. She had truly huge eyes, of a vaguely lightish color that, like everything else about her, was incredibly hard to discern. She wasn't precisely black and white; it was just that whatever colors she wore had a way of disappearing when he tried to concentrate on them. Her headwrap was bright, but he couldn't have said afterwards if it was green or yellow or orange.

"I just don't want to go in there," she said faintly.

"Is there danger?"

"I don't know," she whispered, and then there was a sudden loud crack from the other end of the tunnel.

James spun around, reaching automatically for where his holster would be, if he had any reason to wear a gun in the basement underneath his own office. Light dazzled him, and it took him a moment to realize it was daylight flooding the tunnel from the other end, with Oz's bulk in the widening stripe of morning sunshine between the double doors.

"Well, that took some time," Oz rumbled cheerfully. "The river dragons had to show me where the door was. Some of them have been around since—oh, my, there are all *kinds* of items in here." He poked at the top of a barrel with a claw.

"Way to make an entrance," James said. "Dolly—"

She had vanished. There was only the haze of smoke hanging in the air, considerably thinner now. The room seemed much larger without the old tables, the bar, the shades of long-dead patrons.

James took a slow breath and turned away.

"Where is your friend?" Oz asked.

"She had to go." The tunnel felt less ominous now. It was impossible to be nervous about unseen ghosts or other dangers with Oz looming in front of him, at once comical and lethally intimidating.

The tunnel was easily wide enough for Oz, though low enough that he had to duck his head to avoid clocking himself on a beam. It was, at least, better for dragons of his size than the stairs.

"What is all of this, anyway?" James wanted to know. He tried to pry up the top of a crate. It was stuck fast, the nails rusted into place.

Oz slid a claw-tip under the edge of the lid and pried it up. Nails shrieked and wood splintered, and the top popped off like a champagne cork and slammed against the wall in a puff of gritty dust.

"Oops," Oz said, sound abashed. "I thought it was nailed on harder than that."

"Well, it's open now, anyway."

The crate was full to the top. The first thing was a layer of newspapers so brittle that the edges crumbled when James picked one up. They had various dates, but all were from the late 1920s, years after Dolly's death in 1924. As he dug down further, pulling out more papers, mouse droppings and bits of dry, gnawed paper sifted from between the pages.

Beneath the newspapers there was straw, bone-dry and heavily chewed into long-abandoned mouse nests. The smell was musty and rank. James pulled out a handful of straw and found bottles of heavy brown glass, unlabeled. He picked one up. The still-liquid contents sloshed when it moved.

"I don't know what else I expected to find in a bootlegger's tunnel." James turned to poke the nearest barrel with his toe. It was light enough to move; either it had been empty when it was placed in the tunnel, or the contents had evaporated over the years.

"This place is full of interesting things," Oz remarked, lifting a coil of rope on the end of his claw. Dust sifted out of it.

James went down to the river end of the tunnel to examine the bottle in better light. The tunnel was about a hundred yards long, and as Dolly had said, it came out under one of the piers: actually, he realized, it was the same one he'd been sitting on to feed the river dragons just a couple of hours earlier.

He saw immediately why no one had found the tunnel in the intervening years; in fact, it was likely that no one but Oz could have gotten in, unless they brought a bulldozer. Between the 1920s and now, the harbor's shoreline had been buttressed with a retaining wall of broken-up concrete rubble, rocks, and similar debris. It had covered the tunnel's double doors all the way to the top.

Oz had clawed the rocks and concrete away from the door enough to get it open, though getting out still involved scrambling over a muddy obstacle course, littered with trash that had washed down from above. The smell of mud and fish was overwhelming. Water lapped against the legs of the pier, and the bellies of boats jostled alongside its length. It was like being in his own private little world down here, right on the level of the river.

There was a chorus of cheerful squawking and chirruping, and a half-dozen or so river dragons flopped their sinuous bodies ashore, fluting and chirping at him. They had front legs but no back ones, instead tapering down to a slender and finned lower half, something like an eel.

"Yeah, hi, guys. No fish for you, sorry."

It was dim in the pier's shadow. James picked his way over the rocks, his shoes sliding on mud and slime, until he could look at the bottle in sunlight. It was old, thick brown glass, with a maker's mark on the bottom, nearly full of gurgling liquid that looked as brown as the bottle.

He got a utility knife out of his pocket, and pried at the corroded and stuck-in cork, first with the bottle opener and then the knife blade, until finally it popped out. The powerful smell of brandy was almost enough to overwhelm the fish odor. Brandy wasn't really his drink, but he tested it with a cautious sip. It was eyewateringly strong, but didn't taste spoiled or vinegary.

Soft chirping near his feet made him look down. He'd never been this close to the river dragons before. They were almost close enough to touch. He could see fine whiskers on their narrow muzzles, quivering as they sniffed the air.

"Oh, what the hell."

He poured a little brandy on the rocks. The river dragons scattered with sharp screeches and barks, but came back as soon as he retreated a few steps. Small dark tongues flicked out to lick the rocks. The first one who tried it sneezed and shook its head and then gave a few more eager licks. The others crowded around to join in the licking frenzy.

"And this is how I turned the river dragon population of the Artesia River into a bunch of alcoholics," James muttered.

He scrambled back over the slippery rocks to the half-open doors. There was a badly rusted padlock dangling from an equally rusty chain that looked like it had been holding the doors shut. He should probably see about replacing that, if they didn't want the possibility of curious onlookers wandering in and out.

"Hey, Oz? You still in here?"

"I've found *so many* things," Oz announced in delighted tones.

James shoved his way past the slightly cockeyed doors. "Yeah, good. Look, don't forget that everything in here belongs to—"

He stopped there, unsure how to finish the sentence. The property owners? Was the tunnel even considered part of the building? There might be a decent case for salvage. Or . . . technically, no one knew about the tunnel but the two of them. If there was anything valuable in here, he could bring it up one piece at a time, and—

—and also, you have a one-percenter dragon intern who just offered to pay for an office in a part of town that doesn't smell like fish. And you turned him down. Like you need the headache of trying to sell a few crates of vintage bootleg hooch.

"I could inventory it," Oz offered eagerly. "Would that be helpful?"

"Uh . . . yeah. Yeah, it would." James nudged a dust-covered heap of boards with his foot; they looked like part of a half-finished project to shore up part of the tunnel. "What do you need? I can bring you down some clipboards and writing supplies and the like. I don't have anything your size."

"Oh, I'll just remember it 'til I come upstairs."

"You'll remember everything in here."

Oz nodded, ducking his head to avoid banging it on the

ceiling. Come to think of it, Oz had made occasional comments about the fallibility of human memory before.

"So how does that work?" James asked. "Do all dragons have photographic memories?"

"I have a perfectly normal memory," Oz said. "It's you humans who have trouble remembering things. And no wonder, with those small brains."

"Pretty sure that's not how memory works, or else blue whales would have the best memories on the planet."

"How do you know they don't?"

"On that fun note, I'm going upstairs to do a little research. Close the doors when you're done down here, okay?"

Oz nodded, already turning his eager attention back to the crates and barrels and scattered loose items.

It was all junk, or at least mostly junk, and certainly there was no sign of a body. *Couldn't* be a body; this place had been in use for years after Dolly died, so it wasn't like there could possibly be a heap of bones under a moldering dress in a corner. Still, James looked. Dolly's clear and visible fear of the tunnel kept coming back to him. Something had happened here, something she was afraid of.

But there was no sign of what might have scared her. And the basement was empty of ghosts, although a faint hint of cigarette smoke lingered in the air.

"Dolly?"

There was no answer, and no signs of her ghostly presence like the ashtrays that occasionally turned up in his office. He gathered up the brazier, locked the basement door and the iron gate across the stairwell, and went to look into what exactly had happened in this basement in 1924.

CHAPTER THREE

SHE IS WALKING IN MIST, or perhaps in the rain. Steam curls in the air, breath or smoke or wisps of fog. Everything is gray behind and gray ahead.

Dolly is only truly aware of the passage of time, or for that matter aware of herself, when she is in the world, and those ties have frayed over the years. As the tether holding her to the world grows looser, she has dwindled slowly to a hint of perfume, a trace of cigarette smoke drifting about the warehouse after hours.

But she is anchored more firmly in the living world these days. It makes a difference having a summons to bring her back, punctuating the endless gray days with splashes of color and conversation. It's hard to find her way back to the world without an intangible hand reaching for hers, like James's little ceremony with the brazier and the cigarettes.

He found the summoning ritual in something he calls the internet. She asked him about that. And she remembers the answer, which surprises her. She is remembering more things now.

She doesn't remember her first conversation with James, but he has told her that she arrived spontaneously that first time, filling up the dark space that used to be the Peony Club with color and music and light. Gave me the shock of my life, *he said.*

The Peony.

She used to wear a peony flower in her hair when she worked. Someone . . . someone had put it there for her, tucking it behind her ear. A teasing smile with a boyish twist, a little bit playful, a little bit cruel.

She used to take the wilting flowers home at the end of the night, put them in an empty soup can on the windowsill . . .

The necklace, like the peonies, was a gift. She touches it. There is a cool physicality to its heavy gold setting and rhinestones, there and not-there, like damp fog clinging to her fingertips.

There is . . . something . . .

She stayed for a reason. She's sure of it. Something held her back from moving on after she died; something holds her back still.

It was the most precious thing in the world to her once.

Now she can't even remember what it was.

⁓

AFTER JAMES MET DOLLY, he had looked up her obituary and the circumstances of her death out of pure curiosity. She had never been able to tell him what had happened to her; every time he'd asked, she had evaporated or said she didn't know. So he went to the newspaper archives instead.

He had a vague memory of printing out a bunch of newspaper articles and sticking them . . . somewhere. It took him a solid hour of hunting through loose papers and filing cabinets before he finally found them sandwiched between a flyer for the pizza place next door and a copy of a restraining order from some case he'd forgotten about. It probably would have been faster to just go to the library and search the *Grand Bluffs Register* and *World-Observer* archives again.

But here it was. Dorothy Ann Mott, 1900-1924.

On the late evening of April 27, 1924, when Dolly was 23 and a half, violence had erupted between a riverboat crew bringing bootleg rum up from the Mississippi, and the MacKay brothers, Normal and Geary, who ran the south end of the harbor in the early 1920s. Normal MacKay—what a name, jeez—was killed in the shootout along with one of the riverboatmen and a young barmaid who worked at a gin joint called the Peony.

The shootout was big news for a couple of weeks, and Dolly's death was played as a two-minute tragedy in the papers. So beautiful, so young. The photo of her that stared out of edition after edition of Grand Bluffs' then two daily papers looked even younger than the Dolly that James knew. It was a glamour shot, with her medium-light eyes painted to make them look even larger, and a flower tucked into the blonde hair over her ear.

But eventually she sank to the back page and then slipped off the pages entirely, lost to history.

Flipping through the articles, he wondered how much of the real, living Dolly was missing from the ghost of Dolly, the only version of her he'd ever known. Certainly the woman in these articles, the big-eyed waif gazing out at the reader, was a pallid imitation of a real, living woman who had cried and hated and loved and bled. Was the Dolly he knew *really* the Dolly who had existed in life, or was she more like the newspaper version, a dry caricature drawn together from a few personality traits, with most of her depth missing?

"It doesn't matter, though, does it?" he murmured. If the living Dolly Mott had been different from the basement ghost—less innocent, more complicated, perhaps even petty and cruel—he had never known her like that. Both of them were different shades of the same person, and both were victims of a terrible crime.

Her obituary was tragedy writ in just a few short lines:

buried Saturday . . . survived by three cousins and an aunt . . . No close family, no descendants. An entire life reduced to some scraps of paper and photographs.

He went back to look for the exact circumstances of her death. The articles didn't include much detail, grouping her together with the other victims, but as James combed through them, more details emerged. Dolly had been found hours after the shooting, when her body had turned up on the shoreline later that night. She had been shot twice in the chest and once in the abdomen from fairly close range. It was assumed that she got caught in the crossfire of the shootout on the docks, leaped or fell off the pier into the water, and later washed ashore.

But what if she wasn't? James thought. What if she was actually killed in the tunnel, then her body was dumped to make it look like it belonged to the other shooting?

The type of slugs might tell the tale, if they had forensic science that advanced in 1924; he wasn't sure. But whether or not they did, he couldn't find any mention of it in the articles.

"Coffee?" said a rumbling voice by his shoulder, and James involuntarily flung his handful of newspaper clippings across the room while reaching wildly for the drawer where he kept the spellgun.

"Sorry, didn't mean to startle you," Oz said, pulling back his snout from the open office window. "Here, coffee." He set a cardboard cup on the windowsill, pinched between two claw-tips.

James took a moment to answer while he got his breathing under control. He was going to rearrange the office, he decided. Instead of having the desk facing the door, with the window behind him, he could move the desk around to the side where he could see both the door *and* the window.

"I'm awake now, Oz. Thanks for that." He inhaled the coffee's rich, dark smell. "Although this is appreciated. How's it going down there? Find anything interesting?"

"*Many* interesting things," Oz said happily. He sat back on his haunches, curling his long tail around his hind legs like a huge dog. "Twelve barrels, five crates, two coils of rope, seventeen loose bottles, nine large and seven small and one medium-sized; nineteen boards, not yet sorted by size; one silver item which I believe is a bottle opener; a broken china teacup, human-sized—"

James finally managed to stem the flow by holding up a hand. "Anything valuable? And please don't tell me it's *all* valuable."

"Well, it *is*. But . . . not in the sense you mean. At least I don't think so. In general, it's all the same kind of thing, boxes and barrels, bits and bobs dropped by humans."

"Junk," James murmured. And yet Dolly was deathly terrified of the place.

"One man's junk is another man's treasure," Oz said. "A human said that. It is a very wise statement."

"Yes, well, junk or treasure, let's leave it in place for now." He hesitated and then put the computer to sleep without sending an email to the property management company about it. It would be more of a dilemma if there was a treasure chest of pirate gold in there, but for an old bootlegger's tunnel full of crates, who was really going to care? It had been undiscovered for decades. It didn't matter if it remained secret for a few days or weeks more.

Enough time for him to see if there was anything to find inside.

"Hey Oz, want to take a walk down to the shore and help me scope out a murder scene?"

≈

THE AUKLETS STAGED a cursory attack when he emerged from the building, but when Oz reared up and snapped at them, they changed their minds and winged hastily away.

"I don't even know what they think they're doing," James said. "I'm not leaving. The most they can do is annoy me."

He surveyed the nearly empty parking lot and tried to visualize the approximate location of the tunnel underneath. It must angle from the basement toward the river . . . like so. There was a row of one-story buildings between the warehouse and the water that probably hadn't been there in the 1920s, with various businesses (an engine repair place, the headquarters of a shipping company) behind a long chain-link fence.

"What murder are we investigating?" Oz asked eagerly.

"Dolly's."

"Isn't she—er—"

"Very, very dead. Yes."

They had to circle around the length of the fence to reach the waterfront. In Dolly's day, it would have been a more direct trip from the speakeasy to the pier.

"Why don't you just ask her?" Oz asked, strolling alongside James with a swaying, crocodilian gait. He was a lot less graceful on land than in the air. His tail dragged behind him, snagging occasionally on the pavement.

"I've tried. Either she can't talk about it, or she won't."

In the modern day, there was a broad concrete riverwalk at the top of the steep rubble embankment surrounding the base of the pier. James tried to replace it mentally, roll back the bright sun and the dog-walkers and the marina with its colorful little sailboats and motor skiffs, the same way that Dolly's speakeasy washed in to replace the brick walls and empty basement.

"The shootout was here," he said, pointing along the

riverwalk. "From the pictures, the harbor wasn't as built up then. The pier was smaller and lower, and the bank went right down to the water. They used to unload the rumrunner boats down along the shore there. Then I guess they'd bring it in through the tunnel."

It had been April when Dolly died, cold and clammy, the muddy water barely broken free of winter ice. He pictured it in his mind's eye, darkness and damp fog wreathing the row of piers, ice bumping along the shore.

"According to the papers, they had a dispute over payment, and it erupted into violence. Normal MacKay—yes, that's really his name—and some of his triggermen were up here. The guys in boats were down there. Several people got shot, and two of them died. Dolly wasn't found until later."

James glanced around for onlookers before realizing that it was impossible to be stealthy while accompanied by a dragon as large as most of the boats. He climbed down the rubble wall to the slimy rocks under the pier. Oz followed with remarkable speed and agility, claws clattering on the rubble and sending small rocks skittering into the muddy water.

As the pier shut out the sky, James was struck all over again by how it felt like a different world under here, calm and dim, a bubble of quiet space where the lapping of the water overwhelmed the throb of diesel engines out in the harbor. It was almost like a little slice of the past. He wondered if this was a little more like the harbor had been in Dolly's time, when it was seedier and less developed.

Oz had closed the doors to the tunnel as requested, and James was impressed at how hard they were to see from the outside, even with the concealing debris dragged back. It was dim under here, cloaked in shadows, and one bit of junk-covered riverbank looked much the same as another. Even if you did notice that a door was there, it just looked like some kind of utility access.

"What did you want to look at?" Oz asked. He fastidiously brushed slime off his tail.

"Dolly's body was found here. I don't know exactly where; the papers are long on local color but short on actual relevant details. A map would be nice. But I think it had to have been pretty close to where we are now."

He looked up at the dark mass of the pier looming above them. Even if the pier was smaller and closer to the water, that would have involved some awkward shooting, with the rumrunners down here and the MacKay gang up top. It must have been chaos out here.

"So why would she be here rather than back in the tunnel?" he mused aloud.

Oz looked up with his snout dripping. "What?" he said somewhat indistinctly.

"What are you *doing?*"

"Fishing," Oz said, slightly abashed. He flipped his head back and snapped his jaws on whatever he'd caught. "I'm listening. Apologies."

"Uh . . ." That sort of thing could derail a man's train of thought in a hurry. "Dolly. Right. She worked in the speakeasy and knew all about the tunnel. If she was helping unload the boats, she would have been close to it. Why wouldn't she run inside as soon as the shooting started?"

"Not enough time?"

"Maybe." He turned and looked at the doors, and the short distance between there and the water's edge. "How could they possibly have missed her body, though? It doesn't make sense. If it was here all along, it shouldn't have taken them hours to find it, and if it was any farther out, the current would have caught her and washed her downstream. The papers made it sound like she fell farther out and washed ashore, but that seems unlikely."

"Are they lying?" Oz asked. He sounded intrigued by the possibility.

"No, not necessarily . . . I think what they found didn't quite fit the evidence, and the police or the reporters *made* it fit. They didn't know about the doors . . ." No, if the police were searching the shoreline with any amount of attention to detail, they surely must have found the tunnel; it wasn't *that* well hidden.

"They were being paid not to notice the doors," he went on slowly. "It was the 1920s. The gangs practically owned the cops. A barmaid being caught in a shootout was an unfortunate accident. Manslaughter at worst. But if someone killed her on purpose, that's murder one. It would have sent them down for life."

Oz swished his tail, flicking the tops of the waves. "First a locked room mystery, now a cold case."

"It's not—" Except it actually sort of was. "Look, don't get your hopes up about this, okay? The truth is going to be shabby and vulgar and sad; it always is. And by now, everyone involved is as dead as Dolly. There's no justice here. Just greedy, petty people doing what people do."

"But you still want to do what's right for Dolly."

"I just don't like not knowing the answers to things."

Oz made a grinding noise that suggested skepticism. He glanced toward the tunnel. "What shall we do about that?"

"Why don't you work down there for now? There's plenty of space."

"Ooh." Oz clattered his claws on the rocks. "Now I have my own office! See, I'm working my way up already. This has been quite an enlightening view of the working man's world."

It was sometimes difficult to tell if Oz was being sarcastic.

"Don't get too used to it. I need to let the owners of the building know about it, and there's no telling what its legal status is, or what they're going to want done with it."

"But we are investigating Dolly's death, correct?"

"Yes," James sighed. "We're investigating Dolly's death."

CHAPTER FOUR

THERE WAS LITTLE POINT, he knew, in putting time and effort into solving a century-old murder. There wasn't necessarily even a murder to solve. And, as he'd told Oz, everyone involved was dead anyway. If she had been killed by intent rather than accident, what was he going to do, show up on the doorstep of her murderer's grandchildren?

But he'd never been able to let a puzzle go.

And . . . it was Dolly.

He went ahead and sent an email to the property management company about the tunnel. It was tempting to continue to sit on it, holding it back as his own private space. But this *was*, technically, one of his responsibilities as the building's maintenance guy. It was an easy gig that got him cheap rent, and he didn't particularly want to get kicked out. And it wasn't like the comings and goings of a full-sized dragon were easy to miss, no matter how stealthy Oz thought he was being.

That being done, he continued to poke at Dolly's case. The idea crossed his mind of turning Oz loose on it, but he didn't really want to. He felt proprietary about it. And it was also one of those cases where he'd know what he was looking for when he found it, but he couldn't say exactly what "it" would turn out to be.

A call to the local precinct let him know that there wasn't much chance of turning up the actual case files from the 1920s. The newspaper morgue was what he kept coming back to.

He trawled through the 1920s archives, not just looking for mentions of Dolly's murder, but for anything else that had happened with that block of buildings. He also looked up property records, society pages—whatever he could find that would help him build a picture of Dolly's world.

The city was a boomtown in those days, flush with the cash from illegal hooch pouring in from both directions. It came up the river from the Mississippi, and downriver from local farmers as the state's corn growers figured out they could make a lot more money distilling their product into liquor than shipping it out for hog feed. A steady current of illegal alcohol flowed through the city, and fortunes rose and fell on the tide.

Normal and Geary MacKay had started out as small-time smugglers. They inherited the family dry-goods store, and before Prohibition used the business as a cover to ship in cigarettes and hooch from Canada without paying import duties. With their smuggling bona fides already in place, they were ideally set up to claim a big share of the lucrative bootleg business when America went dry. In just a couple of years they were high rollers on the Grand Bluffs scene, with their names turning up everywhere in a 1920s archive search before they vanished just as quickly. Their star rose, peaked, and fell, and the shootout in 1924 seemed to be the turning point—and the end of the road for Normal.

As for Geary, most of the personal information James could find on him came from a series of later articles that he stumbled upon by accident.

In the late '50s, a crime beat reporter at the *Register* had done a cold-case series, with several of the articles focusing on Dolly's murder. The reporter, whose name on the byline was Winifred Attredge, seemed to have a theory that Dolly had been murdered by her boyfriend Geary MacKay.

Attredge's articles painted a lurid picture of Dolly as an innocent waif, lured in by the MacKay brothers' shiny cars and fine houses and the cash they waved in fistfuls all over the city. The MacKays were paying off the cops and the city council, doing whatever they wanted under the noses of the authorities, until the shootout got the feds' attention and burned up a lot of the local goodwill toward them. Under scrutiny from the FBI, Prohibition Bureau, and IRS, and with Normal dead, Geary had pulled back in and started focusing on legitimate business interests for the most part. He still ran a string of speakeasies until the late 1920s, including what used to be the Peony Club, rebranded under a series of new names. But he drifted out rather than falling. None of the alphabet agencies ever caught him. He lost most of his business empire in the Depression, rebuilt some of it through wartime contracts, but never really made it back to his glory days.

By the time Attredge wrote what were essentially a series of hit pieces on the MacKays, Geary MacKay had become a recluse. Future information was scarce. He died in the 1970s, and his grandson Gerald took over the family business and began building it up again.

No one had ever really been punished for Dolly's murder. A couple of the MacKay family's triggermen had taken the fall for the shootout, doing hard time, but no first-degree murder charges were ever brought. If Winifred Attredge had hoped that her articles would have changed anything, she must have been disappointed.

Surprisingly, she was still alive—absolutely ancient, of course, but there was an address for her, and it wasn't even a care home; it was a private residence up on River Road.

Maybe it was time to start doing some interviews of his own.

~

WINIFRED ATTREDGE'S address suggested a swanky neighborhood; it was just a few streets down from the subdivision where James had first met the Kowalczyks at their cliffside McMansion.

Still, he genuinely wasn't expecting her house to be as nice as it was. It was perched on one of the prestigious clifftop lots, screened from the road by trees. Unlike the Kowalczyk place, it didn't reek of try-hard new money. It was sedately huge, exuding a sense of comfortable importance. The driveway wound around through finely landscaped grounds; there was a rose garden, a pool, and a glassed-in solarium on one side of the house. Vast windows overlooked the river view.

Not what he expected from a newspaper reporter's house. But then again, the 1950s had been a very long time ago. Maybe this was a child or grandchild's house. Maybe she'd invested in Apple stock in the 1980s. Maybe nice properties on the bluffs were just a lot cheaper back them.

He hadn't been able to find an email for her, or a phone number, so he decided to just show up. When he pulled in, there was a woman kneeling in the flower beds alongside the solarium, pulling weeds. She wore a floppy sun hat and a peach-colored pantsuit, and straightened slowly with the careful deliberation of age.

Still, as she walked toward him, he thought that this couldn't possibly be Winifred Attredge, not if she was old enough to work a crime beat in the 1950s. This woman looked perhaps in her sixties. A daughter, maybe? She had a cloud of white hair under the sun hat, and large, red-framed sunglasses balanced on her short nose.

"I'm sorry, I wasn't expecting anyone," she said. "Are you delivering something?"

The usual dilemma: lie in the hopes of getting more information that way, or go for the truth. He decided truth would work best. "I'm James Keeley, a private investigator. I'm looking for a woman named Winifred Attredge. I wanted to talk about a series of articles she wrote on Dorothy Mott's murder."

The woman in the sunhat tipped her head back. She was quite short. "You've found her. Though, off the beat, I prefer Wendy."

"Wow," James said before he could stop himself. "Whatever your secret is, I hope you bottle and sell it."

There was a moment when she looked at him sharply, and he wished he could see her expression better behind the sunglasses. Then she smiled. It was a quick, light, darting smile, a young person's smile, and it was suddenly familiar in the way of a memory of a movie or TV show. He might have seen her on TV, he thought—but when, and where? It might have been in a movie, a long time ago.

"Come in and have a drink," she said.

~

WENDY ATTREDGE WAS A WINE DRINKER. James was more of a

beer or bourbon guy, but he didn't really mind a strong red wine, so he nursed a glass while Wendy sipped hers. They sat in the rose garden, surrounded by flowers. James found himself thinking he should have put on something classier than his beat-up leather jacket.

"Those articles," Wendy said. "My God, that was a long time ago. So long."

"I would never have guessed you're, what, almost a hundred?" James hesitated; it was probably rude to ask, but under the circumstances, he couldn't help wondering. "Do you have any, er—"

"Any what? Are you asking if I have nonhuman ancestry? Fae blood?" There was that light, movie-star smile again. "No, I don't think so. Good genes and clean living, I suppose." She smiled as if at a private joke.

"Sorry. You must admit it's a plausible question."

"That almost everyone else has the tact not to ask." Still, she didn't seem upset, simply amused.

She was very genteel and serene. Oz would like her, James thought. He could easily picture her in a pair of lacy peach gloves to match the pantsuit. Her nails were painted a slightly darker shade of the same peach pink. Her hands looked strong and capable, and slightly large for her small frame: the kind of hands that would have been poised over typewriter keys, back when being a reporter, and especially a crime reporter, was a man's job.

"Well, I'm an investigator," he said. "I do ask questions. I'm sure you can relate. Our professions aren't that different, you and I."

"Actually, most of the private investigators I knew on the beat were absolute bottom feeders. If there was a corner they could cut or a person they could sell out for a quick buck, they'd do it."

"Ouch. You know, I've heard some reporters can be a little bit ruthless as well."

"A little ruthlessness goes a long way in this world," Wendy Attredge said, with a sip of her wine. "What did you want to ask me about Dolly Mott? I have to tell you, that was a very long time ago. I don't know what I'll be able to remember."

"I know. The thing is, I've got a current case," James said carefully, "that involves looking into some of the circumstances surrounding her shooting. I know it was a very long time ago. But there are some questions I had, that you might know the answers to."

"Does it even matter?" Wendy asked. She removed the sun hat and hung it on the arm of her chair, then smoothed down her flyaway white hair. Without the hat, she looked a little closer to her true age. "Everyone involved is dead and gone now. Including Dolly Mott."

"At one time, you wanted justice for her."

"Yes, well, we all want things when we're young and idealistic, don't we?" Her voice tightened. "What relevance could the violent death of a woman a century ago possibly have to anything you're working on now?"

"I know this sounds corny, and I agree, but I want to know the truth," James said. "Her body was found hours after the shootout. You thought someone else might have killed her. You were careful never to cross the libel line, but you suspected Geary MacKay, didn't you?"

"No long 'e.' It's pronounced like Gary," Wendy said. "And what I thought or didn't think matters not at all. He's long gone too, isn't he."

"Did you ever meet him—Geary?"

"How could that possibly make a difference?"

"I just wondered what, specifically, made you point a finger at him."

Wendy smiled slightly. "You have to admit he's the obvious suspect. Even at the time of the murder, there were rumors. Pay enough hush money and you can crush anything. But again—it was long ago. My fires burned brighter when I was young."

"Was he still trying to crush the story in the 1950s?"

"It ran, didn't it?" she said, sipping her wine.

"It ran, but you're very careful to skirt around directly accusing him."

She barked a sharp laugh.

"Mr. Keeley, apparently I need to explain to you how journalism works. Or at least how it worked back in my day. Beyond the obvious liability to the paper, it is not my job to accuse anyone of anything. I'm not a prosecutor or a jury. We tell the public the facts, not what to think about them. They get to make up their own minds."

"But you can't tell me you weren't hoping they landed on a certain conclusion."

Wendy shrugged.

"What made you go for the jugular in the first place? Did you have evidence against Geary that didn't make it into the published stories?"

She gave him a long, intent look from behind her red-framed sunglasses. "You are very determined for someone looking into a murder that happened long before you were born. It's something I see in people writing true-crime books, not private detectives."

"No reason we can't be curious too."

"In my experience, you're mostly motivated by money. Who did you say hired you?"

He wondered if she'd believe that he was looking into it pro bono. "There's something new that's come to light about the case. Or maybe you already know this, but the police didn't take it into account either."

An eyebrow arched behind her sunglasses. "Care to share?"

"You show me yours, I—"

"Mr. Keeley," she said with a hint of a snap in her voice. "I'm not sitting on some secret stash of 1920s murder evidence. I haven't thought about Dolly's murder in years. Either get to the point, or stop wasting my time."

Right. It was the only hole card he had, but he didn't see any reason not to play it. Or at least, he wasn't going to get anything by sitting on it.

"There's a tunnel that connects the old speakeasy to the river. Dolly Mott's body was found very near it. I think she may have been killed in the tunnel and dumped in the harbor."

Wendy went very still. She carefully set the wine glass down on the iron patio table beside her. "How did you find this out?"

"It's under the building where my office is. From the look of things, it hadn't been opened since the 1920s."

"You broke in?"

James smiled. "As you pointed out, we're bottom-feeding scum. It's what we do."

Wendy took a slow breath and picked up her glass of wine. "What did you find in the tunnel?"

"What did you expect me to find?"

Her hand twitched on the wine glass. "What do you mean? It's a general question. As you noted," she added with a tight smile, "I'm a curious person, as well."

Hmm. He hesitated, but again went with the truth rather than a fishing expedition. "Just some old crates and barrels. Turn-of-the-century junk. Certainly nothing of value. I've notified the owners about it. If you want, I could show it to you."

Wendy shook her head. "Completely unnecessary. I told

you, it was a hundred years ago, and it's been over half a century since I wrote about it. I really don't care anymore." She took a breath and rose from her chair. "If that's all, Detective, I really need to finish pruning the forsythia."

It was like a switch had flipped, from cautiously friendly to cold.

"I'm sorry, have I offended you somehow?"

Wendy laughed a little and reached for her sun hat. "It's only that I've outgrown being excited about this nonsense, I suppose. Secret bootlegger tunnels and Prohibition-era murders—it's like something from a melodrama. It mattered a lot when I was twenty-five. I suppose I've moved on."

Yeah, she was the very image of a woman who had moved on, all right. James held out a card. "Here, call me if you change your mind and want to discuss it."

"I won't," she said, but she took it.

He was halfway expecting to be thrown out on his ear, but she walked him back to his car. On the way, he asked one other question.

"Wendy, did you ever hear anyone refer to either of the MacKay brothers as 'Nero'?"

"That was Geary's street name," she said immediately. Not even a hesitation. "Back in the 1920s. Where did you hear that?"

"One of your stories, probably."

"No," she said, searching his face from behind the sunglasses. "I am fairly certain I never used it in print."

"I guess it must have been in one of the old clippings from the 1920s," James lied. "A quote, maybe? I wasn't sure who it referred to."

"Interesting," Wendy mused, her gaze sharp. "I've never seen it in print. Geary MacKay worked hard to bury that side of his life. *Very* hard."

She watched him drive off, and in the rear-view mirror he saw her as he turned out onto River Road—still watching him, standing in the driveway of her anomalously nice house.

CHAPTER FIVE

THE TUNNEL, in Oz's opinion, turned out to be a most agreeable workspace. James was apologetic about it for some reason, but humans got moody about the oddest things.

It was pleasantly reminiscent of the mountain caves of Oz's youth, the sort of places his people traditionally lived. His daughter Neith had quite a nice cave, with a lovely view and excellent hunting, tucked away on a remote mountain in one of the dragon territories in Canada. He should visit her again soon, he thought wistfully.

But for now, he found the cave—er, tunnel made a perfectly functional office, if a bit low of ceiling. Turning on the power to the basement and tunnel had turned out to be merely a matter of finding the right fuse box ("Did I mention I'm kind of a maintenance man here?" James had said, fiddling with switches). Most of the light bulbs had promptly blown out after a century of disuse, but James brought in much brighter replacement bulbs, their steady white light gleaming alongside the dull amber glow of the handful of vintage leftovers.

"We're going to have to get an electrician in here to look

at this place," James said. "It's probably a complete firetrap down here."

"Fire is not a problem for me," Oz pointed out.

"I can't tell if you're joking or not, but unless you have a built-in fire extinguisher as well as fire breath, it would be a problem for you as much as for us if the warehouse burns down around you." James hesitated. "Uh, do you?"

"Not as such." He refrained from pointing out that he was fireproof; it was probably impolite.

Still, a fire extinguisher seemed like a prudent idea, for the humans' sake if nothing else. He added one to his mental shopping list. Especially prudent, he felt, due to James's tendency to light fires in the basement on a regular basis.

And he quite liked the tunnel. With the riverside doors shut, it was pleasantly private. James obtained a brand new lock from the hardware store and spent some twenty minutes with a cordless screwdriver putting on some bits of steel to attach it to, after which the riverside doors were easy to secure.

"I don't really have any way to ask if Dolly minds if you're here," James said, coming in from the basement side in a swirl of cigarette smoke. "She's not showing up for the ritual right now."

"Is that bad?"

"Not really. She doesn't always come." Still, he looked distracted, worried even, to the extent that Oz could judge expressions at human scale. "Anyway," James added, "if she does mind, you'll find out soon enough."

"How?"

"She's a poltergeist. So be on the lookout for cold spots, things moving around on their own, random ashtrays beaning you in the skull."

"I shall keep a very sharp lookout," Oz promised.

What James was mainly having him do right now was

filing. There was nothing in the world so satisfying as organizing things, and James's office was a wonderland of things to organize. It would have been more convenient if Oz could have gotten into the office itself. But they soon worked out a system where James would bring filing cabinets out on a wheeled handcart (Oz was delighted with it; he'd never seen such a thing before) and Oz picked them up and carried them down to the tunnel by way of the river doors. James carried down the smaller items, boxes and the like.

It was quite an impressive hoard of paper and sundry other items James had managed to accumulate. The man never threw anything away. Oz liked that in a human. A disorganized hoard was a travesty, of course, but that was what Oz was here for.

"Don't throw out anything without asking me," James told him, sitting on a barrel as Oz moved crates to make room for filing cabinets. "It could be important. I never would've thought Dolly's newspaper clippings would come in handy, and now look at us. Just make a pile or something."

"A *pile*," Oz scoffed. "I should be ashamed of myself if all I can manage is a *pile*."

The only real problem was that all of James's paperwork was so inconveniently small, but Oz had plenty of practice at dealing with human-sized printed matter by now. He brought some tools with him from the house, his reading glasses and magnifying glass and a selection of different-sized pairs of tweezers.

"Good God," James said at one point, watching him from the basement-side doors as Oz—reading glasses perched on his nose, magnifying glass in one hand and tweezers in the other—worked his way through a pile of nearly microscopic receipts.

"Am I doing it wrong?" Oz asked, looking at him over the glasses. "I have all of your June through September receipt folders organized, but I can start over if you'd prefer a different organizational—"

"No no," James said, taking a breath. "No . . . it's fine. You're . . . fine. This is definitely an experience . . . that I am having." He went back upstairs.

Humans were so idiosyncratic.

Oz took a break every so often to fetch coffee, tea, and snacks. James had made token protests the first couple of times Oz shoved coffee and muffins in his office window, then seemed to acknowledge that it was a sensible arrangement all around. Oz *liked* feeding people, and rarely had people to feed. To be sure, fetching poppyseed muffins wasn't quite as satisfying as bringing a nice fat deer back to the cave to feed a dragonlet, but it was pleasant in a vaguely related kind of way.

He had shared this observation with James, and James didn't seem as pleased with the metaphor as Oz would have expected, but didn't tell him to stop.

After a couple of experiences in the Starbucks drive-through, and flying back to his own house once or twice, he eventually realized that keeping coffee things at the warehouse made the most sense. Soon he had a little kitchenette set up in the tunnel. There was no running water down there, but that wasn't hard to work around; he could just bring water in jugs.

It was getting quite civilized down here, all things considered. He had the kitchenette, complete with fire extinguisher and first-aid kit because it seemed that a workplace ought to have both, and a nice little working space with bright lighting. He had even brought a couple of rugs from his lair for added comfort. There were boards down the middle of the tunnel's floor—for moving barrels, James had explained—but it was hardly more than splinters and dirt, and his tail kept snagging.

He was making himself tea in a cup the size of a human wheelbarrow when he noticed that he was being watched.

"Oh, hello," Oz said to the young woman watching him from the open doors to the basement. The lights in the basement were off, so it was all shadows over there, but he knew who and what she was because he could see the walls through her. "You must be the ghost that James told me about."

She didn't react at first, and he wasn't entirely sure she could hear him, but then she nodded.

"We met earlier, in a sense, but I couldn't get a good look at you." He set the teacup down. "Do you mind if I come over there? Would it bother you?"

After another hesitant moment, she shook her head, so Oz shuffled over to the basement doors. She took a few steps backward into the shadowed recesses of the basement, cut through by shafts of wan daylight from the high windows. It was a rainy day outside, the light dim and gray. Oz recalled that James had said sunlight didn't agree with her.

Even up close, there was still something distant about her, like a far-off figure seen through binoculars. She smelled very strange, for a human. He could smell a trace of smoke, and one of the flowery scents that humans liked to put on themselves.

But normally those smells would be layered with the dozens of other smells that accompanied any living thing. He should have been able to smell her skin and hair, the soap she'd used, traces of whatever she'd had for lunch. And he couldn't. There was just the faint hint of smoke and perfume, as if that was all that was left of her living smell, just as the translucent impression of her physical appearance was what remained of her living body.

Insubstantial she might be, but she still had all the little movements and mannerisms of a living creature. She was fondling the jeweled adornment around her neck, a sort of nervous habit, while she looked up at him with anxious eyes.

"I won't hurt you," Oz said. He lowered his head, resting his chin on his front paws in an attempt to set her at ease. "I can't. No one can. You're dead."

"I know," she said.

It was startling, hearing her speak. Her voice, a shy whisper, was about what he would have expected from someone so small and scared. But it made him realize that just as she didn't have the smells of a living creature, she also lacked the sounds. There should have been an entire many-layered overlay of sound surrounding her, the little rustles when she touched her necklace, the click of the beads on the wrap holding her hair back, the swish of her skirt and the tap of her shoes on the floor. And there was none of that. Her whispered voice was the only noise she made.

"But I can be hurt, you know," she went on, her voice growing stronger and clearer. "Magic can still hurt me. They tried to exorcise me once, in that warehouse up there. I had almost forgotten about that. It didn't work because they didn't know about the basement, where I'm strongest. But they did try. And it hurt."

"I'm sorry," Oz said sincerely. "I would never want to hurt you, or exorcise you. And even if I should try, which I would never want to, James wouldn't let me."

This made her smile, quick and sweet. "He wouldn't, would he? It's so strange, having a friend. I don't think it's happened before—since I died, I mean. And even before then, I . . . don't think I had a lot of friends. Not close ones. But . . ." She frowned and touched the necklace again. "There were people I loved. I stopped remembering them. I stopped remembering everything. And now it's all coming back, only bits and pieces right now, but it *is* coming back, and it hurts. So that's another way I can be hurt, I guess."

"I didn't mean to cause you pain. We can talk of something else if you'd like."

"No, I don't mind. It's almost like talking about my life makes it real again. Like I can keep the people I knew alive by remembering them." She seemed to realize she was running her fingers over the necklace and dropped her hand away self-consciously. "Everyone I knew then is probably dead now. Isn't that strange?"

"Not to me," Oz said. "Dragons are mortal, but we are long-lived. All the humans I now know will be gone long before I will." That was an unexpectedly sad thought.

"Oh, I'm sorry. We are somewhat the same, then, you and I." Dolly held out a hand. "Can I try to touch you? It might not work. When James tries to touch me, I usually go away for a while. But I don't know what'll happen with you. It's an experiment."

"Certainly. Please do."

She approached him cautiously, until she was so near that he couldn't see her clearly; he had to close one eye and roll the other downward. Her fingers brushed his jaw just below the corner of his mouth. Contrary to the impression most humans seemed to have, dragons' scales weren't insensate. The scales themselves had no feeling, but their bases were full of nerve endings, like hairs on a mammal, and this was even more true of the fine scales around the mouth and face.

So he felt her touch him, like a gentle brush of wind accompanied by a chill: a breeze that carried the cool breath of rain.

"You moved when I touched you," Dolly said. "Did you feel that?"

"I did. And you're still here."

"For now, I think." She sounded wondering. "Perhaps it's because we are a little bit the same. You're a magical creature and so am I. Or maybe it's different when I touch first, instead of people touching me." She took a step back, gliding on soundless feet. "Dragon . . . I *fear* that tunnel you're in. And I don't know why."

"James thinks you were . . ." He hesitated."—hurt here."

"Killed. You can say killed. I . . . don't know what happened to me. It's like there's a hole where it should be. I mean, I *do* know, somewhere inside, I think. It's like my other memories, gone but still there. But I can't get a grip on that one. It's as if I'm *made* of memories now, and I . . ." She trailed off, and then whispered a small, "Oh."

Oz raised his head. A red stain had appeared on her dress, blooming under the glint of the necklace. It was more vivid, more *there* than anything else about her. And he could smell its sharp metallic tang, the distinctive smell of blood.

"This is why I don't think about it," Dolly whispered, and vanished.

Oz sat up. "Dolly?" he said.

His voice echoed through the empty basement. He was alone. After a long while, he went back to his work, sparing a quick tongue of flame for his stone-cold cup of tea.

CHAPTER SIX

WITH MOST OF the filing cabinets and other clutter down in the tunnel, James's office felt strange and bare. Drifts of unfiled paperwork, takeout menus, dust bunnies and junk mail had all been picked up from behind the square impressions the cabinets had left on the carpet. After a good cleaning with a vacuum he liberated from a maintenance closet, there was a moving-in feeling to it, fresh and new.

It made him think of the way this office had felt when he first moved into the building, five years ago. Like a world of promise and possibility had opened up in front of him. He was a self-made man with his own business. In those early days, it felt like he could do anything, go anywhere.

Of course, what he'd mainly ended up doing was process serving, repossessions, background checks, the odd bit of private security work, and similarly unglamorous chores of the profession. He smiled slightly; it wasn't as if he had any excuse for going into it with romantic misconceptions about what it would be like. He'd started out, years and a dozen changes of career ago, as an underpaid assistant to a bail bondsman named Bendix, the man who had given him the spellgun. Somehow he must have thought it would be different working for himself. Glamorous fantasies about solving murders and protecting damsels turned out to be nothing but spun sugar; the actual job was dull and everyday, the dangers coming mainly from people he'd annoyed by slapping court orders and custody agreements on them.

Maybe that was why solving Dolly's murder intrigued him so much. It was something straight out of Dashiell Hammett or Raymond Chandler, a tale of gangsters and bootleggers, of an innocent victim and a crime of passion and a bitter injustice ignored by those in positions of power.

With his office temporarily bare, he took advantage of the lack of clutter to pin up printouts and photocopies of the 1920s-era harbor on the wall. Obtained from the library, the newspaper archives, and in some cases the internet, they were black-and-white and blurry, but also painted a picture of a different and less developed Grand Bluffs.

The general outline of the shore was still recognizable, and many of the same buildings were there. Nearly the entire warehouse district had existed already, the differences mainly where the old brick warehouses had been torn down later for modern developments. Upstream the bluffs began, still almost entirely undeveloped and not yet swallowed the city's urban sprawl or the expensive cliffside mansions capitalizing on the view of what had been little more than steep clay banks snarled with trees. Downstream was lower and flatter, going quickly to farmland according to the old map he'd pinned up beside the photos.

The harbor itself was much less built up. The warehouses were there, with their accompanying docks, but as he had guessed, the large wharves hadn't been built yet; the existing docks were much lower. The concrete promenade wasn't there yet either, or the steep retaining wall. When the water was low, mud flats were exposed; the harbor had been dredged in the intervening years. It would have been easy in those days to walk to the water's edge, rather than climbing down the barricade.

And none of this helped him in the slightest.

It made the scene of Dolly's murder easier to visualize, but if anything it made it even more plausible that Dolly might have fallen from the dock or the boat, only to lie in the mud for hours, unnoticed. The harborside in the photos was a semiwild mess of rocky fill and mud flats, where Dolly could easily have sunken into the mud or slipped between two rocks. He had thought it unlikely that her body could have fallen into the river without washing farther downstream, but he now saw it was all too likely; numerous photos showed smaller boats dragged up onto the long, low slope of mud where now there was a deeper dredged-out channel. If she fell off the dock, in all likelihood she would have fallen into mud and ice, not water.

There was a thump from the window as the tip of Oz's snout slammed into it, hard enough to rattle the glass.

James got up to open it, but his sarcastic complaint died unspoken. Oz was obviously agitated, his scales bristling and the neck ruffs raising and lowering in anxious spasms.

"What's wrong?"

"Miscreants!" Oz snapped. "Larcenous pilfering swine! Blackguards! We have been set upon by purloining scoundrels!"

"Someone stole something?" James guessed as soon as he could get a word in. "From you?"

"From *us*," Oz hissed. There was a strong smell of brimstone around him, reminding James that when sufficiently provoked, he *could* actually breathe fire. "Come and see."

~

THE TUNNEL WAS awash in papers. Someone had gone through it like a wrecking ball. The filing cabinets had their drawers pulled out, with every file dropped on the floor. The lids had been unceremoniously cracked off the '20s-era crates that Oz had neatly lined up against the wall, straw ripped out, bottles scattered. An eye-watering smell of alcohol hung in the air.

"Someone wanted to find something," James said, surveying the devastation. Even Oz's cart of coffee and tea things had been torn apart and dumped on the floor.

Beside him, Oz's flanks heaved in deep gasps of suppressed rage.

"The least they could have done," Oz wheezed, "the very *least* was put everything *back*."

"Aren't you glad they didn't, though?" James picked up a file that had been trampled into the dirt. There was a clear shoeprint on it. "We'd never have known they were here, otherwise. It was like this when you came in this morning?"

Oz subsided with a burbling hiss. "I came up to see you straight away."

"Glad you did." James set the file down carefully on top of an overturned and emptied crate. "They were looking for something small, don't you think?"

This got the dragon out of his rage spiral. "Why do you think so?" he asked, his spiny ruff perking forward with interest.

"Because they dug into everything." James glanced at a file cabinet drawer that had been pulled entirely out and turned over. "They even looked at the bottoms of drawers and the backs of cabinets, in case something was taped there."

"Perhaps it is a red herring." Oz's ruff flattened. "They might have only *wanted* us to think that."

"Oz, unlike in your books, real life doesn't have a whole lot of red herrings, and it has damn few criminal master-minds." It was impossible to step anywhere without stepping on papers. He picked up a few more with visible footprints. "They clearly don't give a damn what we think, and they also don't care about being discovered. They just want to find something that, for whatever reason, they think is here. When did you go home last night?"

"Eight twenty-seven," Oz said promptly. "I stayed late and wished to do a bit of indexing at home this morning—I hope you don't mind." He lowered his head; a growl rumbled deep in his throat. "If I had been here earlier, I might have surprised the scrounging curs."

"I was upstairs and I didn't hear anything." Well, upstairs in a technical sense. His apartment was on the top floor, but through several floors and the tunnel itself, he wasn't surprised that he had slept right through whatever had been going on downstairs. "You know who *was* down here, though."

He stuck his head into the basement. It was dim and echoing, the gray light of morning shafting through the high windows.

"Dolly?"

There wasn't even the slightest hint of cigarette smoke in the air. Well, it was too much to hope she'd turn up without being summoned anyway.

"I'll go upstairs and get the brazier." He turned back to look into the tunnel. Oz was down at the far end, trying not to step on anything. "Why don't you start cleaning up down here?"

"Aren't we going to call the police?" Oz asked. "Dust for prints? Trace their DNA?"

"The police aren't going to care. And we aren't supposed to be in here anyway." A thought occurred to him. "Wait, you can tell people apart by smell, can't you? Can you tell anything about who was here?"

"Human," Oz said. "More than one. Beyond that, it's hard to tell. Between the various liquors and those disgusting perfumes your species likes, I can hardly smell anything."

"Would you know them if you smelled them again?"

"Perhaps." Oz sneezed. "It is hard to do when you mask your body smells with perfumes and soaps that change all the time."

James hesitated and went down to the river entrance, where he briefly checked the lock. The new lock was undisturbed, showing no sign of picking, sawing, or forcing.

"Was this locked when you came in this morning, Oz?"

"Yes," the dragon huffed. "I noticed nothing wrong until I entered the tunnel."

So they had come in from the other side. James stopped to check on his way out through the basement entrance to get his ghost-summoning supplies. Everything was still locked up tight, with no sign of damage.

Whoever was in here last night had a key.

~

DOLLY DIDN'T COME in response to James's repeated attempts to summon her. Disheartened, he wandered into the tunnel, where Oz was grumbling as he picked up papers and casually nudged file cabinets back into position.

"Any idea if anything's missing?" James asked.

"Perhaps I can answer once I've catalogued it all. Again." Oz pinched a broken bottle between two claws and picked it up. Liquid dripped sluggishly from the jagged glass. "And I never catalogued the contents of the crates. I hadn't got around to it yet."

"They thought it might be in the crates." Thoughtfully,

James sat on top of an overturned crate. "Even the ones that were nailed shut. They weren't looking for something we brought down. They wanted something they thought was here already."

It was possible, of course, that the searchers were merely being thorough, or, as Oz said, trying to throw them off. But he didn't think so. His office was untouched. Whoever had been down here was looking for something they thought had been in the tunnel originally.

Something from the 1920s.

"It'd really help if Dolly would show up," he added. Cigarette smoke wafted into the tunnel from the half a pack he'd left burning in the brazier.

"I spoke to her," Oz said, looking up from a handful of paperwork clutched in his claws. The other paw gripped his magnifying glass.

"When? Just now?"

"No. Yesterday."

"Oh. Really? How was she? I haven't seen her since we found the tunnel."

"Shy," Oz said. He examined the papers through the glass and carefully, nipping each one neatly with his claw-tips, sorted them in order. "Quite pleasant really. I see why you like her."

"But she was okay. Not too distressed or anything."

"She didn't seem unwell."

That would have to be enough. It was more than he'd had before.

Oz picked up a can of coffee that had managed to escape the destruction, held delicately between two claws, and looked around for a place to put it, but there was nowhere to set it down that wasn't equally messy. With one paw, he flipped over the coffee cart and set the coffee can on top of it.

"Of course they spilled all my tea and left the coffee, which I haven't a particular taste for. Er . . . would you like a cup?"

"Not right now," James said. He picked up a file folder with half a muddy footprint. There were at least two different people who had left tracks down here, and one of them was big. James compared the footprint to his own shoe. He was a size eleven. This guy must be at least a fifteen.

"What is that?" Oz asked, peering over from picking up tea bags with delicate nips of his claws. "A clue?"

"I hope so." James found a discarded file folder and began stashing papers with visible footprints. He briefly considered and then abandoned the idea of dusting for prints. Technically, he knew how and had supplies for it from back when he'd still envisioned private investigation as a much more storied career. But without the ability to actually run the prints, there wasn't much point.

"Wait, are you sorting those?" Oz exclaimed. "I'm only saying, because you have one from May and one from—"

"I'm taking the ones with footprints. It's okay if it leaves some gaps in the files." He ignored Oz's horrified expression. "Listen, if you have a photographic memory, you'll know if anything is missing when you put things back in order, right?"

"Of course," Oz said, in a tone that implied it was self-evident.

"And you never found anything down here that anyone might want enough to break in and steal."

Oz gave a great, rippling shrug. "Humans place value on the strangest objects. Look for yourself. Aside from the crates, it's all in . . ." He hesitated. "Er, it *was* in that plastic tub with the lid."

Oz had collected all the stray junk from the tunnel— bottles, broken porcelain, odd rusty metal bits and bobs—

into a plastic tote. Like everything else, it had been carelessly dumped on the floor. But Oz was right, there was nothing of value here. James tried comparing the heap of scrap to the neatly typed inventory taped to the tote and gave up. It was a waste of time. Whatever they had wanted to find wasn't here.

"Hey, Oz?" he said. "I'm going to do a little legwork upstairs. You gonna be okay down here?"

Oz gave him a look.

"Right. Not like anyone's going to mess with you. Oh, hey," he added. Oz's arrival with the news about the tunnel break-in had derailed a particular train of thought he'd been working on. "You can talk to the river dragons, right?"

"They aren't particularly good conversationalists—"

"I don't want to have a stitch and bitch. I was just thinking about how they still remembered where the tunnel entrance was. Do you think some of them might remember all the way back to what happened the night Dolly died?"

"Oh," Oz said, raising the spiny ruff behind his ears in interest. Then it flattened again. "I wouldn't get your hopes up. They aren't exactly a source of, er, reliable information about anything happening out of the water. If you want a detailed description of every rock and mussel shell on this stretch of river—"

"Yes, okay—"

"Also, they have difficulty telling humans apart, and they aren't especially clear on the passage of time—"

"Yeah, fine, I get it, but ask them, would you?"

"I will," Oz said. He dipped his head to study the mess again. "I'd like to put this in a bit of order first . . ."

"No worries, I didn't mean right now. Whenever you get a chance."

He left Oz grumbling in the tunnel and went back upstairs with the file folder of footprints tucked under his arm.

Aside from Oz and Dolly, there were only two other people, or entities, who knew about the tunnel—Wendy Attredge, and the property management company. And of those two, there was only one who would plausibly have a key.

CHAPTER SEVEN

IN THE FIVE years he'd rented his office, and the two years he'd actually lived here, James had sent his rent and the occasional phone call or email to Harborside Leasing and Management, the company that operated the property as a rental. Now, however, he began to dig for who actually owned it.

It was technically possible that his email to HLM about the tunnel had landed in the inbox of a low-level office peon who decided to go down and trash the place for . . . reasons. A grudge against the company, maybe?

No. That made no sense. He didn't think he was wrong that it was more than vandalism; it was a systematic search for something specific. Most likely, his email had been forwarded on to the building's owner.

Whoever that was.

But at least it was a matter of public record. After hunting through the city's database of property records, James found that the MacKays actually still owned the building, after all these years. The owner of record was Gerald MacKay, grandson of good old Geary MacKay, Wendy Attredge's #1 pick for Dolly's killer.

Now wasn't that interesting. Covering up the old family scandal, maybe?

And if so, just *what* exactly did Gerald MacKay think was in that tunnel?

The MacKays had lost ground from their 1920s glory days, but they were by no means down and out. Gerald MacKay's primary business was import/exports, not unlike his granddad back in the day. It wouldn't surprise James to find out that the MacKays were still involved in a certain amount of off-book "importing" even today; the apple didn't usually fall far from the tree.

But none of that was any business of his. What mattered was that Gerald almost certainly knew more than the newspapers, the police, or even Wendy Attredge about the things his granddad had gotten up to in the 1920s.

And James wouldn't mind knowing what his shoe size was.

~

GERALD MACKAY HAD a large corner office in a downtown office tower, with deep carpet, gold letters on the door, and a well-coifed and fancy-looking receptionist whose sleek modern desk was flanked by fake plants. It was all of the things that James's office had never been and never would be, at least as long as he kept resisting Oz's offers to rent him somewhere nicer.

"Appointment?" Ms. Fancy asked.

Having learned from the Wendy Attredge excursion, James had taken the precaution of, not dressing up exactly, but at least classing himself up somewhat. He'd shaved and put on a nice shirt and jacket, the only ones he owned, rather than the leather jacket that had been bled on and scuffed up in more than one brawl. He gave her his best and most respectable-looking smile.

"No, but I'm with Harborside, the property management company that operates Mr. MacKay's waterfront investments. I'm with the maintenance division, and I really need to see Mr. MacKay about something important."

"You'll need an appointment." She reached for her keyboard. "I'll check his calendar. What was the matter, exactly?"

"I found something in one of his buildings that I need to see him about."

Ms. Fancy nibbled on the end of the pen gripped between her first and middle finger. "Could you be more specific, please?"

"Just pass that along to him. Tell him that I'm the maintenance man at the property on Water Street, and I found something there that I need to talk to him about. I think he'll want to see me."

She gave him a look that clearly suggested it was, for her, a toss-up between doing that or calling security. He was glad he'd sprung for the nicer shirt.

"Name?"

"James Keeley. Double E, another E after."

She dutifully wrote it down and went through the adjoining office door.

It was very tempting to go all heist-movie and poke around on her computer, but he didn't know what to look for, and anyway, she was back in a moment. "You're right," she said. "He'll see you now. Right this way, Mr. Keale."

"And a Y on the end of the E," James murmured, but he followed her.

Gerald MacKay had a corner office of the sort James was used to seeing on TV, but rarely in real life. Floor to ceiling windows framed a view of downtown Grand Bluffs. In front of the window, the office was dominated by a large, heavy wooden desk, and a correspondingly large and heavy man rising from it, holding out a broad hand to shake. His hand all but engulfed James's.

In contrast to the swanky surroundings, his personal style was more that of a used-car salesman. He wore a plaid suit jacket and a broad tie with sunflowers on it.

And he was the absolute spitting image of both his grandfather and great-uncle. James had spent a lot of time during the last few days looking at pictures of the MacKay brothers in 1920s newspapers, and that broad-faced, heavy-jawed, pugnacious look was unmistakable. A general sense of bigness had come across in the photos, but it was considerably more intimidating in person. Gerald MacKay's shoulders strained against his suit jacket, and when he sat down, the chair creaked and reshaped itself around him. It wasn't fat. He was just *big*.

It was all too easy to imagine this guy grabbing a pipe wrench and taking on a rival gang of headbreakers on the Prohibition-era docks.

There was a dusting of white at his temples, but otherwise it was hard to tell his age; he looked somewhere in his forties or early fifties, which made James realize that he'd expected Geary MacKay's grandson to be older than that. If he'd inherited the company in the 1970s, Gerald must have been running it since high school.

"James Keale, is it? Have a seat, please." Gerald folded his big hands on the desk. They were spattered with freckles across the backs.

"Keeley, actually. And you're Gerald MacKay?"

"Call me Gerry, please."

"Geary and Gerry, huh? Must have been some confusing family reunions."

"I was named for my grandfather, actually." Gerry MacKay smiled slightly. "Did you know him?"

"What makes you ask?"

"Most people don't pronounce the name right. But," he added, "you don't look old enough."

"And here I was just thinking you don't look old enough to have taken over running your grandfather's business in the 1970s."

The smile stiffened somewhat. "You said you found something at our Water Street property."

"Yeah, that," James said. "Do you know anything about old bootlegger tunnels under the waterfront?"

"There are always stories about it," Geary said. "People like imagining that sort of thing." His tone was casual, but his eyes were sharp.

"This one is more than a story. I was doing some routine maintenance work and found a hidden tunnel under the building. Pretty sure it connects to the harbor, maybe left over from those days. There were a lot of speakeasies and whatnot along the shore, from what I've heard."

He stopped there, until Gerry made a rolling motion with his hand. "Yes, and?"

"That's all, really. I felt the company should know about it, so I sent in an email but didn't hear back."

"And did you look inside?"

Ah yeah, that's what you really want to know, isn't it? "I took a quick peek. Do you blame me?"

"See anything interesting?"

James shook his head. "Looked like some old crates and barrels, that's all. Nothing but junk. I locked it back up again."

A look of disappointment flashed briefly across Gerry

MacKay's heavy-browed face. *Yeah,* James thought, vague suspicion hardening into certainty. *You want something that you think is in there.*

"Anything you want me to keep an eye out for?" he asked brightly. "I could go ahead and clean it out, maybe store some stuff down there, since it looks like it was used for that purpose anyway. I do odd jobs around the place for reduced rent; it's really no trouble—"

"No need," Gerry cut in. "Just leave it locked up. I'll handle it."

I'll just bet you will. "Sounds good," James said, and rose from the chair. "I appreciate you taking the time to see me."

Gerry rose too, and James couldn't help getting the impression it was something other than politeness; Gerry MacKay didn't like people standing over him. Once again, James was treated to one of those engulfing handshakes, gripping just tight enough to hurt a little bit.

This man likes reminding people how tough he is.

"And I appreciate you bringing it to our attention," Gerry said. He smiled again, one of those traces of a smile that never reached his eyes. "You never did mention whether you knew my grandfather."

"I'm not really sure," James said, and held his eyes—and his hand—for a little longer than Gerry seemed to want to, before letting go. It was difficult not to respond to the alpha posturing with a bit of his own. "We might have met in passing somewhere. Oh, do you mind if I ask a quick question before I go?"

Gerry's gaze was leaden and noncommittal. "I'm a busy man, Mr. Keale."

"It'll only take a minute. What's your shoe size?"

It was satisfying to see Gerry briefly nonplused. "My shoe size?"

"It's a hobby of mine. I try to guess people's shoe sizes."

Gerry snorted. "What did you guess for mine?"

"I'd say oh, about . . . fifteen?"

"Good guess," Gerry said, unsmiling.

"I'm a good guesser," James said, and let the door of the office swing shut behind him.

CHAPTER EIGHT

"—AND this is the last of them." Oz set down the filing cabinet just outside the loading door with a thunk that raised dust in the alley. He was holding it clasped between his hands, the way a human might hold something unwieldy but not heavy.

"Thanks." James gestured to the hand truck beside the door. "Could you . . ."

"Oh. Yes. Of course." Oz picked up the filing cabinet in a one-handed grip and set it firmly in place. "I'd offer to help you get it inside, but . . ."

"You're too big. Yeah." James gave the hand truck an experimental tug. On the whole, the cabinets were heavier now than when he'd trucked them out, because the loose files that had been all over his office were now neatly filed inside. "I'm impressed you got this put back together so quickly."

"It was faster than the first time. I already knew where everything went."

"And there's nothing missing?"

Oz took a deep breath. "Two pages of the invoices for your casework for the office of Bradshaw & Wright, one page of the contract for your Miller case in spring of—"

"Yeah, I took those, Oz. They're the ones with the footprints."

"Oh," Oz said. "Ah. In that case, no."

"I still can't believe you can remember all of that."

"I'm still surprised you can't," Oz said. He scratched at his ear with a claw. "There are also some boxes of items I wasn't sure about. I think most of them are trash, but I didn't want to throw them away without asking. They're still down in the tunnel; if you want me to bring them up tonight—"

"That's okay. You've really done a lot, and in a short time too." James pulled out one of the drawers, just to appreciate the sight of all those neatly arranged file folders. The filing cabinets hadn't looked like this since they were an empty second-hand set with some dollar-store alphabetical folders inside. It had taken approximately a week for James's high expectations to run aground on the reef of his apathetic filing skills, and he'd never actually managed to get on top of it again.

"Do you really think they'll come back tonight?" Oz asked.

"I think I kicked a hornet's nest, and the hornet's gonna do *something*. I'm just not entirely sure what." He patted the top of the filing cabinet. "Best to move these where you're not going to have to sort them three times."

"What if they break into your office?"

"I'm not putting them in my office. There's a bunch of unused office space in here, and I'm stashing them in one of the empty ones." He grinned briefly. "Not that there's anything too important in here, but it'll keep them guessing."

"Should I move the rest of it out? I still have some coffee and tea things down there, and the boxes—"

"No, don't," James said. "It'll give them something to look through. Better than if the place is completely bare."

"And you think you know who 'they' are."

"I still think it's Gerry MacKay, I just can't prove it. The shoeprint is something, but it's not like there aren't other guys out there with size fifteen feet besides Gerry. Or I guess I should say, the guy who calls himself Gerry."

Oz raised an eyebrow.

James reached into his pocket and took out a folded printout of a magazine clipping from the late 1920s. It was the best-quality photo he'd been able to find of Geary MacKay, a rare color photo from a feature on one of Geary's business ventures. Folded up with it was a printout from the Chamber of Commerce website with a recent photo of Gerry. James unfolded them and held them up for Oz's inspection.

Oz reached for his glasses, hanging around his scaly neck on a gold chain, and perched them on the end of his snout, then proceeded to examine the pictures, squinting first one eye and then the other.

"And that's this Gerry fellow?" Oz said after a moment.

"Supposedly, one is Gerry and the other is his grandfather. It's true that you sometimes get family members who resemble each other closely. But that is one hell of a resemblance. And I haven't managed to find a single picture of the two of them together, even when Gerry was a kid. Supposedly Gerry's grandfather died back in the '70s and Gerry took over, but every picture of him I can find from the '70s and '80s looks pretty much like he does now, just with darker hair. And," James added, "here's the kicker. I did a records search on Gerald MacKay. He's got everything you'd expect —birth certificate, social security number, et cetera. But it's all very sparse. Just the basics."

"Is that bad?"

"Human lives, *real* human lives, are messy. You end up with random stuff. Like winning an award in fifth grade and making the paper, say. Or having your appendix out. Maybe it's not that strange that there's not much on Gerry's childhood, since he *was* a kid and there's a lot of stuff back then that didn't get digitized. But there's even less on his parents. I couldn't even find a marriage license. And there's more. The dates don't quite check out. The birth certificate shows him being born in 1960, which isn't too far-fetched for how he looks now, if he's lived a clean life and lucked out in the genetics sweepstakes. But it means he'd have been in his early teens when he took over the company, and as well as being completely far-fetched, that's—okay—hang on—" He scrolled through his phone until he found what he wanted, an old photo of a business association meeting from the mid-1970s, and held it up for Oz. "There's Gerry there, on the left, shaking hands with the old white-haired dude. Does that look like a fourteen-year-old to you?"

"I'm not the best judge of the ages of human hatchlings. Or adult humans, for that matter—"

"Right, got it, so take it from me. This isn't Geary's grand-son, Oz. This is Geary. Otherwise known as Nero."

"But why would he pretend to be his own grandson?" Oz asked blankly.

"Oz. If this is really Geary, he was born in the 1800s. Humans don't live that long."

"Oh," Oz said. "What is he, then?"

"I have no idea. But I plan to find out. In fact, I'm hoping Dolly can tell me, since she knew him back then. Have you seen her around down there?"

"Not other than the one time. She seemed quite nice."

"She is," James said. "I also really want to talk to her about Geary. Even if she can't remember her own death, she might be able to tell me more about him—and I think Gerry, or Geary, or whoever, is in it up to his eyeballs. If he didn't actually do it, he knows who did."

"I don't think I should leave you alone here," Oz said.

"Oz, they're not going to do anything if there's a dragon hanging around the place."

"Yes, that's rather the point."

"Look," James said, "there's next to no chance they'll search while there are still people up and about, right? Some of these businesses stay open late. Go have dinner, do whatever, and come back a little later. I'll still be up. I'm going to set a trap in my office, because that seems like the next logical place they'll move on to after the tunnel."

"Ooh," Oz said cheerfully. "A trap." The tip of his tail swished.

"Right. So go take a nap and you'll be fresh later. Oh," he added, "did you get a chance to question the river dragons?"

"I *did* ask," Oz said dubiously. "It's as I told you. They had no idea what I wanted. They don't care what happens out of the water. I have, however, been gifted two mussel shells, a shiny rock, and a rusted military canteen from the 1940s, which appears to be the closest they could come to understanding what I was asking about."

∿

AFTER OZ LEFT, the building was quiet enough that the creaking of the hand truck seemed loud as James wheeled the filing cabinet back to the empty office he'd picked out to temporarily stash his stuff in. Most of the building was commercial space, and much of it unoccupied. It was already long after hours and growing dark outside. For all his reassurances to Oz, he was still jumpy, and he locked his office door and window before opening the clinking bag he'd picked up from the hardware store.

The motion-activated trail camera was meant to go on a tree, and James took a little while to find somewhere to put it in the nearly bare office. He'd meant to hide it in a light fixture, but it wouldn't fit. He ended up drilling a hole in his desk and taping it underneath.

Taking his Dolly-summoning supplies, he went outside.

It was fully dark now, with all the businesses on the block closed except a bar down the street and the takeout pizza place on the ground floor of James's building, which had no customers as usual.

James walked over to the waterfront, the brazier swinging loosely from his hand. The piers were lit, but it was inky black underneath. He knelt on the southmost pier and leaned as far out as he dared, shining a flashlight underneath —another hardware store purchase; he'd gotten a big Maglite —until he caught the glint off the shiny new lock. No one was messing around under there. A couple of river dragons surfaced and played in the flashlight beam until James swung it away.

He went back to his building with the reassurance, at least, that no one was likely to go in from the river side. It was pitch dark in the stairwell, and he slowed, playing the flashlight over the steps with one hand resting on the spellgun at his hip. It might not be a bad idea to have a light installed out here. Or maybe just stop coming down after dark. He wasn't worried about being jumped while Oz was here.

But there was no one in the stairwell, and he let himself into the dark basement. Reflected streetlight from the small, high windows striped the bricks on the opposite wall.

"Dolly?"

No answer. Not even a single whiff of cigarette smoke.

Too much light ran the risk of making his endeavor hopeless, but he still shone the flashlight around the black pit of the basement, running it across the cobweb-draped shadows. He was alone, so he closed the basement door and locked it, shutting himself into the haunted darkness, and moved a broken chair in front of it to give him some advance warning just in case someone with a key—Gerry, say—tried to come in that way. Kneeling in front of the door, he set up Dolly's brazier. Two packs of cigarettes went in, along with a folded-up newspaper clipping.

It wasn't as nice a picture of Gerry MacKay as the ones he'd shown to Oz. This was a fuzzy black-and-white newspaper photo of Geary and Normal from a few months before the shootout. It had been taken from a distance as the two exited a restaurant, and they were barely recognizable.

But it was a real, physical clipping, not a copy. He'd quietly torn it out of one of the old editions of the *Register* in the newspaper's morgue. They were going to hate that if they ever found out, but he doubted they would; how many people did they get coming in to look through their 1920s bound copies, anyway?

And from his reading about ghosts when he was first working out how to summon Dolly, an authentic object would be much more likely to get her attention than a copy.

James struck a match. Cigarette smoke and the acrid scent of burning paper curled up into the air.

Nothing happened at first. There was no warm gaslamp glow of a 1920s jazz club brightening the walls around him. But, as the cigarettes burned down and he was about to give up, there was something.

Dolly emerged slowly from the dark, as if she'd walked out of a hidden door. Although the basement was still dark and she cast no light, there was a faint luminous quality to her. He could see her easily enough; there was just no indication of where the light was coming from.

Normally she was dressed more or less the same, in a succession of sheer flapper dresses and gloves. But she was wearing something different today. The skirt was short; it barely came to her knees. And there was a coat around her shoulders, made of pale fur with a ruff that framed her pointed chin and set off the necklace glistening at her throat. The way she was holding her cigarette, with her hands tucked under her arms, made James want to warn her not to set the fur on fire.

Of course, there was no chance of that. Dead women didn't burn.

"Low blow, James," she said quietly.

"Got your attention, though. Long time no see, Dolly."

She kept her distance, unsmiling. James took a slow breath, trying not to cough on the smoke curling up from the brazier. He unfolded the recent photo of Gerry. "Do you recognize this guy?"

Dolly didn't answer for a minute; then she said, "Hold it up to the window."

James obligingly held it up. "I thought you could see in the dark."

"No better than you can." She stepped a little closer; he smelled her perfume mingling with the smoke. "That's Nero. He owns the club."

"Otherwise known as Geary?"

"Yes, but I hardly ever heard anyone call him that. He liked to be called Nero." She smiled slightly. "Like a little tinpot dictator."

"And he and his brother ran the bootleg trade on the docks?"

Her smile dropped away. "Yes. Nero was the brains. His brother Normal was his right-hand man . . . his enforcer."

"And Normal was killed in a shootout?"

"No, he—" Her voice wavered. For an instant he lost sight of her; the private light that illuminated her seemed to fade.

"Come on, Dolly, don't go out on me now."

The light came back up, brighter. She looked more solid now, but he could also see bloodstains on the dress. It wasn't uncommon to see bloodstains on the dresses she wore, always concentrated around her chest and side. But this was a lot of blood; it soaked the dress, stained her legs under the hem and painted the ruff of the fur coat with dark tips on each long silver hair.

These, he thought, were the clothes she had been wearing the night she died.

"Normal was the enforcer," Dolly said, her voice stronger. "Normal was the one who . . ." Her voice faltered, but there was something about the *way* she said it, so that her next words came as no surprise. "Normal MacKay is the man who killed me."

CHAPTER NINE

She goes back to the tunnel, in her not-here times. She knows that now. It is the place that has haunted her . . . not dreams exactly, not nightmares, but whatever ghosts have instead.

In her dreams . . . her not-dreams, she runs through a gray world. There are no walls, no ceiling. She can run forever, but not far enough, not fast enough to escape.

"You little thief!"

Gunshots up ahead. She can't go that way.

And she turns around.

She knows how this turned out in reality. But you can't run forever. Eventually, no matter what happens, you have to turn around and confront what's chasing you.

~

"You *do* remember what happened to you."

"I do now," she said calmly, meeting his eyes.

"Why did Normal do it?"

"He caught me skimming." Now that it had come down to it, she looked almost relieved, even resigned, in a way—as if she'd pushed past something that had terrified her and come out the other side, and whatever awaited her there couldn't possibly be worse than the anticipation. "He confronted me in the tunnel. Didn't even give me a chance to say anything. There was a whole ruckus going on outside."

"The fight with the bootleggers."

"Yes, I know that now. I didn't then. I guess he thought what's one more gunshot in the commotion, more or less." Her smile was small and sad. James wished he could hug her, but he didn't dare make a move in her direction. A single touch would be enough to banish her.

Although maybe, tonight of all nights, he would have been able to touch her. He'd never seen her so present, so *there*.

"What happened to Normal after he killed you?"

"I don't know," Dolly said simply. "I didn't become . . . *aware* for a long while afterwards. Long after all of that had already happened."

But James could guess. Normal MacKay had supposedly died in the same dockside shootout that had killed Dolly. But it was beyond belief that he'd accidentally wandered out into the line of fire, when—from Dolly's mention of a ruckus—the shots were clearly audible inside.

No, the only thing that made sense was that someone else had used the shootout to cover a murder, the same way Normal had tried to. And the most likely person was Geary MacKay. Normal caught Geary's girlfriend dipping into the till, and Normal shot her, and Geary shot Normal—could it all be that simple?

Simple . . . except for the matter of a very much alive and well Geary MacKay, a hundred years later.

"Dolly, what are Geary and Normal?"

"What?" she asked, eyes wide.

"The MacKay brothers. What *are* they?"

"They're mobsters, who run the dockside trade—"

"No, I know that part. I mean, I know they're not human. Do you know what they really are?"

"But they *are* human." She looked and sounded baffled. "As human as you and I, well I guess more human than I—James, *look out!*"

Her warning came an instant too late. Something came out of the darkness and collided with the side of his head.

With his knees buckling and stars bursting in his vision, James tried to twist around and grab hold of whoever had hit him. His hand snagged on a jacket or coat, and through the wheeling kaleidoscope spinning around him, he glimpsed a pale flash of a face before a knee connected viciously with his stomach. He went off balance, his bad leg buckled, and he hit the floor.

There was a terrific thump as someone ran into the chair in front of the basement door, followed by rattling the locked knob, a click, and then the rapid clatter of retreating footsteps, running up the stairs outside.

James lay panting, getting his breath and his wits back. Dolly had vanished; the basement was dark. He felt around until he found the flashlight, and turned it on without getting up. The beam shafted through the smoke still hanging in the air from Dolly's brazier, showing him the bare brick walls. The door to the stairwell stood open, and the door to the tunnel was cracked open as well.

They were already in the tunnel when I came down here. They just locked the door behind them, same as I did.

James cursed quietly, and then struggled to his feet, holding onto the wall. The side of his head was sticky when he touched it. His mystery assailant had hit him with something hard, a piece of scrap wood or the butt of a flashlight.

At least it wasn't a bullet. And the person he had grappled with wasn't nearly big enough to be MacKay.

He coughed. The smoke from the brazier was cloying and painful, knifing into his lungs.

Actually . . . that was a lot of smoke for a couple packs of cigarettes.

He risked a step onto the seesawing floor. By the time he reached the door to the tunnel, he was steadier on his feet. He threw the door open.

Smoke billowed into the basement. There were flames leaping in the tunnel.

James was frozen for a bare instant. The crates, the straw, the dry wooden beams—it would all go up in moments, and take the basement and the warehouse with it. Dolly's warehouse.

No, wait. Fire extinguisher. Oz had one down here, didn't he?

Coughing, his head throbbing, James stumbled through the smoke toward the coffee cart. Oz still hadn't gotten around to replacing most of the spilled and spoiled coffee things; the fire extinguisher and an incongruously brand-new first-aid kit sat neatly lined up beside the one undamaged jar of coffee and a handful of spoons.

Because it was Oz, who had never met a job he couldn't over-achieve at, the fire extinguisher was huge, an industrial one that James could barely move. On the other hand, with flames leaping from the boxes of papers to catch the dry, scattered straw, he didn't think it was possible to have *too much* fire extinguisher.

It took James a moment to figure out how to use it. Unlike a small household all-in-one extinguisher, this one had a bottle of propellant separate from the main tank of powder. Once he turned that on and pointed it at the flames, the extinguisher's contents hosed out in a powerful spray that must have traveled a good thirty or forty feet down the tunnel.

The fire choked and guttered. Covering his face with his sleeve, James dragged the extinguisher closer and hosed it around. Dry white powder coated everything nearby, along with char and ash. Tears streamed down his face from his smoke-irritated eyes. He could barely breathe.

Got to get out of here . . .

The fire was out, or at least the glow of the flames could no longer be seen, but the tunnel was thick with searing clouds of smoke. Now that the flames had died, it was almost completely dark. James dropped the extinguisher hose and staggered backward, his head swimming.

He smacked into something so large and solid that he thought at first it was the wall, until arms closed around him: one big hand on each of his wrists, pinning him firmly.

"Hi there," Gerry MacKay's voice said in his ear, on a slight cough. "Let's talk about why you wanted to burn down my building, why don't we?"

CHAPTER TEN

MacKay dragged him out of the tunnel into the basement. Someone flipped on the lights, and James had to close his eyes against their blinding brilliance. He doubled over coughing, with MacKay's hard grip serving a double purpose, keeping him from going anywhere but also keeping him from falling on his face. His head pulsed in time with his helpless coughing fit. He was dimly aware of the spellgun being wrenched out of its holster, and tried to reach feebly to stop it, but MacKay drove him to his knees with a hard hand on his shoulder.

He got his breath back and blinked the tears out of his eyes. He was kneeling on the basement floor with one of MacKay's huge hands on each of his shoulders, and another bruiser type looming in front of him. James blinked, coughed and spat, and did a quick check of the rest of the room. Another of MacKay's guys stood in front of the open basement door. There was the sound of coughing and cursing from the tunnel—one more henchman? Two? Smoke hung heavily in the air, making him cough again every time he tried to draw a deep breath.

MacKay gave him a little shake, a slight increase of pressure from a hand that felt as big as a Christmas ham. "Now then, let's have a little talk about what you were burning in there."

James finally managed to drag in a breath. "What *I* was burning?"

Goon Number Three stumbled out of the tunnel door, wheezing. "Boss, it's a godawful mess. Can't even tell what he was trying to set on fire in there."

"That's because I was trying to put it *out*, you idiots," James got out between strangled coughing fits.

"Yeah, so what was your plan, anyway?" MacKay hauled him up by a grip on the scruff of his neck. James wasn't a small man—he was a shade under six feet, topping out at about 180 when he hadn't been working out much—but MacKay dragged him around like a kitten. "Tried to destroy evidence, but it got out of control?"

"Evidence of *what*?"

MacKay gave him another shake, harder this time, rattling his teeth. "That's what you're gonna tell me."

Goon Number Two stretched out his hand, cracking his knuckles. "Just give the word, boss."

"Where did you find these guys?" James asked.

That mouth was going to be the death of him one of these days. MacKay spun him around and drove a fist into his already sore ribs.

"You know what I want," MacKay snapped. He pulled James up by a fistful of his jacket. "Where's the necklace?"

"The what?" James gasped out, genuinely baffled.

"The necklace. *Her* necklace. You found it in there, didn't you?"

"I have no idea," James got out between gasps, "what you're talking about." The smoky air felt like knives stabbing his lungs.

MacKay smothered a cough. "Can't breathe in here. Denny!" he snapped at one of the hirelings. "Get the harbor-side door open and let it start airing out in here. You two, let's get him somewhere more congenial to having a casual chat. Somewhere," MacKay added as he strong-armed James toward the basement door, "that no one's going to hear you scream."

James let his knees wobble, trying to look weaker than he was. It wasn't that much of a con in his current state. He glanced around for the spellgun, and found it tucked into the waistband of Number Two, just out of reach.

One of his feet struck the brazier with a ringing clatter. It rolled away, scattering ashes and bits of cigarettes. None of the intruders paid it any mind; it was just another item of trash, part and parcel of the broken chairs and fallen bricks scattered along the walls of Dolly's basement.

But MacKay paused in the basement doorway, with James's jacket fisted in his meaty hand. He looked over his shoulder. "Hell of a thing to be back here," he muttered, and then he reached over and turned off the lights, plunging them back into darkness.

As MacKay forced him up the stairs, James murmured, "You really are Geary MacKay, aren't you?" and felt the two giant hands—one in his jacket, one squeezing his shoulder—tighten painfully for a moment.

"You just concentrate on walking, clever boy," MacKay muttered. He pushed James up the stairs, a little too fast for James to entirely keep his feet under him; he kept barking his shins on the concrete steps.

At the top, there was a pause while Goon Number One, the one who had been guarding the door, locked the wrought-iron gate. MacKay leaned forward over James's shoulder.

"Okay, buddy, last chance," he said into James's ear. His

hot, cigarettes-and-whiskey breath brushed the side of James's face. "Do you have the necklace here? Save us a trip, we might thank you."

"I don't know what necklace you're talking about," James ground out.

But he couldn't help remembering the ever-present gleam of what he had taken for gaudy paste jewelry at the hollow of Dolly's slender throat. *Normal caught me skimming*—maybe what she'd taken wasn't money from the till, but jewelry.

If that was the case, though, where was it? And why would Gerry, or Geary, or whoever the hell he was want it back *that* badly? It had been a hundred years.

Unless this isn't really Geary MacKay; maybe he really is Geary's grandson as he claims . . .

No. There was no doubt in James's mind, not after seeing the look on MacKay's face as he had glanced back into the abandoned basement that had once been alive with music and lights. That was the face of a man looking back into the past.

"No answer?" MacKay said. "So that's how it's gonna be." He shoved James forward. "Walk casual now. Just some friends coming home from a boys' night out." He threw a meaty arm over James's shoulders in a parody of comradeship. His other hand, lower down, shifted its pincer grip to James's wrist. "Car's right around the corner."

James tried to look around, made more difficult when he could barely move his head. It was late at night in an industrial part of town, but there were still a few lights. The pizza takeout was still open. He might scream for help—

Yeah, and get his neck broken for his troubles. MacKay's arm felt like a tree trunk across his shoulders.

Try to throw MacKay, grab the spellgun, and make a run for it?

If it was just MacKay, he might have tried it, but there

was one thug in front and another bringing up the rear, and both of them had the kind of ill-fitting jackets that spoke eloquently of guns underneath.

Salvation, when it came, fell from the sky.

James felt the draft of air and, through pure habit, ducked. A couple pounds of furious, clawing auklet smacked into MacKay's head instead.

MacKay let out a gargled, "What the *fuck*!" and let go of James, who stumbled away. A second auklet swooped through the space where James's head had been.

James dived for Goon Number Two, who had the spellgun. He went low, rammed a shoulder into Two's stomach, and clawed around the back of the man's belt for the gun. He got an elbow in the back of his neck for his pains, but he staggered away, coughing, with his hand wrapped around the spellgun's grip.

He spun around to find MacKay engaged in single combat mano-a-auklet, and both of MacKay's hired help drawing their guns. Goon Number One had his gun out already, so James fired at him out of pure instinct.

He never had any idea what was going to happen when he pointed the spellgun at anything. Usually it was nonlethal. In this case, however—

There was the pistol's sharp bark and a green flash, and a small cube, about the size of a Rubik's Cube, clattered to the pavement.

Number Two stopped with his gun halfway out of its holster. MacKay, who had finally managed to claw the auklet away from his face, stared at the cube and then at James.

"Yeah, you two think you can shoot me before you're next?" James asked, backing away in the alley. The more space he could put between them, the less chance they'd actually manage to hit him with pistols in the dark. "Or you could just leave." Movement out of the corner of his eye alerted him, and he fended off another auklet attack one-handed, feeling small claws gouge his wrist.

MacKay hesitated. He reached down and picked up the cube. It was dull and unreflective, like granite. "What'd you do to Hank?"

"I'll do it to you and the other guy if you don't leave." James's voice scraped his raw throat. It felt like he had a three-day cold. "Or maybe I'll just do him right now—"

"Fuck no, I'm out of here," Number Two announced. He holstered his gun and retreated, hands in the air.

"Oops, looks like your ride is leaving."

"You are a dead man, Keale," MacKay declared, backing away after Two.

"It's not—Okay, fine, call me Keale or Nancy or whatever you want. Don't forget to collect your other guy from the tunnel, because I sure don't want him!" he yelled hoarsely after them.

As soon as they turned the corner, James indulged in the coughing fit he'd been desperately holding back. With the spellgun still pointed down the alley, he backed up to the side door, and fumbled at it with shaking hands until he got the key into the lock. He edged down the hall and then found that the lock on his office door was broken. The knob spun, and the door swung loosely open on the dark office.

There was next to no chance they'd bothered to leave a guy there, but James still dodged to the side. He reached in to turn on the light, and carefully swept the room with the gun. The drawers of his desk had been dumped. The camera was ripped off its tape and smashed on the floor.

"Bastards," James muttered. He turned off the light but didn't bother trying to close the door. Then he went upstairs.

The bottom floor of the converted warehouse was offices, the two middle floors were hired-out storage space (usually about half full of crates and God only knew what), and the top floor was apartments, of which James's was currently the only occupied one. His door stood open. James sighed deeply, coughed a little, and then did the same turn-on-the-light-and-clear-the-room procedure as in his office. It took a little longer, since there was a bedroom and bathroom to clear as well.

It looked like MacKay and company had been busy up here before they'd come down to the basement. The furniture was overturned, couch cushions slashed open, drawers pulled out and dumped.

"You guys have a damn *key*," James muttered as he closed the door only to have it swing open again. They'd kicked in the door anyway. It was a message as much as anything.

He dragged the overturned couch in front of the door, for whatever that was worth, and flipped up a chair to sit on for a few minutes, until the shakes eased up a bit.

Then he called Oz, who answered on the first ring.

"Oh, James, hello! I was just thinking about calling, actually. I've had the best idea for a place to watch the building; there's a flat roof next door and I could easily—"

"Oz," James said. It came out in a hoarse bark, and the dragon fell abruptly silent. "Yeah, sorry, you were right, I should've had you stay, and—" He broke off to cough for a minute. "Could really use a dragon bodyguard right about now."

CHAPTER ELEVEN

"THIS REALLY CANNOT BE BORNE," Oz declared, surveying the charred wreckage in the tunnel. All the lights were on in the tunnel and basement, pitilessly exposing the damage to boxes, crates, and timbers, all of it coated in a fine layer of powder.

James had waited upstairs until Oz showed up. He'd spent most of that time in the bathroom, dabbing at his soot-smudged, bloody face with a dampened dish towel. He had a feeling that it hadn't done much to improve his appearance, based on the look of horror Oz had given him upon arrival.

"Yeah, well, they'll be back. They own the damn building." James kicked at a charred scrap of cardboard. The fire had started in the boxes of scraps and receipts, and spread to some of the straw-filled crates before he'd extinguished it. "I think there's not much question of moving out now. It's not like I can stay in a building where the landlord is literally trying to kill me."

Oz cleared his throat. "Er, about that offer, I'm still entirely available to pay—"

"Not now, okay? We can work out the details, whatever details need to be worked with, when I don't feel like I smoked a pack of Dolly's cigarettes and got smacked in the skull with a bowling ball." He coughed again. A wet, heavy feeling had settled into his chest, clinging like the cold damp of a winter fog. Being in the smoky tunnel wasn't helping, even with the doors on both ends open.

Oz hesitated and turned to look at him. "You really should be in a hospital."

"I'm fine." James said. He coughed again, trying to stifle it.

"You keep saying that."

"Can you smell anything?" James asked, making an effort to steer the topic away from his health.

"Nothing except smoke and some sort of chemical they must have used to start the fire. Ugh." Oz sneezed, and rubbed at his snout with the back of his paw. "Terrible."

"Oh," said a soft female voice.

Dolly was standing in the doorway to the basement. With all the lights on, her body seemed to waver, so translucent that James could see the wall through her. But she was there. He'd never seen her manifest in the light before.

Even more extraordinary, she cautiously stepped into the tunnel. She was wearing the fur coat and the bloodstained dress, her hands clasped in front of her.

"Hello, miss," Oz said politely. He sneezed again and pawed at his nose. "Pardon."

James wasn't sure whether stepping toward her would break whatever tenuous control kept her here. "I wasn't sure if I'd see you again," he said, and smothered a cough. "After you told me about Normal, I thought that might've been your —unfinished business, y'know?"

"No," Dolly said softly. She looked all around, taking it in with her wide eyes. "It's not that. Not exactly. I . . . I haven't been here in a hundred years, but in some ways it feels like I never left. Does that make sense?"

"It does," James said gently.

She brought up a hand to touch her neck, curling her fingers around the necklace glittering in the hollow of her throat. He'd seen her do that before, come to think of it. She often touched it when she was upset. It had always seemed a nervous habit to him, like the way she played with her cigarettes.

She didn't have a cigarette right now, he realized. It was the first time he'd ever seen her without one.

"Dolly," James said, "who gave you that necklace?"

"This?" She looked started, and pulled her hand away from it. "Oh, it was a gift from Nero." She seemed to see him for the first time. "Oh, *James*. What did they do to you? Are you all right?"

"I keep trying to get him to go to the hospital," Oz said.

"I do *not* need a hospital."

Oz took a step forward, ducking his head to avoid the low ceiling beams. James braced himself for Dolly to vanish, but she seemed too fascinated, looking around at everything. She lightly ran her hand across the top of a crate that had escaped the fire unscathed. Her ghostly hand didn't stir a single fleck of the powder that dusted it.

"Dolly, did you see who did this?" Oz asked.

Dolly shook her head. "I'm sorry. I didn't. All I saw was someone moving in the dark."

"I think I know who it was anyway," James said. "I still don't know why, but there's only one other person I told about this tunnel, and that's Winifred Attredge, the reporter who—Dolly?"

Dolly's ghostly outline rippled like a reflection in a puddle. For an instant she was almost completely transparent, but then she solidified and stabilized, and raised her eyes to meet his.

"Winifred," she whispered, and clutched the necklace in both hands. "*Oh.* That was my most precious thing. That was why I couldn't leave, the reason I had to stay—And I forgot. I *forgot.*"

James had to stop himself from reaching out to touch her. "What did you forget?"

"Winifred. Wendy. My *daughter.* Oh, James." Tears flooded her eyes.

It wasn't a movie star that Wendy Attredge reminded him of, James thought, dizzied by the sudden click of recognition. It was Dolly, with her rare, beautiful smile.

"I went home to her from the bar every night." Dolly's voice faltered and then came back stronger. "It was what I looked forward to through every shift. An old woman in my boarding house watched her for me. I used to pay for it out of my tips. Did you—did you meet her? What's she like?"

"She's lovely," James said. "She looks just like you." And he was only now seeing it.

Tears washed over Dolly's eyes and flooded her cheeks. She buried her face in her hands.

"I just wanted her to have a good life," she said through her fingers.

"I think she did. I think she had a very good life indeed. She was a reporter. She tried to find out what happened to you." Through her hands, Dolly gave a wet little laugh that made James smile. "But there's something I don't understand. If she's your daughter, she must be almost a hundred years old. She didn't look anywhere near—" But answer followed question, as quick as thought. "Geary is her father, isn't he?"

Dolly nodded wordlessly. She wiped at her eyes before reaching into her small, beaded purse for a handkerchief. It was a living woman's gesture; it made him want to reach out even more overwhelmingly.

Instead, he asked, "Does Geary know?"

"I never told him," Dolly said quietly. She blew her nose and wiped her eyes again. "I couldn't hang that on her, not until she was old enough to understand who and what he was."

And it all circled around to that. "Which is what?"

"A bad man," Dolly said. Her voice was calm and steady. Sniffling a little, she tucked her handkerchief away. "Even when I loved him, I knew he was no husband or provider. I was swept up in the charm and the delight and . . ." She plucked at the lapels of the fur coat. "The presents. I never had nothing like this, growing up. Please don't judge me for it."

"No one judges you," Oz rumbled, and nudged James.

"No, no, I wasn't even thinking that." His thoughts had been somewhere else entirely. "But Dolly—what *is* he? He was here earlier tonight, and I *know* it's him, not his grandson. He's got to be almost a hundred and fifty years old."

"Oh, that!" Dolly's face cleared. She looked bright and animated all of a sudden, with her fingers curled over the necklace again. "That's the special gin. Probably for Wendy too, come to think of it."

"The special what?"

"Come on," Dolly said, and she walked briskly down the tunnel. There was nothing at all unsure about her now. The fur coat belled out behind her, as if she really was physically moving. James and Oz stepped aside to let her by, and James felt a draft of chill air as she passed, like a winter breeze.

She strode down the tunnel to the open door leading into the fish-stinking darkness under the pier. James expected her to vanish there, but she didn't, though her outline wavered and she hesitated briefly when she crossed the threshold of the door onto the shoreline. But then she went on, passing through the rocks until she came to a halt at the water's edge.

As before, in the basement, she was faintly luminous. She looked like reflected starlight.

James came up carefully beside her. She was gazing out at the water, looking distressed. "It's so different."

"It's been a hundred years."

"I guess that's so. I wonder if they'll come?" Before he could ask who, she put two fingers in her mouth and whistled two short notes, then whistled again.

Oz shuffled up on James's other side, quiet in the way he sometimes could be when he wanted to; the only sound was the dry rustle of his tail dragging over the rocks, hardly audible over the lapping of the water. Out on the river, a boat horn sounded. Ropes creaked somewhere; there was the noise of distant traffic on the bridge, and a low, long train whistle.

James rubbed idly at the auklet scratches across the back of his hand. He was tired, and his throat and head hurt. It was Oz, however, who spoke first. "May I ask what is supposed to happen next?"

"Next," Dolly said, "we see how much has changed in a hundred years."

She started to raise her hand to her lips to whistle again, but just then the tone of the lapping water changed. It was a boat, pulling up to shore, the way they raised waves to precede them—no, it was a lot more waves than that, with a lot of splashing.

Dark, wet bodies swarmed onto the shore, all but invisible among the rocks: river dragons. They poured out of the river onto the shoreline. It was impossible to count them in the dark, but from the flashes of their scales, the gleam of their eyes, James could tell there were more than he'd ever seen in one place at a time.

Dolly stood among them like a softly glowing statue, while the tiny dragons cavorted around her, ecstatic. One of them tried to rear up and put its paws on her skirt, and gave a startled *yawp* as it fell through her leg instead.

"My little friends," Dolly said. Her voice broke. "You remember me."

She crouched and held out her hands. The small dragons tried to thrust their snouts against her hands and arms. Bafflement was clear in their body language when they went through her instead.

"I thought you said they didn't remember her," James murmured to Oz.

"Perhaps," Oz answered quietly, "I didn't ask the right questions."

From where she crouched among the rocks, with the wavelets washing through the spill of her long coat, Dolly looked up at James. "They were my only friends," she said, and wiped the back of her hand across her eyes; her cheeks glistened with tears again, looking like quicksilver in her lambent radiance. "My mother took in laundry for a living, but she was often ill. I worked with her from the time I was a small girl. I didn't have much time for play, but we used to bring loads of laundry to the river. It was bedsheets mostly, linens for the cheap hotels around the waterfront. And I made friends with the river dragons. Oh, no, sweetheart, I can't take that." One of the dragons was holding up a piece of river glass in its small, webbed front paws.

Undaunted, the little dragon offered it to James. "Uh, thanks," James said, leaning down to take it. The edges of the glass were worn smooth so that it felt like a lump of stone.

Now more of them came clamoring to offer gifts to Dolly, bright shells and lost fishing lures and a pull tab or two. One of them held up a ring, cheap and silver with a gaudy stone that was probably glass. It might have come from a vending machine.

"They brought me gifts like this in the old days, too." Dolly's voice hitched again. "It's been so long."

"They like showing people their treasures." James looked up at Oz. "I, uh—they bring me things too, every now and then."

"I know," Oz said, his deep voice gentle. "Remember when we first met, back at the beginning of all that business with the stolen cars? I told you the river dragons recommended you to me. Most people ignore them. Some like to take pictures of them. But few listen to them, and pay them enough attention to be offered their treasures of the deep."

Dolly looked up from where she crouched waist-deep in a swarm of wildly waving, squeaking dragons. "They can talk? I mean, you can understand them?"

"Not entirely as you and I do." Oz bowed his head to solemnly touch noses with one of the little dragons. "But they have their own way of speaking. I think you understand them almost as well as I."

James looked down as a river dragon nudged at his leg, and he took a cats-eye marble from a small, clammy paw. He stuffed it into his pocket with the wet shells and pair of broken tortoiseshell eyeglasses that had already been given to him.

"No, my little darlings," Dolly said gently. She stood up. "I can't do anything with your pretties anymore." She smiled wistfully at James and Oz. "Oh, but they gave me lovely things back then. Mother used to think I'd stolen them. But we did need the money, and she was sick all the time; she had a bad heart. Sometimes the dragons would find truly valuable things that rich ladies had lost, fine pieces of jewelry and silver-backed hand mirrors and even coins from the river bottom. Sometimes I would wear a bracelet or a necklace for a little while, pretend it was mine—"

Oz raised his head abruptly, scenting the air.

"What's wrong?" James asked him, low. Dolly tensed, looking alarmed, for all that she wasn't even physically there at all.

Oz shook his head. "Don't worry about it. Go on, my dear."

But he turned and looked back into the tunnel. James placed his hand on the butt of the spellgun.

"Oh. Well." Dolly gathered the coat around her, clearly rattled. The fur ruff hid the bloodstains, all but a few dark traces. "Mother died, but I kept taking in laundry, and went out drinking afterward—we all did, you had to, if you were going to spend your days with your arms up to the elbows in river water. I went to the Peony a lot, and Nero—I mean, Geary ended up liking me. But it was the special gin that really got his attention."

"And what's that?" James asked quietly. He took a step closer to Oz, placing the dragon's bulk at his side. Not many enemies could get past Oz. But, as he knew from experience, there were still some.

Dolly relaxed a little. The river dragons were starting to lose interest in what they couldn't touch or scent, sliding back into the water. Whatever was alerting Oz didn't seem to be concerning them. And Oz, at least, didn't seem afraid or worried, merely intrigued by something.

"I don't know," Dolly said. "They brought it to me, of course. It was one of their little presents. I think there must have been a wreck on the river, years ago. Some of the odder things the dragons used to bring me were shipwreck salvage, and I think this was too, all muddy and strange. There were bottles and bottles of it."

"What was it, though? Alcohol?"

"Sort of." Dolly laughed a little. "You know what I think it might be? Some kind of fae wine. Or maybe even water from the fountain of youth. Whatever it was, Geary got rich off it. People would pay absolutely *anything*."

She held out an arm, the fur coat glimmering in the starlight radiance that surrounded her. Real fur then, James thought. He didn't know fur, let alone fur from the 1920s. Something high-end, he now thought: not fake, not rabbit. There was a luster to it, like the rippling fur of a living creature.

"Most of the money went to Geary, of course, but some of it came to me, mostly in presents, but there was cash too, more cash than I'd ever seen. You can't really imagine how these people spent money, James. It was just . . . *fistfuls* of it. They'd go out for dinner and give handfuls of cash in tips to the waiters and the taxi drivers. It was no wonder most people liked them. The people in the nice neighborhoods didn't like the violence, but the working stiffs, people like me —they *loved* the MacKays. What did those nice people in their nice houses ever do for us, anyway? Everyone wanted to work for the MacKays if they could, and they dreamed of working their way up to *be* them. You could, then. It was that kind of a time."

Oz whipped around abruptly, his tail rattling across the rocks. The spiny fringes behind his ears pricked up, making him look like a cat on the hunt.

"Oz—"

"Stay here, tell me the rest of the story later," Oz said quietly, and with that he was up and over the rocks and into the tunnel with one of his deceptive bursts of speed.

James drew the spellgun.

"Are you in danger?" Dolly asked.

"Probably not." Not with Oz here. He hoped. "When you

said Normal caught you skimming, you weren't talking about money, were you? It was the, ah, the special gin."

"I didn't take *much*," Dolly said defensively. Her hand closed over the necklace again. "I wished—I wish—that I'd never told Geary about it in the first place. But then, I'd not have had the nice things, and the money I put aside for Wendy's future. There was never enough of that, though. I had to spend so much on doctors." She swallowed, her face pained. "It was the same problem as my mother. Her heart. But then I thought of the gin, and I was right. It helped."

"Wouldn't that have kept her a baby forever?"

"What? Oh, no—when I called it a fountain of youth, it's not *that*. It just keeps you healthy."

"It's a little more than that. Geary still looks like he did in the 1920s. That was a recent picture I showed you."

"Really?" she said, surprised. "Maybe when I died, he stopped selling it and kept it for himself. The only place he could ever get it was from me. The river dragons certainly wouldn't have brought it to *him*."

No wonder Geary had turned around and killed his brother when Normal killed Dolly. She was the goose who laid the golden eggs.

"Why does Geary want the necklace?"

Dolly touched it reflexively. "I had a little compartment that I used to smuggle it in. Maybe he thinks the necklace is the key to getting more? I never told him about the dragons—"

From the tunnel, there was a sudden "Aha!" in Oz's deep voice, along with a thump and a yelp.

Dolly flinched and her outline wavered, but this time she didn't vanish. The handful of river dragons who had stuck around through Dolly's story dived into the water with a chorus of otter-like squeaks and barks.

"Right," James muttered, and went into the tunnel to see

who or what Oz had caught. Although he thought he might have an idea.

Oz was crouching in a very catlike pose at the far end of the tunnel, his tail swishing back and forth. "I *thought* I heard someone sneaking around back here. It's all right, James, I have her."

"Her?" Dolly said softly, from behind James.

"Yeah," James said quietly. "If Geary didn't set the fire, it had to be Wendy."

Wendy Attredge was trapped in a cage of Oz's claws.

CHAPTER TWELVE

"LET HER UP, OZ."

"Are you sure that's a good idea?" Oz asked. He was holding Wendy with both hands, pinning her to the floor like a child who had just captured a frog or bird—which was about her size relative to him. Wendy lay flat on her back, breathing slowly.

"You're scaring the life out of her," James said, holstering the spellgun. "Let her up."

A few steps away from him, Dolly had gone pale, literally so. She was barely more than a faint outline under the bright lights in the tunnel.

Oz lifted his paws away carefully, one at a time, and shuffled backward; the low ceiling and close walls of the tunnel gave him little room to maneuver. Wendy sat up cautiously, never taking her eyes off the dragon. Her flyaway white hair was mussed, her green wool coat stained with dirt and soot.

"Returning to the scene of the crime?" James asked pointedly.

When Oz made no move to attack, Wendy stood up.

There was a certain stiffness to it, age more than injury. She brushed off her legs. "I have no idea what you mean."

"Oh, come on. I know you set the fire and clocked me over the head."

Wendy let out a low laugh. She smoothed down her hair, combing her fingers through it. "If you want a confession, you won't find one here."

"No, but what if I have answers for you?" James asked, and her sharp eyes snapped to him. "That's what you've wanted your whole life, isn't it? Answers. About yourself, about Geary MacKay, about what happened to your mother."

He stepped aside, and Wendy saw Dolly for the first time. Wendy went pale, then red, two bright spots of color pinking her cheeks.

"What is that?" she asked, her voice a dry rattle.

"You've seen pictures of your mother, haven't you?"

"Of course I . . ." Her hot gaze went quickly to Oz, then back to James. "How are you *doing* that?"

"Dolly," James said, "say something."

"Winifred," Dolly whispered, and Wendy jumped, an all-over flinch.

There was a moment of tense silence, and then Oz asked brightly, "Tea?"

Wendy jumped again. James carefully reached for her arm and helped her sit on one of the unburned crates. Stunned, staring at Dolly, she went with him like an automaton.

"Oh bother," Oz said. "I forgot, there's only coffee. I could run and get—"

"Just make the coffee, Oz," James said over his shoulder. "Or whatever you want to do."

"Not my favorite, but oh well." Oz whistled cheerfully as he worked, and the smell of perking coffee filled the tunnel. That seemed to wake Wendy up.

"I have to get out of here," she said in a dazed voice.

Dolly, meanwhile, had just been looking at her, staring at her and drinking her in, while clutching one hand on the fur coat's lapel and the other on the necklace.

"You're *grown*," she murmured, her voice wondering. "Your chin, it's just like Mother's chin. And those are *my* eyebrows."

"Sugar?" Oz asked. "Cream?"

Wendy shook off James's attempt to put a hand on her arm and jumped off the crate. "Let me *go*. This is insane. That's not my mother."

"Well, technically it's her ghost—"

Oz slurped from a washtub-sized cup, winced, and began tearing open creamer packets, wielding the tip of his claw as delicately as a letter opener. "Ugh. Coffee. What a waste of perfectly fine caffeine. Actually, this is *quite* bitter—never buying this brand again—"

"Oz," James said, as Wendy backed away from Dolly's beseeching hands, "could you *shut up* about the damn coffee, already?"

He wasn't sure whether he ought to try to physically stop Wendy from leaving. What was he going to do, tackle her? Dolly was already on the edge of vanishing, her edges wavering as distress faded her like an old photograph.

"How did you do this?" Wendy demanded of James. "A spell? Technology? Is that a hologram, or is it actually affecting my brain somehow?"

"It's her, Wendy. I'm not tricking you. *We're* not."

"Liar!" Wendy snapped.

Dolly made an unhappy sound and disappeared.

James had begun to reach toward the empty air where she'd been (*and what then, drag her back from the ether somehow?*) when Oz said, "James?"

There was a distressed, uncertain note in his voice. James turned just as Oz wobbled, took an uncoordinated step forward, and then crashed to the floor, upsetting the coffee cart. A flood of coffee from Oz's dragon-sized coffeepot washed over the floor.

"It's about damn time," Wendy snapped.

There was a warning note in her voice that went straight to James's hindbrain. He was already drawing the spellgun as he spun around, and by the time he came to a stop, looking down the barrel of a small but efficient semiautomatic, he had it out and pointed at her.

"I thought he'd never drink it." Her voice still shook a little, she still looked rattled, but her hand was rock steady on the gun.

"You drugged the coffee."

"Poison, actually. Hard to calibrate a dose for something that size." She was regaining self-control by the moment, the shaken look fading into the core-deep confidence that must have carried her through a life as the daughter of a dead single mother, as a self-made and successful woman in a time and a profession that hadn't welcomed either. "He *might* survive."

James started to move in Oz's direction.

"Don't," Wendy snapped, with a small jerk of the pistol's muzzle. "Step away."

He might be able to shoot Wendy before she could get a shot off; the spellgun's effects could be unpredictable. But she looked like she knew her way around that weapon in her hand.

"So you're just going to, what, kill me and walk away without knowing why you are the way you are, or what happened to your mother?"

"I know enough," Wendy said shortly. "More than you do."

"Did you know Geary MacKay is your father?"

This made her jerk, her eyes going wide. She *hadn't* known.

"Yeah, that's right. He and Dolly had a thing going in the 1920s. Her ghost told me."

"There are no ghosts here," Wendy said, but now she sounded unsure.

"Really? You're a hundred years old and you've only aged, what, sixty or seventy? And you don't think ghosts are a real thing?"

"I know ghosts are real; I just don't think you've somehow discovered my mother's ghost in an old speakeasy tunnel."

"Actually," James said, "she haunts the basement." He tried not to look at Oz, keeping his eyes on Wendy. He couldn't even tell if the dragon was breathing.

"You're lying. You'd say anything if you think it'd get you out of here."

"Yeah? And what do *you* want? You used to be a reporter; you wanted the truth. You spent years digging into your mother's death."

"I got old," Wendy said. Her mouth twisted. "I got tired."

"And cynical, and ready to make moral compromises. I get it." Damn it, he wished he could get closer to Oz. Actually, the dragon wouldn't make a bad barricade; Oz's scales were bulletproof. "But the person you used to be is still in there somewhere—"

He heard the gunshot before he felt it. The echo rolled around the confines of the tunnel. There was a brief moment when he couldn't entirely take it in. Wendy's hand should have moved, but it hadn't; she looked as shocked as he was, frozen in a single stunned instant.

Sensation caught up with him then, a feeling like a punch to the lower chest. Wendy started to turn, her shocked attention off him for a bare instant. There was movement behind her, at the door into the basement. James fired blindly in that direction and dived for cover, rolling behind Oz's scaly bulk.

There was a shocked yell, and a different voice—Geary

MacKay—snapped, "What are you doing down here, talking him to death?"

He had bare seconds; Oz's bulk was a temporary reprieve, and Wendy was only a few yards away. The only thing he could shoot at without breaking cover was the lights. With a normal gun, he'd have had to shoot out the light bulbs one by one. Instead, he aimed at the light switch. His hand was shaking. It felt like there was something heavy and hot wedged under his ribs.

Come on, gun, I don't know how you work but I hope you understand what I need.

He shot the light switch.

The tunnel plunged into utter darkness, taking down not just the tunnel lights but the basement lights as well.

James laid a hand against Oz's scaly side. This close, he could feel the very slight stirring as Oz's rib cage expanded. The dragon was still breathing, but he felt cold to the touch. Oz was never cold; he always felt like there was a banked furnace inside.

"Sorry," James whispered. "I'll come back."

He scrambled to his feet and started for the river end of the tunnel.

In the dark, he bounced off crates, stumbled into walls, and at one point his hand glanced off something warm and moving and obviously alive and human. There was a yell, and the sharp flash of a gunshot. James fired the spellgun point blank. The tunnel flashed green, and he wasn't sure if it did anything, but then he was out into river wind and lapping water and the smell of mud.

It was hard to get a deep breath. James pressed his fist to the shirt and jacket over the gunshot wound. It was on the left side of his sternum, but low. Not the heart; he wouldn't still be walking around if that was the case.

But there was nowhere a bullet could hit the human torso

and not wreck things inside. When he tried to breathe, it felt wet and strange.

Behind him, he heard yelling and arguing in the tunnel. At least two voices, one male and one female.

Should've known I couldn't trust her when she set fire to the building, hit me over the head, and left me to burn. You know, most people would've realized that was a warning sign.

The lights were out all up and down the docks, he realized gradually as he stumbled over the rocks in the dark. Whatever the spellgun had done to the lights in the tunnel had also blacked out this entire part of the city. There were still lights across the river, wavering in the water, and he realized that he was aiming for those only when he stumbled into ankle-deep mud. River water washed over his shoes, and he staggered to a panting stop, half doubled over, one arm wrapped around his ribs.

He couldn't swim across the river; what was he doing? *Think, James.* He had to climb the retaining wall somehow. As he started to turn back, there was a sharp clatter not too far away. MacKay and Wendy would be out here too, searching for him.

"James!"

It was a female voice, a loud whisper. Dolly floated ahead of him among the rocks, illuminated with her own soft light. She stood out like a beacon, and she seemed to realize it, because she faded back among the rocks, but he could still hear her voice. "Over here. There's a place to hide."

Gasping, with blood welling hot between his fingers, he tumbled into the crevice between two rocks that she'd found for him. Colored spots danced in front of his eyes.

When his vision cleared, Dolly was crouched in front of him. "I'm sorry," she whispered.

"Not your fault," he ground out. He pulled back a little of

his blood-soaked shirt, but it was too dark to get a look at the damage. His chest felt strange and hot.

"She's my daughter. I can't believe—"

"Kids don't always turn out like their parents. They are who they are." Definitely a plus, in his case. "Listen, can you go for help?"

She was already shaking her head. "The building is closed up. Everyone's gone. There was a janitor and I tried manifesting to him, but he screamed and ran away. People usually do that, except for you."

"And you can't get any farther from the warehouse?" He tried to tear off a piece of his shirt, but his fingers slipped on the sodden fabric. This looked easier on TV.

"No, I've never even been this far before."

James gave up on trying to make a bandage and rolled up the shirttail instead, pressing the ball of sticky, bloody shirt to his chest. The night air was cold on his blood-wet flank.

It was too dark under the pier to see how many shots he had left in the spellgun. The gun was magic, but it took actual bullets, charmed ones that he had to buy on the black market. He'd fired three times—or, no, was it four? He was starting to have a hard time keeping his thoughts straight.

I can barely breathe and I'm losing blood fast. This is bad.

"James!" Dolly said sharply, leaning into his face. "Don't pass out."

"Shhh." A light stabbed across the rocks. James pushed himself up, sucked in a breath at the knife twisting under his ribs, and peered down the shore.

They were out with flashlights, at least two people. MacKay and Wendy? Hard to say . . . but just then the person at the edge of the water turned, and he caught the glint of the flashlight's reflected light on white hair.

Blinking hard, struggling to focus, he took aim with the spellgun.

"James, don't," Dolly said softly. "Please."

Down by the water, Wendy was looking straight at him.

"Damn it. She saw you." No help for it now. She was coming this way. He trained the gun on her.

"I said no!" Dolly snapped, and she thrust out with both hands, striking the muzzle of the gun.

The spellgun wrenched to the side, and the shot went wild, striking the underside of the pier. There was a green flash, and the pier began to rain, a drenching shower exactly one pier-width across.

James realized that he'd lost his grip on the spellgun only when it slipped out of his wet hands to clatter down among the rocks.

Damn it. This isn't good . . .

And then Wendy was standing over him, her gun pointing down at him. There was something pale and filmy in the way. It took him a dazed moment to realize it was Dolly, standing between them with her hands held out.

"Wendy, stop!" Dolly cried.

"Whatever you're doing—" Wendy began.

"It's not me." He had to grind it out, propping himself up with one hand on the rocks. He kept wanting to cough and knowing it would be a terrible idea.

"Wendy," Dolly said. "It's me. My beautiful baby, please don't do this."

Wendy's face, filtered through Dolly's filmy body, was a study in shock and horror.

"I'm so sorry I left you behind," Dolly went on desperately. "I didn't mean to. I tried so hard to get back to you, to *stay* for you—"

"Did you find him?" MacKay's voice cut across Dolly's,

Geary MacKay struggled toward them over the rocks, slipping and sliding. He had a flashlight in one hand, the beam stabbing in front of him. James couldn't see much of the rest of him in the dark, but he caught an occasional gleam off the gun in MacKay's other hand.

"Yes, he's up here," Wendy called down. "Are you seeing this?"

MacKay barely spared a glance for Dolly's ghost. It was too dark for James to see his expression. "It's a trick," MacKay snapped. "Ignore it. Does he have the necklace on him?"

"I don't know, I—I haven't—"

MacKay shot her.

Dolly's scream pierced the night; even MacKay flinched. Wendy made no sound. She simply looked surprised as MacKay's gun cracked again, and the dark stain blooming over her lower abdomen was joined by another blossoming on her chest.

She began to fall, crumpling slowly among the rocks. Dolly screamed again, reaching for her daughter with desperate, ethereal hands that passed through her body without touching it.

James dug down for a final burst of energy and leaped forward in a last desperation move.

He caught Wendy with an arm around her waist, felt her body jerk again as MacKay fired once more at both of them, and then they were tumbling—bruising, agonizing—to the water's edge. Somehow he managed to hang onto the presence of mind to keep them moving, kicking out against the rocks as they fell into mud and shallow water and then deeper water, and the cold current caught them, and took them.

CHAPTER THIRTEEN

Dᴀʀᴋ ᴡᴀᴛᴇʀ ᴄʟᴏsᴇᴅ over James's head. He hadn't had time to get a breath, could barely breathe anyway. Muddy water flooded his mouth. He choked on it, managed to gasp in air when his face broke the surface, then went under again. Somehow he kept hold of Wendy, though he had no idea why. He didn't even know if she was still alive.

In the tumbling confusion of water and mud and brief, desperate gulps of air, he didn't at first recognize that there was something more purposeful to the bumping and jostling. It wasn't until his knees hit mud, then his hands, that he realized he was out of the water—half out, anyway, with Wendy sprawling limply in the shallows, tangled around him.

And all around them were river dragons, catching at them with small claws, pushing and bumping with their noses and their sinuous, muddy bodies, shoving them farther out of the water.

James collapsed. His face went under. He tried to push himself up, and a wet ripping feeling tore through his chest. He collapsed again. Agonizing coughs wracked him, and when he tried to suck in a breath, water filled his mouth.

"James!"

He knew that voice. Through the water, through the darkness swallowing him, he clawed his way toward it.

"James," Dolly said again, and he peeled open his sticky, muddy eyelids.

He was lying on his back; he could dimly feel water lapping across his lower body, his legs lifting and settling with each surge from the harbor. River dragons crawled on and around him. He still had the urge to cough, but it somehow had become easier to resist. It wasn't hard at all if you just didn't breathe.

"James, wake up."

Dolly was bending over him. She was so faint that he could barely see her, a crayon tracery of a woman against the night.

"James, *listen*," Dolly said. "They brought it. They had it all along. Gifts from the river bottom." She laughed, a small pained sound. "James, can you hear me?"

He managed to suck in a breath. It hurt viciously, knives stabbing at his lungs. With an effort, he rolled onto his side, and rolled up against Wendy. She was limp, with water lapping at her still body. He couldn't see her face or tell if she was breathing.

His view was abruptly blocked by a river dragon pushing its whiskered snout into his face. James made a feeble, flailing effort to fend it off. He struggled to suck in another breath, and gave up. It was just too much effort.

His cheek sank into the mud. One eye was half covered with mud, the other half open. He had a dim sideways view of the muddy shore, and the claws of the river dragon resting in the mud a few inches from his nose.

And the bright glint of something tangled in those claws.

The little dragon chirped softly and thrust it at him.

"My necklace." Dolly's voice was a breath on the wind.

"It's been on the bottom of the harbor all this time. James, open it. What you need . . . it's inside."

James fumbled at the necklace with nerveless hands. The world was narrowing, gray fog closing in from the sides. Dolly put her hands over his, and somehow he seemed to feel her skin as a colder sensation through the ice creeping into his limbs.

"Turn it over. The catch—like so—"

She moved her fingers, showing him what to do. Dazed, clumsy, he followed along. There was a faint click and a hidden compartment swung open. A tiny vial—glass chased with gold—fell into his palm.

"Can you open it? Don't check out on me, gumshoe. There's a little cap at the top—yes, there . . .don't drink it all, you need to save some for . . ."

Her voice faded to a faint buzzing in his ears, but he managed to tilt the little tube toward his half-open mouth. A sudden floral taste burst on his tongue. It was like chewing up an entire mouthful of rose petals, so intense it was cloying, almost nauseating. James choked, and then suddenly he could breathe again, though each breath felt like it was tearing through his wet, painful lungs.

" . . .takes a little while to take full effect," Dolly was saying. "James, can you hear me? You need to give the rest to Winifred."

"Oz," he whispered, and opened his eyes. His voice was raw. Shakily he sat up, clutching the precious vial against his chest. "Oz needs it."

"Don't let her die. Please." Dolly's voice was as faint as the rest of her. It was clear that she was struggling with all she had to hold onto what little remained of her mortal presence. "She's my daughter. *Please.*"

James coughed wetly. He clutched Wendy's shoulder, and she rolled limply toward him in the mud.

It was impossible to tell if it was too late. Wendy's eyes were closed, her mouth slack. James tipped a few drops from the vial into her parted lips. His mouth still tasted like roses, not as intense as that first shocking taste, but syrupy and not entirely pleasant.

But it was working. Each breath he drew was easier. The grayness began to retreat from his vision, the ringing from his ears.

"Wendy?" He could barely hear Dolly now. She had faded almost entirely.

James stoppered the vial. No matter how potent this stuff was, they were going to need the rest for Oz, if Oz was even still alive. "Come on," he muttered, giving Wendy a little shake. She rolled bonelessly under his hand.

And then she stirred, the smallest twitch.

"You better be worth it," he rasped out, and choked on another painful cough. Carefully, he tucked the vial into an inside pocket of his jacket.

Wendy didn't answer, and if Dolly said anything, her faint voice was lost in the slap of the wavelets on the shore, and the muddy plopping and squeaking of the river dragons. When James looked up, there was no sign of her. He and Wendy were alone on the shore.

It looked like they had washed downstream a few hundred yards from the pier. Here, the bank was tangled and steep, strewn with rubble and trash. The river made a long slow curve, and the lights of the docks glimmered upstream, with a block of darkness in the middle where the power was still out. Headlights flowed across the river on the Lincoln Boulevard bridge.

James sat with his hand on Wendy's shoulder while his breathing steadied, the ache in his lungs receded, and energy returned slowly to his leaden body. His mouth still tasted of perfumed roses. Wendy's body contorted with each shuddering breath, but she began to relax against his leg, her breathing growing easier.

No wonder Geary MacKay had been willing to kill for just a single vial of this stuff.

The necklace lay on James's thigh, corroded and muddy. He balled it up and stuffed it into a pocket. Time to examine it later, when Oz's life wasn't slipping away. He still wasn't entirely sure that he could stand up, but he was going to have to try.

"Hey." He gave Wendy's shoulder a harder shake. "You in there?"

Wendy groaned weakly. The river dragons, who had mostly gone quiet—he'd almost forgotten about them—set up an excited babble of squeaking.

"Hush! You little idiots are gonna get me killed."

He got hold of a double handful of Wendy's sodden coat and dragged her a little higher among the rocks and rubble, struggling along in an awkward three-limbed hobble, using his free hand as much as his legs. Wendy was stirring now, trying to help and not doing much more than uncoordinated flailing. When he dropped her, she coughed and rolled over. James wobbled, caught himself on the rocks, and sank to his knees next to her. He started patting her down. Wendy tried weakly to fend him off.

"What are you doing?" she demanded hoarsely.

"Seeing if you have any more little surprises before I get a knife in my back."

"Ugh. Get off." She rolled over, wheezing, and managed to get her hands and knees under her, then fell again. "How," she panted, and spit out a mouthful of mud. "He *shot* me. And you."

"Trade secret," James said.

"You have some of it." Wendy coughed again, deep and wet. "The elixir."

"And you poisoned my intern. What'd you give him?"

Wendy dragged in a ragged breath and ran her hand through her wet hair, swiping it out of her eyes. "It's a neuro-toxin and paralytic, refined from snake venom."

"How long does he have?"

There was a moment's silence. Then she coughed and said breathlessly, "It's hard to figure the dosage exactly. He's too big. I put in a lot, just to be on the safe side."

"So I would've just dropped dead if I drank any of that coffee, huh?"

Wendy didn't answer. A boat passed by, out on the water, long and low and strung with running lights, passing under the bridge. James had a brief, wild thought of hailing it and asking for a ride.

"Why did you help me?" Wendy asked hoarsely.

"Because your mom asked me to."

He stood up carefully, holding onto a wiry tangle of brush growing out of the bank. His legs wobbled, but held him.

Come on, Oz, tell me dragons aren't that easy to kill.

Wendy spat out more river water and made an attempt to lurch to her feet. James released a sigh that seemed to tear its way out of his sore chest, and offered her a hand. She glared up at him through the wet, muddy hair hanging in her eyes, and then took it. Helping her up almost sent him over again, but he managed to stay on his feet.

Some rescue party I'm gonna be.

"Think you can climb out of here?" he asked, stifling a cough. "Because if you can't, I'm leaving you behind."

"I can climb," Wendy said between her teeth, and to prove it, she began struggling doggedly up the bank, leaving him behind.

James cursed, grabbed a handful of brush that turned out to be full of stickers, and struggled after her. He had to give her a boost over some of the steeper parts; she returned the favor by turning around and giving him a hand up.

"What were you doing, teaming up with Geary MacKay?"

Wendy coughed, but it was sounding better, less of a deep wet bark and more of a dry getting-over-a-cold kind of coughing. "It's a longstanding business arrangement. I found out a lot of things in the 1950s that he didn't want getting around, not the least of them the secret to Geary's eternal youth."

"You knew about the elixir." Right. With everything else, it hadn't quite registered on him that she had known exactly how he'd healed her on the riverbank.

Wendy coughed again and paused to struggle over a particularly unwieldy section of concrete rubble that made up the bank's retaining wall. "I don't tell anyone about his side tipple, and he keeps me in the style to which I have, unfortunately, become accustomed."

"You were *blackmailing* MacKay?" James panted. His chest felt damp and heavy, aching with every gasping breath. "Those are some polished stainless steel cojones you've got there, woman."

"I'll take that as a compliment," Wendy gritted out.

They stumbled out onto an industrial frontage road running along the river. An abandoned factory reared up in front of them, windows broken out, soot-stained bricks plastered with ivy. There was no traffic and no sign of anyone nearby.

"So is there a plan?" Wendy wanted to know. She rested her hands on her knees, catching her breath. The river had washed off most of the blood, but there were visible bullet holes in her wool coat.

"Get Oz, try not to get shot." He heaved a few breaths. It was getting easier.

He started jogging up the road, but had to slow to a fast

walk as his healing lungs protested. Wendy caught up a few minutes later, wheezing.

James couldn't help thinking that another sip from the vial might restore him to full health, taking away the wet heat in his lungs and the exhaustion weighing him down. His bad leg felt better than it had in weeks.

And it might be Oz's last chance. So don't even think about it.

The frontage road ended in the interchange at the base of the Lincoln bridge. After getting through that, they entered the dockside tangle of small roads, dead ends, chain link fences and old warehouses, most of the latter repurposed now as apartment buildings or retail space.

"It's all changed so much," Wendy murmured as they circled the harbor's small marina. "When I was a girl, this was a slough. Smugglers used to tie up here."

Sailboats and motor cruisers bobbed in the marina's dredged-out, manmade bays, most of them dark. One showed a flash of light as someone opened a door and went into the small cabin.

"So what do you know about how all of this works, anyway?" James asked quietly. "You lived a hundred years just because you got a few doses of the stuff as a child?"

"I don't know much more than you do. It's most likely fae in origin. There are stories of fae elixir that can heal any ill."

"Why'd you try to burn the warehouse down?"

Wendy grimaced. "Why do you think? I like the arrangement I have with Geary. I don't need anything upsetting it, whether it's Geary MacKay getting his hands on a whole new supply, or some private detective sniffing around, uncovering old secrets." She hesitated. "Is he really my father?"

"Sorry to break it to you."

"I don't particularly care. I grew up with a foster family that I loved. My real father died back in the 1950s."

The lights were still out on the entire block. They passed

the closed Starbucks. To their dark-adapted eyes, reflected cityglow gave light enough to see by, if dimly.

"Does Geary know?" Wendy asked softly.

"I'm not sure. Dolly said she never told him."

"Dolly." Her voice was wondering. "You keep talking as if —you believe it, don't you? That it's really my mother's ghost."

"As far as I know. Can we hurry it up here?" He was all too aware of the minutes ticking past. Oz was tough, but *how* tough, exactly—that was a question he didn't want to find out the answer to.

The warehouse loomed ahead, an inky shadow against the slightly brighter sky. James touched his pockets, wishing he had a weapon. He gave a passing thought to climbing down the river barricade and trying to find the spellgun, but he no longer had a flashlight and doubted he had a prayer of locating it by feel in the dark.

"Stay up here," he whispered to Wendy.

"I know I look old," Wendy whispered back fiercely, "but I've covered stories in war zones. I'm not some fragile flower."

"I don't want you up here for your sake, I want you up here because you've already tried to kill me twice."

She didn't answer, but he was aware of her presence behind him as he made his way carefully, by feel, down the basement stairs, placing his feet as softly as possible to avoid making too much noise in the years' accumulation of trash and leaves. There was a soft crunch and a whispered curse behind him as Wendy failed to do the same.

The door to the basement stood half open. There was only darkness inside, but James heard voices, very faint. He risked a glance around the doorjamb. The basement was pitch-black, but there was a quick strobing flicker of a flashlight in the tunnel.

James stepped inside, and his foot came down on the tipped-over brazier.

With all his senses on high alert, he noticed the instant that his foot contacted a curved, unexpected surface instead of the flat floor. He jerked his foot back, stumbled into Wendy, and then into the wall. The brazier rolled with a soft clank, but at least it didn't go shooting off to clatter against the wall.

The voices in the tunnel hushed. "You hear that?" someone said.

James froze, his hand pressed to crumbling brick. He glanced back to see what Wendy was doing, but she was no longer in the doorway. She had slipped into the dark basement while he was distracted.

Great. She *probably* wasn't planning to slip a knife into his back, but the skin on the back of his neck itched.

A flashlight stabbed from the tunnel and raked across the interior of the basement. Shadows leaped and grew, a dancing patchwork spreading behind every pile of bricks and piece of broken furniture. James pressed his back against the wall. If the flashlight landed right on him, there was no chance they wouldn't see him, but it was a cursory inspection and the light withdrew a moment later.

In the darkness, he moved forward.

The basement was a nightmare to feel his way through blind. He felt ahead with his toes, caught himself more than once just before stumbling into broken chairs and old construction scraps.

He was halfway there when the room began to brighten.

At first he thought the lights had come back on. But this was the warm golden light of Dolly's time. It was the flush of color and light that usually came along with Dolly when he summoned her; she brought the entire speakeasy with her, or at least a simulacrum of it.

Except he hadn't summoned her this time.

"Damn it, Dolly, not now!" he muttered.

At least now there were places to hide: tables, chairs, dancers, the gleaming wooden bar. The Peony Club was coming to life around him. He had never seen it like this before. Normally the ghostly nightclub had a dim, translucent quality; it was brightest around Dolly's bar, fading into shadows and darkness away from her.

Tonight, it was so vivid that he might have walked right back into the 1920s.

Dolly had brought the club and all its patrons with her. Men and women in Roaring 20s dress sat at tables or whirled each other around the room. A jazz band was playing on a raised stage at the far side of the room that James had never even known was there; it was opposite the bar, so Dolly's light had never reached that far. At first they played in silence, but sound came up slowly, like a radio being dialed in: music and talk and laughter and the clink of glasses.

It all happened in moments. He was feeling his way through a dark basement, and then it flushed into life around him.

James took a few quick steps back, behind a flowering potted plant. It was a shock when his fingers accidentally trailed through the leaves without a hint of physical contact. Everything looked perfectly solid and real. The air, which had been chilly a moment ago, had grown warm as if from assembled bodies packed into an actual basement. It smelled of cigarette smoke and perfume and alcohol.

The walls were painted. James had never realized that before. What was, in his time, bare brick with perhaps a trace of crumbled and faded paint was vividly splashed with huge pink and red and white flowers, framed in richly detailed greenery. Peonies, he guessed, not that he'd know a peony if he stepped on one.

The mural continued all the way to the ceiling, over the top of the windows that existed in James's time. At first he thought the windows had been added later, then noticed the plywood nailed over them and painted to match the rest.

James couldn't see Dolly anywhere, but he wasn't actually sure if he would have recognized her, at least not at first glance. There was too much visual clutter, too many women in a dazzling array of 1920s finery.

Wendy, at least, was easy to pick out. She stood across the room, staring around her. The bright lights revealed her sodden, bedraggled state, plastered in mud and poorly washed out bloodstains. James knew he must look just as bad.

The club patrons didn't notice, of course. They weren't really here; all of them had died decades ago. They danced and drank and smoked and went through the steps to dances that had gone out of fashion before James's parents were born.

"Okay, who turned on the—what the *fuck*," Geary's voice said, just out of sight.

James risked a glance around the potted plant.

Geary stood in the open doorway to the tunnel, slack-jawed in shock. One big hand held a gun, dangling forgotten by his leg.

If his expression earlier that evening had been that of a man gazing wistfully into the past, this time it was a man staring down the throat of his own personal hell.

He took a cautious step into the room, then another. A woman trailing smoke from a cigarette in a silver holder brushed past him, and Geary flinched back violently, stumbling halfway into a male club patron in a pinstriped jacket—literally *into* him; his elbow sank through the ghost's solar plexus.

"Hello, Geary." Dolly's soft voice carried across the music.

Geary whirled, half-raising the gun.

Dolly stood in the middle of the dance floor. For the first time since James had met her, she was in full, living color, not a sepia-toned shadow of herself. Her hair was dark gold, brown at the roots; James had never realized it was bleached. The coat was a rich silver-gray, the dress beneath it a burnished autumn orange. The necklace was gold, set with large green stones.

And her blood was crimson, soaking the dress, staining the coat, trickling down her legs into the straps of her gold-and-orange sandals.

White-faced, Geary aimed the gun at her—as if he thought bullets could hurt her. Dolly only smiled a little.

But there was something damn familiar about that gun.

He's got the spellgun.

The one kind of gun that could hurt a ghost.

CHAPTER FOURTEEN

IT WAS hard to be entirely sure. The gun was a short-barreled Colt .38 Detective Special—not exactly uncommon. It was black and nondescript. James always used shoe polish and paint to cover the illegal runes on the gun's grip and barrel.

But it was the right size and shape, the right apparent model.

Which meant Dolly was in acute danger.

Maybe she knows. Maybe she doesn't care.

But more likely, she just thought it was an ordinary gun, and therefore no harm to her.

Wearing a slight smile, she walked toward Geary MacKay. The patrons moved aside for her. Blood dripped from her dress, leaving a trail of gleaming droplets on polished wooden floorboards that were cracked concrete in James's time.

And Geary was panicking visibly with every step she took. Dolly was half his size, but the big man looked terrified —as well he might, with his long-dead lover's ghost walking across an equally long-vanished dance floor toward him.

"Would you like to dance?" Dolly asked. She held out a hand. Blood glistened on her fingers.

From across the room, Wendy stared with wide, shocked eyes. Her face was the face of a woman watching reality tugged sideways out from under her feet.

Geary aimed the gun with both shaking hands—and, under the golden lights of the club, James glimpsed the wink of a rune on the barrel. They never stayed hidden for long, no matter how often he renewed the paint.

It was definitely the spellgun.

He sucked in a breath and yelled, "Hey, Geary! Over here!"

Geary spun toward him, Dolly flinched, and the entire club vanished in a heartbeat, plunging them into total darkness.

Geary fired the spellgun anyway. There was a green flash in the dark, and a startled yell from Geary. Startled, but not pained, so his aim must not have been true; otherwise the shot would have rebounded from James onto him.

Without the lights of the club, the basement was a black pit. James gave up stealth for speed and stumbled across the floor. He tripped over something, a broken chair or other piece of wooden junk that went clattering across the floor. An instant later there was the muzzle flash and deafening bark of a normal gun.

Damn it. The spellgun could hurt Dolly, but it was harmless to James. Ordinary weapons were the exact opposite.

But it gave him an idea of where Geary was, which also meant he knew where the tunnel was, where Oz lay dying.

James stumbled into the wall much sooner than he expected. His hand slapped dusty brick. There was another shot and muzzle flash; chips of brick stung his face. That was way too close. Even in the dark Geary was a crack shot.

James dropped to one knee and groped for loose bricks

on the floor. Another gunshot chipped the wall above his head. His hand closed over something rough and gritty and about the right size. He hurled it out into the middle of the basement and heard it shatter on the floor.

No more gunshots. Geary was too smart to fall for it, but now he was unsure of James's position, at least.

James crouched with one hand resting on the floor. He couldn't tell exactly where Geary was either—or Wendy, for that matter. He felt around for another brick.

"Boss?" a voice said, echoing in a way that suggested its owner was back in the tunnel.

A flashlight beam stabbed into the basement, lighting up Geary's big, blocky shape in the tunnel doorway. He'd switched the spellgun to his off hand and drawn another one, a small square Glock. James didn't get a good enough look to guess at the size of the magazine, but it was almost certainly carrying anywhere from seventeen rounds to thirty or more.

"Give me that, you moron," Geary snapped. He tucked the spellgun into his waistband and reached for the flashlight, tucking it under the Glock. At the same time he ducked back through the tunnel door. He had to know the light made him a target—or it would, if James had a better ranged weapon than bricks.

James dived away from his current location as the flashlight strobed over him like an MGM searchlight. It caught him briefly, a flash of a leg and shoe in the glare, and a quick spray of gunfire ripped up the floor.

James jinked left and slammed into the opposite wall, colliding hard enough to hurt. The beam swept his way. This was a freaking shooting gallery, and he was the target.

Think. He had the lighter he used on Dolly's brazier, for all the good that was to him. The vial of elixir, which he needed. And the—

Oh.

He ducked as the flashlight strobed over his head, and pulled the wadded-up handful of Dolly's necklace out of his pocket. "Looking for this?" he called, and as the flashlight whipped back his way, he gave the necklace a hard overhand throw, up and over so that it arced through the beam and caught the light with a brief propeller-spin of its glittering chain and overly large paste jewels.

Geary dived for it, the flashlight beam sweeping the floor. James ran for the tunnel door.

He had only the vaguest sense of where the other guy was, but ran smack into him anyway, a wall of muscle wrapped up a suit that smelled of aftershave and cigars. In the dark, it was a quick, furious grapple of a fight. They tangled each other's feet and went down hard. There was the skittering sound of a gun bouncing off somewhere in the dark. James slammed the heel of his hand into an unshaven chin, snapping Aftershave's head back, and got an elbow to the skull for the trouble, splintering the darkness into a shower of stars.

His tiny advantage—being on top—evaporated when Aftershave rolled them over and used his superior bulk to pin James down. He got in a lucky kick on James's sore knee, undoing whatever good the elixir had done for it.

Eyes watering with pain, James wrestled his other leg free and drove it between the thick thighs attempting to pin his own. As Aftershave rolled off with a groan, James followed it up with a stomp to the stomach and a couple of kicks to the general vicinity of the face.

"I'll handle him," Wendy's voice said abruptly out of the dark, making him flinch wildly with the adrenaline flooding his system. "See to your friend."

At this point he wasn't going to turn down help from any source, no matter how dubious. James felt his way through the dark, and slapped a hand against Oz's scales, lacerating his palm from the feel of things.

Right now he didn't care. Oz was stone cold, no different from the air in the tunnel. There was no sign of movement of the dragon's great side. James felt his way along Oz's body, slicing up his hands some more.

Where's your damn head . . . why are you so LONG . . .

He found Oz's head eventually, nearly getting a neck spine through his palm. Even lying down, Oz's head was almost as tall as James's waist. James felt across the finer scales on the dragon's face, found his way to cold, rubbery lips like the seal on a refrigerator door.

He thrust an arm inside, pushing Oz's jaws apart with sheer desperate strength. Oz's mouth was damp and cool. James pushed one hand as far down Oz's throat as he could reach, and with his other hand, groped for the vial in his pocket.

If it was broken, or had fallen out with all the running around—

But it was still there. He popped the cap with his teeth; the cloying taste of roses flooded his mouth. With his thumb pressed over the opening, he reached carefully down Oz's throat until both his arms were jammed as far into Oz's mouth as he could reach, his shoulder pressed up against the great rubbery lips. Teeth like daggers dug into his upper arms.

If Oz moved or spasmed, he would bite James's arms off.

Hazard of the job.

"This better work," James muttered. He removed the thumb stoppering the vial, and tilted it by feel, pouring what was left of the contents onto the back of Oz's tongue.

The scent of rose perfume swelled into the tunnel. There could only be a few drops left in the vial, but it was as powerful as if someone had spilled a whole bottle of dollar store perfume in here.

"Come on, come on." Unsure what else to do, James rubbed a hand across the back of Oz's tongue, trying to get him to swallow. It was cold and slimy and rough. "This is horrendous. I'm going to have nightmares. I hope you appreciate my sacrifice here."

I hope you're alive to appreciate it.

As he crouched on the tunnel floor with both arms buried in Oz's mouth, awareness of all his various hurts flooded back to him: his headache, the wet-concrete feeling in his lungs, the hot throbbing in his knee and the blood trickling down his palms. He couldn't see what was happening on the other side of Oz's bulk, although he'd heard a few worrying thumps and another gunshot that made him flinch, nearly lacerating his arm on Oz's teeth.

Doing CPR on a dragon seemed both risky and highly unlikely to work, but he was about to give it a shot.

"You bitch!" MacKay yelled, and there was a green flash that briefly lit the cave.

"Don't use all my ammo, you son of a bitch," James muttered. "That stuff's expensive. Come on, Ozymandias, tell me you're not that easy to kill. Come *on*."

Oz's body contorted abruptly. James yanked his arms back just before the massive jaws snapped shut.

"Oz?"

In the darkness, he felt his way over Oz's muzzle and throat, trying to locate something like a pulse or breath. Oz was perfectly still, just long enough to give James a minor heart attack, but then the dragon's cold body shuddered and sucked in a rattling, stentorious breath.

James dropped on his ass and leaned his shoulder against the dragon's massive head. Oz was breathing regularly now, sucking in air in labored gasps.

"Yeah, you're not allowed to die your first week on the job, damn it," James said, patting the dragon's jaw with one sticky hand. "Now let's just see what—"

A flashlight stabbed him in the eyes.

He started to lurch to his knees, but collapsed back against Oz when Geary MacKay's harsh voice said from behind the light, "Move and you'll be spitting out lead."

James squinted against the glare. He couldn't see MacKay very well behind the light, but he could see enough to tell that the gun in MacKay's big hand, clamped above the flashlight, was the Glock and not the spellgun.

"Where's Wendy?" James asked.

"Taken care of." MacKay stepped forward, almost bumping into Oz's muzzle. "I'm going to give you one chance to answer. How much of Dolly's hooch do you have, and where—"

Oz gave a deep, pained groan, and MacKay jumped back, almost dropping the flashlight.

"What the fuck!" he snapped, swinging the gun to point at the dragon's muzzle. "You're supposed to be dead."

Oz groaned again, and lurched, raising his head slightly. His eyes were cracked open just enough to gleam in the flashlight glare, but as far as James could see, he didn't seem to be tracking. James wasn't even entirely sure Oz was conscious.

"Wai—" MacKay began.

That was as far as he got. A ball of flickering, sickly yellow flame burst out of the dragon's mouth. The backwash of heat was tremendous. James threw both his arms over his head.

When he lowered them, the tunnel was rapidly filling up with smoke, lit by the flickering glow of a dozen new fires all the way from Oz to the riverside doors, which were themselves smoldering. There wasn't enough left of Geary MacKay to fill a very small, fireproof box.

Oz's head flopped to the tunnel floor with a tremendous thud.

James ran to grab the fire extinguisher again.

When he was done putting out the flames, he threw open the slightly charred riverside doors to get some air inside. The tunnel was full of reeking smoke. James stood in the doorway for a few minutes, gulping in great gasps of cleaner air.

As he stood wheezing, the lights in the tunnel, and all the way back to the warehouse, abruptly came back on.

"Thanks, Municipal Power and Light," James murmured. He coughed and tried to kick the door a little wider to get more air in the tunnel. The stench was awful. "Better late than never."

He pulled his sleeve over his mouth and limped back over to Oz.

"I feel dreadful," Oz groaned.

"Yeah, I think you just puked fire. Are you planning on doing it again?"

Oz coughed and didn't answer. James risked standing in front of the dragon's mouth long enough to look for the spellgun.

The Glock and flashlight had fused into a twisted hunk of metal, but the spellgun, perfectly unharmed, lay in the charred remains that had once been Geary MacKay. James found a slat from a crate to scrape it out with, but when it didn't so much as scorch the wood, he ran the back of his hand over it, then touched it and found that it was only mildly warm.

"Huh," James murmured. He patted Oz's side. "You okay here if I go look around a little?"

"Urgh," Oz mumbled, dazedly blinking his dinner-plate eyes.

Taking the spellgun with him, James went to check on the other combatants. What looked like a large block of concrete in the corner turned out to be a statue of one of MacKay's guys, possibly the one he'd shot with the spellgun back at the beginning of all of this. There was blood on the floor, but no sign of anyone else around.

He found Wendy and Dolly in the basement. Wendy was lying on her back, her body rigid and eyes open, staring at the ceiling, with Dolly bending anxiously over her.

"He shot her with your gun," Dolly said. She wrung her hands. "I don't know . . . I can't tell . . ."

"It does something different every time." James crouched to feel for Wendy's pulse. It was slow and strong. "It doesn't even necessarily hurt them. The auklet gang are fine; they're just birds."

"This isn't permanent, is it?"

"Probably not." At least she wasn't an actual statue like the other guy. He'd seen her blink a couple of times already, so he didn't think so; it was acting more like a paralytic. "There ought to be at least one more of Geary's guys around here."

"I think he ran off after your dragon friend incinerated Geary. Everything is a bit of a blur." Dolly was no longer covered in blood, but she still wore the coat, buttoned up the front with the ruff tucked under her chin so he couldn't tell if she had the necklace or not. "Are you okay, James?"

"Oh, yeah, I'm wonderful. Of course," he added, "she poisoned the coffee and the entire place is a godawful mess and has been on fire twice in one night, so . . . I think I'm just going to sit down here."

He was still sitting on the floor when Oz lurched into the basement, wobbling with every step. "Oh," he said, "there you are." He stumbled over, weaving, to prod Wendy with his nose. "Is she dead?"

"Spellgunned. Probably wear off soon. I hope."

Oz lay down with a thump. "I've never been poisoned before," he said faintly. "My head hurts. It's not very pleasant."

"Welcome to the club. I mean, not the poisoning club. The feeling-like-shit club." James leaned back against Oz's side. There was some warmth to the dragon now, radiating through the scales like an old iron radiator. Much better than the deadly chill from earlier. "Do you need a doctor or anything? I don't know how that works for dragons."

"I'll be fine. Sleep will restore me."

Wendy stirred and rolled over. "Geary," she said thickly.

"Dead," James muttered. He cracked an eye open. "If you try anything, I'm giving Oz orders to sit on you."

Wendy sat up. One of her hands was tightly clasped into a fist. She slowly unkinked the fingers, one at a time—and there was Dolly's necklace, the muddy chain dangling.

"It's not valuable," James said, his head tipped back and resting against Oz's side. "Geary only wanted it because he guessed the elixir was inside."

Wendy tucked it into a pocket of her filthy pantsuit. "Then I'll keep it." She looked nervously sideways at Dolly. " . . . Mom."

Dolly beamed. There was a long, awkward silence. Then James said, "So there are a couple of dead guys in there, one of whom is Geary MacKay, and a guy who's a statue. I guess we should do something with them at some point."

"How do you normally handle this sort of thing?" Wendy asked.

"*Normally?* Normally I don't have dead bodies in the basement!"

"What do you think of burying them in the tunnel?"

"Underneath the building I live and work in?"

Oz cracked open an eye. "I have a great deal of hunting woods behind my house. It would be no hardship to put them there. Now please be quiet, my head hurts."

"Not sure I like the idea of burying them in the woods either," James muttered.

"By all means," Wendy said, "call the police and explain to them how you aren't responsible."

The woods it was, then.

CHAPTER FIFTEEN

IT TURNED OUT THAT, magic elixir or not, recovering from being shot in the chest took a while. The elixir hadn't replaced the blood he'd lost, and James spent a few days feeling slow and stiff and achingly exhausted, dragging himself between his top-floor apartment and the office. There was also a deeply unpleasant afternoon when a slowly growing ache in his chest resolved into sharp stabbing pain— that suddenly stopped. He didn't find out why until taking off his T-shirt that evening. Something hard and pebble-like dropped out. He crouched and picked it up, thought at first it was a bit of gravel until its squashed shape registered. His body had pushed the bullet out.

Better than having it in, he decided.

They disposed of Geary's remains in Oz's woods. Burying them in the tunnel probably *would* have solved the problem, and also would have been horrifying in a way that James found he couldn't quite articulate to Wendy and Oz. So, under the cover of darkness, they transported Geary's remains, along with the statue, to the forest preserve behind

Oz's mansion. They buried Geary in the deepest part of the woods. The statue they left in a nice spot under a tree overlooking a pond and not too far from a trail. He might destatue at some point, in which case he'd probably need to be able to find his way out.

James was never quite sure what had happened to the guy he had inadvertently cube-ified. Either the cube had been in Geary's pocket—in which case, no coming back from that; sorry, dude—or it was in the statue's pocket, or . . . hell, it could have been taken to Goodwill for all he knew.

After helping transport Geary to a final resting place, Oz vanished into his mansion and didn't come out for days. James was halfway expecting him to just not come back at all, but when he finally showed up he seemed as cheerful and willing as always, though perhaps a little gray around the lips and eyes, where the scales were thin enough that his skin showed through.

Work was slow as usual. James did a couple of paperwork searches for an attorney in town who kept him on retainer, which could be done from his chair by computer and phone, and that was it.

Dolly came and went in her normal fashion, but she was a bit more colorful, more *there*—and she no longer wore the necklace.

Wendy stopped into James's office a week later. Nattily dressed, with a hat cocked jauntily over her silver hair, she was still walking carefully and using a slender cane with a carved maple head.

The gold and green necklace was clasped at her throat, setting off the jewel tones of her metallic gold blouse and dark green skirt.

"Keeping that, huh?" James asked, pulling around the one guest chair for her.

Wendy glanced around the office. He was slowly putting it back together, but hadn't felt up to moving the filing cabinets back in yet. The wall was still papered with pictures of the harbor, and her gaze lingered on them for a time.

"It's a memento," she said, touching the necklace lightly. The gesture was very Dolly-like.

"I wouldn't think you'd want mementos of a father like Geary."

Wendy's smile was brief and lupine, reminding James that she was Geary's daughter as much as Dolly's. "It's more a cautionary tale." She took her hand away and curled it over the head of the cane. "In any case, I thought I might see how you were doing—and update you on a few small business matters."

"Such as?"

"Such as," she said with a thin smile, "Geary MacKay seems to have vanished, leaving no one running his business empire."

"Right," James murmured. Geary wasn't officially dead, as such. He had simply disappeared. "Who's his heir?"

Her smile took on that lupine quality again. "Geary didn't have a will. Probably because he thought he was going to live forever."

"What happens to his business empire, then?"

"A good question, that. It's a handy thing, isn't it, that he'd been working closely with a silent business partner who also happens to be his maiden aunt."

"That's . . . legal?"

She moved a hand in a curt gesture that was very emphatically *not* one of Dolly's mannerisms. "If I learned one thing from Geary, it's that legal and illegal and perhaps even the finer points of blood relationship depend in large part on the people whose palms you grease and the lawyers you can hire. Money is vulgar, but it makes the world go 'round. Or at least makes it more convenient in certain ways."

"Yeah, well, that may be, but Geary's original boardwalk empire disintegrated when the IRS and FBI started asking awkward questions, and he ended up buried in the woods in an unmarked grave. So it's good to keep in mind, money and lawyers can only take you so far."

Her thin brows, neatly plucked and traced with brown eyebrow pencil, arched toward the brim of her hat. "Is that a threat?"

"Jeez. No. Not my style. Just a reminder, maybe, that hubris took down Geary. Don't make the same mistakes he did."

"Hmm."

She sat back in the chair; he recognized the careful stiffness in the way she moved, grimly covering for lingering pain and weakness. She crossed her legs and assumed a position of deliberate casualness, with her hand clasped on the knob of the cane.

"So tell me what you want, Mr. Keeley."

"Want?" He was genuinely thrown. "I'm not trying to blackmail you."

"Of course not. But I've found that business arrangements can be more harmonious. Or at least a reminder of our mutual obligations to each other. After all, I'm going to be your landlady." That smile again. He was liking it less every time he saw it. "And we are the ones who know where the bodies are buried, as they say."

James stared at her for a minute.

"Well, if you're offering," he said after a minute, "there *is* one thing I want. The basement."

"If I get it, you can have the entire building."

"I don't want the building. I just want the basement. And the tunnel."

"Why?" Wendy asked. She sounded genuinely curious, and she tilted her head, listening with her whole body. This was the reporter side of her, he thought—what was left of it.

"Because," he said, "it would make a nice, dragon-accessible office. And your mom likes it down there."

FAE AND FLATFOOT

KEELEY & ASSOCIATES #3

Fae and Flatfoot

CHAPTER ONE

"DOLLY, I don't want to upset you, but you can't keep scaring away construction workers like this. We just lost our third crew, and I'm starting to scrape the bottom of the Grand Bluffs construction market."

Dolly wrung her hands. She was semitransparent in her distress, and the ghostly echo of a 1920s speakeasy faded in and out of existence around her, revealing shadowy glimpses of a nearly empty basement with heaps of construction supplies and half-finished interior walls. The brightest place in the room was right around her, as if she stood in a spotlight.

"I just don't *like* them here," she burst out, and the smell of cigarette smoke in the air intensified. "It's my basement. It's been my basement for a hundred years. And they're noisy, and they're crude, and I don't *want* them."

James let out a long breath and sat down on the end of a pile of stacked lumber. It was almost midnight, the barely healed gunshot wound in his chest throbbed with a deep ache, and he didn't want to spend time he could have been asleep arguing with a ghost. But she was a sweet ghost, and he liked her, and it *was* her space.

"You agreed that I could have my office down here, because Oz doesn't fit upstairs."

"I agreed *you* could be here. I'm just fine with *you* being here. And Oz, of course." Dolly conjured a cigarette out of thin air, in a slim silver holder, and smoked while she began pacing. Her short flapper dress whipped around her and the beads on her headwrap clattered against her short blonde hair. "It's *them* I don't want."

"We have to remodel so I can use the basement to work in. I can't run a business out of an unfinished basement with spiders in the corners, Dolly."

"It was fine when I worked here!" she burst out. "It's not *that* bad!"

"Dolly," James said, as gently as he knew how, "that was a hundred years ago. You said it yourself. Dolly . . . look around."

She turned her head, a little thrust of her chin. Surely she'd looked before; surely the 1920s facade wasn't the only thing she had ever seen down here.

But ghosts were, in part, about belief. And James felt like a grade-A heel as he watched the translucent echo of the Jazz Age club, with its soft lighting and colorful wallpaper and the faintest hints of long-dead patrons spinning each other between the old mahogany tables, fade slowly away to leave behind the patched concrete, the heaps of building supplies, the single bare light bulb casting stark shadows into plastic-draped corners.

"Oh," Dolly whispered, one sad little word.

"It's been a hundred years," James said softly. "You know nothing lasts that long. Not furniture, not wallpaper, not ideals . . ."

"Not barmaids," Dolly said in a brave, tiny voice, and smiled a little.

Months ago, he might have expected her to vanish, disrupted by the intrusion of reality into her 1920s fantasia. In the early days after he first met her, anything from a shaft of sunlight to James reaching out to touch her had broken the illusion and made her disappear. There had been times when he had even doubted his own sanity, his own judgment of whether she was real or not.

But lately, she had seemed ever more strongly anchored in his reality. And it occurred to him now, as he supposed it should have earlier, that Dolly standing up for herself and rejecting the construction workers was actually a huge step forward for her, personally inconvenient as it was for him. He knew she'd used her poltergeist abilities to run off unwanted intruders from the old warehouse before, but had she ever really made such a determined and persistent statement about her own desires and needs?

"Dolly, listen. We can negotiate this. If you really don't want them here—"

The door to the basement slammed open, accompanied by a cold draft, and the electric light flickered as if a strong wind had just blown through the room.

Dolly winked out like a popped soap bubble.

At least he was used to her swift comings and goings. James touched his side, where his gun wasn't, and turned slowly toward the door.

A woman stood there.

She was tall, the crown of her silver hair nearly brushing the doorframe, and she carried her own eerie inner light. It lit nothing and cast no shadows, but it streamed out from her, silvery cold.

Her skin was white, her hair like polished steel. She wore a white dress that trailed off her bare shoulders, and it was carried by dozens of small butterflies with electric-blue wings, holding it off the ground so that it touched nothing.

"Are you James Keeley of Keeley and Associates?"

Her voice was unexpectedly normal, with a husky undertone. It was a sexy voice, a whiskey voice, but it wasn't filled with eldritch music; it didn't bend him like a willow wand.

"Yes, ma'am," James said slowly, taking his hand very carefully from the pocket where his phone was. "Can I help you?"

The butterflies bore her train as she . . . he would have said *glided*, but in truth she walked, though each step of her white boots was as graceful as a ballet dancer's. She approached him, and as she came closer, he saw there were butterflies on her body as well as those carrying her train. They perched on her shoulders, opening and closing their wings; they walked about in her hair like strange, moving ornaments.

Eeriest of all were those on her face. Her expression remained serene as they crawled over the corner of her mouth and above her white brows.

"I saw the sign on your door," she said. "I must say I find these minimal surroundings agreeably different."

He had a blank moment when he couldn't imagine what she meant, and then remembered the card taped to his office door upstairs: IF CLOSED DURING REGULAR OFFICE HOURS, CHECK BASEMENT.

It had never occurred to him that someone wouldn't understand midnight was not included in regular office hours. After spending this much time with a ghost and a dragon, he probably should have.

She was now standing in front of him, her train undulating gently with the subtle movements of the butterflies, and James belatedly realized she was waiting for something. He jumped off his pile of lumber and gestured her to another. "Would you like to sit, my lady?"

"Thank you," she said politely, and took a delicate seat on the end of a protruding 2x12. The butterflies very gently let her skirt trail to the ground.

"You have the advantage of me, ma'am." James took the seat opposite her, resting his hips on the stacked ends of a pile of drywall. His chest throbbed when he breathed too deeply. A painkiller and eight deep hours on his mattress upstairs . . . that was what he craved. Not whatever the hell this was.

"I'm sorry?" she said.

"You know my name. I don't know yours."

Her slight, frosty smile deepened, and he knew then, for certain, what he was dealing with. She was fae. *Fuck.*

"My name is not for mortal ears, but you may refer to me by my sobriquet, Prudence."

There was a moment when he wasn't sure if he'd heard right. "Prudence?"

"Yes."

"I . . . uh . . . okay." He had a brief, mad impulse to ask her if he could call her Pru, but squashed it. "What can I do for you, Prudence?"

"You are a detective? One who finds missing things?" A butterfly walked delicately past the corner of her eye and crawled into her hair. She never twitched.

"Yes," James said carefully.

"An item has been stolen from me. I would like to make a bargain with you to retrieve it."

"What's the item?"

"I do not wish to tell you."

"Gonna make it hard to recover, then."

"You need only find the person who took it from me. The thief is one of my own kind, a greater fae who is known by the sobriquet Victorious."

Great. More fae. "That's basically unhelpful as far as

finding him, unless he shows up on Google. Got any more specific info? Any idea where he might've gone?"

She seemed briefly baffled. "You are a detective, are you not? I should not need to tell you how to do your job."

"Yeah, well, I don't know how it works in Fairyland, but 'some dude named Victorious who stole a thing' is not actually helpful over here. Do you know what name he's using in the human world? Where he lives? Little description of either him or the thing he stole, maybe?"

"Oh," she said, and smiled. It was a weird, icy smile, edged with frost, that didn't reach her cold, cold eyes. "Of course."

She moved her hands, both of them together, in a shape that might describe a vase or an hourglass—or a human head and shoulders. Beneath her trailing, pale hands, a face took shape in the air: inhumanly symmetrical, with light brown skin and dark purple hair trailing down from a center part.

"Victorious," she said, gesturing forward, so that it floated in the air toward James.

. . . who decided to try pushing his luck. "I can't do much with it like this. Can I get a photograph?"

He was halfway expecting her to ask what that was, but instead she turned her hands palm to palm, and as she moved her palms together, the image in the air flattened and drifted down until an 8x12 glossy rested in James's hand, gently warm and slightly sticky as if fresh from the developer.

"And what did he take?"

"That I cannot tell you." She held out her hand. One of the blue butterflies crawled out onto her fingertips. "This will alert you when you are near it."

James extended the photo, holding it by the edge, rather than his hand. The butterfly crawled onto it, and then, unexpectedly, melted into the picture so that it was perched on Victorious's hair like a strange ornament.

"Okay then," James murmured, handling the photo with

the caution of a live grenade. "When did he take off with the, er . . . thing?"

"It was only a few days ago. Time does not pass quite the same on this side of the Veil. Certainly less than two of your weeks."

"See, that's helpful information. Any idea where he is?"

"In your world somewhere." She sounded impatient.

"This city? Another city?"

"I do not know."

"Well, do you know where he came into our world? That'd be a starting place."

"Not exactly," she said. "Somewhere near this city. I cannot pinpoint it more closely than that."

"So he stole something and showed up around here somewhere and went somewhere after that."

"Yes," she said, wholly oblivious to his sarcasm.

"Okay . . . let's say through some miracle of detective work I do actually find him. Suppose he doesn't have it anymore, destroyed it or sold it or something."

"I doubt that very much. We have little need for human money. It's the having that my kind cares about. He wants to have it so I cannot. He won't give it up."

"But if I can't get it back from him, what does—"

"You *will*."

"Lady," James said, stopping just short of a sigh, "I've done repo work before, all right? I just want to know what you want done if he doesn't still have it, because there is a lot of that in this business."

"Then alert me to his location, and I will proceed from there. If he *does* have my stolen possession, you will recover and return it."

"And you're not going to tell me what it is."

"Does it matter?" she asked archly.

Did it? Maybe not, because he didn't think she could

possibly make it worth the trouble. "And what are you planning to pay for this?"

He was fully expecting her to look blank. *Payment? Don't know it.* Instead she said promptly, "A favor."

James opened his mouth and closed it again. He'd heard of fae favors. They could be incredibly powerful. Also worryingly binding. But . . . powerful. It was not something to be turned down lightly.

Would it really be that bad? Do a little legwork, try to find this missing thief of hers. He'd done worse things for worse people.

"And if I refuse?" he asked.

"Then I will remove your memory of this conversation and this visit. It will be as if it never happened. And we shall both go on with our lives."

James was already on his feet, stomach clenching into knots as his hands clenched into fists. "No. No, no, no. *No one* messes around in my head."

"Then you'll take the case?" she asked, with a trace of a smile on her pale lips.

"Those can't possibly be the only options."

"Regretfully so. You may decide which you prefer. I will only take a little of your memory. It is not a precision art, so it might destroy the last few days' worth of memories, and perhaps anything closely associated with them."

"*What*? No. Stay out of my head."

"In that case," she said, rising, with the butterflies picking up her train, "bargain accepted. I look forward to working with you."

Damn it, why had he left the spellgun upstairs? James started to take a step after her, then realized he couldn't. He was frozen in place, unable to move or even to speak. All he could do was stand like a statue, heart pounding, staring at her as she walked away.

In the doorway, she turned and looked back. Her eyes glimmered like a cat's. "I shall return in three days to see if you are making progress. In case you need to contact me sooner, please dispatch the butterfly I have given you."

She whisked her train after her, and the strange paralysis broke. James took a stumbling step forward, his breath catching with a gasp.

Wonderful.

CHAPTER TWO

"I DON'T SUPPOSE you know anything about fae."

"No one knows that much about fae," Oz said. Too large to fit inside, the dragon was curled in the alley outside James's office window with his chin resting on the windowsill. "Not even me. They are not more powerful than dragons, obviously, because that's impossible, but they are *quite* powerful. Particularly the greater fae."

"Greater fae as opposed to what?"

Oz settled into lecture mode. "Broadly they are divided into the greater and lesser fae. Lesser fae are the brownies and boggans and leprechauns. Like Murphy, that vile thief." Oz spoke the name with a disgusted curl of his lips. "Greater fae are very rare on this side of the Veil. Usually they come here on business of their own, and their intentions are seldom good."

Great.

"And what's the Veil?"

Oz blinked his great dinner-plate eyes. "You don't know what the Veil is?"

"I'm asking, aren't I?"

"Hmm." He gave a quick all-over flick of his scales, rippling down his long gunmetal body. "It is the boundary between the fae world and our world."

"Yeah, I guessed that part. But, I mean, where is it? Is it like a portal, or a magical screen door, or . . .?"

Oz gave him a puzzled look. "It's everywhere."

"Ah."

"Their world lies one step below our world. One must only open a doorway through the Veil to pass between. However, most places do not contact closely enough to make a door between. There are a few old doors, made in the early days, and thin places where new doors may be made. The fae guard these locations closely, as you might expect."

"Yeah, I guess I wouldn't want the riffraff barging in through my back door, either."

"But from what I understand, any point could be made a point of contact with sufficient effort. The fae are always with us, but a step to the side."

"Not worrying at all," James said.

"May I ask why you're so curious about the fae? Not that it isn't a fascinating topic, it's just that you haven't previously seemed to—"

"Because one of them hired me last night for a repo job."

Oz's head went up, the frills around his ears and the base of his jaw lifting. "Is that wise?"

"No," James said. "I really don't think so. She didn't exactly give me a choice, though."

"Did she *hire* you?" Oz asked. His frills flattened. "Or make a bargain with you?"

"Er . . . isn't that basically the same thing?"

"No! One is magically binding and one is not."

"How would I know?"

Oz lowered his great eyelids slowly. The look on his long-jawed face was strangely familiar, but it took James a moment to place it as the outward reflection of the way *he* felt when he was trying to explain human things to Oz, such as football or retirement accounts.

"Did the word 'bargain' occur at any point?" Oz asked.

"Several times," James admitted. Another of those slow blinks. "Look, if you think I'm an idiot, just say so, damn it."

"I don't think you're an idiot," Oz said. "What did she ask you to do, *exactly*?"

"Find the missing thing and bring it to her."

"In those exact words?"

Oz always seemed to forget that most humans didn't have his near-photographic memory. "As well as I can remember, yeah, that's the gist of it."

"*Precision*, James. That is the key to dealing with fae."

"You know when this would have been really useful to know?" James said. "Last night."

"What does it feel like?" Oz asked eagerly.

"What does *what* feel like?"

"Being bound by a fae bargain. I've always wondered."

"I'm not—I—" James took a breath. A trapped feeling had settled around him like a noose. "How do you get out of it?"

"Er, I'd have to do some research. If it helps at all," Oz said, "from what I understand, it's considerably more binding on her than on you. You can choose not to do it."

"I can?" The noose loosened slightly.

"Yes, well, if you don't mind having an extremely angry fae pursuing you to the end of your days."

"But that's all. No magical side effects."

"Probably not."

"Probably?"

"I'm not an expert on fae!" Oz said. "I told you that."

"Well, do you know any experts on fae? Because I could really use one right now."

"I can ask around," Oz said.

"Yes, thank you. In the meantime, I guess the other way to get rid of her is by finding the thing she wants found, so I may as well get to it."

"Hmm. What does she want you to retrieve?"

"No idea. She won't tell me."

The neck frills lowered again. "Not to criticize how you do your job, but I would think that would make it difficult to recover."

"I don't have to find the thing. I just have to find the guy who has it." James held up the picture that Prudence had given him. It was still slightly warm to the touch in a way that he found unpleasant; it made the thing feel eerily alive. "That's going to be tricky, since he's only been here for a few weeks tops, and wouldn't exactly have left a paper trail."

"But this is what you do, is it not? I look forward to seeing a master at work," Oz said. He clattered his claws on the pavement outside the window in an excited little flurry of taps.

"You might have to wait longer for that, because I'm taking a shortcut. Oz, you know I don't like you paying for things, in general."

"I know it well," the dragon said, with a long-suffering sigh that gusted faintly brimstone-smelling air around the office in a whirl of loose papers.

"Yeah, so I'm finally going to take advantage of those deep pockets of yours. I need to buy something expensive, and I have to pay with cash. Can you get the money for me?"

Oz perked up attentively. "How much money?"

"I'd say about thirty thou—"

"On it!" Oz said, and beat his wings with a tremendous downdraft that sent papers swirling around the inside of the office.

"Wait—"

Too late.

Oh well, when it came to quantities of cash in the tens of thousands, denominations didn't matter all that much. While Oz was gone, James went back to doing what he had been doing when Oz showed up that morning: getting on the darknet and looking into what it would take to get a finding spell cast.

Magic was tightly regulated. An artifact like the spellgun that he carried, disguised as a normal gun, would earn him a nice little felony if he got caught with it. Lower-level spells were legal, their practitioners performing openly, but a spell like the one he wanted would have resulted in a lot of paperwork, leaving both his name and the existence of what he wanted done on file.

Which was the reason the magical black market existed, of course.

He hadn't dealt with them much because they were so expensive. With magic, like anything else, you got what you paid for—but a cheap, incompetent mechanic would merely leave you by the side of the road. A cheap, incompetent magician might accidentally turn you into a rubber duck, give you a horrible disease, or blow up three city blocks.

And magic could very easily get loose. There had been a rogue magicstorm a couple of years ago down in the railyards, when an unlicensed spell had slipped the bounds of its practitioner's control. It had resulted in a rain of hedgehogs across downtown, a stand of oaks developing sentience (one of them was apparently getting a university degree in structural engineering; there had been an entire feature on the news about it), and a Union Pacific coal car eating two brakemen. Not to mention strange effects on the weather lasting for months. There had been some very interestingly colored snow last winter.

And that was why magic had such tight legal controls on it. Magic was dangerous. Magic was *hard*. Magic, as a trade, was like surgery: expensive and time-consuming to learn to do, requiring talent and focus to do well. Any idiot could pick up a scalpel, but you wouldn't want them cutting into your brain.

James couldn't even imagine the skill, effort, and cost it had taken to make an artifact like the spellgun.

But it also meant that if you wanted something magical done, you had your choices of going with the few and restrictive legal options, or rolling the dice with someone willing to practice magic without a license. In general, in the past, he had felt it was better not to take the chance. Anyone he could afford was probably too poorly trained to be safe.

Now, though, he could get a proper tracking spell done. And, while he was at it, perhaps a consultation about breaking fae bargains.

CHAPTER THREE

"So you just had thirty thousand dollars laying around," James said, hefting the briefcase.

"I believe you mean *lying* around," Oz said loftily. "And no. That would be ridiculous. It was in a safe."

"Right." James resisted the urge to open the briefcase and count it. Or just stare at it. He'd glanced inside already, and tried not to react to that amount of money all in one place.

Oz scowled. "I should come with you for protection."

"And I'd love to have you, but it's not a good idea. People in the black-market magic trade are a jumpy bunch. Showing up with my own personal dragon is a good way to make sure they never talk to me again."

"I'm not *your*—"

"Oz." He lifted the briefcase. "This is your contribution to the current job. Now I'm going to go buy us a tracking spell, and we can go looking for our rogue fae."

"I'm definitely coming for *that*."

"Of course you are. And I'll call you if I have any problems. Good?"

"Good," Oz muttered, with a hint of a growl in his tone.

The meeting place James had gotten from the practitioner was a motorcycle repair shop. As requested, he pulled up just after closing time, the Trans Am purring into a parking spot in the nearly deserted gravel lot.

The CLOSED sign was out, but there was a man in a plastic lawn chair sitting in front of the door, reading a magazine. He got up when James pulled in. He was heavyset, with a pink scalp showing through close-cropped gray hair, and an oil-stained gray T-shirt straining across a beer gut. He was in no way out of shape, however; his arms were ropy with muscle, his hands capable and quick, with a powerful grip when he shook James's hand. The short nails were stained permanently black around the edges.

"Hell of a ride you got there," he said.

James hadn't quite gotten past thinking of the car as slightly pretentious, but it *was* extremely satisfying to drive. "I figure no point in waiting for midlife to have the car part of the crisis, right?"

The mechanic grinned, crinkling the skin around his sharp, dark eyes. "Max Guerrera."

"James."

Max's eyes flicked down to the sliver of the gunbelt just visible under the edge of James's jacket. "Anything magic needs to stay in the car."

Good guesser, or was he actually able to tell by looking? James hadn't met anyone else who could spot the spellgun as something other than a normal gun without the runes showing. He unbuckled the gunbelt and tucked it back into its usual place under the seat. Max watched with his arms folded and no sign of judgment, just a wary alertness.

"Also might want to leave anything electronic you don't want to lose."

James dropped his phone in the change tray. "Want me to leave my underwear too?"

"If you don't have magic undies, it's fine." Max held out a hand to the shop door in an "after you" gesture. James picked up the briefcase and went inside.

Despite the CLOSED sign, the door was unlocked. The shop inside was exactly the kind of place it looked like from the outside, small and smelling strongly of motor oil and coffee. There was a tiny waiting area with two chairs and a pile of magazines, the TV in the corner tuned silently to a news channel.

Max closed the door and casually flipped the deadbolt. James tensed, wishing he'd thought to bring a nonmagical weapon. He could kick the door open if he had to.

Max took something out of his pocket that looked like a tire pressure gauge, one of the cheap ones with the pop-out end. "Okay, gotta do a quick thing first. Stand still." He moved it briefly in the air, up and down, side to side.

There was a small *pop!* and the TV screen went dark.

"Fuck me, I always forget to turn the damn thing off," Max muttered. "Ah, sorry 'bout the watch. Digital, is it?"

James glanced down at his watch. The screen was blank.

"I did mention the electronics issue." Max stuck the gauge back in his pocket. "Okay, you're clean. C'mon into the back."

"What were you checking for?" James asked as Max opened a door behind the front desk. There were black smudges all around the doorknob.

"Wires. Spells. Whatever. Can't be too careful."

The shop was, once again, just what the outside of the building suggested. Most of the lights were off. In the dim shadows, James had an impression of motorcycles in various stages of repair, shelves of tools, oil-stained service bays. The air smelled of metal and oil and exhaust.

"You a car man, James?" Max asked. He took out a heavy, jangling key ring and unlocked a door in the back.

"Not really, I mean no more so than anyone. I've been

picking it up a little from a friend who's into it. He's the one that gave me the Trans Am."

"Nice sort of friend to have."

"Yeah," James said under his breath. A very useful friend. Who he wished he'd brought with him after all.

The door opened onto a small storeroom. Max shifted a couple of crates of oil aside, moving them effortlessly with his powerful arms, and unlocked a padlock on a trapdoor set in the floor. When he swung it up and turned on the light, a flight of wooden stairs led downward.

James's level of tension had continued screwing itself tighter, and he balked, all too aware that he had a suitcase full of cash and no weapons. "There are people who know where I am."

Max snorted. "Trust me, if I wanted to bump you off, I wouldn't have to go through a whole puppet show to do it. Down there's where the magic happens. Literally." He gestured. "After you."

Nothing ventured, nothing gained. James descended the steep wooden steps into an unfinished basement, with a dirt floor and rough cinderblock walls. There were worktables along the walls, half hidden in shadow, their contents a clutter that could only be glimpsed.

"Dirt absorbs magic," Max remarked from a few steps above. He closed the trapdoor and then swung a second trapdoor up into place from below, this one nearly a foot thick and, from the look of it, very heavy. It was like being sealed into a bunker. "Anything that spills out will be grounded in the dirt and concrete, so the feds don't get a sniff of it and also because this town doesn't need more sentient oak trees."

James couldn't help grinning despite his nervousness. "That wasn't you, then?"

"Thanks a lot for the vote of confidence." Max hopped off the bottom step, with lightness and grace belied by his size, and flicked a switch on the wall. An entire array of halogen lights above the worktables sparked to life, lighting up the basement like a photography studio.

The light revealed an array of paraphernalia that was part high school chemistry lab and part machine shop, with a dash of the genuinely occult. Among the ordinary equipment and tools, James saw a brazier similar to the one he used to use for summoning Dolly, a bird's skull with bones as delicate as papier-mâché, a collection of herbs in neatly hand-labeled bottles, and a foot-long birch wand with symbols scratched into its sides. There was a sink down here too, and a chemical vent hood.

"Not to jump straight to business," Max said, "but let's have a look." He nodded to the briefcase.

James opened it. He still wasn't over the sight of square-bound stacks of cash in neat rows. It looked like a television prop.

Max took one out and flipped through it. His quick gaze flicked over the rows and columns. "Looks legit. I'll just point out that cheating me isn't a good idea, in case you got your hands on some fairy money that turns to dead leaves in the morning, or the like." He smiled slightly. It wasn't warm. "I don't know where you live, but I'm confident I can find out."

"I'm playing you straight."

"Hope so. You wanted a tracking spell, right?"

"Yeah." James set the briefcase on the seat of a stool; it was the only clear space in sight, other than the floor. "What kind of turnaround can I expect?"

"You're paying for a rush job, so . . . now." Max crossed to the sink and began washing his hands. Over his shoulder he said, "I already set up the main components of the spell. "Do you have an object belonging to the target?"

"No, sorry. Can you do it without one?"

"What do you have? Name? Photo?"

"Photo and an alias."

"I can do it," Max said. He dried his hands on a cotton shop towel. "It'll be a little less reliable, that's all. More of a chance of false positives. Let's see it."

James held out the photo. "The name I was given was Victorious."

Max took it, and nearly dropped it. "You never said anything about fae being involved."

"Is that a problem?"

"Is it a—fuck." He ran his hand over his face. "Okay, look. I can do it, but it'll cost you double, because of the risk and the extra precautions to keep the spell from being traced back to me. Half now, half tomorrow. Cash."

"Okay," James said. "I'm good for it." He had no doubt that Oz would be, anyway. If the dragon could come up with thirty thousand on the spur of the moment, sixty shouldn't be a problem.

Max gave him a narrow-eyed look. "And you didn't even bat an eye. You must *really* want this guy."

"More like I don't have a choice and I doubt I can find him any other way, since it's not like he's gonna be paying his electric bill as 'Victorious.' Unless," James added hopefully, "you happen to know a way to break a fae bargain."

"Oh, one of *those* kinds of things. No, that's way outside my skill set. But I can set you up with a basic tracker." Max held the photo by the very corner, as if he didn't want to touch it any more than he had to. "Part of the deal, though— I'm not involved. You were never here. You finger me for this in any way, you won't have just the fae to deal with."

"I was never here. Got it."

Max nodded, a brief jerk of his chin. "Stay out of the way and be quiet. I'll let you know when I need you."

He went to a cleared space on one of the workbenches.

There was a collection of small objects in the middle of a chalked circle.

James stepped a little closer, trying to watch unobtrusively. He'd seen magic performed, of course—who hadn't?—but not the ritual kind.

The items in the circle were an antique compass, an old-fashioned brass key, a lawn dart from the days when they were still made of metal, a gray-barred bird feather, and the shoe token from a Monopoly game. Max carefully slid the photo underneath them and arranged them on top, compass in the middle, the rest ranged around it.

"I need something of yours." His tone was careful, the words quiet. "Doesn't matter what. Metal, if you have it."

The dead watch had a brass band. James stripped it off and handed it over.

"Why metal?" he asked as Max rearranged the objects to make room for it.

"Holds a charm better than just about anything else. Wood's second best. Earth and stone tend to resist it. Plastic takes a charm easily but sheds it quickly, too fast for anything permanent." He looked up from careful, fussy rearranging, and jerked his head toward the stairs. "Step back now, over there is good, and do me a favor—turn off the lights while you're there."

James did as asked, moved to the stairs and flicked off the light switch. The room plunged into sudden darkness, oppressively flat and black.

And then, at the worktable, light came up slowly. It was a soft ruddy glow, tinged with gold: a sunset kind of light. James couldn't tell where it was coming from. It seemed to be ambient, generated by the air itself.

The light brightened, gilding Max's thick frame, glossing the cinderblock walls, painting a fine line of gold on every bristling hair on Max's scalp and forearms. It seemed to have a physical presence, or at least *something* was tickling James's skin and prickling down the back of his neck, like a static electric charge.

There was a sudden cascade of snapping, popping brilliance, like a string of fireworks erupting down Max's arms and across the workbench. James threw his arm over his face protectively. When he opened his eyes, he saw nothing except blackness filled with blooming purple spots, and for a moment he thought he'd gone blind.

"You can turn the lights on," Max said into the darkness. His voice cracked wearily.

James did so and squinted against the glare. The blotches in his vision were fading to a faint bruise-colored glaze. He came over to the workbench cautiously.

"It's not gonna bite you. At least not now." Max looked washed out, almost gray. He reached for a thermos on the edge of the worktable and took a swig, then grimaced. "Blegh. Magic aftertaste. Gotta remember not to leave the coffee down here." He picked up something off the table. "Here, have a look."

The individual items in the chalk circle, except the photo, were gone. What remained was James's watchband with the compass embedded where the face of the watch used to be, lying on top of the perfectly undamaged photograph.

Max picked up the watch and deposited it into James's hand. It was slightly warm to the touch. The compass needle rotated loosely, pointing nowhere in particular: first at one wall, then another.

"It doesn't have a fix yet," Max said. "Do *not* take one here. Or anywhere near my place. It's possible that a skilled enough practitioner can backtrail it. I suggest taking your first fix someplace you don't care about too much." He tapped the side of the watch with a thick fingertip, where the old buttons remained, embedded now in the compass's case.

"To take a fix, press and hold each button in turn for about fifteen seconds. Needle points the direction; the level, that little inset bubble there, shows roughly how close you are."

"Thank you." James fastened it around his wrist. It felt like his old watch, but slightly heavier. He slipped the photo back into his pocket.

"Once you take a fix, it'll point to the same location until you take a new one. If your target is on the move, you might need to reset it frequently. I'd suggest keeping the resets to a minimum if you can." Max reached for a grease-smudged rag on the edge of the workbench and mopped his forehead. He was sweating as if he'd run a marathon. "In passive search mode it's not easy to trace, but every time you power it up, you give the other guy a shot at getting a fix on you, too. Oh," he added, "there's always gonna be a little magical leakage, but not so you could home in on it from a distance. Practitioners will be able to tell, but only from up close."

"That's how you knew about my gun."

Max smiled briefly. "Yeah, but that thing, it's miles beyond what I can do. What I make here are a kid's crayon scribbles, and that piece is a Rembrandt. I'd love to look at it sometime, if you don't mind."

"Maybe. I can't promise anything."

"Yeah," Max said. "First you gotta survive fucking around with the fae."

❧

JAMES DIDN'T SUPPOSE it mattered all that much if he used the compass at his office, since Prudence had found him there anyway, but just to be on the safe side he drove to a park overlooking the river. He left his phone in the car and walked out along the bike path. Without the watch's time-keeping function, he counted down the seconds instead, pushing the buttons as indicated.

Nothing visibly changed for a moment, and then the needle abruptly ceased its aimless wobbling and swung around to point steadily southeast. At the same time, the small air bubble in the level rolled toward the side, stopping about halfway.

James tilted the compass, turned it around, even held it upside down. Both the needle and the bubble in the level stayed rock solid.

He regretted not asking more questions about how to read the level as a distance indicator, but he guessed that having the bubble partway over, but not all the way, meant that his target wasn't right in the city, but probably not in, say, France.

Well, at least that made his next move easy.

CHAPTER FOUR

"What is a road trip?" Oz asked.

"Yeah, so, it's like . . . you're on a trip. On the road. Look, I am definitely going to want backup for this one."

"You don't need roads. I can carry you."

"You mean—on your back? Uh, no. Thanks anyway. I'll drive."

They were down in the basement of the warehouse, with early morning light glinting through the recessed, ground-level windows up near the ceiling. He'd wanted to try summoning Dolly rather than just abandoning her without a word.

Sometimes she could stay away for days after a shock like she'd had with the fae, but she showed up as soon as smoke began curling up from the brazier. These days, she often showed up without being summoned, but it remained the only way he had of getting hold of her when he really wanted her, a sort of afterlife telephone.

"I'm sorry about the other day," Dolly said, tangling her fingers in the strap of her beaded clutch. "Hi, Oz."

"Hello," Oz said, resting his chin on a pile of building supplies. "James is taking me on a road trip to find some fae."

"*James.*" Dolly turned her concerned, one-step-left-of-monochrome gaze on him.

"I didn't exactly have a choice. Look, I've got the spellgun, and . . ." He held up his wrist. "Magic compass."

"Ooh." Dolly came over to have a look. James held out his arm for her inspection. To his surprise, she drifted her cool fingers around the watch, brushing them over his wrist like little prickles of cold air. There had been a time, not long ago, when she couldn't have held the contact without vanishing.

"Can you tell if things are magic by looking at them?" James asked. His conversation with Max had made him curious.

"Sort of," she said, frowning. "Your gun looks very bright, but this . . . it's just a sort of gentle glow. Like Oz has."

"I glow?" Oz asked, raising his head.

"Something like that. I don't know quite how to describe it. It's not really with my eyes that I see things." She looked around the basement, blinking, and it struck James that her 1920s milieu hadn't come with her this time.

"Are you going to be all right here?" he asked her. "I might be gone for a couple of days, I'm not sure yet. I haven't had a chance to look into finding a new work crew, so you'll have the place to yourself while I'm gone."

"Things change," she said with a wistful note in her voice. "I know it's not 1924. I just . . . forget, sometimes. And . . ." Her gaze lingered on the piles of construction supplies. "This is making it so much harder to forget. That's all."

"Dolly . . . if you could have us do anything at all with the basement, what do *you* want us to do with it?"

She turned to him, wide-eyed, and it seemed shocking to

him, all of a sudden, that he had never thought to ask her. He had just assumed . . .

—no, it hadn't seemed *relevant*, he thought, kicking himself now. He had thought that preserving the building for her was enough. But it was her home, and unlike him, she couldn't leave.

"I . . . I don't know. I never really thought about it." She frowned. "I never had a choice about it."

"Then you should. I don't have to have my office down here; it would just make it easier for me and Oz if I could. Or maybe it would be possible to remodel part of it like a 1920s nightclub, if you'd like that better. I could have an office over in the corner."

She was looking brighter and brighter—literally as well as figuratively: she was about as solid as he'd ever seen her, gleaming faintly with traces of her own inner light. "Can we do that?"

"Oz is paying for it. You'd better ask him."

Dolly turned to Oz.

"Well, of course," the dragon said, as if it was no big deal. Which, to him, it probably wasn't. "That's the . . . one with the tables, correct?"

"You should probably leave the details to us," James said.

Oz dipped his head graciously. Dolly looked starry-eyed.

"It'll still mean work crews down here," James warned her. "Probably for months. And I'll have to completely redraw the plans. Maybe I could look up photos of what the Peony Club used to look like, and make part of it look like that again. We could have your bar in the corner, the way the place looked when I first came down here and met you. What do you think?"

"I . . . I don't know," she said, uncertain again, twisting a hand in her skirt. "I haven't had to—make decisions, James. Not in a very long time."

"Well, think about it and tell me what you want to do."

Dolly nodded, and vanished abruptly. Usually the nightclub came and went with her; this time, with the nightclub absent, her departure was more like the sudden extinguishing of a blown-out candle, rather than the gradual fading of the speakeasy decor around him.

"I can't believe I never thought of asking her what she wanted. I know she's a ghost, but she's a person too."

Oz sat up, resting a clawed forepaw on a plastic-draped stack of drywall. "I would not have thought to ask. I would have just done it. I am learning a lot from you, James."

"Yeah, well, *stop* learning from me, idiot. I've been taking her for granted for months." He slapped the exposed brick of the wall. "Look, are we getting on the road this morning or not?"

～

HE DROVE out of town on a highway glazed with morning sun, a giant takeout cup of coffee in the cup holder and Springsteen on the stereo. The Trans Am purred. He hadn't had a chance yet to take it out and really put it through its paces. There was still a slight ache in his chest, deep in the lower left quadrant where a mobster's bullet had barely missed his heart not that long ago, but he hadn't needed ibuprofen this morning and he could take a deep breath without pain. He felt energetic and cheerful and *healthy*, for the first time in a while.

Since Oz could easily outpace the car while flying, the dragon had taken his own bearing off the compass, then headed off to leave the other half of the payment at Max's garage. James wished he could be a fly on the wall for *that* conversation.

He was about twenty minutes into the drive when his

phone rang. "Payment delivered," Oz said cheerfully. "I shall fly ahead and scout for you. I'll catch up soon."

"Are you flying right now? Holding a phone?"

"It's a hands-free headset. I had a special one made in my size. The phone is belted behind my ears."

"Yeah, well . . . be careful. In the city they're used to dragons . . . well, sort of used to them. The countryside's a different thing. Don't get yourself shot."

"As if guns would damage me anyway," Oz said smugly.

"That's not the—well, okay, it *is* the point, but anyway, don't go around freaking people out too much, all right?"

As he drove onward, the compass needle continued to point solidly southeast. James pulled off after a couple of hours to stretch his legs, get something to eat, and take a new reading. Oz touched down behind the Trans Am in the McDonald's drive-thru line, graciously endured the startled babbling from the staff, then ordered 100 burgers to go.

While they were waiting for the order, James sat in the parking lot on the Trans Am's hood and pushed the buttons. The needle wobbled slightly and stabilized, pointing in more or less the same direction as before. The bubble was a bit closer to the center of the level.

"You know, I have to say this is an extremely inefficient way to consume a cow," Oz remarked, delicately unwrapping a burger with the tips of his claws. He did two of them like that, then gave up and started eating them wrapper and all.

"Only for you." James ate a handful of fries and wiped the grease off his hands. "Let's roll. I can eat in the car, and you can catch up." He held up his phone. "Call if you lose track of me."

"Radio check," Oz said brightly, touching the earpiece with a claw.

"Stay in touch."

James drove on for another hour, with Oz intermittently

visible in the sky, off to the side or behind him. The needle continued to point ahead for a while, then started rotating slowly off to the side. Since it pointed to a fixed location, this meant the road was starting to diverge from where he needed to go.

James took the next exit and meandered down country roads, following the arrow. It was a gorgeous time of year, late summer heading into early fall. He drove past farm stands and U-Pick signs, apple and cherry orchards, fields thick with corn and soybeans. It made him think in a surprisingly not-unpleasant way of his Michigan childhood, the little rural roads and farms.

He took another fix—no change—and consulted his phone's map app before he found a long, straight road heading in the right general direction. As he got up to cruising speed again, he checked the side mirrors reflexively —there was little other traffic—and found that he'd picked up company.

There was a giant black dog running on either side of the car. They had come out of nowhere, and they were effort-lessly keeping pace with the Trans Am. Each of them was as big as a small horse.

Okay then.

Since he had a long straight stretch of road, James pushed the pedal down. The needle crept up to eighty, then ninety. With the car's top down, the wind lashed his hair; it was exhilarating at first, and then unpleasant.

The dogs seemed to float alongside, showing no sign of exertion.

"This is a pleasant race," one of them said, and James jerked the wheel—not a good idea at ninety-five. He tapped the brakes and began to slow.

"You guys are some kind of fairy hounds, I take it?"

The wind caught and snatched his words away, but the dogs seemed to have no trouble understanding him.

"We are guardians," said the one on the left.

"You are too close," said the one on the right. "You bring magic. We can smell it."

"We suggest you turn back now."

"Sorry," James said. "Can't."

In answer, one of the fairy hounds fell behind the Trans Am, and then the car abruptly and wildly slewed to the left.

James clutched the wheel, fighting for control. He risked a glance into the rear-view mirror, and saw just enough to let him know that the hound had clamped onto his rear bumper with its teeth.

"It's nothing personal," the other one said, and then latched onto the driver-side mirror with its jaws. Its huge teeth, gleaming between heavy black lips, were only a few inches away from his white-knuckled hands on the steering wheel. He could feel its hot breath and a spray of sweat or saliva.

The car was now sliding all over the road, dragged by their weight. That mirror was going to give—and then a couple of tons of dragon hit the dog from above like a swooping hawk, caught hold of it, and lifted it away. That side of the car lifted off the road for a moment and then thumped back down as the mirror broke away from the car's frame.

The shadows of dragon and dog flickered over the car and then James lost sight of them, too busy fighting the car's slewing.

He stomped the brakes and brought the Trans Am to a stop in the middle of the road. The hound's enormous head appeared over the rear bumper, and as James twisted around in his seat, it put one dinner-plate-sized paw on the trunk.

"Nothing personal," he said, and shot it in the face at point-blank range with the spellgun.

He never knew what to expect every time he pulled the trigger. This time, the dog tumbled backward off the rear bumper . . . in slow motion. It hit the pavement, rippled all over, and bounced in a strange slowed-down way.

Oz thumped down beside the car. "Well, that was exciting, wasn't it?" he said cheerily. The cheer dropped away when he got a look at the car. He gasped in horror. "Oh, my gracious."

"Yeah. Oz—"

"What have they *done* to this *automobile*? The barbarians!"

"Oz—"

"Are those *claw marks* on a pristine, vintage paint job? And the mirror! Is that what that canine miscreant was carrying? The bodywork is quite repairable, but a vintage, matching mirror—I must go look for it at once."

"Oz!" James pointed behind the car. "There's a dog back there, very slowly preparing to attack us. How about we clear out and worry about the car later."

"Oh." Oz looked over the car's trunk at the dog, which was, with excruciating slowness, rolling over to get its feet under it. "What happened?"

"Spellgun. Did you see where these things came from?"

"No," Oz said, his gaze drawn magnetically back to the scratches on the car's paint. "It was as if they appeared out of nowhere—"

"Great. So I guess we can expect more surprises."

"—but I was distracted," Oz went on. "So I might have missed the moment when they arrived."

"Distracted by what?"

The dragon frowned and turned to look down the deserted road. "There is something strange about this area."

"What do you mean?" James glanced back at the dog. It was progressing in its glacially slow effort to stand up. He figured that he had a few more minutes before it had any hope of getting close to the car, but he really needed to stop sitting here in the middle of the road in case another car—

Huh.

The road was completely deserted. Not a single farm truck, produce wagon, or buggy had passed him the entire time they had been sitting here. It was downright eerie now that he'd noticed it.

"I cannot seem to fly properly here," Oz said. "I keep losing my way. It was actually quite difficult for me to find your car. I tried to call you, but there was interference."

"Magic?" James said.

"Almost certainly. Have you noticed any difficulties staying on course?"

"Not other than the dogs." James glanced back again at the dog, which was now standing up and snarling in a slow-motion way that suggested it would very much like to resume tearing pieces off the car, or off him.

It also seemed to be moving a little faster than a moment ago.

"The spellgun makes me immune to spells and glamours." James popped the car into gear. "Listen, we really need to roll. If our presence here is still a secret, it won't be for long. Let's not hang out and wait for a supernatural nuke, all right?"

"Yes, of course." Oz spread his wings. "I will reconnoiter."

"Actually, I'm not sure that's a good idea. If you stay close to me, you might be less affected by whatever's messing with your head."

He started rolling in a low gear, driving slowly enough that he had to feather the clutch to keep from stalling the engine. The compass had begun to rotate, pointing off the road at a slight angle. Oz walked beside the car with the swaying alligator-like gait that the dragon typically used when walking on land—for a minute or two, anyway. James looked down at the compass, and when he looked up, Oz had fallen behind and veered off to the other side of the road.

"Oz?"

He braked and backed up. He had to wave to get Oz's attention.

"This is very strange," Oz said, taking a few quick steps to catch up. "It is disorienting."

"We might be able to tie you to the car. I don't know if I have anything to use for—"

"Look out!" Oz snapped, and reared up over the car, spreading his wings.

James didn't see where they came from, but the creatures arrowing down at them from the clear blue sky were eagle-sized and nasty-looking, and there were half a dozen of them. Bat wings, stony gray skin. Gargoyles? He slammed on the brakes and shot one of them with the spellgun. It burst apart in a cloud of sand that rained over the hood of the car. Oz swatted another one out of the air—it hit the pavement with a crunch—and launched himself off the ground with a tremendous downbeat and gust of wind.

"Oz, no—"

Another of the gargoyles, or whatever they were, came swooping in over the windshield. James snapped off a wild shot, and it turned into a cloud of purple smoke that swept over him and smelled faintly of roses.

When the smoke cleared, the sky was also clear. No gargoyles, and no Oz.

"Oz?" James reached for his phone. "Oz, can you hear me?"

There was a fuzz of static. He caught, for a moment, Oz saying in frustration, "I can hear you; I just can't *find* you." And then nothing.

Shit. He looked at the compass. It was pointing into the woods alongside the road at about a 45-degree angle. Behind him on the empty, sun-drenched road, the hellhound was making its way toward him with plodding but singleminded determination.

He put the car in gear and drove forward a few hundred yards, until he came abreast of a gravel driveway branching off the road, framed with trees. A cheery-looking sign read THE GUNDERSONS WELCOME YOU! The compass pointed straight off into the trees.

"Oz?"

No answer at all.

James turned onto the driveway. The boxelder and pin oak along the road gave way to ranked rows of apple trees, low and shrubby, stretching away on both sides. Beyond them, he glimpsed the top of a house, just visible over the trees.

Then the car's engine and all its electronics died abruptly. It coasted to a stop.

Well, shit. He cranked the key. There was a dry clicking, but nothing else.

James got out of the car. The orchard was very quiet. The narrow lane of the driveway showed no sign of anyone driving over it recently.

He hesitated with his fingertips on the compass's side buttons. From what Max had said, this stood a chance of giving his quarry a fix on his location. Balanced against that, he needed to know if his target was on the move.

He pressed the buttons. The needle rotated abruptly to point at about a thirty-degree angle to its previous heading. The bubble in the level was very nearly centered.

Great. His quarry was close . . . and moving.

And he'd just lost his wheels, his backup, and his air support.

"Still got you, though," James muttered, reloading the spellgun. The gun's charmed ammunition was expensive and rare, available only on the black market. He'd come out here with all the ammo he had, a full load of six cartridges in the gun and two more in his pocket. Now he had five shots left.

First things first. Get away from the car before he found himself at ground zero for a supernatural nuke. He could retreat, but it would mean going on foot, leaving the car, and there was no guarantee Oz could get to him on the main road either.

So he went forward, down one of the green lanes between the apple trees, spellgun in hand, moving as quietly as he knew how.

CHAPTER FIVE

IT WAS ALMOST UNNERVINGLY beautiful here. The sun was warm, the trees loaded with ripe and nearly ripe apples. But James jumped at every slight sound, the fall of a leaf or the rustle of what might be a bird or something worse.

There was some visibility between the tree trunks but not much. The compass still pointed off at an angle into the orchard. He didn't dare risk taking another reading. His head might as well have been on a swivel: behind, in front, off to the side.

There was little warning—a slight scuffing sound, perhaps. He whirled around in time to see one of the enormous hounds, either recovered or a different one, bounding at him in great leaps down the lane between the trees with its slavering jaws wide.

James fired at it. The shot was semi-wild, but the runes on the gun flared, and between one leap and the next, the creature came down not on solid ground, but on a gaping hole that hadn't been there an instant ago. The ground sealed up over it and he was alone.

"Wow," he whispered, staring at the perfectly untouched grass swaying gently in the wind. What *couldn't* this thing do?

Only four bullets left. Better hope Victorious didn't have an army of those things.

There was sunlight visible up ahead. James reached the edge of the orchard, and crouched in the shade of the apple trees, surveying the farm.

It was a peaceful, pastoral scene that met his eyes. A green expanse of lawn stretched to a white farmhouse with a panel truck in the driveway. GUNDERSON APPLE ORCHARDS was stenciled on the side. Behind the farmhouse was a barn and more ranks of orchard trees, rambling over gently rolling hills.

Nothing moved. There was no sign of Oz. He checked his phone: no reception.

Great.

He was preparing to move out when something soft and furtive fluttered in his pocket.

He nearly screamed, and jerked his hand up and away from his side. The feeling was a strange soft tugging against his jacket. Something was moving in his pocket, as if an insect had crawled inside.

And that was exactly what it was, he found out an instant later, when Prudence's electric blue butterfly crawled out of his pocket and took to the air on its delicate wings.

The butterfly would alert him to the stolen object, she'd said.

It fluttered through the sunlight, headed not for the house, but for the barn. James tried to keep his eyes on its dancing blue dot as he circled around the edge of the orchard, then used a corral fence for cover.

The farm remained dead quiet.

The butterfly vanished around the corner of the barn.

James followed with the gun at the ready—which turned

out to be a good thing when something enormous, scaly, and toothy erupted in his face. He squeezed the trigger on pure instinct, and a wave of cold washed over him as a great weight slammed into him. He was knocked to the side and landed painfully in the grass, while the huge creature (dragon? gargoyle?) crashed to the ground next to him.

There was a small giggle from nearby.

James rolled to sit up, twisting around so that he could point the gun in that direction, and then lowered it.

In the long grass beside the weathered clapboard wall of the barn, a little girl was sitting with her legs tucked under her. The butterfly was perched in her hair.

There was no sign of anyone else. James glanced warily at the enormous scaly heap of whatever-it-was. The gun had frozen it solid; the scales glistened with ice. Very slowly and carefully, he stood up.

The little girl didn't flinch or look afraid. Instead she held out her hand. "I want that," she said in a clear, childish voice.

James had no experience at estimating children's ages, but if he had to guess he'd say she was probably somewhere in the general three-to-six range. She looked like a normal child, not supernaturally beautiful, no fangs or horns or wings, just a cute and chubby little girl with brown hair past her shoulders. Her blue dress was richly embroidered in silver and gold, but it was torn and stained, smudged with dirt.

And the queenly stare she directed at James clearly announced that she expected to be obeyed.

"This is a gun," he said.

"Give it to me," the little girl ordered. "I want it."

"Yeah, no, it's dangerous. You can't have it."

"I said *give*," she wailed, and then her face screwed up and turned red.

"Jeez," James muttered, glancing around. There was still

no sign of anyone or anything nearby. The pastureland beside the barn sloped away gently to more apple trees, serene in the sunlight.

The little girl screamed at the top of her lungs.

"Jeez, kid, shut *up!*" James took a quick step forward, and then felt something like a soft punch in the back, and an abrupt shower of something prickly and powerfully pine-smelling cascaded off him.

James spun around, raising the gun. His feet slipped in heaps of pine needles all around his feet.

Victorious, instantly recognizable from his picture, was standing no more than twenty feet away at the edge of the corral fence. He wore black leather despite the heat of the day, and the hand upraised toward James was covered in some kind of glove that sparkled faintly as if covered in black rhinestones; his other hand was bare.

And he looked absolutely baffled.

"That should have gone through you like a knife through wet paper." Victorious had a lighter voice than his muscular build suggested. "What *are* you?"

"Immune to magic," James said. Only when he was holding the spellgun, but the fewer people who knew that part, the better.

But he'd *felt* that, which gave him an idea of how powerful that spell had been. Normally magic slid off him with barely a tingle.

Behind him, the little girl was still screaming.

"Nikki," Victorious said, raising his voice. "Nikki, are you hurt?"

The only answer was further enraged screams. The child threw herself down and ripped up handfuls of grass.

"I didn't hurt her," James said.

"I know. She does that." Victorious's tone was, for an instant, deeply weary. "What did you do to my guardians?"

James glanced toward the flash-frozen mound of scales, melting slowly in the sun. It was definitely something gargoyle-adjacent, built to elephantine proportions. "Only what I had to do to stop them from attacking me. No idea what my dragon is doing to the ones that are still out there, though." He could only imagine Oz's reaction to being referred to as anyone's dragon, but Oz wasn't here to defend himself.

"A dragon? Of course you brought a dragon. And how did you get through—no, if you have some form of magical immunity, the don't-notice-me wouldn't have worked on you." Victorious frowned, his fine-boned face growing pensive. "You must be a very powerful mage."

"Yes," James said solemnly. "Very powerful."

Nikki subsided to small whimpering sobs, lying facedown on the grass. Victorious went around James, giving him a wide berth and keeping him in sight at all times.

"Nikki." Victorious crouched beside her and placed his ungloved hand in the middle of her back. "Sit up, child. This is unseemly."

"He won't give me the *thing*," Nikki sniveled into the grass.

"Here, child, have a sweet," Victorious murmured, producing a box from his pocket.

Nikki sat up, covered in grass, her face wet with tears and snot. She took the chocolates he handed her and stuffed them into her mouth.

"Hey," James said, taking a step forward. "What are those going to do to her?"

Victorious gave him an exasperated look. "They are chocolate. Don't you have chocolate here?"

"They're not drugged, or fairy food, disappears by the light of dawn . . ."

"It's broad daylight," Victorious said.

Nikki leaned against him, worn out from her tantrum,

but the way she drooped onto his leather-clad arm spoke of trust. Victorious stroked her hair, then jerked his hand away as if stung.

"What is this?"

He carefully plucked something from her hair with the gloved hand and held it up. The electric blue butterfly was pinched between his thumb and forefinger. Victorious's face twisted, and he squeezed it in a quick, convulsive motion, crushing it.

"You're working for *her*. One of her mercenaries. Of course you are."

The gloved hand snapped out, and James couldn't decide whether to brace or dodge or run. Instinct took over and he ended up trying to dodge and run at the same time, tangling up his feet. As he went down, he felt something whiplash against his neck and race down his arm with an electric crackling sting.

James rolled to his feet and scrambled back a few steps. He'd never actually tested the limits of the spellgun's ability to protect him from magical attacks, and wasn't even sure if it had limits—but if it did, fae magic was probably the thing that would do it. His arm tingled fiercely from shoulder to fingertips. He switched the gun to the other hand.

Victorious was still crouched on the ground with Nikki nestled against his side, gloved hand outstretched. "And *that* should have spread your head in a fine red mist from here to the road. Yet," he added, his voice turning curious, "you walked in here openly. What do you want?"

"I was hired by a lady who calls herself Prudence to retrieve something for her." James nodded to Nikki. "She didn't tell me what it was. Guess now I know. What does she want with the kid?"

"She will not have her."

"Not saying she will. I'm just curious why."

Victorious lowered his hand slowly, frowning at James. "You know, I am starting to believe you, if only because it is such a ridiculous lie I can't imagine that anyone would try. You really don't know?"

"Listen, Michael Jackson, I never met Prudence before two days ago, never wanted to meet her, and wouldn't be here if she'd given me a choice about it. All she said was that you stole something from her and she wanted it back." Nikki had fallen asleep, drooling, in Victorious's lap. "What *is* she? Why is she important? She looks like a normal kid."

"She is," Victorious said. "Do you know what changelings are?"

"I thought that was a myth."

He shook his head. "It's not that common anymore, but it still happens."

James carefully sat on the grass; talking to someone who was sitting down was giving him a crick in his neck. He laid the hand with the spellgun in his lap, keeping it pointed in Victorious's general direction.

"So she was kidnapped from her real parents?"

"She was taken as an infant," Victorious said. "She doesn't remember her parents. The Summerlands are all she knows."

"Still not explaining why you re-kidnapped her." Oh. Wait. "Are you returning her to her parents?"

"What? Of course not," Victorious snapped. "They don't even remember her."

"Right, okay, that's not fucked up at all . . . So you fae take kids from their parents, take them through the Veil, and—what happens to them then?"

"They are pets," Victorious said quietly, stroking Nikki's hair. "Pampered, spoiled, indulged. The woman you know as Prudence found Nikki very entertaining. But fae grow easily bored. A toy is only valuable until its owner ceases to find it fun and pretty."

He hesitated, and adjusted the sleeping child to a more comfortable position in his lap, resting his gloved hand on her head.

"I am—or I should say, I *was* the horsemaster of Prudence's guard. Keeping the stables for the Wild Hunt is no mean feat. But it was then to me that the care and feeding of her living toy also fell. I had never met a human before, let alone a human child." He was quiet for a moment, looking down at the little girl. "Fae do not have children often, and rarely in the normal human way. Our children are not like human children. We are born, or made, with a good deal of our adult abilities already. This is why human children fascinate us so. Prudence greatly enjoyed playing the role of mother to Nikki, but whenever she wearied of her, which was often, she gave her to me until she wished to see her again."

"What happens to Nikki if she goes back?" James asked quietly.

"Most likely nothing bad, for a time. Prudence always covets that which she does not have—fae are like that—so losing Nikki will have renewed her interest for a while. A few days, a few months. But her patience with the child was already growing short." He lifted the hair away from Nikki's sleeping face. "Step closer. She won't wake."

"You did drug her," James said tightly. He rose—Victorious tensed—and kept the gun out, arm loose at his side, as he took a couple of cautious steps forward.

"I wished to talk to you without her hearing," Victorious said. He lightly brushed the child's tear-stained cheek with his fingertips. "See here."

The scars were parallel stripes, such as long fingernails might have scored. They just missed the edge of Nikki's eye, vanishing next to her ear.

"It is a short and not altogether pleasant life for Prudence's favorites," Victorious said quietly.

James looked down at both of them, jaw clenched. "What's in it for you, then? You stole her out of pure kindness?"

"Don't be such a cynic. There is kindness in us, sometimes."

"Yeah, I haven't had much to do with fae, but I know what I've heard, and I haven't seen much so far to think it's wrong."

"And do you always believe everything you hear?" Victorious smiled thinly. "Though, to be fair . . . I don't know myself why it mattered so much. I threw everything over for this worthless brat, my position at court and my lady's favor. And now here I am, run to ground by some common human ruffian."

"Hey."

"Run to earth, cornered, and grasping at straws." He laid an arm across the child's sleeping body, and as he looked up from his position on the ground, it occurred to James in shocked realization that Victorious was afraid of him.

Victorious had no idea how powerful James was, or what else he could do.

In all honesty, neither did James. The spellgun could incapacitate Victorious, but he had no control over how it did it, or what the effects were. It could easily be lethal; sometimes it was. It also might not work on elder fae the same way it did on lesser magical creatures, in which case he was only going to get one opportunity to find out.

And if he took Nikki by force, what then? Take her back to Prudence, the woman who had left those scars on the child's face?

"Fuck," James muttered. He kicked at a tuft of grass. "Okay, tell me something. That blue butterfly—does Prudence know where I am now?"

"Probably not precisely." Victorious watched him with a wary gaze. His eyes were faintly silver, catching the light. "The spells I've raised around this place should confound even her formidable abilities, else she could have found me without needing the help of human hirelings. But she will have a much better idea of where to look."

"Great." James glanced up at the vivid blue sky, which now seemed slightly threatening, as if a fae air strike might fall on them at any time. "Look, can we talk in a place where there's something to sit on other than grass? And I wouldn't mind having my dragon here."

"Your dragon? I don't think so."

"He's also my secretary."

Victorious gave him a long, thoughtful look, then scooped up Nikki and rose gracefully to his feet. "Your dragon must stay wherever he is, but you may come with me."

CHAPTER SIX

INSIDE, the farmhouse was cozy and homy, cluttered to the gills with toys, games, and books. James chose not to holster the spellgun, carrying it instead lowered beside his leg, where he could have it up in an instant if he needed to.

But no danger threatened. The house lay still and quiet in a sleepy afternoon silence; dust motes floated in the sunlight shafting in through the curtains. Victorious swept some toys onto the floor to make space and laid Nikki on the living room couch. He carefully covered her with a knit afghan that had been thrown sloppily across the couch back.

"What did you do to her, anyway?"

"A simple sleep spell." Victorious moved a couple of open jigsaw puzzle boxes from the end of the couch and sat down by Nikki's feet. "It won't hurt her." He reached for a box of tissues on the coffee table and began to clean up her face.

James had to move some toy cars and video game cartridges from a chair so that he had a place to sit. There were toys scattered everywhere, on the floor and the furniture, and items of kids' clothing that looked clean and unworn, in contrast to Nikki's torn blue and gold dress.

He fingered one of the toy cars. It was a chunky baby toy, clearly not belonging to whatever child had owned the video games or the jigsaw puzzles. There were some dolls on the coffee table, next to cartridges for games like *Grand Theft Auto*. Few of the children's clothes were even close to Nikki's size; there were a bunch of baby things and some jeans and shirts sized to fit a teenager.

"What happened to the people who lived here?"

Victorious looked up sharply. For a moment he didn't answer.

"If they're dead," James said, "the odds of me helping you just dropped. A lot."

"*Helping* me, are you." Victorious dabbed his tongue on the tissue and wiped a smudge off Nikki's cheek with a distinctly parental air.

"I'm thinking about it. But I'm not going to leave you loose on Earth to go around killing people."

"They're in the basement," Victorious said. "We fae are not indiscriminate killers, no matter what you think of us; what point would there be? They are sleeping, as she is. But much more deeply. They will not age or come to harm in that state."

"You realize I'll have to verify that."

"Be my guest." Victorious gestured. "The basement door is that one by the stairs."

James looked, and couldn't stop a reflexive flinch when a shadow by the basement door turned out to be one of those enormous hounds, sitting so rock-still that he hadn't even seen it. But it was alive and aware. Its gleaming liquid eyes turned briefly toward him, and one ear twitched.

"It won't bother you," Victorious said. He wadded up the tissue and dropped it on the floor. No wonder the house looked like a hurricane had hit it. "Unless you do anything to threaten me, that is."

James edged carefully around the dog. It was shaped like a giant wolfhound, with a long straight muzzle and floppy ears, but it was a dead pitch black that seemed to absorb all the light in the room. Even up close, it was like a silhouette of a dog.

Steep stairs led down to a partly finished basement that looked like it was used as a game room. There was a big-screen TV, a pool table, and some couches. And there was a family of six, fast asleep. Mom, Dad, and the kiddies, plus Grandma. They lay on the carpeted basement floor in various uncomfortable-looking positions, but they all had pulses and were breathing. Feeling deeply weird about the whole thing, James moved Grandma's arm to a less awkward angle and put a blanket over Mom and the baby before he went back upstairs.

The dog didn't appear to have moved, and it remained statue-still as James maneuvered around it going the other way. Only its eyes followed him.

Victorious was where James had left him, on the couch with Nikki, lightly stroking her hair. A steaming mug had appeared on the coffee table during James's absence. "Refreshments," Victorious said, nodding to it.

"Yeah, no." James perched on the edge of the chair, his skin crawling with unease.

"Are you reassured as to their condition?"

"I'll be more reassured when they wake up."

"Then you will remain unreassured for a while longer."

James checked the load in the gun, not that his three bullets were going to multiply, but it was mostly just so Victorious could see him doing it. "Any more of those dogs around?"

"I'll tell you of my defenses as soon as you tell me about yours."

"Fair enough." James hoped Oz was doing okay out there.

In all likelihood the dragon was simply flying around in frustration, trying to find the place through the obfuscation spells protecting it.

"So tell me something else, then," Victorious said. He sat back on the couch and pulled Nikki's head into his lap. "Does Prudence have you under a compulsion?"

There seemed to be no reason not to answer honestly. "Not exactly," James said. "She made a bargain with me, and didn't give me much choice about taking it."

Victorious smiled thinly. "What *exactly* did you agree to do for her? Were you only to find us, or was there more?"

"I'm supposed to bring back the item she said you stole from her, which I guess would be Nikki."

"Hmm." He smoothed back the child's hair. "Precision matters a great deal with us."

"So I've been told."

"Do you remember if she said where you were to bring Nikki? To her? To the Summerlands?"

"Uh . . ." He had been unable to retrieve the exact words when talking to Oz about it, but it was like jogging a witness's memory—asking specific questions could bring forth half-forgotten details. James ran his thoughts back to the dark basement, and Prudence shining in the darkness, brilliant and cold. The butterflies with their feet tickling her arms and face, the chill precision of her eyes on him. "She said she wanted me to find and return it. Her. Nikki."

"Return it . . . to her? To Prudence?"

"Well, that part's implied." James met Victorious's silvery eyes, saw the sharp flash there. "Or is it?"

"Not necessarily." Victorious looked down at the little girl's sleeping face. "To return something is to take it back where it was before. Where it belongs. And there is somewhere else she belongs: with her human parents."

In the silence that followed, the refrigerator compressor

came on with a sudden hum. Both Victorious and the hellhound guarding the basement door flinched. It was only the slightest movement, barely perceptible, but it was a sign of how on edge they all were. James's nerves seemed to be vibrating like a plucked guitar string.

"Would that actually work?" James asked.

"If you're right about what she said, it ought to."

"But that's not even slightly what she had in mind."

"It doesn't matter what she had in mind," Victorious said. "It matters what she asked for. *Exactly* what she asked for."

"What's to stop Pru from just snatching the kid away from the real parents?"

"She can't," Victorious said. "She made a bargain. Once the child is back where she belongs, Prudence can't touch her."

"Really."

"She has no choice. We are not like you. And of course," he added, with something vaguely like a smile, "we rely on humans not knowing that."

That hung in the air between them for a minute.

"What about the parents?" James said. "Will they go along with it? You said they didn't remember her."

"They don't," Victorious said, "but that's because they don't realize she was ever taken at all. We leave a replacement behind."

"A . . . child? But I thought you said the fae don't have—"

"Not a real child." Victorious's tone was impatient. "We make a simulacrum of a child from a tree branch or a stone, and leave it with the parents in place of the old one."

"You know, new parents can be sleep-deprived, but I'm pretty sure they'd notice their baby is now a rock."

Victorious gave him a look of deep exasperation. "It looks and behaves like a baby. It just isn't one. Usually the new baby will appear to die, withering as it is separated from its parent tree, or simply crumbling back into sand. Or the parents will realize what it truly is and abandon it."

"Great. So they think their baby died, and now you're going to show up with this kid and explain that their baby didn't die, she was taken by fairies."

"You don't think they'll accept her?"

"I don't know," James said with a sigh. "Oh hell, yeah I do. I don't have kids, but I guess most parents wouldn't look a gift miracle in the mouth if it meant their child returning to them safe and sound."

"Wouldn't look a—"

"Human saying. Well, sort of."

Victorious said nothing, only looked down at Nikki and continued to stroke her hair. James sat in silence for a moment, the gun dangling down beside his knee. The refrigerator compressor clicked off. Otherwise the house was almost entirely quiet, devoid of all the usual sounds that should have gone with the warm, family-oriented decor, voices and laughter and a television playing in the background.

James's childhood home had been nothing like this. There was still some deeply buried part of him that ached for it.

"What about you?" he asked at last. "Are you willing to hand her over?"

"Do I have a choice?" It was a gently rhetorical question; Victorious seemed to speak more to himself than to James. "Prudence will find me sooner or later . . . most likely sooner, as it has taken her only a few days this time. I can't win against her. At least this way, the child will be safe."

James was not at all confident about that, but hell, if it got him out from under Butterfly Lady's thumb without turning the kid over to her, he was willing to risk it. They'd have some breathing room, at least. "Right. Got any idea where her parents live?"

"None at all. I was not involved with the original theft."

James glanced down at the compass on his wrist. The needle was swinging idly now, its purpose fulfilled. "Do you know how to do a tracking spell?"

"Oh, *that*? A trivial matter."

"One other condition," James said, and Victorious raised an eyebrow. "I am *not* calling you Victorious. First of all, it's definitely not a human name, which means anyone who overhears me talking to you is going to know something's off. And also, I feel ridiculous."

Victorious's silver eyes narrowed. "Feel free to suggest another option."

"Vic," James said. "From here on out, you're Vic."

CHAPTER SEVEN

IT WAS A VERY different experience setting out from the Gunderson farm in the Trans Am with two passengers, one curious fae who had clearly never ridden in a car before and one extremely fidgety and upset child in the backseat.

"I do not see why we can't simply ride your dragon," Vic said, struggling with the seat buckle after James explained it to him.

"I am not *his* dragon," Oz declared coldly. He was sitting on his haunches with one clawed paw resting firmly and possessively on the trunk of the Trans Am. "And your ilk may not ride me *anywhere*."

"That's why," James said.

"I hate this," Nikki announced from the backseat. "Take me home."

Vic had awakened her back at the house to pack a few things—the Gundersons' things, technically, since they had fled the fae realm with nothing but the clothes they were wearing, but James had decided to pick his battles. Then she'd cried and screamed all the way down the driveway to the car, wanting to go back, saying she was hungry, complaining about one thing or another that she wanted—James had had to stop Vic several times from going back to pick up specific toys she wanted to bring. By now the family would be waking up back at the house. James had hung around long enough to see them begin to stir before he'd gone to join the others at the car.

"Are you well back there, little one?" Vic asked, twisting around in the seat.

"No!" Nikki screamed at the top of her lungs, and kicked the seat in front of her, which happened to belong to James. "I hate you!"

"Can't you put her to sleep again?"

"I will if I must, but I think she'll like the journey. She has been so few places." Vic leaned between the seats. "We're going for a ride, little one. You'll like it."

"I want to go *home*!"

"Me too," James muttered, and checked the compass. Vic's renewed charm had been nothing like Max's workmanlike magic. Vic had simply passed his gloved hand over the compass and concentrated for a moment, and now it was pointing in a southerly direction. "You need to collect any of your, er, guardians before we take off?"

"They are here," Vic said. He opened his gloved hand, displaying a collection of toys in his palm. They appeared to be carved of glossy wood. James glimpsed a couple of dogs and a horse before Vic closed his hand over them and put it in his pocket.

"Right. Let's roll."

They left the farm behind, with Oz's shadow passing over them now and then. Other traffic slowly began to reappear, occasional cars or farm trucks passing, and the road was busy again by the time they merged onto the freeway.

"So what are the odds Prudence is tracking us now?"

James asked, trying to ignore Nikki steadily kicking the back of his seat.

"I crushed the butterfly, so that will help, and I still have a few concealment spells on us. They are less effective when one is moving, but . . ." Vic's smile was fierce. "A moving target is also more difficult to hit."

"Comforting." James glanced at the gloved hand resting in Vic's lap. "Is that the only weapon you've got?"

"Oh, are we having that discussion about mutual defenses after all?" Vic's gaze, in turn, went to the spellgun. James had left the gunbelt on and prominently displayed, despite the discomfort of driving like that.

"I'm mainly concerned about not being turned into fae flambé."

"By me, or by Prudence?"

"Given that I'd be equally dead either way, I don't see that there's a big difference."

"I don't intend to harm you," Vic said.

"That's nice, but keep in mind there's a dragon overhead who'd be pissed if anything happened to me, and also, I'm driving a metal death machine at seventy miles an hour."

"It would be nice if killing you would fix my problems, but it won't." Vic gazed out the window at the passing fields, golden with late summer wheat. "One immediate problem, certainly. But Prudence will only try again, perhaps with someone less obvious, or more ruthless."

"Thanks, I think."

As the miles slipped away, James realized that the kicking had slowed and then stopped entirely. Also, there had been a surprising lack of complaints for the last few minutes. He glanced into the backseat in the hopes that Nikki had fallen asleep. Instead she was pale-faced and hunched over.

"Shit." He veered onto the shoulder. Vic clutched at the door.

"What is it? Are we in danger?"

"No, I think she's carsick." James wrenched open his door, started to fold his seat forward—there were no rear doors—and then realized he had absolutely no desire to handle a carsick child when her caretaker was *right there*. "Your seat comes down—yeah, like that—"

"She does this in carriages as well." Despite his haste, Vic's hands were gentle on the shivering child. "That's it, you're going to be all right. Do you have water in the car?"

"Yeah." James fetched a water bottle, as Oz thumped down on the highway shoulder behind them.

"What is it? Where are they? I shall fight—"

"No fighting, everyone is fine. The kid's sick, that's all."

Vic and Nikki sat on the grassy margin that sloped down into the ditch. She didn't seem to be actively ill, just limp and unhappy, draped against her caretaker's side. James handed the bottle of water over Vic's shoulder.

"Can you drink some of this, little one? Small sips. It's just like those times you feel unwell at court."

"No," Nikki mumbled, but she obediently took a couple of sips. Vic wet a handkerchief and wiped her sweaty forehead, then snugged an arm around her and held her close. It caught and hooked in James's chest, the trust on her pale face and the obvious care and affection in the way Vic handled her.

He turned his back on them and wandered back up to the shoulder, where some of the passing motorists were slowing to snap phone pictures of Oz—who was posing, wings raised.

"I never knew you had such a vain side."

Oz lowered his wings carefully, folding them along his back. He had one foot in the ditch, but was still perilously close to traffic. "You'd think they've never seen a dragon before."

"I told you, dragons aren't common around here. Not outside the cities, and not this far south."

"Provincials," Oz sniffed.

"Snob." James sat on the hood of the car. From the grassy verge came the sound of Vic speaking softly and soothingly to Nikki, too low to make out the words.

"I quite relate to your dislike of him, you know," Oz said, leaning in to mutter in a deep basso mumble that could probably be heard at a distance even over the traffic noise. Oz's idea of a whisper usually wasn't.

"I don't dislike him," James said. "I mean, I don't *trust* him, but . . . why do you have it in for the fae, anyway?"

Oz drew his head up in indignation, neck ruff flaring. "It's the *car*, James. Haven't you seen what he did to your car? Philistine," he grumbled in Vic's general direction.

Vic's shoulders stiffened and he turned to look over his shoulder.

"I would be quite happy to challenge your creature to a duel, James, when this business is concluded."

"His—what? Yes," Oz snapped. He reared up on his hind legs and stretched out his wings, causing a string of cars to veer wildly into the left lane to avoid him. "I accept."

"No you don't! No one is dueling anyone. God," James muttered. "Look, we need to get the kid back in the car. I know you don't want to knock her out, but I don't really think we have a choice if we want to make any progress today."

"I know," Vic said, and he stood up, lifting Nikki with him, her head cradled against his shoulder. He laid her carefully in the backseat.

The afternoon slid away under the Trans Am's wheels. They were driving through Iowa now, mile upon mile of green-gold farmland. James glimpsed Oz now and then, far out across the table-flat landscape, his shadow flickering across the corn and soybeans like a small low-scudding cloud. The compass pointed steadily south.

Vic was quiet, keeping his thoughts to himself, the hand with the glove curled loosely on his thigh. James listened to the radio, flicking from one classic rock station to another when he could find them. Mostly it was country and NPR out here.

"You know," he said, "I wasn't expecting you to be this reasonable about it."

Vic glanced sideways at him, a flick of silver eyes. "Because I am fae?"

"No—yes—I don't know. You're obviously attached to that girl."

"So I shouldn't want to let her go?"

"It would be understandable."

Vic said nothing for another ten miles or so. At last he said, "It is tempting, to have and to keep. But I didn't take her from the Summerlands so that I could hold onto her as if she were my own possession. It has become clear to me over the last few days that I don't know how to raise a human child. She should be with her own kind."

"Human parenthood doesn't come with an instruction manual either. I don't think you're doing too bad."

Vic grimaced.

"Well, okay, I mean she's an intolerable brat who could really use a bath, but she's only, what, five or six? I'm guessing she'd settle down a lot if she had more of . . ." James shrugged. "Whatever parents do, I'm not one. Structure. Schoolwork. Kids her own age."

"None of which I have any idea how to provide for her."

There was nothing he could really say to that. Vic was right, was the thing. Human parents might have to start out on beginner mode, but at least they had the instincts for it, and the cultural expectations for it, and their own memories of growing up. What kind of parenting could you hope for from a race of ageless, powerful beings with no children of their own?

Yeah? said a deeply buried corner of James's mind. *He's better at it than your parents were, and you know it.*

"Hey, listen," James said, and Vic's silver eyes flicked his way again. "Looks like we're a ways out yet, and I'm getting hungry. The kid hasn't ever been to a restaurant in her life, has she?"

⌁

THEY GOT TAKEOUT from an Applebee's, because James doubted it was a good idea to try to deal with Nikki in a sit-down dining situation. There was a small park area with some picnic tables, and they sat there to eat, while Oz, who claimed he wasn't hungry, stretched out along the edge of the parking lot like some kind of baroque ornamental wall. Most people passing by appeared to take him for one. Every once in a while James saw one of them do a violent double take when Oz blinked or twitched a wing.

Nikki turned out to be surprisingly subdued and polite when she was getting what she wanted, in this case a helping of nearly everything from the kids' menu: a corn dog (that Vic eyed dubiously), chicken strips, fries, a mini-cheese-burger, and a kid-sized slice of pizza.

"I want to feed your dragon," Nikki said, and Oz stirred and cracked open an eye.

"I'm not his dragon," he rumbled.

Nikki grabbed a handful of chicken strips and hopped down from the bench. Vic reached out to pull her back.

"It's okay," James said. "He's good with kids." Actually he had no idea if that was true, he'd never even *seen* Oz with kids, but at the very least he trusted Oz not to eat one.

He did have a moment of doubt when Nikki trotted up to Oz's enormous head, which put in perspective just how much bigger the dragon was, and how easy it would be for the child to disappear between those great jaws. Oz lifted a lip, baring huge fangs, and James wondered if the dragon was aware of Vic's battle-ready posture, the gloved hand half raised. But Oz was only opening his mouth a little, providing a tiny aperture so she could stick her fistful of chicken nuggets fearlessly between those huge teeth. Vic was perfectly still, rigid with tension, and James held his breath, watching Vic more than Oz.

Nikki jerked her hand away and dashed back to Vic, giggling. Oz made an elaborate show of chewing and swallowing what for him must have been an almost imperceptibly tiny snack. He raised his head politely so that he could dip it to Nikki, causing a minor fender-bender elsewhere in the parking lot. "That was most flavorful, young lady."

Nikki giggled again and hid her face against Vic's leg.

~

IT WAS EARLY EVENING, and Nikki was asleep again in the backseat, when the compass—which had been trending south-southwest for the last hour—swung gradually around to point to the side.

They had just passed an exit for a town called Bennett. James took the next exit, and found a state route going west. The setting sun glared in his eyes, painting the world in shades of orange and gold.

"Have you thought about what you're going to say to them?" he asked.

"The truth," Vic said. He glanced into the backseat. "I see no benefit in lying."

"You're just going to tell them their kid was abducted by fairies."

"If you can think of a better story in the next twenty minutes, please do share it."

The compass needle changed angle again. James turned onto a road that ran string-straight toward a water tower and grain elevator, silhouetted against the brilliant evening sky. The needle pointed off to the side at a steep angle, and James found a side road that took him through the outskirts of a small town, driving on cracked pavement between small, tidy ranch houses.

The road dead-ended at a little park beside a pond. There were a number of people out and about in the balmy evening air: couples wandering hand in hand, parents watching their kids play, a few people fishing at the edge of the water. What passed for a parking lot was more like the grassy edge of a field. James parked among the trucks and SUVs.

The car's engine pinged in the abrupt silence. He looked down at the compass, pointing steadily into the park, and got out of the car.

The air was warm and mild. There was no sign of Oz. James turned back to see Vic getting Nikki's sleeping form out of the backseat. With Nikki's head propped against his shoulder, Vic followed James. His calm was starting to crack; he looked nervous.

The compass pointed toward the pond. There were some trucks pulled onto the grass until they were almost at the water's edge, with teenagers in the truck beds, laughing and chatting with each other. Nearby, a small playground featured bright-colored equipment, all but gleaming in the growing dusk. As the sun slipped below the table-flat edge of the world, parents had begun gathering in their children.

It hadn't occurred to James that the family might have other kids, but the needle was indisputably pointing that way. There were only a couple of families left now. A harried-looking pair of moms were collecting several small kids off the monkeybars. The needle didn't point that way; it was aimed at the playground's edge, where a woman sat on a bench with a small child beside her.

As James got closer, he saw that the woman was pointing to objects, one at a time. "What is that? Cloud," she was saying. "What is that? Swing. Oooh!" She pointed at herself. "Who am I?"

The child sat with her legs tucked under the bench and her arms curled against her chest, and didn't look like she was listening much, but at this she looked up and broke into a toothy grin. "Mama."

"That's *right!*" the mom said, grinning back, her face lit up. The girl's whole body curled up in a spasm of joy, and her mom bumped noses with her, eliciting another full-body delighted squirm and a little squeal.

There was another bench nearby, and James sat on the far end, leaving enough space that the mother barely glanced at him.

The little girl was obviously Nikki.

She was well cared for, clean and neat. Her hair was pulled into two pigtails, but it was the same silky brown hair. Those were the same soft little arms and legs, though she had them curled up as if she wasn't quite sure how to hold them.

And it was the same face, even if there was a slight vacancy in her eyes and a tendency for her gaze to drift away from her mother. Her slightly detached gaze drifted over James, snagged for a moment—he smiled at her, and she gave a little tug of her mouth in return, almost reflexive, and kept looking, just looking at the world. Her gaze floated past Vic, who had stopped at the end of the bench, holding Nikki and staring in shock.

"Oh look, there's Daddy with the car," the mom said. She scooped up the other Nikki and kissed her forehead. "Let's go home and have a snack. Snack?"

"Snack!" the girl said, and curled up against her mom, with the same trusting affection that Nikki—Vic's Nikki—showed for him.

The mother walked away, carrying her child. James sat for a moment. He wasn't sure what to do. Dusk was gathering now, and the kids at the trucks had broken out flashlights and looked like they were kindling a bonfire.

"So about that changeling thing, Vic . . ."

"It's not supposed to work like this!" Vic's composure had deserted him; he looked near panic. "They *die*! They're not real children."

"Really? You sure about that? Did you ever go back and check afterwards?"

Vic plunked down on the other end of the bench, adjusting Nikki automatically in his arms. James twisted around to follow the other Nikki and her mom to the parking area, where a small SUV waited for them. The dad had the door open and was rummaging around in the back. Mom set down the other Nikki and they started buckling her into some sort of complicated contraption.

Oh right, kids that age were supposed to have a car seat; he'd forgotten about that.

"She was made from a willow branch," Vic said softly. "There's someone at court who makes the finest changelings from his own private willow grove, and Prudence commissioned him because she wanted the best. I saw it . . . the changeling . . . before they took it through the Veil. It was a perfectly formed baby-like doll, but when next I saw Nikki, the real one, I realized the difference. The real one was so much more animated. She screamed all the time. The fake one had been so quiet. It never made a sound. It didn't even want to eat."

"*She* seemed pretty animated to me," James said. He followed the progress of the SUV as it backed out of the parking field and turned around on the small road. "I mean, she's obviously a little bit . . . delayed, but you'd never think she wasn't an ordinary human child."

"But they *die*!" Vic said. There was a desperate edge to his voice, as if he needed to convince himself too. "We make them for ourselves too, you know. But they never really come to life. They don't grow properly. They don't cry. Maybe they last six months, or a year. But they never last *that* long. Always, they wither and fade."

"Maybe it's not them," James said. "Maybe it's you." He twisted back around on the bench, to look at Vic with Nikki draped across his lap. "Perhaps, with loving parents, they actually *do* turn into real children. Perhaps they always have."

"But," Vic said blankly. He looked down at Nikki, his face a mix of fear and horror that was uncomfortable to look at.

"We could always give her back anyway," James pointed out. "They could raise them as twins."

"No!" The word was barked out. Vic took a breath and modulated his tone. "If there is already a Nikki here, then her place is taken already. She doesn't *belong* here."

"Think maybe her parents would feel differently about that? Might be a good idea to ask them."

"I mean magically." Vic shifted Nikki's weight in his lap, her head drooping against his shoulder. "Our entire solution to this problem was based upon putting her back as if she was never gone. If we leave her here now, with her place already filled, Prudence can take her back with impunity."

"Do you know that for sure? Because, not to keep harping on this, but you were wrong about the changeling thing, and this is a *lot* to hang on the exact dictionary definition of 'return'."

Vic took another deep breath and released it through his nose. With each word bitten out precisely, he said, "I am not willing to risk Nikki's life on the chance that it won't work."

It was almost fully dark now. Firelight, flashlights, and headlights gleamed from the direction of the teenagers' pondside party, and someone was playing music with a heavy beat. When Oz landed behind the benches, darkness had swallowed the park so completely that only a few people looked over at the loud thump and the firelight catching on Oz's scales. He mantled and then folded his wings.

"I hope that I am not stating the obvious, and perhaps you've already noticed," he said. "But you still appear to be in possession of a child."

"Thanks," James said. "Hey, you remember back at the start of all this, when I asked if you could find me an expert on fae bargains?"

"I haven't had an opportunity to—"

"I know, I know, but I think it might've just jumped to the top of my priorities. Is there such a thing as a fae contract lawyer?"

"I hope for your sake you didn't sign anything," Vic said.

"No, I didn't sign anything, do you think I'm a—okay, don't answer that."

"Perhaps you *should* have had it in writing," Oz said. "That way you would have the exact terms at hand."

Vic flicked his firelit eyes up to the dragon. "I don't suppose *you* know the exact words of the bargain he made."

"No! I wasn't there, and he can't remember, not with the necessary degree of precision. It is quite vexing."

Dragon and fae shared a rare look of commiseration.

"You're seriously ganging up on me?" James said in disbelief. "Great. Hey, Vic—while we're figuring out our next move, you could probably wake her up and let her run off a little energy on the monkeybars."

"That's a good point. I don't like leaving her asleep this long anyway." Vic blew on Nikki's brow, and her eyes snapped open. She gave a little gasp and sat up.

"We are at a place of human playthings," Vic said. "Do you like it?"

"Humans make their places *dark*." Nikki said it casually, as if she wasn't human herself, and squinted into the night. "The lights are pretty. I want some."

"I have lights." Vic raised his gauntleted hand, and light flickered around it in firefly glimmers, spreading and flowing, casting rainbow reflections on the playground equipment, on Oz's scales and James's compass watch. The light played across Nikki's fascinated face and reflected in her wide-open eyes.

"What do you want to see, little one?"

"Make a dragon," Nikki said in a rapt voice.

Vic twisted his fingers like someone making a shadow puppet. And it was a shadow puppet that took flight off his fingertips, but one made of rainbow light. Crude and unformed at first, it took on detail and dimension, until it was a perfectly formed miniature dragon that swooped around their heads, making Nikki giggle. It ducked in to swipe its claws through James's hair—he felt something, not physical exactly, but a sort of tingling—and dived at Oz's head.

"A derivative facsimile of the original," Oz scoffed. He held himself still with resolute dignity as the dragon-in-miniature swooped through his head and out the other side, then flew back in and came out his nostril.

Nikki was half in hysterics with laughter, wriggling with delight until she started to slide out of Vic's lap. Smiling, he caught her with one arm and pulled her back up, while the fingers of his other hand moved in small gestures, controlling the dragon of light.

James laid his arm along the back of the bench. The night was beginning to cool, running chill fingers up his spine. It wasn't fully autumn yet, but it was starting to feel like it.

"What options do we have?" he asked, and Vic looked over as more creatures danced off his fingers, small winged horses and dogs that moved in liquid leaps.

"Options? Run, I suppose." Vic flicked his fingers, banishing the creatures. Nikki set up a banshee whine. "No, dear, no more creatures for you now."

"But I *want*—"

"Nikki." He took her by the shoulders and gave her a small shake. "My sweet, we are in *danger*. We are not at court anymore. You cannot have all the things you used to have."

Nikki began to cry, not a scream this time, but a tiny, helpless sobbing. Vic pulled her against him and looked at James over her head. "Why are you helping us?" he asked quietly. "All you have to do to be free of Prudence is to turn us in."

"To be completely honest, I'm not actually sure."

"It is because he is a decent and honorable man," Oz declared from above James's head.

"You can tell he hasn't worked with me very long," James told Vic. "Look, I'm a pragmatist. I know Prudence's type. They give you a little job, you do it, and the next time it's a bigger job, and you don't have any choice in that one either. Helping you two get away might make her think twice about making a deal with me next time."

"Justification," Oz coughed.

"Did I ask you?"

"Your reasoning makes sense," Vic said. "I simply don't know how—"

Something fluttered out of the sky, dropping lightly onto Vic's hair, like a falling leaf. He reached up and plucked it off.

It was a butterfly.

Soft wings brushed James's ear. The butterfly that had landed on Vic was the advance scout for a multitude that came tumbling out of the night, whirling around the benches and the playground equipment. Oz snapped instinctively at the swarm. James scrambled to his feet and drew the gun, while insectile wings and feet tickled his hands and face. It was like being caught in a sudden swirl of autumn leaves, and then, just as suddenly, the butterflies all settled on the backs of the benches, on the grass, on Oz's scales and the shoulders of James's jacket.

And the Wild Hunt came out of the dark.

CHAPTER EIGHT

THEY WERE ALL MOUNTED, but only a few rode horses. Some were mounted on great stags, some on tigers, some on elephant-sized Ice Age megafauna or even stranger creatures bristling with spikes and extra limbs.

The riders were as diverse as their mounts. Most of them wore light armor of leather, metal, or wood. Some had horned helmets; some wore skulls; some had long braids, or swirling cascades of unbound hair. They were every color that a human could be, and a few that humans couldn't.

Their leader rode a monumental black horse with not just one unicorn horn, but two, twisting and black, arranged in a line like a rhino's. The rider was built to match the horse, a massive slab of a woman, with one broad, scarred hand lightly resting on the reins and the other holding a spear that lay alongside her leg against the horse's shoulders, pointing forward. Branching elk's antlers rose from her helmet.

She brought the horse to a halt in front of them. The rest of the riders ranged out around them. Oz turned in place, wings half spread, trying to decide which direction presented the most threat. James had to push against the dragon's scaly flank to avoid being crushed as Oz tried to get in front of him.

Vic stood up slowly, holding Nikki. The child was utterly silent, petrified.

"Really, Valor?" Vic said, looking up at the woman on the horse. "Against *me?*"

The woman shrugged, rippling her massive shoulders. Her scaled armor caught the light whenever she moved.

Oz made a hissing sound like a boiling-over kettle. "You are wearing dragonskin."

James had never heard that tone from him before. It was low and bitter and dark. A soft light kindled around Oz's mouth: the glow of dragonfire, blue with orange tints like an old gas stove.

"Yes, it is," Valor agreed. She thwacked one hand against her scaled and well-muscled thigh. "Best for deflecting almost anything, dragonskin, from arrows and heat to the common lower-level spells. In fact, I could use a spare set. Are you volunteering?"

Oz crouched and lowered his head. The glow in his throat built, lighting up the scaly ridges around his eyes and the lowered, spiny frills behind his vestigial ears.

"Oz," James said softly. He had the spellgun out, but lowered, resting against his thigh. *Three bullets left.* Not enough. Not nearly enough. "You can't take them, Oz. Not all of them."

"Perhaps not." Oz's voice was a hoarse basso rumble; smoke escaped when he opened his mouth. "But I can take *her.*"

Valor raised her spear, and purple sparks flickered down its length. "Can you, wyrm? You are welcome to try."

Oz hissed and opened his jaws. James steeled himself and laid a hand on Oz's flank. It was almost painfully hot to the touch, like a hot-water radiator.

"Oz, if you fight her here, you'll kill people."

It seemed impossible for the teenagers not to have noticed anything—but they hadn't; the music playing now was country, and some of them were tossing things that sparked and popped into the bonfire. The Wild Hunt, and everything happening over at the playground, was invisible to them.

"Glamour," Vic murmured, seeing James's gaze drift in the humans' direction.

Oz let out a shuddering, gusty breath that withered the grass in front of him, and raised his head, rearing back onto his hind legs so that he was taller than everyone in the company except one riding a sort of elephant-giraffe-thing. "I shall not fight you here, for it wouldn't be honorable to harm bystanders."

"Ah," Valor said. She set her spear in a hook on the saddle that was clearly designed for it, and rested her fist on her mailed thigh. "You have come to your senses. I appreciate your recognition of your own inability to defeat me."

"I am *not*—" Oz spluttered.

The company fell back just then, Valor among them, parting for another rider to come through. Prudence rode on the back of a unicorn only slightly larger than a deer, and just as delicate. It seemed to James that, although the pale creature moved with grace, it seemed exhausted from carrying the weight of a full-grown and exceedingly tall woman on its back.

Prudence rode sidesaddle, but without a saddle, merely a richly embroidered blanket draping down on both sides. What held it, and her, on the unicorn's back had to be magic. She used no reins, steering the unicorn with no visible means of control. A train of butterflies trailed behind her like a swirling blue skirt.

The Wild Hunt saluted, fist to forehead, as she rode past.

Vic did not; he straightened his shoulders and wrapped his arms more tightly around Nikki. The child pressed against him, visibly terrified.

"Oh, Carysto," Prudence said, and her voice, though soft, carried to every one of the assembled company. A rustling seemed to pass among them, like the whisper of a wind rattling dead autumn leaves. James wouldn't have thought it was possible for Vic—Carysto—to tense further, yet he did, stiffening until it seemed his spine would snap. "Carysto . . . why do you betray me? Steal from me? I am so disappointed in you."

"I offered to buy her from you when you tired of her."

"But I was *not* tired of her, Carysto. You took something of *mine*."

Her voice lashed like a whip. There was magic in it; James felt it, a sting against the protection the spellgun gave him. Several of the assembled Hunt winced. Vic staggered, his knees almost buckling before he stiffened his legs through sheer force of will. In his arms, Nikki gave a sharp wail of mingled fear and pain, and began to cry.

"See what you've done now? You've made her cry. Give her here." Prudence held out one long, pale arm. "Come to me, sweetling. I will soothe you as always, give you nice things to eat and make you smell nice and look pretty. *Look* at the state of you, all dirty and bedraggled. My poor pet. What can he possibly offer you that I cannot?"

Nikki sniffled, and then a wan, fragile hope bloomed on her small face, and she squirmed and held out her arms to the woman on the unicorn.

Oh yes, James knew that look, knew it from the inside out. *This is my mother. She loves me. This time, she won't hurt me.*

This time will be different.

Prudence rode closer. "Here, sweet little pet. Let me take you."

"No," Vic said. Ignoring Nikki's squawk of protest, he tightened his grip on her and turned his shoulder to Prudence, shielding the little girl.

"Carysto, Carysto. I see some correction is in order."

At a small gesture from Prudence, several of the Hunt moved in, drawing their weapons. One of Oz's wings dipped to curve over James, pinning him between the dragon's hot side and the warm, living mass of the wing. James shoved at it, pushing it aside so that he could see what was happening. And also so that he could breathe.

He was just in time to see Vic whip around and, holding Nikki in one arm, lash out with the glove. A blue-white snake's tongue of lightning burst from his fingertips and branched through the air. It seared the night and vanished in an instant, leaving James's vision a branching network of blinding afterimages. Horses screamed. James blinked to try to clear his sight. One of the Hunt was down; the formation of the rest had broken and they were fighting their panicked mounts back to steadiness. Some had raised weapons to protect themselves; some of these weapons were smoking.

Prudence had not moved. She sat still and calm on her unicorn, just a few feet in front of Vic, not a hair or a butterfly out of place.

As sparks flickered around the glove, Vic curled his fingers. There were shouts among the Hunt. Dark tongues of shadow curled out of the night to wrap around their mounts' legs, crawling upward with frightening speed, pulling on their boots and legs, pinning their arms. The ground itself seemed to be coming alive with questing tendrils of living black smoke.

"Get on my back," Oz said out of the corner of his mouth.

James holstered the spellgun and clambered up Oz's side. Oz cocked his front leg to offer a step, but it was still a scramble, and James lacerated his hands and tore the knee of his jeans on the sharp edges of Oz's scales. There were many reasons why he profoundly disliked riding dragonback, but the risk of intimate injury was definitely one of them. There was also nothing to properly hang onto and nowhere to sit that didn't make it feel like he was straddling a sawhorse.

In the time it had taken him to mount up, things had changed yet again. Several more of the Hunt were down, and Vic had taken an arrow through the meat of his forearm, just above the gauntlet. Teeth clenched, he was still wielding it. He knocked away a glancing blow from a sword and whirled around, Nikki's hair flying out, to catch a spear in his gloved fist and yank it away from its owner.

The mounted riders coursed around him, taking turns striking at him, while Prudence remained on her unicorn, hands folded, watching.

No wonder Vic had been so impressed by the spellgun. He had just taken down several members of the Wild Hunt in moments, singlehandedly. But the magic that was capable of doing that had splintered on the spellgun's shield.

Not for the first time, James wondered what the hell it was, and where it came from.

He drew it, keeping it down by Oz's neck, where it would be hidden from a casual glance.

So you take out one of his attackers, and then what?

Three bullets. A lot more than three of them.

"And with a damn kid in the middle of it," James muttered. He jockeyed for a shot, but there was no clear angle that wouldn't risk hitting Nikki and Vic, or at least causing them blowback from whatever the gun decided to do to its target. Still, if one of the Hunt looked like they were going to hit the kid, he was shooting them anyway, consequences be damned . . .

How could they *not* hit the kid, as chaotic as it was?

And yet . . . they weren't.

Vic was bleeding from a dozen wounds, but Nikki didn't have a scratch on her.

Because they can't, James thought. Because they didn't dare. Not with Prudence right there, watching. Right in the middle of things. They didn't dare harm Nikki any more than they dared to lay an accidental blade on Prudence—in fact, he saw one rider pull her stag wildly to the side to avoid running into Prudence's cloud of butterflies. The stag's feet slipped on the grass; stag and rider went down hard in a tangle of limbs and hooves and antlers.

Oz spread his wings. "I can get us out of here," he said, low.

"Carrying them?"

"If I can get hold of them."

But it was over before they had a chance. It was the drag-onskin-mailed rider, Valor, who struck the deciding blow. Hampered by his need to defend Nikki as well as himself, Vic left his back open. Valor rode in, bringing her spear forward. Vic sensed her coming at the last minute and swung around, raising his hand. He had no time to do more than that. The spear pierced his palm, with Valor's strength and the entire weight of the war-unicorn behind it, and drove all the way into his chest, punching in just below his right collarbone.

Nikki screamed.

James lurched forward on Oz's back, raising the gun. If he shot Prudence, maybe it would be like cutting off the head of the snake. The others might give up.

But he couldn't get a good shot at her. There were too many of the Wild Hunt in the way. And he could only catch glimpses of what was happening with Vic until suddenly the scrum cleared, with Valor dancing back on her war-unicorn and wrenching the spear free. The glittering black glove on Vic's blood-covered hand disintegrated in a crystalline shower of bits of dark glass.

As Vic fell to his knees, he released the final defense: his guardians. They seemed to come out of nowhere, erupting from thin air. There were half a dozen hellhounds, as well as the giant scaly thing that James had shot at the house, and a demonic skeletal horse with eyes of fire and dead hide hanging off its bones. They formed a defensive perimeter around the blood-covered, kneeling man holding the child.

The Wild Hunt cut them down, one by one. Each of them turned into a brief pillar of flame as it died, sending up sparks like the bonfire that might as well be in another world.

As the last of the guardians fell, Prudence abruptly kicked the unicorn into motion. She rode through the rest of the Hunt, who fell back and left her unimpeded.

Even on his knees and swaying, Vic tried to twist his body to wrap it around Nikki.

"Carysto," Prudence said sharply, a rebuking tone, and Vic shuddered all over. Fae names had power; it was why they didn't hand them out casually to mortals or to each other. In that, it seemed, the folklore was true.

Prudence touched the unicorn's neck, and it lashed out one perfect hoof, kicking him in the injured shoulder. As he reeled, she leaned down and scooped Nikki away from him.

Nikki offered no resistance, too shell-shocked to do anything except to let herself be manipulated like a doll. Prudence stroked her hair and then wheeled to look toward James, acknowledging him for the first time.

"You have served me well," she said, with a gracious dip of her head. "The stolen property is returned, the traitor in custody. All is well, and our bargain is concluded. One favor of mine is now yours to call upon."

James wet his lips, and managed a jerky nod. A fae favor was the sort of gift of which kings had been made, in the old days. There was almost no limit to what they might do.

"Wait," Vic croaked out. He had managed to get back to his knees, and from there, staggering, swaying, to his feet. "I . . . I ask you—no, I demand—"

"You?" Prudence wheeled her mount around. One of her hands curled possessively over Nikki's hair. "You are in no position to demand *anything*."

"A duel," Vic said. He sucked in a harsh breath. "I challenge you to trial by combat for the child."

Prudence stared at him for a moment, then she laughed sharply. "You challenge *me*?"

Vic stood shaky but defiant, blood running off his fingers. There was still the stub of an arrow protruding from his forearm, broken off jaggedly a few inches above the skin. "It is my right."

"You couldn't defeat me even at the best of times, but if you really insist—"

"Hey," James said clearly, his voice ringing out across the field between them. "So. About my favor."

Oz shifted under him. James kicked him lightly in the ribs.

The Wild Hunt turned, as one, to look at him.

Prudence's smooth brow creased in a slight frown. Her butterflies rippled as if in a light breeze.

"Is now really the time?" she asked in a tone just a slight shade away from annoyed.

"It is exactly the time. You have to grant my favor, right?"

"James," Oz rumbled.

"Hush—so, here it is. I want you to give the kid back and let them go."

Prudence stared at him for a long, silent moment. A couple members of the Wild Hunt laughed, and Valor tossed back her head and reached up to adjust her horned helm. "You human fool," she said. "She doesn't *have* to grant any foolish wish made by a—"

"I accept," Prudence said.

"Oh," James said. He'd been tensing for a fight. "Oh, uh, thanks."

"I *shall* grant that favor." She swung Nikki abruptly around, and all but hurled her through the air at Vic. Somehow he managed to sway into position to catch her one-armed. "And I also accept your challenge, Carysto, to ritual combat for the child."

"Wait," James began.

"If my champion wins," Prudence said, looking triumphant, "we take the child *and* you, Carysto."

"And if I win," Vic said hoarsely, "we go free, all of us. You will no longer pursue or attempt to harm us."

"Yes, of course," Prudence said. "I accept your terms."

She looked triumphant, as well she might. Right now, Vic didn't look like he could fight a flock of sparrows.

"Uh, hey," James tried again. "Wait. I said—"

"I heard you," Prudence said impatiently. "Your favor is granted. All business between us is done. Why are you still here? I have a duel to arrange."

Oz cleared his throat in a deep rumble. "You mentioned something about champions," he said. "How does that work, exactly?"

It was Valor who spoke up from her war-unicorn's back. "Either party may appoint a champion to fight for them. It is how duels are done. I presume I will represent you in this, my lady?"

"But of course," Prudence said, with a gracious tilt of her silver head.

Oz tipped his head back to fix James with one enormous eye.

"Oh my God," James groaned.

"It will not affect *you* in the slightest," Oz rumbled.

"Don't be an idiot."

"But I *want* to," Oz growled, the banked-fire glow heating up again. He stood up straighter, arched his neck, and mantled his wings, emphasizing his size next to most of the Wild Hunt steeds. James had to clutch at his neck spikes to avoid being tipped off. "I choose to fight on his behalf."

"Oz!" James kicked him in the ribs. Oz merely shrugged, a quick ripple of his scales, like an annoyed horse shaking off a fly.

"Oh, how interesting," Prudence declared. She brushed a hand over the shining cascade of her gown, smoothing away bloodstains where Nikki had left smears of Vic's blood, restoring it to its former perfection. "It is of course up to my opponent."

"I . . ." Vic was at a loss for words, staring at Oz. "You would do this?"

"I would be *extremely* happy to do this," Oz growled, with smoke leaking out of his half-open jaws. "On the condition that if we win, we shall *all* be set free, the four of us, not to be pursued, harassed, or harmed in any way."

"My lady," Valor said, with her fierce gaze fixed on Oz. "I would be *very* pleased to accept this challenge for you."

"Wait, now," James protested. He'd thought he had a perfectly good and relatively nonviolent solution nailed down, and now everything seemed to be spinning out of control around him. "Oz can't—that is, he's my steed, we're a package deal, if one of us fights so does the other."

Oz gave a low, rumbling growl. "*James.*"

"I have no problem with that," Valor said. She patted the neck of her black war-unicorn. "That means Savage can fight too, with your permission, my lady."

"I am not your steed, James," Oz rumbled.

"Steed, business associate, when in Rome, right?"

"I am *far* more capable of fighting them than you are."

"Oz," James muttered, stretching out along the scaly neck

so he could murmur close to the dragon's ear. "Magic gun, remember?"

"Oh," Oz said, perking up.

"If they don't find out and take it away from me. *Capisce?*"

"Is that Italian?"

"Oz, *hush*, they can hear you."

Prudence was giving them both a narrow-eyed look of distrust. Oz raised his head and flattened his ruff while arching his wings over his back. "Where shall we fight? Here?"

"Of course not," Prudence retorted coolly. "We shall go to the arena. You may have some time to recover and refresh yourselves beforehand."

She moved her hand, stirring a wave of butterflies, and James's world seemed to turn sideways.

For a moment there was a strange, disorienting feeling of two different places existing simultaneously: the field, the bonfire, the sky full of stars overhead, traffic passing on the nearby highway—and somewhere different, wilder, *deeper*. There was a suggestion of the massive dark boles of redwood-sized trees around them, and stars overhead, but stars that blazed more brightly and fiercely than those of Earth ever had. The cool air smelled of pine needles and mosses and wild things. The field was the unreal place, paper-thin compared to the age and depth of this forest.

And then the field seemed to crumble and blow away, and there were dark trees above them, rustling in the night wind. The smell of pine needles and leaf mold was almost strong enough to be unpleasant, old and musty and decayed.

Prudence glimmered softly in the dark, like a beacon for the others to follow.

"Come," she said, her voice brisk. "To the palace. Someone bring Carysto and the child. It would be a shame if he drops dead of that wound before he has a chance to watch his champion lose."

No one in the assembled company moved to help, though Valor started to move her hand on the reins of her war-unicorn and then seemed to think better of it.

"Oh for . . ." James muttered. "Come on, Oz."

Oz hesitated and then heaved out a gusty sigh and walked forward in his slow, swaying, tail-dragging style. James had never ridden him on the ground before, and it was profoundly uncomfortable, a swaying up-and-down move-ment that jarred his ass at each step and threatened to make him seasick.

He holstered the gun, all too aware that if he made it look like too much of a threat, they might take it away. If he had to fight them all flat-out, he would lose. But the gun was not just a weapon; it was the only defense he had against what-ever glamours or other spells they might cast against him. Right now it was more useful to him as a harmless-seeming personal item than for any short-term self-defense he could muster with it.

Oz stopped beside Vic—covered in blood, on his knees, good arm wrapped around a shell-shocked Nikki. He looked up at them with a kind of weary, helpless despair.

"Get on," Oz said. He jerked his snout impatiently at his back.

Vic stared at him blankly. James was already sliding off Oz's back to lend a hand by the time the fae managed to collect himself enough to start trying to stand up. James hesi-tated and then tried sliding an arm under Vic's injured shoulder.

"No," the fae rasped out. "Take her."

He handed Nikki to James, who now found himself with a scared and half-limp little girl clinging to him.

"Uh, hi, kid." James smoothed down her hair. "You okay?"

Nikki twisted around, wrapped her arms around his neck, and buried her face in his shoulder.

Gritting his teeth, Vic managed to climb up to Oz's back without assistance. James struggled after him, trying to climb one-handed while keeping Nikki away from the sharp edges of the scales.

This put Vic in front, slumped over Oz's neck, while James was stuck sitting on the dragon's low-slung back—which, he found out as soon as they started moving, made an even less comfortable seat; Oz's swaying locomotion was even more pronounced here.

"I don't feel good," Nikki mumbled against James's neck.

This better not be a long trip.

CHAPTER NINE

AS IT TURNED OUT, it wasn't. With Prudence's butterfly-flecked luminescence at the head of the procession and Oz in the middle, flanked by unfriendly-looking fae guards, they wended their way out of the trees and onto the grounds of a vast, rambling complex of buildings.

In the darkness, the fae palace shone with light. There was no coherent design or architectural style. It was a byzantine mishmash of slender towers and glassed-in solariums, domes and pagodas, flying buttresses and verandas and gardens. They rode through gardens lit with colored lanterns and tens of thousands of . . . was it appropriate to call them fairy lights here? Among the lanterns and the lights and the ornamental trees, there were dancing specks of color that James took for pastel fireflies until one landed on the back of his wrist. It was a miniature winged horse, the size of a bumblebee.

Prudence brought the unicorn to a halt. "We shall provide you rooms in the palace. Your dragon will go to the stables with the other mounts."

"Stables?!" Oz started to rear in horror. At the yelps of

dismay from his riders, he slammed back to all fours. "I am not a *horse*."

"It's nothing like it sounds," Valor's war-unicorn said, and James felt Oz jerk in surprise. "It's actually just as nice as the palace, but with amenities that are made for us instead. Nice pastures and indoor accommodations built for four legs instead of two. You'll like it."

Oz growled low in his throat. "We shall not be separated."

"He's right," James said. "We're staying together."

"Your dragon won't fit in the palace," Valor said. She rode up alongside Oz, who pulled his head back and wrinkled his muzzle in a doglike, silent snarl. "You are our guests for the night. Honor dictates that we will not harm you."

"Excuse me if I don't entirely trust your honor right now," James said.

"I personally guarantee your safety," Valor said, touching a hand to her chest.

"*You* do." James glanced at Prudence. "What about her?"

"Such melodrama." Prudence glissaded off the back of her unicorn. A pair of retainers came up with a bridle that looked like it was made of cobweb and starlight, finely spun and softly luminescent, which they slipped over the unicorn's head. "I give you my word that no harm will come to you or yours tonight, human knight." She smiled, displaying small, sharp-looking teeth. "What kind of fun would *that* be?"

Oz twisted his neck around to give James a dismayed look.

"They're telling the truth," Vic said, between harsh breaths. "We do not break our word. We *can't*."

"Is it possible to put us up in the stables too?" James asked.

"It's possible, I suppose," Valor said. "But Victorious needs medical attention. You would probably like a bath. We can provide both more easily in the palace."

Vic grunted, and then with effort he stirred, twisted

around, and began, with difficulty, to climb down one-armed from Oz's back.

"Seriously?" James demanded.

Vic struggled with the climb, his blood-covered hands slipping on scales. Oz grudgingly bent a knee to give him a step down, but he ignored it and slid to the ground on his own, holding onto the dragon's side. He raised his good arm wordlessly for Nikki.

"Yeah," James muttered. "Right." He handed her down and climbed down after her, then held out an arm to take her back. "No, look, you can barely stand up. You want to go facedown on top of her? Give her to me."

Vic handed her over without argument. Nikki wrapped her arms around James's neck and tucked her head under his chin.

"I don't like this," Oz growled.

"Me neither, but if they decide to stab us in the back, would it really make that much of a difference if we're together?" Privately, he thought Oz might have a better chance at getting away without being burdened with the rest of them, but he wasn't going to say it.

Valor dismounted from her enormous two-horned war-unicorn as well. It looked as if she ought to need a step to get down—the saddle was probably eight feet in the air—but she landed gracefully with a jangle of armor fittings, and took off her horned helm to reveal tousled, short-cut dark hair. She was a few inches taller than James.

"I'll show you to your rooms," she said.

"And I will show you the stables," the war unicorn said to Oz, with a toss of its head. "I cannot *wait* to have this saddle off. There is an itch under the saddle blanket that I cannot reach."

James pressed a hand to Oz's warm side. "Go. We'll be fine."

"If you intend betrayal, I shall make you regret it," Oz rumbled, but he turned and shuffled off with the unicorn, casting frequent glances back over his shoulder.

James followed Valor into the palace, with Nikki still draped on his shoulder. He wished he believed his own reassurances.

≈

THE PALACE WAS as labyrinthine inside as out, but their rooms were nice, several interlocking chambers with comfortable-looking wood-and-velvet furniture. Softly glowing pastel globes provided a lovely, gentle light that was very relaxing, if not much good for reading. A pair of wide glass doors opened onto a balcony.

Vic, who had barely managed to stay on his feet for the walk, wobbled to the nearest couch and sank onto it, leaving bloodstains on the plush, jewel-blue seat cushions. Valor knelt before him with a soft jangle of armor and weapons. "Let me," she began, reaching for his bloodied arm.

He pulled away with a soft hiss of pain. "Don't touch me."

She hesitated, then rose with a short nod, and stood looking down at him. James couldn't help thinking how terribly out of place they both seemed in these chambers, Valor in her armor with her sweaty and mussed helmet-hair and smudges of blood on her face, and Vic in black, covered in his own blood. They looked like what they were: warriors, not courtiers meant for soft, pastel surroundings.

"For what it's worth," Valor said quietly, "I'm sorry it came to this, Carysto."

Vic shuddered at the sound of his real name. "Little late for that," he said, his gaze fixed on the floor.

Valor grimaced, and turned away, taking in James with a quick sweep of her knife-edged gaze. Her eyes were a clear, reflective violet. "I'll have a healer sent up. And it seems you could both use clean clothes and something to eat."

She left, closing the door behind her. James was unsurprised, when he tried it, to find it locked. Or not precisely locked so much as sealed, absolutely unbudging whether he tugged or pushed against it.

"Don't bother," Vic said from the couch without looking up. "We're prisoners, not guests."

Nikki perked up a little at the sound of his voice. She had been so still and quiet that James had wondered if she might have fallen asleep. He carried her over to the couch and set her down on Vic's uninjured side. Vic put an arm around her.

"Is it safe for me to eat the food here?" James asked.

"You think they'll poison you?"

"I'm more worried about not being able to leave. 'Don't eat the food' figures heavily in a lot of fae folklore."

"Don't worry about it," Vic said. He tried to shift position on the couch and grunted in pain. "If they want to keep you here, they have much more direct ways of doing it."

"Thanks, that's reassuring."

"It wasn't meant to be."

"Yeah, it's not." James sat on the arm of the couch. "So, want to let me know what I've gotten myself into? What's gonna happen in this duel? You better tell me it's not to the death."

"It goes on until one combatant yields. For whatever it's worth," Vic added, "Valor is honorable, and I expect she will not kill a surrendered opponent. She rarely does."

"Rarely."

"Do you want false hope or truth?"

"That bad, huh?"

"I suggest you make your terms very clear before the duel, including the expectation of safe passage afterwards. Also . . ." Vic sucked in a breath and visibly steeled himself, straightening his shoulders and just barely failing to hide the spasm of pain on his face. "You are not honor-bound to follow through with it. I am the one who called the duel. If you choose to back out, I will fight instead."

"Yeah, you won't last ten seconds against her, in the shape you're in."

"What do you get out of this?" Vic asked. "I find it hard to believe you're doing this out of pure altruism."

"Hell if I know. Give me a favor, why not? One of the special fae kind."

Vic smiled slightly. "I am disgraced and cast out. I have no ability to grant you any sort of boon. However, whatever I *can* grant will be entirely at your disposal, whether you win or lose."

The door opened with no knocking or other warning, whisking aside to admit a pair of fae in long robes. One, in a peach-colored robe, carried a large silver tray; the other, wearing plum-colored robes decorated with silver beads, a bundle of clothing.

A round, short, human-looking woman followed them inside. It was only when she knelt in front of Vic that James noticed the cloven hooves showing beneath the hem of her skirt.

"Hi, Bronze," Vic said with a wan smile.

"Well, you are in a state, aren't you?" the little woman said. She plucked Nikki unceremoniously from his grasp. Nikki started to cry. "Oh, stop. Adaira—take this, please, clean it up—"

Pink Robe reached for the child, who tried to squirm away.

"I'll do it," James said.

He half disbelieved that he was actually volunteering to take care of the kid, all the more so when Nikki clamped onto him like a distressed, trusting limpet. She had Vic's blood all over her and didn't seem to have noticed.

"Clothes," Vic said, over the top of Bronze's head as she pulled the blood-sodden fabric from his shoulder.

Pink Robe, unspeaking and unsmiling, handed James a clean shirt in dark jewel blue and a child's yellow dress with butterflies stitched delicately around the hem.

"Uh, thanks, I guess. Is there a bathroom?"

She pointed.

It was not precisely a bathroom so much as a bath grotto. The place was done up like a little rock cave, lit with the same soft pastel lighting as the rest of the suite. There was no door. He wasn't sure if he would have recognized its function if not for the toilet, which at least was reasonably familiar. *What happens when fae need to take a shit* was not a question he had previously thought to wonder about. Apparently they did it in very nice toilets, with carved wooden pedestals and ornate tanks, but nevertheless recognizable as toilets.

Which meant the boulders beside it, overgrown with moss, with a small flow of water trickling down between the rocks, might be some kind of shower. Despite the lack of door or shower enclosure, some degree of privacy was provided by boulders cozily framing the toilet and—ornamental waterfall? shower? . . . bidet?

James set Nikki down on a rock. "Gonna clean you up, okay?"

There was no sign of towels or washcloths, or toilet paper for that matter. He tore off a handful of moss to scrub at Nikki's hands and face. It immediately grew back, sealing over the exposed rock, so yeah, that probably *was* what that was for.

Nikki was uncharacteristically easy to handle, pliable and uncomplaining through a combination of exhaustion and trauma. She held up her arms obediently, and James peeled her out of her blood-stained blue gown, scrubbed her down with handfuls of moss, and got her into the clean yellow dress.

"Is Mother here?" she asked when her face popped out of the dress's neck hole, speaking for the first time since they had entered the palace.

"Not at the moment." He tried to think what he would have wanted from a strange adult at her age. His childhood experience with adults had been generally not that positive. But then, hers wasn't either. "Stay there while I clean up, okay?"

She nodded and sat on the rock, swinging her legs. James changed his shirt, washed his face and hands in the water trickling over the boulders, and scrubbed at the stains on his jacket with moss.

"You hungry?" he asked her.

She shrugged and kicked her legs harder. It made him think, abruptly, of a cold night—a neighbor—CPS—adults asking him questions. *Are you cold? Are you hungry? Did your mother lock you out? Where is your father?* Questions that had no answers. At least, he didn't remember what he'd answered.

There was silence from the main room of the suite. At some point, the voices and quiet rustling had stopped.

"Come on," James said, and held out a hand. Nikki took it and hopped off the rock. She came with him, obedient. Trusting. It was a strange feeling and he didn't know what to do with it.

Vic was alone in the suite. He had been stripped to the waist and heavily bandaged, and was sprawled on the couch, looking weary and faded and even less human than usual, exhaustion drawing him down to an ethereal pallor. But he cracked open an eye, and grunted faintly when Nikki flung herself on him.

"There's food," he said, his voice a thready whisper.

Although it had been sitting out while they were in the bathroom, the hot items were still piping hot, the cold ones still perfectly cold. Most of it was pastries, finger food, and other small items. Nearly all were familiar or at least recognizable, though they came from a mishmash of cuisines: pastries, sushi, steamed buns, cocktail shrimp, little cakes. There was a carafe of coffee and a decanter of wine.

James poured himself a cup of coffee and took that and a croissant out to the balcony, closing the door carefully behind him.

The night was lovely, neither too hot nor too cold, with just a hint of a breeze. The balcony was about three stories up, and a sprawl of gardens lay below it, picked out in fairy lights and lanterns. He glimpsed people walking on the paths, most of them couples, strolling arm in arm. Beyond the gardens were more buildings, windows softly glowing, framed by a dark tide of trees. From this high up, he could glimpse a lake or other large body of water glimmering beyond the forest, reflecting the starlight.

He didn't dare relax here, but it really was beautiful. The little colored lights of the miniature pegasi danced on the soft night air. Curious, they ventured close to James, their tiny hooves skimming over the backs of his hands like the faintest brush of a feather.

"James!" said a voice from just below the balcony.

James jumped and dropped his croissant over the side. The pegasi fireflies scattered.

"Oh!" said the voice from below. "Thank you. Bit small though . . ."

"Oz?" James whispered, leaning over.

The dragon was standing on his hind legs beneath the balcony, stretched up the wall. His wings were half-spread for balance.

"What the hell are you doing here, Oz?"

"Looking for you," Oz retorted in what he probably thought was a whisper, easily loud enough to be heard by everyone on this side of the building.

"Problem at the stables?"

"No, they're quite nice. Although I feel they should change the name to something more inviting, such as 'accommodations for four-legged guests.'" He paused. "Except some of the residents have six or eight. I shall continue to ponder."

James leaned on the railing. "I feel like Juliet on this balcony, but if you're Romeo . . ." He waved a hand, vaguely indicating the dragon's everything.

"I know," Oz said, preening.

"How'd you find me, anyway?"

"By smell, of course." Oz curled a lip back from his huge teeth. "Are they treating you well? Do I need to bite anyone?"

"Please don't bite anyone. Not before the duel, anyway. And I'm doing fine. They fed us and everything."

"I dislike this. I want to fight them now and get it over with."

James hung over the railing, looking down at the dragon's massive head. "Why are you even *here*, Oz? Why did you volunteer to fight?" He couldn't help being aware that he was echoing the same question Vic had put to him earlier. *What do you get out of this?* He didn't know if Oz would have any more of an answer than James did.

"Because it is right," Oz said promptly. "Also, because I would greatly enjoy crushing that wretched dragonslaying fae in my fangs."

Okay, so at least one of them had a reason.

"And also," the dragon added, "because you cannot fight them alone."

"I can't—You're the one who volunteered us! I wasn't even planning to fight them in the first place."

"Really? You would have walked away and let them take the child?"

James was silent.

Oz cleared his throat. "I don't always understand the ways of humans or fae, but I do know what it is to have children and want to protect them."

"That's right," James said, floundering for safer conversational ground. "I completely forgot you're a parent. You have a daughter, right? Neith or something like that?"

"Yes, Neith." Oz sounded pleased. "Of course, she is grown now. But it seems like only yesterday that she was a tiny dragonet, hunting mice and learning to use her little wings."

James grinned at the mental image. "I should meet her someday."

"She is reclusive and not overly fond of humans," Oz said. "But I will ask. She visits me in the city sometimes. What of you, James—do you have children? Pardon if that is a rude question. I do not know at what age humans become sexually mature, but I assume you're past it."

"I—uh—yeah, definitely past it. No kids, though. It just never was a thing that happened. And, to be completely honest, it wasn't really something I wanted. I doubt I'd be good at it."

"Why not?" Oz asked, looking up at him. "It's a thing all humans must have the ability to be good at, isn't it? Unless you have a reproducing class, like bees. But I don't think humans are like that. At least your fiction suggests that you are not."

"No, we're not; anyone can have kids. But some people have a much better grounding in—Look, neither of my parents was what you'd call the parent type. I don't really have role models."

He rested the coffee cup on the railing. It was still piping hot, as if freshly poured.

"My dad checked out when I was a little kid, and Mom never really wanted to be a mom in the first place. The older I got, the more I grew up, the more I looked like him, and the worse she was. Not like . . . I mean, I wasn't abused, exactly. I had food and a place to sleep. But she—"

He hesitated, on the verge of admitting truths he hadn't ever said out loud, not to anyone.

"—wasn't that much of a mom," he said, and laughed a little, mostly at himself. Apparently the darkest edge of everything his mother had been, everything she'd done, was going to stay locked up, the way it had been for all these years. "Anyway, I ran away from home when I was sixteen. Moved in with an old guy called Bendix."

"I've heard you mention him before," Oz said. "He's the one you got the gun from."

"Yeah, but that was years later. I did some work for him, summer job kind of stuff. When I left home, I asked if I could work for him full time, and he figured out pretty quick that I was actually crashing on a classmate's couch. After that, I slept in Bendix's back room and helped out with his work. He was a bail bondsman and skip tracer. All illegal as hell, since I wasn't eighteen yet, but Bendix wasn't the kind of guy who got too fussed about that. He had a pretty checkered past himself."

He wasn't sure why it was so easy, all of a sudden, to dump all of this on Oz. It helped that Oz didn't have the same frame of reference; Oz had no idea what human childhoods were normally like. He wondered if Oz even understood half of what he was saying. He probably could have admitted the rest of it, but he didn't want to, now that the danger—the moment of greatest openness—was past. It was easier to just move on, the way he had done with her, and from her.

"We had a pretty big blow-up and I left town. I didn't hear from him again, didn't really even think about him, 'til I got a certified letter from a lawyer in the mail. Bendix had died and left me the key to a safe deposit box, and what was in the box was the gun. So yeah, that's my entire experience with parenthood."

There was silence for a little while, but it was companionable this time, or at least peaceful, until sudden burst of laughter from down in the garden broke their shared reverie.

"That doesn't mean you wouldn't be good at it," Oz said quietly. "If you wanted it."

"Yeah, well, it's not really in the cards for me soon anyway, since the woman I'm closest to these days died back in 1924." James pushed off from the railing. "And we have a big day ahead. You better get back to the stables, or whatever you want to call it, before they notice you're missing and call out the guards. Get some rest."

"I don't think anyone is paying that much attention," Oz protested, but he thumped back to all fours. "Good night, James. I trust that you know what you are doing."

That makes one of us, James thought as he went back inside, fingering the spellgun's grip.

The common room was deserted. He glanced into the adjoining bedrooms until he found the one with Vic and Nikki. The little girl was asleep, wrapped in a blanket. Vic lay beside her, stripped down to a pair of loose pants. He appeared to be sleeping as well, bandaged chest raising and lowering almost imperceptibly.

Both of them helpless, at the mercy of the fae.

James cursed quietly under his breath, and went to see if he could make good on his advice to Oz and catch a little sleep before the duel.

CHAPTER TEN

THE FAE CAME for them at first light. James had been up for hours. He'd caught a couple hours' sleep on one of the beds, lying on top of the richly embroidered coverlet, but it was restless and unsatisfying. He ended up wandering the suite and nibbling on the snack buffet. Eventually he took a plate and a cup of coffee—still perfectly hot—out to the balcony.

Under the gradually brightening sky, details of the palace's baroque architecture emerged slowly, one roof and column and portico at a time. The gray light of dawn washed out the colored lanterns, but brought out subtle colors in the building faces and balconies and towers.

Beyond the palace, beyond the trees, the water he had glimpsed last night was faintly luminous in the clear morning light. It stretched to the horizon, and he caught sight of the black triangles of distant sails plying the shining water.

They were too far inland for this to be Lake Michigan, but there was no reason why geography on this side of the Veil had to correspond to the other side. It wasn't like there were huge forests in Iowa either.

The door to the suite opened. James set down his coffee and went to face whoever had arrived.

It was Valor, accompanied by several stern, martial-looking fae in white and gold livery. Her dragon-scale armor had been polished until it gleamed, and she had the helm tucked under her arm. When not matted down with sweat, her dark hair turned out to be curly.

"Is that what you're wearing?" she asked with a disdainful look at James's beat-up jacket and jeans.

"Not up to your standards?"

"I would have expected armor. We can spare some, if you like."

He frankly couldn't see how it would make a difference. There was no way he could beat someone like Valor through physical force alone. He would rather be unencumbered.

"No thanks," he said, tucking a thumb into a belt loop of his jeans. "Don't need it."

"You'd be wise to take her up on it." Vic spoke hoarsely from the bedroom doorway.

He looked a little better than last night, but only a little. A dark green shirt hid most of the bandages, but not their stiff bulk or the slow, careful way he was moving. His eyes were sunk in deep hollows.

"I've got my own defenses, thanks."

"If you say so." Vic limped to the buffet, picked up a sesame-speckled bun, and put it down. Valor watched him carefully the entire time, her gaze shadowed and uncertain. Vic looked up and met her eyes defiantly. "Are we ready?"

"I believe we are," she said. "My people can watch the child—"

"She's staying with me," Vic said in a tone that left no room for argument. He went into the bedroom and came out carrying a sleepy Nikki.

"Don't *want* to get up," Nikki complained.

"It's important, child. Hush."

"I'm *hungry.*"

"There will be food where we're going." But he reached for a pastry on his way out the door.

As they fell into step in the hallway—Valor in the lead, livery-clad fae flanking and following them—James's head began to fill with a whirl of questions he hadn't thought of asking Vic earlier, when it was just the two of them. *Cut me some slack, it's my first duel, after all . . .*

He dropped back to walk with Vic, who looked up wearily from a fretful Nikki.

"So, about Valor," James said quietly. "How does she fight? Is she going to come at me with magic, or run over me with that unicorn, or what?"

"Her preferred weapon is the spear." Vic grimaced and shifted Nikki's weight, pain visible on his face, but shook his head when James made a motion to take her. After a moment, he went on. "If you have a chance to choose weapons, you should probably ask for combatant's choice. She will likely choose the spear, but you'll be able to fight with . . . that." He tilted his head almost imperceptibly toward James's holster. "They are unlikely to allow you to use it otherwise."

One shot from the spellgun, maybe two to take out the war-unicorn, ought to end the duel in moments. Could it really be that simple?

"How do I get the option to choose?"

"It's random. Could be her, could be you. If it's her, you'll most likely end up fighting with a spear. How are your spear skills?"

"Uh . . . it doesn't look that hard? Pointy end toward the person you want to stab?"

"Nonexistent. Got it. Try not to end up with a spear. Out of curiosity," Vic added, so quietly James could barely hear him, "what weapons *are* you skilled at? Bow, dagger, sword . . ."

"Gun."

"I was afraid of that."

It was hard to say for certain, in the maze of the palace, but James thought they were traveling a different way than the route that had brought them inside last night. He was sure of it when they exited not into the gardens, but onto a broad, curving avenue, lined with flowering trees, that took them to a great field.

He had been picturing an arena with stadium seating, but this was probably more appropriate to the faux-medieval stylings of the fae. Colored banners snapped along the borders of the field, and a variety of spectators had already shown up, some in pavilions draped in colored silks, others mounted on horses or other creatures. Some had brought chairs. There was lively activity around a large tent that appeared to be serving breakfast.

James spotted Oz easily, since not many of the fae mounts were his size. It appeared that Oz had also been offered armor, and had taken full advantage of it. The dragon was resplendent in a horned headpiece of some shiny black metal that glittered against his gunmetal scales. An armored carapace with a built-in saddle arched over his shoulders and curved around his chest into a gleaming breastplate with spiraling designs picked out in jewels.

Well, James thought, at least it would be easier to sit on that than on Oz's bony spine.

"*That's* what you're wearing?" Oz said when he caught sight of James.

"Yeah, I've heard it already, thanks."

"We are representing Earth here, you know. The very least you could do is attempt to cut a good figure," Oz complained, but he crouched and held out his leg for James to mount up.

From Oz's back, James had a better view of the field. Too good, maybe. He was all too aware of the vast size of it and the sheer number of people who were there, ranged along the edges of the trees in the sharp, clear morning sun. On the far side of the field, the trees were half occluded by low-lying ground mist, but banners snapped brightly above the mist, and the vivid colors of tents and pavilions could be glimpsed.

He had lost sight of Valor when she peeled off from their company at the field, but from his higher vantage point he spotted her again as she crossed the edge of the field toward the war-unicorn who waited for her beside a silver and gold pavilion.

James had been doing reasonably well up to this point at keeping calm, mostly by not thinking too hard about what was ahead, but now his heart began to pound. He wiped a sweaty palm on his leg.

"Don't worry," Oz said, twisting his head around on his supple neck. "We shall stomp them."

Prudence arrived on her unicorn. Her dress today was a frothing white cascade with subtle gold embroidery, its ruffles and frills swamping the narrow hindquarters of her small mount. Butterflies frosted her head and bare shoulders. "Ah, Carysto, there you are," she said, and seemed to relish his flinch when she spoke his true name. "Come join me in my pavilion, you and the child. We shall have an excellent view."

"I'm good where I am," Vic said.

"Don't stand on pride. And I do mean stand. You've not even a single supporter left in court to bring you a chair." She rode closer. Vic twisted around with visible pain to put his body between her and Nikki, but with Nikki's head resting on his shoulder, Prudence was still able to reach over and brush a finger down the child's cheek. "I'm sure you'd like some sweetmeats, wouldn't you, pet?"

"Stay away from her," Oz rumbled, lowering his big head.

"Oh, aren't you *defensive*, how lovely. I look forward to making pets of you both."

"Not part of the deal," Oz said promptly.

"I don't believe it was specified *what* I might do with you, specifically. If my champion wins, of course." She beamed up at them. "I shall see you on the field."

With that, she rode off, trailing butterflies. Oz gazed beseechingly after her.

"Are you sure I can't bite—"

"Not yet, but if we have to fight our way out of here, you can bite her all you want." This seemed to mollify Oz somewhat, and James looked down at Vic. "Any parting advice?"

"Don't die."

"Thanks, I'll be sure and remember that."

Vic stepped closer to Oz's scaly shoulder, and said quietly, "She sometimes leaves her left side exposed. It's a bad habit I tried to train her out of, with only moderate success. Watch for it."

"Will do," James said, doubting if he would even recognize what an exposed left side looked like.

"Combatants to the field!" a high, fluting voice cried. James didn't see who or what had spoken, but Valor and her war-unicorn rode out, and Oz lurched forward.

The saddle was definitely more comfortable to sit on than Oz's bare spine. Something tapped against James's thigh when the dragon moved, and he discovered that the saddle had straps. After some fumbling with the buckles, James got the saddle's harness fastened around his legs and waist. It looked like it was meant to hold him on through any sort of maneuvers, even upside down in midair.

"Think we get to keep all this if we win, Oz?"

"Oooh." Oz lifted the spiny frills behind the helmet, intrigued. "I would very much like to add this to my hoard. It doesn't match the rest, but I can have a separate room built to display it."

"There you go, another reason to win, aside from the avoiding horrible death and fae slavery options."

Valor and her mount had stopped at the approximate midpoint of the field. Oz swayed up to stand in front of them and dipped his head politely to the war-unicorn, who gave him a small, polite nod in return.

Another creature approached them across the field—and *creature* was the only word that fit. Its body was vaguely leonine but huge, with high, humped shoulders, a lion crossed with a buffalo. Hawklike wings mantled above its back, and its hindquarters tapered down to the flat segments of a scorpion's tail curled above its back, with a stinger as big as both of James's hands together. Its face, framed by the ruff of a lion's mane, was disturbingly humanlike, although the jaw projected forward in an animal's snout and its large eyes were sunk in shaggy brow ridges; the overall effect was a bit like a rhesus monkey.

"Manticore," Oz murmured out of the corner of his mouth.

"Good morning, Arbus," Valor said cheerfully. "How's the wife and kids?"

"Oh, you know how it is." The manticore's voice was a deep rumble with a slight, discordant sibilance to it. "Can't complain. We have some new eggs hatching any day now. How are your sisters?"

"Hope slew threescore frost giants this past fortnight, or so she claims. Her trophy room looks a bit bare for all of that."

"Some are late bloomers, but all get where they are meant to be in the end," the manticore said philosophically.

He turned to James. "You stand as champion for the challenger?"

"I do," James said. "And if I win, we go free, back to Earth, and you guys leave us alone. Agreed?"

The manticore quirked a shaggy brow at Valor.

"Yes, of course," she said. "And if I win, you shall clean my boots with your tongue."

"Uh. Is that negotiable?"

"Is yours?"

To be fair, if he did lose, he was probably going to have worse problems than some minor humiliation. "Yeah, okay. Agreed."

Oz growled faintly.

"Yes, then, with that settled," the manticore said briskly, and whipped out a clipboard. "Here are the rules. Bystanders may not be intentionally harmed or used as shields or hostages, but incidental harm is at their own risk. Only the selected weapons are permitted on the field. The first to die or yield loses. Breaking a rule means forfeiture. Do you agree?"

"Agreed," Valor said, her voice clear and her purple-glinting gaze fixed on James.

James swallowed, his throat tense and dry. "Agreed."

With a flourish, the manticore ref pulled a coin out of thin air, a heavy gold one. "The challenger will choose: grain or castle?"

It took James a moment to realize that they were both looking at him. "Grain," he said.

The ref flipped it and slapped it to the back of his wrist. The movement was familiar enough to be startling in this strange place. "Castle. Defender chooses weapons."

"That was rigged," Oz grumbled. James kicked him in the side.

"Bare hands," Valor said. "No weapons."

"Hey," James began, but subsided at a look from the referee.

"Combatants, remove your weapons."

Valor gave James a slight smile and began taking off an unreasonably large number of knives, passing each down to a small winged creature who appeared out of nowhere to take them.

"That a weapon?" the manticore asked, nodding to James's gunbelt.

He was tempted to say no, but there was all too much chance they knew what modern Earth weapons looked like. Valor, from her expression, almost certainly did. "I have to keep it on. It's a . . . custom of my people. I can't fight without it."

The ref gave him a long, steady look. So did Valor.

"I won't use it," James said. "On my honor."

The fuck he wouldn't, if he really had to. But that would mean breaking the rules, which meant they'd have to grab Vic and fight their way past a bunch of pissed-off fae, who could quite easily follow them back into the real world.

The ref turned to Valor. "The defender may decide."

"If I can't wear it, I'll be forced to forfeit," James said. "There'll be no fight. No glory in that, right? All these people showed up for nothing."

Valor still looked skeptical, but she gave a terse nod. "I will accept. On your honor."

James was half expecting a sarcastic comment out of Oz, but there was none. Right, he kept forgetting honor was a thing Oz thought he actually had.

"Combatants will withdraw to each end of the field."

Valor settled her horned helm over her short hair and saluted, fist to forehead. James awkwardly returned the gesture. Valor wheeled the unicorn around and galloped downfield. Oz spread his wings and retreated in a series of little gliding hops. When he neared the trees, he turned around and folded his wings. Valor and her unicorn were little more than a dark blot at the far end of the field.

"I don't like this, Oz," James muttered. "She can't possibly think she can beat you barehanded, unless she's way stronger than she looks. What's she up to? She's not going to pick a fight she doesn't think she can win."

"Perhaps she is choosing an honorable out to allow us to leave with the child," Oz suggested.

"Trust me, Oz, that was not the face of a woman who's planning to throw this fight."

"Begin!" the referee shouted.

CHAPTER ELEVEN

Valor kicked her unicorn into motion. The drumming tattoo of powerful hoofbeats resonated through James's chest.

Oz spread his wings and took to the air. "No one said anything about flying being dishonorable, right?" he asked anxiously.

"Pretty sure it's fine." James peered over the side of the saddle. "In fact . . ."

It turned out they weren't the only ones. Gossamer wings of pale violet light unfurled from either side of the war-unicorn's powerful shoulders. Between one rapid-fire drum-beat of hooves and the next, it launched into the air, running from grass to sky as effortlessly as breathing.

"Well, that answers one thing. I guess now we know why she wasn't worried about going up against a flying opponent."

Oz wheeled around in midair. The unicorn galloped upward at a steep angle, racing toward them. Its widespread, transparent wings did not beat; they seemed to function merely to keep it aloft, with its legs providing the actual locomotion.

That's another advantage we have, James thought. *We're swifter and more maneuverable in the air, and they'll tire out faster —wait, what's she doing?*

Valor had one mailed fist clenched on the unicorn's reins. She raised the other, empty, with the fingers curled, and brought it forward in a throwing motion.

With no warning, Oz folded his wings and dropped. He was almost too late. A blinding afterimage of electric blue light seared the air where they had been. Even with his stomach in freefall, James flinched from the heat of it.

Oz snapped out his wings and leveled out, jarring James painfully against the saddle. They had lost a couple hundred feet of altitude, and there was a scorched smell in the air.

"You okay?" James gasped out. All his internal organs felt like they'd slammed into each other like cars on a derailing train. He was glad for the straps holding him to the saddle.

"I think so." Oz sounded shaken. He twisted his head around, looking at his side. There was a sooty mark across the scales behind the saddle. It looked like it had just missed his wing.

"Hey!" James yelled at the ref, who was casually hovering not too far away with rapid, fluttering wingbeats. "She's cheating!"

"She didn't use a weapon. Spells are permissible as long as they don't require components to wield."

"Shit! How much magic does she have?"

"Whatever battle spells she's learned," the ref said. "You may use your battle magic as well."

Fan-fucking-tastic.

"But you *do* have magic," Oz said, low, as he beat his wings to bring him back up to Valor's level.

"Only the gun! Which I can't draw without forfeiting."

Valor was doing nothing at the moment. Her unicorn stood in midair, occasionally stamping an impatient hoof. She seemed to be waiting to see what they would do next. Oz circled her slowly in a long glide.

"Doesn't the gun protect you from magic?" Oz asked.

"It protects me. Not you." A major oversight that he was now severely regretting. "In fact it might make it worse. If a spell rebounds off me, it'll hit you. And, at a thousand feet, she doesn't have to hit *me* with a lightning bolt or a sleep spell; she only has to hit you. We'll be equally dead either way."

"We could land—"

"Yeah, where she's faster and more maneuverable, and we can't easily get away."

Valor seemed to come to a decision. She urged her unicorn forward. Her hand, held low at her side, whipped up and overhand. James was watching for it this time, started to yell a warning, but Oz was also alert and barrel-rolled wildly to the side. Only the straps held James to the saddle; there was a weightless instant, the disorienting flash of green grass above his head, a sense of gravity and momentum playing tug-of-war—and a ripple in the air as whatever she'd thrown at them missed them, barely. The wind of its passing ruffled his hair.

Oz leveled out, breathing hard. "I take it biting is now on the table."

"Please. Yes. Bite anything you can reach."

They were below Valor and the unicorn again, having lost more altitude in the last attack. Oz beat upward, arrowing straight at them. Valor waited, and as they closed on her, abruptly the wings of light vanished, and she and the unicorn plunged downward. Oz's jaws snapped futilely, mere feet from the unicorn's flying mane. The unicorn's wings caught the air below them; its hooves found purchase, and it broke into a short gallop before wheeling around.

"Oh, now it's on," Oz growled. He folded his wings and dived like a hawk.

This time, from above, he had the advantage; there was nowhere Valor and the unicorn could go. Instead, purple light bloomed across Valor's armor and the unicorn's glossy pelt. When Oz hit, jaws wide open, his teeth slid off as if he'd tried to bite a glass sphere. Momentum carried him onward, though he did knock the two of them off balance. As Oz wheeled around for another go, James looked back and saw Valor hauling herself back into the saddle.

"Of course they have a freaking shield. Of *course* they do."

Oz's sides inflated. "Cover your face," he said thickly. James could already feel the heat baking up from below. He threw an arm over his face and pulled his legs up as well, and hoped Oz had the control not to fry his rider as well as his target.

He'd seen Oz use fire only once, while half-conscious and drugged. This was something entirely different from that weak, sickly flare. It was a searing white beam, erupting from the dragon's throat and lancing through the air toward its target with a deafening crack that suggested the air itself was being superheated in its path. James, peering below the arm flung across his forehead, felt as if the skin on his face was blistering, as if his hair might catch on fire.

Valor dived—straight into the path of the beam: Oz, anticipating her, had aimed slightly below. She yanked the unicorn's reins and they rolled wildly to the side, tumbling in freefall. The beam clipped the violet shield with an explosion of sparks, and as Valor and the unicorn tumbled, the shield winked out. For an instant, they were falling helplessly, and then the light-wings bloomed again and the unicorn caught itself, stumbling, just above the treetops. Valor was hanging onto the saddle; she clung for a shaken instant before hauling herself back up.

James cautiously lowered his arm from his face. He fingered at his cheeks to make sure nothing was burned. The skin felt tender, as if with a mild sunburn.

"Good Lord. Uh . . . how many of those do you have in you?"

"Not many." Oz's sides heaved, panting. "I won't be able to do it again for a few minutes."

"Think she knows that?" But Valor was already galloping toward them again, the unicorn tilted at an angle as if it was racing up a hill, though there was nothing but sky under its hooves. "Of course she does."

Valor gripped the saddle with one hand and trailed her other through the air, fingers spread, like a child trailing a hand over the side of a boat into lake water. The air rippled visibly around her fingers.

Oz hovered, wings beating hard, watching to see which way to dive. When the movement came, the shimmering spread out in a series of ripples expanding from her fingers, like a net made of air.

And that was exactly what it was. Oz tried to roll out of the way, but there was nowhere to go. The ripples closed around them, and Oz let out a shocked yelp as his wings were pinioned to his sides and he began to fall.

James couldn't feel much of anything, except a sort of fizzing against his skin. Wherever the strands of sky-rope contacted his body, they melted, banished by the spellgun's magic-nullifying properties.

Which did absolutely nothing to help Oz.

Oz managed to wrestle one wing most of the way free, enough to keep them from being in total freefall—but they tumbled wildly, spinning around, sky-ground-sky. James began struggling with the straps on the saddle.

"What are you doing!" Oz roared.

"I think I can get those off you. Just have to—get *to* them—"

As the last strap came free, he was horribly aware that his tenuous grip on the saddle was the only thing between him and death. Centrifugal forces pulled at him as Oz jinked this way and that, managing to stay in the air one-winged by sheer frantic effort. James had no idea where Valor was, and couldn't spare the attention to find out.

Instead, keeping his grip on the saddle, he swung his legs onto Oz's flexing, muscular neck. He had only been guessing, but he was right: wherever his body touched, the distortion of the invisible net faded to nothing. Oz gave a sudden gasp and thrust out with a foreleg that had been pinned to his body and was now abruptly free.

"Whatever you're doing, James, I—ah!"

Oz's wingtip clipped a treetop, scattering leaves and twigs. They'd lost nearly all their altitude. As Oz strained to keep them from colliding with the trees, James tried to clamber down to the dragon's pinned wing without losing his grip on the saddle.

Before he managed to do more than free the base of the wing, they hit the ground in a clear space between the trees. Oz threw out his forelegs to break their fall, but his chin smacked into the ground and he plowed up a tremendous furrow of overturned earth, sod, and bushes. James hung onto the side of the saddle until they ground to a halt and the shower of dirt and twigs stopped falling.

"Oz? You okay?"

Oz spat out a mouthful of dirt and blood. "Hurry!" he ground out. His pinned wing jerked spasmodically as he tried to free it. He struggled to get to his feet, but one foreleg wouldn't take his weight, and he fell over again, back legs still entangled with invisible bonds.

James half-climbed, half-fell from the dragon's back to the churned-up ground. "Stop thrashing around before you crush me."

Oz went still, quivering with adrenaline and stress. James had never touched his wings before, and it felt strangely intimate now. The great spars of his heavily muscled wingbones were covered with scales like the rest of him, but delicate, as fine as those of a grass snake. The powerful muscles were warm to the touch, flexing slightly under James's hands. He felt the slight fizzing on his skin as the bonds dissolved, parting one by one.

The shadow of Valor's unicorn swept over them, flickered across the trees and circled back around.

"James—"

"I know!"

Valor and her unicorn thumped to the ground in a quick drumbeat of hooves, just a few dozen yards away in the clearing. Hissing furiously, Oz exerted a tremendous effort and tore his wing free of its remaining bonds. His sides huffed up; it looked like he was gathering another burst of flame.

Valor moved her hand in the same overhand throwing gesture she'd used to throw lightning at them before.

It was Oz she was aiming at, and on the ground, he couldn't dodge. James had a split second to choose to roll out of the way, or—

He jumped in front of Oz.

CHAPTER TWELVE

HE HADN'T BEEN ENTIRELY SURE the gun's protective field could stand up to the full force of those lightning attacks— but it did. There was a sharp snap like the sting of a rubber band across his chest and face, and the searing flash grounded in a nearby tree with a deafening crack. The tree was torn in half, slowly parting to fall two ways in a crash and swirl of leaves.

For a moment Valor was frozen in total shock, staring at him with her hand upraised.

"Up, up!" James yelled, scrambling into the saddle.

Oz gave a tremendous downbeat and launched himself skyward. James fumbled for the straps and then gave up on trying to fasten them midflight and concentrated on holding on.

"Did you see the look on her face!" Oz chortled. "How did you know that would work?"

"I didn't."

Oz twisted his supple neck around a hundred and eighty degrees to give James a horrified look.

"What? It would have *killed* you, Oz."

"Not necessarily!" Oz said indignantly. "Dragons are quite resilient! It would most likely only have hurt." He sounded, James thought, somewhat less than certain, but was back to full indignation a moment later. "Do *not* do anything like that again."

"Right, next time I'll just let her fry you. Speaking of which . . ."

Valor was aloft again, her unicorn galloping up an incline of empty air. But she was falling behind; when it came down to wings versus hooves, she couldn't outrun them in the air.

On the other hand, they couldn't win by running away from her.

"What's she doing now?" James asked warily. Rather than pursuing them, Valor continued to climb; she was merely a speck against the sky, high above them.

"I don't care. This time I *will* burn her," Oz snarled, wheeling around with wings outstretched.

"I wouldn't get too close. She's clearly got something in mind."

"I don't need to get close. I only need to get her in flaming distance."

"Yeah, well, your flame range seems to be about her lightning range, so try not to get us killed, would you?"

As Oz winged back around, James kept a watch on the tiny figure with its violet flare of wings. Valor had stopped in midair and was just sitting there on unicorn-back, watching them from above.

She's definitely up to something.

Oz huffed up his sides, smoke spilling out of his mouth. James threw an arm over his face and added "asbestos armor" to his mental shopping list.

Heat seared James's face, prickled his skin, frizzed the ends of his hair. In the same instant, he glimpsed the unicorn's wings wink out like a popped soap bubble. But it was just *before* the fire hit her . . .

"Oz, look out!"

Valor and the unicorn plunged like a rock; then the light-wings snapped out, and the tremendous momentum of their plummeting fall turned, instead, into a glide aimed straight at James and Oz. Valor snapped out her hand, and this time a sword of purple light bloomed from her fingertips.

Her targeting was near-perfect, her speed and Oz's surprise combining to make her impossible to avoid. The two mounts slammed into each other with a terrific shock that nearly knocked James—still untethered—out of the saddle. As he scrabbled for a handhold, he looked up and saw the sword coming directly at his head, with Valor's grim face behind it.

He threw out an arm uselessly to block it, as if *that* would do anything—but it did; the sword evaporated as soon as it contacted his skin.

Valor's hand slid past his arm, throwing her off balance. She half-fell over the back of his saddle, rolled onto her shoulder, and hooked a hand through the gunbelt. She gave it a tremendous yank that felt like it bruised everything between his rib cage and pelvis, and pulled his hips off the saddle.

James kicked at her face. Valor hung on tenaciously. Her horned helm had been knocked off in the struggle; with her short hair fluttering in the wind, she dangled from Oz's saddle, held up by nothing but her grip on the gunbelt. The unicorn was nowhere to be seen. Struggling, clawing at the saddle, and trying to kick her, James was pulled inexorably after her.

Valor got her other hand into the opposite side of the gunbelt—now she was wrapped around his legs, while James tried desperately to hang onto the saddle and struggled to bring up a knee to kick her somewhere vulnerable.

Valor wrenched her hands apart, and the leather stretched before the buckle snapped. The belt slithered out of its loops, and she slipped quietly over the side and fell, one hand triumphantly gripping the gunbelt.

She didn't fall far. The unicorn glided in, moving like it was sliding with its hooves on ice, and Valor fell across its back and struggled upright. James caught glimpses of this in between climbing back into Oz's saddle, wheezing for air. His entire midsection felt like one giant bruise, and there was a stabbing pain in his chest whenever he tried to breathe. He was not *nearly* healed enough for this level of physical activity.

"That cannot possibly be a legal move!" he yelled at the ref as soon as he had enough breath to get it out. The manticore was winging lazily nearby, staying well back from the combatants. "She had a sword!"

"No rules were violated," the manticore intoned. "Weapons of entirely magical nature are intrinsic to the natural abilities of the combatants and therefore legal."

"I don't think we're getting fair ref calls here," James snapped, rubbing at his tender ribs.

"I *knew* they were nothing but cheating blackguards, the lot of them." Oz sounded scandalized.

"Dunno if it's cheating exactly, but let's just say I don't think they're above taking her side over ours whenever they feel like it."

"That sounds suspiciously like cheating."

"Tomayto, tomahto." James peered over Oz's wing. The unicorn was below them, stamping in the air while Valor divided her wary attention between keeping an eye on them and examining the gunbelt.

"Okay, let's try her trick, then. Oz, drop me on her."

"Is that a good idea?" Oz asked.

"Probably not, but look, she's way more experienced at this than we are, she's got a bigger box of tricks, and now she's got my gun. What have we got to lose?"

"Your life?" Oz muttered, but he folded his wings and stooped in a hawklike dive. His body huffed up with clear intentions of flaming.

"Oz!" James yelled past the screaming wind. He bent low and clung to the saddle with both hands, his legs pressed so tightly to Oz's sides that the muscles shook with tension. "Oz, be careful, I need to get the gun back—!"

"Misdirection," Oz said out of the corner of his mouth, and opened his jaws wide. Smoke trailed from the corners of his mouth like contrails.

Valor hastily looped the gunbelt over the front of the saddle and wheeled the unicorn around, but Oz made no attempt to either flame her or hit her. Instead he abruptly checked in midair above her with wild backbeats and flipped upside down.

James was totally unprepared. The cool, graceful action-hero slide off the saddle that he'd planned was instead a frantic, clawing fall. He smacked into Valor from above with all his limbs flailing. His chin cracked the top of her head and he saw stars.

At least Valor was caught just as thoroughly off guard. She let out a startled squawk as they both tumbled off the unicorn's back. The unicorn dodged sideways and, with the grace and aplomb of a performing circus horse, intercepted them before they plunged into the trees below.

Valor landed on her back on the saddle, with James on top of her. They rolled around wildly. She tried to punch him in the throat; he kneed her in the stomach and the bruising jolt from the armor went all the way up to his groin. He managed to get a fist in her hair, but she jammed her hand under his chin and thrust back with a snap that might have broken his neck if they hadn't almost rolled off the unicorn again.

On the ground he had no doubt that she would have defeated him in moments. James had a lot of scrappy fighting skills picked up over the years, but she was far stronger, more experienced, and almost certainly knew actual martial arts attacks that probably had names and everything.

But she didn't seem to expect someone pulling her hair and trying to knee her in the chest. The unicorn's broad back rolled around wildly under them, catching them every time they nearly fell off, but the effect was like brawling on top of a wide, rolling log.

"Just let us leave," James gasped out, getting a hand around her throat. She rammed an elbow into his side with an impact that felt like being hit with a two-by-four. He was really regretting not having armor right now. "All we want to do is take the kid and—*erk*—"

Violet sparks burst behind his eyes with a snap of electricity that he felt in his back teeth; there was a metal taste in his mouth. But Valor stiffened and spasmed at the same time. She recovered first, and punched him in the neck.

Ears ringing, he felt himself going over the unicorn's side, the sense of tremendous space opening up under him, and grabbed wildly for anything to stop his fall. Instead he got a grip on Valor's broad, mailed body, and she went over the side with him.

There was a moment of stomach-lifting freefall before they rebounded off something rubbery and trampoline-like that turned out to be Oz's wing. Oz lifted his wing and redirected them toward his back. Still grappling, they rolled down his wing and thumped against the saddle.

Valor threw out a hand and pressed it to Oz's flexing neck. "Desist or I kill your—"

James kicked her in the face. Her head snapped back; her hand slipped off Oz's neck, and, overbalanced, the rest of her followed.

It was on pure autopilot that he lunged and caught her.

For a terrifying, weightless moment, they both hung on the edge of a thousand-foot plunge. Then Oz rolled the other way, and they toppled back into the saddle, James half flattened under Valor's armored bulk. Their faces were less than a foot apart, their bodies pressed together. He felt her heartbeat like a series of explosions, and the shocked fear was glass-clear on her face before it iced over into a look of glacial calm. Almost casually, she pinned his arms.

"So the way I see it," James said more calmly than he felt, looking up at her with her armored weight crushing his lower body and the back of his skull grinding into the backrest of the saddle, "I just saved your life."

Valor bared her teeth in a fierce smile. "Savage would have caught me."

"Really?" James said. "Are you absolutely sure about that?"

She leaned down, speaking through that vicious smile. "If you expected gratitude, perhaps you should think twice before saving an enemy next time."

"You know what I think?" She was half crushing him; he could barely breathe.

"Not much, I expect."

"Ha ha. I think you're not actually trying to kill me."

"Your defeat is assured, human."

"Yeah?" James said. "Then how come this fight is still going on?" There was a fierce "Ha!" from Oz, which James chose to ignore. Instead, he said, "So here's the thing. I don't think you're actually fighting at a hundred percent. I think if you were, you'd have wiped us off the map in the first couple of minutes. We're just not in your league."

"Hey! I object!" Oz snapped, twisting his neck around

with his ruff flattened. "Speak for yourself. I am *entirely* in her league. Above and beyond it, even."

"Oz, shut up."

Valor straightened slightly. She was still crushing his lower body in a way that might have been suggestive if she wasn't all but breaking his spine, not to speak of his pelvis. She also still had his hands pinned.

"I thought you agreed they were cheating to win," Oz said huffily.

"The ref's definitely not on our side," James said. "But you don't really *want* to win, do you?"

Valor let out a snort. "There is little honor to be gained from defeating an enemy such as you."

"But losing to an enemy like me would be worse."

"Well," she said, "obviously."

The delay in the fight was starting to attract attention. Valor's war-unicorn swooped above them, so near that his dangling hooves nearly brushed Oz's neck. The ref was also moving in for a closer look.

"You'd better hit me if you want this to look good," James pointed out.

He realized his mistake as soon as Valor balled up a mailed fist, but it was too late. The fist smashed into his cheekbone; the world exploded in fireworks.

He came back to reality dazedly with Valor's hand knotted in his hair and her gauntleted fingers wrapped around his throat. Oz was sweeping wide circles in the air with his head twisted all the way around and his teeth bared, inches from the back of Valor's head.

"It appears," Valor said in a tight voice through barely moving lips, "that we have a questionable situation here."

"Questionable," James choked out.

"I have clearly defeated you."

"No you have *not*," Oz snarled, the gust of his hot breath washing over them, and the saddle rolled as his sides inflated.

"Oz," James gasped, "keep in mind humans aren't fireproof."

"But you saved me earlier," Valor said, frowning down at him. "This means that by fae law, I *owe* you. And your dragon, it seems, is prepared to kill me if I kill you."

"Damn straight," Oz declared, smoke seeping out between his teeth.

Valor tightened her grip on his hair, enough to bring stinging tears to his eyes. "This feels suspiciously like a standoff."

"Guess so," James wheezed out.

"Sir dragon," Valor said to Oz, "take us to the ground, if you wouldn't mind."

"How about I bite your head off instead."

"Try it and I will pull his head off his neck."

"Or we could land," James got out.

Oz hissed fiercely, but James felt the drop in his stomach that meant they were descending. Valor eased up on her grip on his hair a little . . . but only a little.

They landed in the middle of the field. He was aware of this mainly by the vague awareness of a vast green space around them. The ref and Valor's war-unicorn both dropped to the grass beside them.

"Do you declare victory, champion?" the ref asked.

"I do not," Valor said, and James twisted his head ever so slightly to the side so he could appreciate the manticore's expression. "In fact, I have a difficult point of honor to contend. This *human*—this pathetic weakling, this lesser being, this sniveling worm—"

Oz's sides huffed up again. James, afraid to say anything at this point for fear of knocking their fragile truce out of kilter, kicked him in the ribs as hard as one could while bent backward over a saddle.

"—saved my life," Valor said. James genuinely couldn't tell whether she was playacting or not. She sounded absolutely disgusted. "He did not have to. It would have been very easy for him to let me fall. I cannot ignore this; my honor requires that I acknowledge it."

"Your steed was waiting to catch you," the manticore declared.

"There is no guarantee, is there? I cannot fly without Savage."

"How can you be sure he did not save you to have you in his debt, as an intentional ploy?"

"Does it matter?" Valor asked. "If it was a ploy, it was quite a clever one, that perhaps not more than one in ten of our people would have even thought of. He could quite easily have killed himself in the attempt. Few among us, I think, can boast of such courage."

While Valor debated the referee, the spectators had been drifting in from all over in small clumps, mounted and on foot and in some cases in small chariots or coaches. Foremost among them was Prudence on her small, browbeaten unicorn—a very different sort of steed from Savage with his heavily muscled draft horse's body. She carried a drowsing Nikki in front of her, the child's head drooping against her breast. Maybe one reason why Nikki was so hard to deal with was because she'd spent very little of her life actually being awake.

Vic stumbled along beside the unicorn. There were cuffs on his hands and a guard flanking him on each side.

"Let it be known," Valor said, "that I *could* have won, quite easily—"

True, James thought.

"But I refuse to owe anyone a favor," Valor snapped. "I

discharge this debt by granting him a victory not of skill, but of honor."

And she released her grasp and sat back in the saddle. James sat up, trying not to cough too overtly.

Murmurs passed through the gathered assemblage. Vic, who had been slumped against the silver haunch of Prudence's unicorn as if his legs would barely hold him up, straightened up with a shocked look.

Prudence's butterflies lifted from her body in a swirl, as if a breeze had passed through them. Her inhumanly beautiful face twisted in a way that made it suddenly ugly.

"You defeated this wretch," she snarled. "Finish him!"

Valor drew herself up. "I was in position to defeat him only because he gave me the opportunity. To kill him now would be the worst kind of base, honorless cowardice." She turned to fix James with her direct gaze. "Do you accept this discharge of my debt, human? I owe you nothing now."

"Uh . . . yeah. Debt accepted." And he stuck out a hand without really thinking about it.

Valor stared for an instant, then grasped his hand and squeezed it in a hard, businesslike clench of her mailed fingers that felt like it left bruises to match the ones that were almost certainly purpling on his face and turning his torso to a mass of black and blue.

Savage trotted up. Oz turned his head and hissed. James kicked him in the ribs again. "Knock it off," he muttered.

Valor leaned over to retrieve the spellgun and belt, still looped over Savage's saddlehorn. "Your weapon."

Hauling Nikki like a doll, Prudence stood up on her unicorn's back, balancing easily in her bare feet, to bring herself up to their level. "I forbid this," she snapped. "You are my champion. You cannot concede. I will not allow it."

"I didn't," Valor said. She vaulted from Oz's back into Savage's saddle, landing with a solid thump. "I was beaten, admittedly through a base and underhanded trick. Would any of you have done differently?" she demanded of the assembled crowd. "Allow a human to incur a debt over you?"

The murmurs suggested that they were, while not precisely happy with James's technical victory, at least prepared to accept its validity. Vic looked dazed.

"There would be no debt if you killed him!" Prudence snarled.

"I have not killed a defeated opponent in two centuries," Valor said. She smiled slightly. Sitting loose and confident on the back of her gleaming black unicorn, she looked every inch a winner. "I do not plan to start now."

Prudence whirled on the ref.

"It is a legal victory," the manticore said, raising his hands. The stinger tail pulsed in time with his words. He didn't look happy about it, but neither did he look like he was about to turn on them. "All has happened in accordance with proce- dure. Victorious's champion won the fight, and you are both bound by the terms of the arrangement."

A shiver seemed to pass through the air, like a silver chime just out of earshot, felt rather than heard. Magic, James thought. The fae were powerful, entirely out of the league of humanity, but they were bound by their own rules just as surely as humans were subject to gravity and age and the need for food and sleep.

Prudence's delicate hands curled like claws, and for an instant her sharp, perfect teeth pressed into the swell of her lower lip, raising bright drops of blood. Then she turned on the unicorn's back, the butterflies ruffling around her.

"Cut him free," she said, and the guards moved to obey. James noticed that they touched the shackles only with gloved hands, and the skin on Vic's wrists was blistered and welted where the bonds had touched.

But he held up his arms without complaint when

Prudence handed Nikki down to him—dropped her, rather —and clasped her to his chest.

"So the deal was, if we win, we can leave, right?" James said.

If looks could kill, Prudence's expression would have dropped him in his tracks.

"If we win, we shall all be set free, the four of us, not to be pursued, harassed, or harmed in any way," Oz quoted himself. His neck spikes were perked up at a jaunty angle.

From the look on Prudence's face, she was looking as hard as she could for a loophole, but in the end, she only gave a brief, tight nod.

CHAPTER THIRTEEN

I T   W A S   D O W N R I G H T   anticlimactic coming out of a fae portal into small-town Iowa.

James thought it might have made the transition easier if it was anything other than the middle of the day—sunset maybe, or the middle of the night with an eerie wind blowing. Instead there was a bright noon sun overhead, casting small pools of shadow and knocking any vestiges of chill off the humid late-summer air.

Valor had brought them out where they had started from, beside the pond in the park. The playground area was deserted, but there was a family having a picnic on the grass and a couple of teenagers fishing in the pond. James's Trans Am was still where he'd left it, now parked beside an older, dirt-covered Chevy Suburban.

Vic rode on Oz's back with Nikki in his lap. Oz looked less than pleased about this arrangement, but was putting up with it with the long-suffering air of a cat enduring an unwanted brushing. James walked alongside. They were escorted by an entourage of silent, mounted fae guards, led by Valor.

"So nobody just noticed us materializing in the middle of nowhere?" James asked.

"We're under a glamour," Valor said. "I'll drop it in a minute, when we leave."

"You seem to be taking your defeat awfully well. Is this going to blow back on you?"

"Blow back?"

"You know. Get you in trouble."

She rested an elbow on the saddle's pommel, leaning over Savage's neck to give him a smile. "Why would it? This isn't my first duel, nor my first defeat. It was clear that I would have beaten you."

"So you claim," Oz muttered. Savage flattened his ears.

"But you won through base human trickery. The court will be talking about it for *years*. I'm sure it will help cement your kind's reputation as sneaks and tricksters, which will only benefit you in the long run."

"Fae think *we're* tricksters?"

"Of course," Valor said, sounding surprised. "Your kind's inclination for mischief is well known."

She straightened in her saddle and raised a fist to the rest of the guard, who faded back through the portal, one by one. On the other side, the vast trees of the fae forest rustled in the wind.

"It was nice meeting you, and a shame we had to fight," Savage said to Oz—startling James once again, who had all but forgotten the unicorn could talk.

"It's not your fault," Oz said magnanimously. "I appreciate the hospitality, and invite you to enjoy mine, if you are ever in the area."

"I don't know if I shall be, but I will remember it."

Vic had been riding in silence, lost in thought or possibly on the verge of passing out, with Nikki still sleeping her charmed sleep in his lap. Now he raised his head and turned to look at Valor. "I am in your debt," he said.

"You most assuredly are not. I lost fairly, because of the human's cunning treachery, of course." She glanced at the child in his lap without much interest. "I still don't know what's so fascinating about that creature, but I hope you enjoy having it."

With that, she rode through the portal. It winked out behind her, and there was an outbreak of exclamations from the family on the grass when they noticed the dragon who had shown up out of nowhere.

"You know, she could have taken us home," Oz remarked.

"My car is here."

"I can give you another car."

"Oz, I swear, please stop trying to give me things."

The picnicking family had their phones out and were taking pictures of Oz, who stretched his neck and preened. James slapped his shoulder. "Come on, let's roll."

The Trans Am had a piece of paper tucked under the windshield wiper. James expected a ticket, but it turned out to be a polite notice that there was no overnight parking at the pond. Small towns. James crumpled it up and stuffed it into his pocket.

Oz sniffed and prodded with his claw at the twisted metal post where the side mirror had torn off. "You damaged a vintage automobile," he growled at Vic.

"It was self-defense," Vic said defensively, hitching Nikki up against his shoulder.

"You owe me repairs."

"Oz, you can afford to have it fixed," James said.

"It's the principle of the thing!"

James looked thoughtfully at Vic, who was still more than half bandages and looked like he was barely staying on his feet. "What *are* you planning to do next, anyway?"

Vic gave him a dazed look, and slowly shook his head. "I didn't even expect to be alive." He adjusted Nikki against his shoulder again, his one good arm tiring. "You can drop us off somewhere. We'll be fine."

James thought of the imprisoned farm family, the entire neighborhood warped around Vic's presence. He wondered what, exactly, he'd unleashed on the mortal world. "Actually, it might be better for me to take you back to Grand Bluffs." Vic started to shake his head again. "Look, you've got no money, no mortal identity, no job. And you've got a mortal child. We can figure out what to do about her birth family later, I guess there's no rush, but she's going to have to go to school, you know that, right? She'll need immunizations, doctor visits, all that stuff. You know anything about that?" Vic just looked blank. "Yeah, that's what I thought."

Oz snaked his neck around to look down at the three of them. "They can stay with me."

"Er, what?" James said.

"Yes. That is an excellent solution." A look of smug self-assurance settled over Oz's long face. "Fae are not the only ones who can provide hospitality. Ha! I shall show you hospitality. I have a mansion of my very own, shared with none—er, except the rooftop gargoyle—and a hunting preserve I think you ought to find quite satisfactory."

James punched him in the shoulder. All he did was bruise his hand on the scales. "Oz, do you think that's a good idea?"

"Why not? What is that human saying—keep your friends close and your enemies closer?" Oz squinted at Vic and Nikki, eyes narrowing to slits. It was a worrying expression. "I will keep a *very* close watch on you. And under my tutelage, you shall repair this automobile."

Vic seemed slightly shell-shocked, not entirely tracking the conversation. He stared at Oz for a little while before answering at last. "That would be . . . appreciated. I think. I have no clear idea of the hospitality obligations in this world. How long would you allow us to stay?"

"Stay as long as you want, the depths of my hospitality are bottomless, unlike the miserly ways of your—*what?*" Oz demanded when James reached as high as possible and grabbed the end of his muzzle to try to shut him up.

"They're *fae*, Oz. Well, Vic is, at least. Be careful what you promise, remember?"

"Oh. Ah. Right." Oz looked down his nose at Vic. "There will be contracts. *Many* contracts." He rattled his claws. "I am planning them already."

"On that note, we have a long drive ahead of us," James said. He unlocked the car. "Let's get on the road, why don't we?"

"Ah," Vic said, giving the car an unimpressed look. "I was going to wake Nikki up. It's not good for her to leave her in faesleep too long. But she seems to be not very—er—"

"She's going to have to learn to ride in cars eventually. There are a lot of them here."

Oz cleared his throat. "It would be much faster if you'd all simply ride back on me. Yes, even you," he added, fixing Vic with another stare. "If you're to be my houseguest, I *suppose* I could let you ride on my back when necessary. Don't get used to it."

James twirled the Trans Am's keys in his hand. They had relinquished the saddle back in the fae lands, and he had an all too vivid sense-memory of riding Oz's narrow, hard spine. Then again, spending hours with a carsick Nikki didn't sound like a laugh a minute, either.

"What say you fly them back, and I'll drive the car? I could use the time to clear my head."

Oz crouched down, offering a knee politely. Vic scrambled on with difficulty, Nikki slung over his bad shoulder. He got Nikki propped in front of him, and then passed a hand across the child's eyes.

"Wake up, little one. Look where we are."

Nikki blinked slowly and rubbed her eyes. "Where's Mommy?"

"Mommy isn't here," Vic said, and bared his teeth slightly. "But you've got me. And look, you get to ride on a dragon."

"You'll be all right here?" Oz asked James, cocking his head to look down.

"I'm capable of driving back to Grand Bluffs on my own, Oz. See you there."

Oz spread his wings and took off with a great downbeat, sending James stumbling back in a slipstream of dust. The last thing James heard was Oz saying cheerfully, "So how do you feel about classic cars?"

~

He had plenty of time for second thoughts, driving north through the long golden Midwest afternoon, with AC/DC on the stereo and the Trans Am eating up the miles. If Prudence decided to seek some sort of revenge, having Vic in town was the absolute last thing he needed. A thousand miles away might be too close.

Not to mention the hassle of it all. He didn't need to get himself mixed up with a displaced fae and a spoiled human child. And he had no illusions about who was going to get stuck with the headache of explaining things like taxes and childhood vaccinations, since Oz had only the loosest grasp on the conventions of human culture himself.

Still . . . it didn't just feel right to turn them loose on the human world—either for their sakes or that of the random bystanders who would have to deal with them.

He stopped for gas and bought a bottle of aspirin from a

convenience store clerk who gave him a look that made him suspect his bruised face was turning a variety of lovely colors. His head hurt, his chest hurt, and even turning slightly left or right made him gasp in pain.

Next time, he thought, *if they want to give you armor, take the damn armor.*

He reached Grand Bluffs at sunset, with the river off to his right shining like polished brass under the setting sun. There were a couple of texts from Oz on his phone, which he ignored for the moment while he swung by his building to take a quick shower and change into clothes he hadn't been wearing since yesterday.

Under the lights of his bathroom, he winced at the bruises girdling his stomach and mottling his ribs. At least he didn't seem to have done too much damage to his healing chest injury. The bullet scar was still pink and fresh, but not sore or bleeding. The bruise under his eye was starting to puff up. He probed his split lip with his tongue.

He examined the shirt he had picked up in the fae lands. It was a silk so fine that it seemed to glide, waterlike, through his fingers. Did you have to get it dry cleaned? Launder it with regular laundry? For perhaps the first time in his life he looked for a care tag, but naturally there wasn't one. It was probably spun from spider silk under the light of the full moon or something equally bizarre. He dropped it in the hamper.

"James!"

James spun around, caught himself with a pained gasp. At least he still had his pants on. "Hi, Dolly. I didn't know you could get all the way up to the apartment floor of the building."

The ghost was standing in the bathroom doorway. She didn't reflect in the mirror, something he realized he had never wondered about before.

"Only sometimes," she said. "I've been keeping an eye on it for you. Wow, you sure do get hit in the face a lot. Are you okay?"

"Long story." He reached for a T-shirt. "Any action while I was gone?"

"None at all. How long *were* you gone?"

"Just about a day and a half," he said, muffled, through the shirt. Dolly couldn't reliably tell time in her noncorporeal state. Tugging it down, he added, "I've got a heck of a story to tell you, but first I have to get over to Oz's for a little while."

"Come down to the basement first," Dolly said. "I want to show you something."

~

NOT MUCH HAD CHANGED. The piles of lumber were still where they'd been, everything stopped in mid-construction, a reminder that he was going to need to look for a new contractor who wouldn't be scared off by having an unhappy poltergeist hanging around the place.

Dolly had drifted downstairs with James; now she pointed to the wall behind the building supplies. "There. Take a look and see what you think."

He started to ask what she meant—and then he saw.

The wall was brick, old and crumbling, with traces of paint left from the long-ago days of Dolly's time, when this basement used to be a speakeasy called the Peony Club.

Now, the wall had been scratched up, as if someone had taken a knife or claw-sharp fingernails and gone to work on it.

"Uh, Dolly . . ."

What *was* this, some kind of poltergeist temper tantrum? But before he had a chance to ask, he took a step back and suddenly saw the pattern to it.

It was a map, of sorts. No, a blueprint. There were dense notations scratched along the edges.

"You asked me what I wanted," Dolly said. She was all proud smiles, fairly glowing in her delight. "So I've been working on it. You can change anything you like, of course. I looked at your plans too." She pointed to the sheets of contractors' paper, which had been neatly rolled up when he left, and now were unrolled and spread out on the floor. "So it's really just yours with some modifications. What do you think?"

He didn't quite have the heart to tell her that if the basement had been slightly eerie before, having a poltergeist scratch a complex web of diagrams on the wall wasn't doing anything to make it less creepy. "I think it looks good, but I'm going to need to take some time with it. And transfer it to paper, obviously." And sand down the wall before the new contractors saw it and ran screaming like the last batch.

"Oh, yes, of course. I just wanted to tell you about it. Go have fun." She faded, but her lipstick smile lingered for a second or two, Cheshire-cat-like.

Sweet but weird. Exactly what you wanted in a poltergeist.

He went upstairs to get his jacket. When he picked it up, the stiff corner of the photo poked his hand. He pulled it out and looked at it, tilting it toward the light. Vic's serious face stared back at him.

It seemed like a normal photo now. It was no longer warm to the touch. But he still didn't trust it. No sense taking chances.

He got one of the lighters he kept around for lighting Dolly's summoning brazier and set the photo on fire in the sink. Flames curled up the photo, blackening and occluding Vic's face. When there was nothing left but ash, James washed the remains down the sink and headed out to see how Oz's guests were settling in.

～

THE MANSION WAS ALL LIT up, gleaming across the dark lawn. James parked in the sweeping drive. He would never be comfortable in Oz's world, but he couldn't help thinking of the first time he'd been here, and how much more out of place he'd felt then.

He knocked, got no answer, and let himself in through the vast double doors.

"Oz?"

There was the sound of music and voices coming from upstairs, which as he recalled was a large open living space, dragon-scale, like a living room scaled up to fit inside a ballroom. Before he'd made it halfway to the great sweeping staircase, however, he glimpsed Oz's quick, shadowy movement as the dragon launched himself from the top of the staircase. "Oz—" he began.

He didn't get any farther than that. The dragon, which definitely was *not* Oz, crashed to the floor with one set of enormous claws curled over James, knocking him down.

He had seen Oz pounce on people before, generally people who were trying to kill them, but had never fully appreciated how absolutely terrifying it was. He lay on his back, staring up at the dragon. Where Oz was gunmetal-colored, a sort of iridescent blue-gray, this dragon was sleek black, with startling, blood-red eyes like a pair of huge, glittering rubies.

"Oh, more humans." The dragon sounded disappointed. "Is this one for dinner?"

"No!" Oz said sternly from the top of the staircase. "No eating the guests. Oh, hello, James. I see you've met Neith."

359

"Hi," James squeaked out.

Neith lifted her foot and James scrambled quickly backward out of reach, his heart thumping like a rabbit's. Oz landed beside his daughter, making James realize how much smaller Neith was; she'd seemed enormous when she was on top of him, but seeing her and Oz side by side, he now recognized that she was maybe half Oz's size. Did dragons grow throughout their lives, like carp? He tried to stifle a half-hysterical laugh. There was enough adrenaline flooding his system right now to fuel a dorm full of exam-cramming college students.

Oz held out his vast paw, offering a claw delicately. It took James a moment to realize what it was for; then he caught hold of it and Oz helped him to his feet.

"I wasn't expecting to find your lair full of vermin, Father," Neith complained.

"Be polite," Oz admonished. To James, he said, "After our conversation yesterday, I decided to invite my daughter to visit, as we discussed. And here she is."

Neith scratched behind her ear with a claw. It was a very catlike motion. Compared to Oz, her entire suite of body language was less . . . *civilized* was the first word that came to mind, but that wasn't quite right. *Humanlike*, he thought. There was something more predatory about Neith. Oz had spent so much time around humans that he had either picked up some of their mannerisms, or learned to tone down his natural feral twitchiness so he didn't freak them out. There was something about Neith that made James reluctant to turn his back on her.

"I'm going hunting, Father," Neith said. "Do you want to come?"

"Not yet. Let me get my guests settled and see if they need anything first."

Neith clattered off, and Oz turned toward the staircase.

There was something different about it, but James had to get closer to realize what it was. The last time he'd been upstairs, Oz had to carry him. The risers on the stairs were scaled for a dragon, too far apart for a human to climb without a struggle or possibly mountaineering equipment.

Now there was a human-scale staircase that went up the side of the big one, like a pedestrian walkway alongside a highway bridge.

"Do you like it?" Oz asked anxiously, one large paw resting on the dragon stairs as James tested out the new staircase. "I thought this would be more convenient for small guests."

"Thanks, Oz." There was no railing, which presumably Oz hadn't even thought of, not being used to guests who couldn't fly. This became more alarming the higher up he got. On the other hand, Oz would catch him if he fell. Probably. "This is really thoughtful."

"Well, you're remodeling your entire office to fit me. It was the least I could do."

The upstairs had undergone a certain amount of redecorating as well. In addition to the dragon-sized couches and other furniture, there were small groupings of human-scale furniture, looking like dollhouse furnishings in the grandly scaled upstairs.

"You had human guests before, didn't you?"

"I did, but it hadn't occurred to me that anything tailored to my comfort would be inconvenient for them." Oz looked slightly abashed; the tip of his tail twitched. "I suppose I assumed the auto club *preferred* to stand."

James patted his flank. "Hey, I never even noticed my door was too small for people your size. Not your fault."

"Oh, that's true." Oz brightened.

Vic and Nikki were nowhere evident, but James followed the sound of a television to the far end of the loft, where a floor-to-ceiling velvet curtain turned out to be concealing a home theater setup. It was dim inside, but not entirely dark, lit by a wall screen that wouldn't have been out of place in an actual movie theater. There were dragon-scale couches here too, but they were low enough that James could have easily scrambled onto them.

Vic was stretched out, asleep, while Nikki lay beside him with her chin propped in her hands, enraptured by the cartoon playing on the screen. They looked doll-sized on the giant couch.

James ducked out again and let the curtain fall back into place, leaving them to it.

"As you can see," Oz said in what he probably thought was a whisper, "they are quite worn out from the day's exertions."

"What about you? You fought Valor and then flew back from here from Iowa."

Oz stretched a wing casually; it went all the way up to the ceiling. "I expect I'll be sore tomorrow. It was good to get a workout. It's easy to let myself go with all these modern conveniences." He grinned; it was a terrifying sight. "I expect a bit of light hunting will wind me down for sleeping. Would you care to come?"

"I hope you don't mean on foot, because I think Neith would consider me prey."

"Oh, she was only joking," Oz said, though to James's ear he didn't sound entirely convinced. "No, I was thinking perhaps you'd like to ride. We made a good team, I thought."

James thought so too, but he wasn't prepared to admit it. "One condition," he said, and Oz perked up, looking alertly attentive. "Do you have anything around here we could use for a saddle?"

EPILOGUE

"Dolly?" James called into the dim space of the basement.

It no longer echoed as it once had, now that interior walls had started going up. The speed of the transformation was startling. He was starting to be able to see the shape of the place in his head: a lobby and foyer, offices and conference space. Part of the interior warehouse floor had been knocked out for an indoor entrance, and light shafted down from above, filtering through bare wall studs as if through forest trees.

James flicked on the lights, and the bare bulbs dispelled some of the place's mystery and illuminated the outlines of the office it was going to be. He'd asked the workmen to leave the brick walls bare in the lobby—a large, dragon-accommodating space that encompassed the new inside entrance as well as the tunnel doors—and meant to decorate it in a 1920s style. It might be a selling point if clients knew the place used to be an old speakeasy. And Dolly was already happily planning the decor.

He trailed his fingers over the exposed brick, which still showed faded, crumbling traces of the bright paint that had once livened up the basement nightclub. Maybe they could paint it again, if not in the main lobby, then in the conference room opening off it.

A section of framed-in studs, half covered in drywall and half open, divided the lobby from what would become the conference room. He walked through the open wall, and stopped dead.

"Hello, James," Prudence said with a chill smile.

She stood at the far end of the room. The light around her had a strange, chill, gray quality, like the cool clarity of winter daylight after a snowstorm.

James drew the spellgun; it all but leaped to his hand, pointing at her before he had consciously decided to draw it.

"You have to stay away from us," he said. "It was the deal."

She took a step forward. Butterflies lifted around her in a swirling cloud. "That is *not* the deal. I may not harass, pursue, or harm you, and I'm not here to do any of those things. Actually, quite the contrary. I merely wished to stop by and offer a nod to you for your victory. I appreciate a worthy opponent."

"I don't have any desire to be your opponent," James said. "Or your anything."

"Hmm. We shall see what the future holds." That chill smile again, cool on lips like frosted plums. "But you have your own defenses this time, don't you?" She glanced at the spellgun, and there was a brief frisson of . . . *something* that crossed her face, a little flicker of surprise or even something vaguely like awe. "I knew I shouldn't have let you keep that device. Well, the mistake was mine. I won't make it next time."

"I don't know what you're talking about."

"No, of course not." And then, unexpectedly and worry-ingly, she laughed. "You have no idea what you've got there, do you?" She answered her own question immediately. "Of course you don't. Humans love to meddle with things they don't understand."

It was a game, he told himself. Another mindgame. Before now, he'd never even had a hint about the spellgun's origins or what it really was. She couldn't possibly know. Or did she?

"So it's fae, then," he said cautiously.

"Fae?" She laughed again. "Gracious, no. We wouldn't mess around with such things as *those*."

She disappeared in a cascade of snowflakes, fat and large, tumbling like dead butterflies through the air to collect on the bare floor.

After a long while, James cautiously holstered the spellgun. Its familiar weight on his hip no longer felt comforting. It felt like a grenade with the pin on the verge of falling out.

She was messing with you. He prodded at the melting snowflakes with the toe of his boot. They were already dissolving into a slushy puddle. *She doesn't know what it is any more than you do.*

But she had seen *something*. Something he couldn't. And now he really wondered what that something was.

Next:
The origins of the spellgun!
Dick and Demon
(Keeley & Assoc. #4)
Available on Amazon!

GHOSTS BEARING GIFTS

A KEELEY & ASSOCIATES BONUS STORY

THIS STORY TAKES place after Fae & Flatfoot. *It originally appeared as a bonus Christmas story on the mailing list.*

∾

IT WAS SNOWING OUTSIDE.

Dolly was aware of it in the same distant way that she was aware of the leak in a second-floor water pipe in the office-converted warehouse, the same way she knew there were people in the pizza parlor and the pull-tab place on the ground floor. The snow was a cool softness settling over the roof, where she sent a little bit of herself to check on the auklets nesting under the air conditioning unit. They were tucked in, rustling little bundles of feathered heat.

She made a mental note to tell James about the leaky pipe. It might freeze. She was a lot better at remembering things these days.

"Make me something fun!" a small, imperious voice commanded, and Dolly was drawn back to her current task.

She pulled herself—all of herself—into the basement

offices of Keeley & Associates. The basement had changed a great deal over the last few months. There was a wide staircase coming down from the warehouse above, opening into a lobby with comfortable furniture and flowers in vases and a solid, antique wooden bar that functioned as the reception desk.

The walls had been painted to match the old paint job, back in Dolly's time when this had been a speakeasy called the Peony Club. James had offered to do the entire lobby speakeasy-style for Dolly's sake, but she didn't really want that. Having more modern furnishings around the bar helped remind her where and when she was. But the paint was nice. The once-bare brick was splashed with vivid red and pink and white peonies, adding a dash of color to the otherwise classy but rather drab interior of the office.

"Dolly!" the child's voice ordered, and Dolly settled herself as firmly as possible in the here and now. She was sitting, or pretending to sit, on one end of a couch—plaid-covered, with sagging springs, it had been upstairs and was now down in the new office pending the arrival of nicer furniture. On the other end of the couch, a small child was curled in a fuzzy blanket with ponies on it. Her brown hair was done up in two neat pigtails.

"What would you like, Nikki?" Dolly asked. "Butterflies?"

A shudder seemed to run through the girl under the blanket. Nikki shook her head vigorously.

"No butterflies, okay. Let's see."

Dolly concentrated. She was getting better at this. For most of her ghostly existence, all she had ever done was drag a little portion of the 1920s into the real world with her. She didn't have much control over it. The club came with her, and left with her.

But since James had begun calling her back into the world, since she had confronted her own murderer and past, she had started to gain some mastery over her poltergeist abilities as well. She had haunted the building for almost a century, and in that time she had been a reactive force for the most part, chasing off tenants she didn't like and wrapping herself up in her ghostly version of the basement nightclub where she had worked as a living woman. Her loss and anger and sorrow had echoed through the building, helplessly driven by her almost uncontrollable emotions. She was the reason why most of the apartments on the third floor were vacant. James was the only person in years who had been willing to confront her as herself, to talk to her and learn about her and, eventually, help her resolve her murder.

Now, she curled her hands together, cupping them around each other, and opened them in a wide flourish. Horses like the ones on Nikki's blanket burst from her fingers.

She still didn't have as much control as she wanted, and as usual, her attempt to create ghostly illusions became wrapped around her memories of the past. The horses galloped out of her fingers in shades of pastel, but by the time they gained their footing, they were the milk and draft horses of Dolly's childhood.

Nikki sat up and giggled as the horses clattered around her, full-sized now and not pastel at all, but rather workaday brown and gray. They were in harness, snorting and puffing out clouds of steam into the cold air of a December long past. By the time Dolly had died, horses had almost entirely given way to noisy, smelly gasoline trucks, but when she was Nikki's age in the first decade of the 1900s, it was still horses that pulled the milk and ice wagons, horses who pulled the farmers' wagons to markets and carried the policeman and drew firemen's engines to a fire.

Summoned from her memories, a pair of heavyset bay draft horses with gleaming white socks and white-blazed muzzles galloped through the wall, their red harnesses jingling. The firehouse Dalmatian ran alongside the horses, guide and companion. Firemen on their steam engine in their smart red jackets—one driving the horses, two clinging on behind—were little more than an afterthought, blurred as in the background of a photograph.

Dolly, as a child of Nikki's age, had had eyes only for the horses.

The horses pulled up, snorting and stamping. Nikki leaned out with a small hand extended toward the black and white firehouse dog.

Dolly's horses snorted and circled while Dolly tried to free herself of the memories of the past and concentrate on the dog. It was limping slightly on a crooked hind leg— kicked by a horse, perhaps? She never quite knew what she would bring to the future with her, not just conscious memories but everything she had absorbed over twenty-three years in Grand Bluff's slums. But it reached up to touch its nose to the girl's hand.

Dolly shivered as Nikki brushed her fingers through the dog's ghostly fur. She used to vanish when mortal beings touched her or her creations, and it was still hard not to. Around her, the ghost horses and dog and the faint echo of a snow-covered early-1900 street scene rippled like a wind-tossed reflection in a pond.

"Dolly?" James called down the stairs, and the horses and dogs rippled again, going transparent. It was only with effort that she hung onto them.

James came down the stairs with snow on his hair and shoulders, and Nikki's father Vic behind him. Dolly leaned back on the couch with her hands locked around her knee over a silken fall of skirt, and watched Vic scoop up Nikki and bounce her in his arms. Once, she had done that for her own daughter. Now that daughter was grown and gone and old.

But Dolly was still here.

"How's the babysitting going?" James asked. He leaned over the bar, quasi-casually, and dropped the shopping bags behind it. There was no chair behind the desk, since at this point the closest thing they had to a receptionist was a sixty-foot-long dragon who curled all around the office with his chin resting on the bar top when he was doing receptionist duty.

He tended to scare off any but the most desperate clients.

"We're having fun," Dolly said brightly. Watching Nikki hold up her arms for her fae dad to scoop her off the couch had brought back memories of Wendy greeting her with small cries and chubby arms held out in welcome. She had to fight it down, then: the surge of memory wanted to bleed out of every surface. If she wasn't careful, the entire room would be full of Wendy.

James jerked his head at her, signaling her wordlessly to follow him. Glad for the reprieve, she hopped off the couch —she wasn't technically sitting on it, but she was getting better at pretending—and followed him through the dragon-sized door into the connecting conference room.

"Do you have any idea what kind of things six-year-old girls like?" James asked.

"Sorry?"

James blew out a breath and sat on the edge of the polished wooden surface of the conference table. There were snowflakes lightly dusting his scruffy dark hair. He reached over with the toe of a snowy boot to push the door shut.

In an undertone, he went on, "Today I have been through four toy stores, six big box stores, and an adult toy store that we went into by accident before I could explain to Vic that it had the wrong kind of toys. I've listened to enough versions of 'Jingle Bells' that I'm about to flip over the one-horse open sleigh myself, I have *had* it with rocking around the Christmas tree, and all I want for Christmas right now is for Mariah Carey to retire from the music business."

"Christmas?" Dolly said.

"*Please* tell me you already had Christmas in the 1920s and I don't have to explain it to you too."

"No, I ..." She heard/felt/saw the world shifting into gray murk and fiercely thought, *Not now!* For much too long, her instinctive reaction to any kind of distress was to go away. Decades had slipped by like that. She got hold of herself and stabilized, anchoring herself once again in the mortal world. "No, I ... I just didn't know."

"Oh," James said. He looked surprised. "Sorry—I forgot. Time doesn't pass for you quite the same as it does for us."

"It's just harder to keep hold of, that's all." She had known it was winter. She should have noticed. She reached out now, noting the sad plastic wreath in the window of the pizza parlor on the first floor of the warehouse building. Maybe she had already noticed and forgotten; it didn't happen to her as much as it used to, but it did still happen.

"Yeah, so Vic is taking Nikki down to spend Christmas with her birth family and Other Nikki, but somehow actual Christmas shopping for her never occurred to anyone until today. Not that Nikki has a clue what Christmas is either. But Vic's determined to do it right, so Oz and I took him Christmas shopping, which I have to tell you is an *experience*—"

There was a loud bump from the high-up windows of the conference room. The basement office's windows were all narrow and high, recessed just under the ceiling at ground level on the outside. James got up and stretched to undo the catch and open it. The tip of Oz's muzzle thrust inside, dislodging a shower of snow over James and the chairs along the wall.

"Thanks, man," James said, brushing off his hair and neck. "Use the door, maybe?"

"No time, I am off to obtain the further accoutrements of Christmas holidaying," Oz said cheerfully. "I wanted to ask if there are any Christmas accoutrements you desire."

"You didn't even know about Christmas until I told you about it this morning."

"All the more reason to do it properly!"

"How close is Christmas?" Dolly asked.

"Day after tomorrow," James said.

She was shocked all over again. "That soon?"

"But the gifts—" Oz began.

"Do what you want, okay? I don't care," James said.

"It *is* traditional to give gifts, is it not? And decorations? Oh! I just had the most marvelous idea for decorations—"

"Oz, go knock yourself out, just leave me out of it!"

"I shall improvise then," Oz said, and delicately closed the window with a clawtip.

"If you give me another car I'm going to fire you!" James shouted after him. He brushed at the melting snow on his collar. "So yeah, you see what I've been dealing with all afternoon."

Dolly couldn't help smiling. "He means well."

"Please tell me you're not all aboard the North Pole Express too."

"I—no, but—Don't you like the holidays?" she asked.

"It's more just not wanting to deal with it."

There was a loud crash from the outer office, and Vic yelped, "Nikki, not the lamp!"

"Case in point," James groaned, and went out to deal with it. Dolly was left in the conference room, gazing at the melting snow on the carpet. After a moment she stepped up onto one of the chairs—she could just levitate, but it felt less strange doing it this way—and looked out at the snow piling up against the window.

∼

AFTER THE OFFICE emptied out for the night, she wandered the building.

Christmas, she thought.

It hadn't been as much of a big deal in the 1920s as it seemed to be now. It was more of a children's holiday and an opportunity for adults to drink and party and play games. Adults giving gifts to other adults was not quite as much of a thing.

Still, she remembered Nero's hands clasped over hers, his big fingers carefully fastening diamond studs to her ears. *A beautiful gift for a beautiful girl ...*

She touched her hands to her earlobes and was not surprised to find the studs of those same earrings there.

No, she thought firmly, and banished the diamonds, replacing them with a dangling pair of red brass shells that were one of the first things she had bought for herself with Nero's money.

There was no way to erase the man from her past; he was woven through too much of it. But she could still choose to hold onto those pieces of her past that she had chosen for herself.

She walked in perfect silence down the dark hallway of the warehouse's top floor, outside James's apartment. She would not violate his privacy, but she wandered into the unoccupied apartment next door and, for a moment, made it snow so that she could conjure up a whirling white dress to go with it. Snowflakes rained from the ceiling of the empty room, and outside the window, the real versions swirled on the night air.

She walked out through the wall, leaving the room dark and still behind her, and meandered down through the building's floors. The antique pipes groaned in the walls, reminding her that she had, after all, forgotten to tell James about the leaking one. She toed the growing puddle on the second floor with a beaded slipper.

If I were a living woman, maybe I would remember more.

Maybe I would be able to buy gifts too.

∾

IN THE MORNING, Oz came in early and decorated. Sort of.

He brought in greenery, an explosion of it. Branches, mostly—not wreaths, not even evergreens for the most part. Just branches. Some of them had dead birds impaled on the twigs, contributed by Gneiss, Oz's gargoyle housemate, who clearly understood Christmas even less than Oz did.

"I'm not going to say anything," James remarked to Dolly. "Because if I do, he'll probably empty the holiday decoration shelves at Target and it'll look like Santa's workshop threw up in here."

They were in James's personal office behind the larger reception area. It was still a work in progress; there were drop cloths on the floor and the walls were spackled and unpainted. Dolly sat on the edge of James's desk while he rummaged through the drawers.

"Do you really hate it so much? Christmas?"

"I told you, I don't hate it," he said with a shrug, and went down to one knee, rifling through the bottom drawer contents. "I just don't want to fight my way past an eight-foot blow-up Santa and all his reindeer on my way to the conference room."

Dolly laughed. Then she sobered. "What do you want for Christmas, James?"

"Peace on Earth, goodwill toward men," he said without missing a beat.

"I'm serious." She could ask Oz to buy it on her behalf. She was sure he would be happy to help out.

"Me too," James said. He sighed and took a handful of files out of the drawer. "You know, it's like things spontaneously disorganize themselves just by existing in my office. It's a good thing Oz alphabetizes things for fun, because I swear I haven't even touched this since the last time I turned him loose in here and yet the Bradbourne file is nowhere to be found."

"Isn't it the one on top of the sawhorse there?"

"*Yes*," he said, and pounced on the file, absently kicking the desk drawer shut with half its files still scattered around on top of his desk.

A complete mystery, she thought, amused, *how things keep getting moved around in here.*

"And when I get this done," he said, as she trailed him out into the conference room, "I get to go Christmas shopping *again*. See, this is what I hate about this time of year, besides the Muzak and the jingle-jingle everywhere. It's not that I hate Christmas per se, it's the mutual obligation. I was doing perfectly well at ignoring it, and now I have to try to buy a gift for an independently wealthy dragon. Do you have any idea how much of a pain in the ass that's going to be? Especially on Christmas Eve."

"You don't have to. I'm sure Oz wouldn't mind."

"No, he *will* mind but he'll pretend not to, which is worse. Especially since he's probably planning to give me a Corvette or something."

Dolly laughed. "What kind of thing would you like instead?"

375

"Don't you start too." James tossed the file on the conference table. It slid across the polished surface and bumped into a bowl full of dirt. Shoved into the dirt, there were twigs, and neatly impaled on each, there was a bright red berry. "I'm not really a Christmas person, Dolly. I didn't have a great childhood and I really don't have a lot of warm fuzzy Christmas memories."

"Oh. I'm sorry." It wasn't as if her own childhood was that swell either, and she thought about bringing that up, but the moment slipped away before she could decide on something to say.

"Anyway," James added, "if you're fishing for gift ideas, I—look, not to be rude, but—"

"I know. I can't exactly buy anything." She looked down at her hands. They looked perfectly normal, just like her regular hands, but how would she know what her hands were supposed to look like? She didn't know which pieces of her were missing anymore.

"Don't feel bad, Dolly. It just keeps it from being awkward. It's not like we could get you anything either."

"I *know*," she said, and this time apparently some of her stung feeling trickled through into her voice. James looked up from leafing through the folder.

"Sorry, Dolly. I'm being a dick today."

"You always are," she said, and when he raised an eyebrow, she hastened to explain, "No, no, it's not meant to be insulting. It's a joke. Because you're a detective? Oh, that's one of those things people don't say anymore, isn't it. *Nuts*."

"Sort of." He smiled crookedly. "I like it when you use dated slang. It's very you."

"I guess I'll forgive you for the Christmas thing, then." She sat on the edge of the desk, taking pains to make it look like she was actually sitting on it. "What's the case?"

"Mmm. Old divorce case from last year. Not that interesting. I did a little bit of legwork for the wife's attorney, that's all. The guy's getting divorced again and her lawyers were going to take the opportunity to see about adjusting her alimony, so they wanted a consult on the dirt I dug up last time." He lifted a shoulder in a shrug. "Dirty laundry and paperwork, that's the lifeblood of this business. It's not all hundred-year-old cold cases and fae duels." He rubbed his chest. "Which is good, because I don't think my constitution can handle it."

"Are you still hurt?" Another thing she no longer had a good grasp on was how much time it took regular, mortal people to heal.

He gave her a reassuring smile. "Just a twinge now and then." The smile faded to something a little softer. "*Is* there anything you want, Dolly?"

She was genuinely caught off guard. "What do you mean? For Christmas?"

"For Christmas, or anything else, honestly. I don't ask that often enough. I keep forgetting that we're all you have of the outside world anymore. So just let me know if I can do anything for you."

She was desperately, deeply touched. "I—" She began, opening her mouth.

She was going to ask if James could find out if Wendy wanted to come see her for Christmas. She still didn't know how to behave around her adult daughter, the daughter she had last seen as a baby who was now an old woman. But Christmas was for family, wasn't it? If there ever was a time when she might be able to sit down with her grown-up baby and be a family for a little while ...

But, no, she told herself with grim determination. It wasn't fair to ask James to be a go-between for her on a holiday he didn't even particularly like.

It was enough just to know that he would bring her things if she asked him.

"Not right now," she said, shaking her head.

His eyes crinkled up a little, and he tipped his head to the side. There were times when he almost could've been a moving-picture idol, when he looked at her that way. He had a little dash of that old Hollywood charm and didn't even seem to know it.

"You sure?" he said. "It seemed like you were going to say something."

Dolly shook her head again, very firmly. "No," she said, and leaned over the case file. "Tell me what the lawyers are looking for, and maybe I can help. I was pretty good at picking up bits of blackmail material when I worked for Nero. People talk to barmaids, and it was useful for keeping up with the competition and giving Nero a little dirt when he needed it."

James gave her a quick glance, and laughed a little. "Dolly, sometimes it's easy to think of your time as a simpler and nicer time than ours. I appreciate you shooting down any illusions I might have about that."

❧

BUT SHE FIGURED it out that night.

She held onto herself overnight, afraid that she might slip some time and come back days later, with Christmas a week or a month gone. Instead she spent the time working on the thing she had in mind.

She didn't think James would take it the wrong way. Maybe Christmas wasn't his kind of thing, but she knew that he liked hearing her talk about the city back in the old days. James was ... well, not old-fashioned exactly, but there was something a little out of place about him. Like he was always

378

looking for the place he belonged. Maybe that was why he liked her stories of the war days and the 1920s so much.

Anyway, she thought he would like this. It wasn't a Christmas present, not exactly. It was just a gift, a random gift, no strings attached, such as friends gave to friends.

She worked on it all night down in the basement, coaxing out details she'd half forgotten, relearning how to conjure smell and sound. By the time the darkness outside the high basement windows lightened to gray, she was tired in a strange metaphysical way, but also deeply satisfied.

Oh baby, she thought, *you are good at this.*

When she heard and sensed James's footsteps on the stairs leading down from the warehouse, she brought up the lights on the 1920s.

It was a different version of the Peony Club than he would ever have seen before. The nightclub ambiance that always used to come with her automatically, without Dolly having to do anything, was a half-remembered vision of the club as she had experienced it night after night—a generic vision of the sights and sounds so familiar that it was as if she had absorbed them into the very pores of her body.

This was specific.

When the lights brightened, the office was revealed in the best approximation she had been able to remember of how they used to decorate the Peony Club for Christmas.

Brilliant red streamers draped the walls; red paper bells dangled from the ceiling. There was crepe paper everywhere —she remembered they'd gone wild with it, in a brilliant display of whatever colors were fashionable that year. For this she had chosen pastel lavender and yellow because she liked the contrast with the vividness of the Christmas reds.

But that was only the start. The bar was decked out with garlands and a fully stocked assortment of the expensive liquors they used to bring in specially from Canada for the holidays. There was a tree in the corner, the fat bushy kind that looked so much more *right* to her than the taller, pointier trees that were more fashionable nowadays. Nero used to prefer the new electric strings of bulbs to light the tree, not least because they were less likely to burn down the club, but since she didn't have to worry about that, she had decked it out with candles. She liked their warmer, softer glow. Her mother had never been able to afford a tree when she was a child, but they would light some candles on the windowsill, and—oh, the soft golden light took her back there.

And more! Glittering tinsel everywhere, and soft curls of cotton snow along the walls and dusted across the top of the bar. But she hadn't stopped with fake snow. Back in the old days, Nero had made confetti snow burst and fall from the ceiling onto the delighted dancers. It was the bar's servers, of course, who had to clean it up after. She used to hate that stuff. But she loved its ethereal look when it was falling, so there were snowflakes drifting gently down from the ceiling, vanishing on the floor except where she remembered to have them collect on chair seats and the edge of the bar.

"I know you said you didn't want a lot of decorating." She found herself shy now, suddenly worrying that he wouldn't like it. "I just thought you might like to see what the bar looked like in the old days. I can make it go away, if you want."

"No ... no, Dolly, I don't want." He stopped at the bottom of the stairs, looking around with a wondering expression. Ghostly snow drifted down around him. To indulge herself a bit, Dolly made the snowflakes linger on his hair and shoulders, setting off the dark brown scruff of his hair and the wrinkled brown leather of the jacket.

"Back in my time, we used to decorate the club for Christmas," Dolly explained. "I tried to remember how it was done and recreate it. I don't remember everything exactly, so some of it I had to make up."

James raised a hand as if to touch her and then dropped it. "How long can you keep this up?"

"I don't know. I'll have to find out." She grinned. "It's kind of fun. Like running a marathon. Is there anything else you want me to add? I can—"

And then she saw who was behind him, standing on the stairs, and the entire carefully assembled tableau flickered as if a wind had gusted through it.

Wendy stood there.

It was still hard for Dolly to look at her full-grown daughter and see how old she had become. Wendy's hair was white, tucked up neatly today beneath a red hat with a few real snowflakes melting on the brim. She wore a tasteful suit-dress in dark jewel colors, a deep red jacket and skirt with a sweater and stockings of a violet so dark it was nearly black. She carried a cane of dark-colored wood with a brass handle. Her boots had buckles.

And she was staring at Dolly with a look that went straight down to the core of whatever was left of Dorothy Mott, the living woman and mother who had died in 1924.

Dolly took a few steps forward and then stopped. She couldn't touch Wendy anyway, and she was suddenly terrified that even trying would rupture the thin thread that still bound her to the mortal world.

"Mother," Wendy said, a single fragile word.

"So," James said, "I'll just ..." and he made a hand gesture toward the conference room and fled.

Wendy carefully descended the remaining steps. She stood in Dolly's snowfall—Dolly focused hard on maintaining the careful illusion of real snowflakes—and looked around with a wondering expression at the tree with its

381

candles gleaming through the snow, at the bar and the crepe and all of it.

"Is this really what it looked like?" she asked.

"Mostly," Dolly said. Her voice came out small, and she discovered that she was slipping again, sliding away from the world. She cleared her throat and held onto the real world and her presence in it with all she had. "We used to decorate. Like this. Um. Not the snow, though."

Wendy gave a small, sharp laugh. "I didn't think you had indoor snow, no."

"We sort of did. There was confetti."

"Really?"

"It got down my shirt and up my stockings. It was amazing, the places I'd find it. I used to shake it out at home and ..." She faltered, but went on. "It made you laugh. You used to try to catch it, like this ..."

Before she even thought about it, caught up in the memories that were already trying to bleed into the world around her, she grabbed at the air, miming tiny Wendy in Mrs. Sorenson's borrowed, too-big crib.

And Wendy laughed.

It was like time stopped for Dolly. That was *the laugh*. That was what used to welcome her back home after each long, exhausting day at the nightclub. And that was what held her to the world: not a hope of vengeance, not anger or hate, but love. Even after she had, for so long, forgotten what it was that she loved—forgotten Wendy—until she had recaptured those memories because of James.

"Oh," Wendy said, a strange small sound, and Dolly looked around and realized that things had changed.

The Christmas nightclub had melted away. Instead she was standing in the small, drafty attic room she used to rent while she worked at Peony's. She had all but forgotten the details, but her subconscious remembered.

There was the low ceiling, the single small window with a candle standing in it. *Oh,* she thought, *it's Christmas* ...

There was the old chest she had of her mother's, the pitcher and washstand where she remembered so vividly having to break the ice every morning. And there were the new things, the ones she had bought with the money from Nero. She remembered the nice walnut dresser that she had bought brand new from a downtown department store, when she had never believed she would own a new piece of furniture in her life. The store had even sent two men to carry it up the narrow stairs from the street. A careless handful of pearls and other jewelry lay scattered atop it, all of it paste, but glittering and nice. There was a good party frock draped over her chair, more dresses hanging under the eaves. The bed was heaped with pretty coverlets.

And there beside it was the borrowed crib. Wendy's crib.

Dolly walked toward it slowly. It was as if she moved through her own memories. For *she* was there in the memory, the real her, the living her, kneeling by the crib and reaching through its wooden bars to tickle the baby who squirmed inside.

"Is that me?" Wendy asked softly, and the ghost of Dolly looked around and found her daughter beside her.

"Yes," she said just as quietly. It was as if speaking loudly could disturb the memory.

For memory it was. She couldn't believe how vivid and real it seemed. She could feel the chill in the air and smell the familiar scent of her own perfume and the lingering rich, earthy taste of the expensive cigarettes Nero bought for her. She watched herself lean over Wendy, kicking in the crib, and hold a handful of jewelry to the child's parted lips. That was the necklace, the one that—

The one that the real, modern-day Wendy was wearing, she realized with a feeling like a kick beneath her ribs.

That necklace had spent a century at the bottom of the Grand Bluffs harbor. Back in the time of this memory, she used to use it to hide the magic healing elixir that kept baby-Wendy healthy.

"That smell ..." Wendy breathed, her voice so soft it could barely be heard.

There was an additional smell in the air, Dolly realized, half-smothered by perfume and powder. It was the light, cloying floral scent of the elixir.

"I do actually remember this, I think," Wendy said in that same quiet voice.

Dolly looked at her, at the strong lines of her daughter's face, creased with the hard marks of a life deeply lived. "Really?"

Wendy nodded and turned to look at Dolly. When Wendy was a baby, Dolly had seen nothing at all of her father in her, but now she saw Nero's hawklike quickness, and even a little of his cruelty, in Wendy's sharp dark eyes.

"I didn't think so," Wendy said. "But I do. Only flashes here and there. I was so young. But that *smell* ... I remember a woman bending over me. I remember the taste of flowers and the rattling of beads and pearls. I think that woman was my mother."

"I think," Dolly said, in the faint whisper of a voice that was all she could manage, "that she was, too."

They both watched the young Dolly—and how strange was it, seeing herself from the outside?—as she picked up the baby from the crib and held Wendy's small, kicking body against the shoulder of her work frock. The dress was yellow, Dolly noticed, with lavender ribbons and trim. Real? Or just because she had picked those colors for the Peony decorations? It was so hard to know the difference these days, when memory was all that was left of her.

And then she took a deep breath and banished it.

The attic went away, along with all of its furnishings and memories, and finally, shimmering into ghostly insignificance and then fading entirely, the mother and child. She kept the candles though, relocating them to the edge of the bar in the real world. She tried to reconstruct some of the Christmas ambiance of the Peony Club, but couldn't get what she'd had before. What she ended up with was more like the old ghost club, a semi-instinctual reflection of several different Christmases rolled into one.

She held onto it anyway.

Wendy was still staring toward the empty space where the mother and child had been. Her profile was hawklike, and also made Dolly think of Nero more than her own scoop-dip nose.

"I wasn't expecting that," Dolly said, and Wendy dropped her head and huffed out a quiet laugh that somehow sounded much less familiar, less like her laugh as a baby.

"Well," she said, "we're both new to this," and she raised her head and turned to look at Dolly and smiled, and there was much less of Nero in that smile than Dolly would have expected.

~

IT WAS both a sorrow and a relief that Wendy couldn't stay all day. They chatted for a while, and then Dolly found herself flagging and Wendy pled exhaustion, and at that point Oz barged in via the river door and further conversation was impossible.

"Is that *real snow*? How did you do that? I am thrilled and delighted! I had no idea Christmas was such a *cold* holiday ..."

Wendy made her way out, with a smile over her shoulder at Dolly, and James found his way back in. Dolly retreated and continued to make it snow while an exchange of gifts occurred. Oz appeared to be sincerely excited over the day planner James had given him, while James accepted a coffee mug.

"You don't like it," Oz said. "I could have given you a car, but you didn't want a car—"

"Another car. You already gave me a car. Actually, the car just about covers all the holidays for the whole year, right? So technically you've given me my present already, and it's great."

"Oh," Oz said cheerfully. "That's true." He clasped the day planner in his claws. "I must write something in this *immediately*."

Dolly could feel herself winding down to a thin thread of energy, but she still followed James back into his office, where he sprawled in his chair with a booted foot up on the desk, and then looked up at her.

"So this sure is a thing I own now," he said, turning the mug where she could see it. It said WORLD'S BEST DETECTIVE.

Dolly laughed. She was too tired to contain herself; she flopped on the edge of his desk and laughed helplessly, losing containment of herself just a bit around the edges.

"It's not actually that funny." James sat forward. "Are you all right?"

"I'm fine—I just—your face—"

Eventually she contained herself before she laughed herself into oblivion and fake-sat on the edge of his desk like a motion-picture dame. "You know you'll need to drink all your coffee out of that from now on or you'll hurt his feelings."

"I know," James sighed. "It'll make a great impression on our clients, I bet." He shifted papers to set it on the desk.

From the main office came a plaintive, "If you wouldn't mind, I can't find anything, all this *snow*—"

Dolly smiled and let it go, releasing the illusion and finding a good deal of her energy spiraling off with it. She was really *very* tired. "Where are Vic and Nikki?"

"They drove down to Iowa yesterday," James said. "I think I mentioned they're spending Christmas with Other Nikki—er, I probably should try to break him of the habit of calling her that. I just hope he doesn't do it in front of her parents."

Dolly giggled.

"It wasn't actually that funny ..."

"I think I'm getting punchy," she admitted. She held her hand up and inspected the wall through it. "Very tired, in fact."

James looked up sharply. "You gonna be okay?"

"Oh yes." She was strangely confident of that, actually, even as she felt herself fading away. "I'm just tired. Like you get. I'll be back. It might take a week or two, but don't worry about it."

She was losing her grasp on the real world entirely, but she wasn't done yet, not quite. She leaned over and kissed him on his forehead, her lips brushing the skin she couldn't feel.

"It was a lovely present," she said. "Thank you. Merry Christmas, James."

He might have said, "Merry Christmas, Dolly," but the gray swallowed her; there was only the faintest trace of his voice. But she went into it content, suffused with a full-body feeling of happiness. She knew that she would come back, and she was nothing but happy as the world swept away from her and the gray washed gently in.

AUTHOR'S NOTE

I hope you enjoyed this book! If you liked it, leaving a review or a rating is always very welcome.

Dick & Demon, Keeley & Associates #4, is up for preorder and will be out on June 30, 2021.

I send out free stories on my mailing list every month or so. Follow this link: https://www.subscribepage.com/laylaslist

You can also join my Facebook group where you can contribute prompts for future stories and read sneak previews of upcoming stories and novels.

OTHER WORKS & SOCIAL MEDIA

I also write paranormal and sci-fi romance as Lauren Esker.
https://laurenesker.com/

Find me online!

Website:
https://www.laylalawlor.com

Mailing list:
https://www.subscribepage.com/laylaslist

Twitter:
https://twitter.com/Layla_in_Alaska

Facebook page:
https://www.facebook.com/MagicMayhemMystery/

Instagram:
https://www.instagram.com/icefallstudio/

You can also join my Facebook reader's group.